# UNFORGETTABLE DAYS

*Recent Titles by Margaret Pemberton from Severn House*

THE FOUR OF US

# UNFORGETTABLE DAYS

Margaret Pemberton

**Severn House Large Print**
London & New York

This first large print edition published in Great Britain 2006 by
SEVERN HOUSE LARGE PRINT BOOKS LTD of
9-15 High Street, Sutton, Surrey, SM1 1DF.
This title first published 2005 by
Severn House Publishers, London and New York.
This first large print edition published in the USA 2006 by
SEVERN HOUSE PUBLISHERS INC., of
595 Madison Avenue, New York, NY 10022.



Pemberton, Margaret
Unforgettable days. - Large print ed.
1. Military spouses - United States - Fiction
2. Female friendship - Fiction
3. Vietnam War, 1961-1975 - Missing in action – Fiction
4. Vietnam - Fiction
5. Large type books
I.Title II.Pemberton, Margaret. White Christmas in Saigon
823.9'14[F]

ISBN-13: 9780727875488
ISBN-10: 0727875485



Except where actual historical events and characters are being described for the storyline of this novel, all situations in this publication are fictitious and any resemblance to living persons is purely coincidental.

Printed and bound in Great Britain by
MPG Books Ltd, Bodmin, Cornwall.

# ACKNOWLEDGEMENTS

Many people gave assistance to me during the writing of this book, but my deepest debt is to Ms Carolyn Nichols, Bantam Books, New York. Her enthusiasm and encouragement gave me the courage to embark on a subject that would otherwise have daunted me. For two years she gave unstintingly of her valuable advice and time, sharing with me her personal library and her deep interest in all things Vietnamese.

My thanks and acknowledgements are also due to the following: the staff of the American Embassy, London; the Beverly Hills Hotel, Los Angeles; the California State Division of Veteran Affairs; the Caravelle Hotel, Ho Chi Minh City; the Colindale Newspaper Library, London; the Foreign Languages Publishing House, Hanoi; the Imperial War Museum, London; the Jefferson Hotel, Washington; Travis Air Base Information Centre, California; the Thang Loi Hotel, Hanoi; the War Museum, Hanoi.

I owe special thanks to Madame Dai, Bibliothèque Restaurant, Ho Chi Minh City; Diethelm Travel, Bangkok; Mr Geoffrey Hann, Hann Overland Travel, London; Dr Bich

Nguyen, London; Mr Richard Pugh, the British Epilepsy Association, Leeds; Mr Robert Radcliff, Hutchinson, Kansas; Mr Richard Tomlin, London; Vietnam Tourism, Hanoi; Mr Ron Wilson, Civil Aviation Authority, London.

Also, my sincere thanks to Mrs Diane Pearson, of Transworld Publishers, London, and my literary agent, Miss Carol Smith, London, for their friendship and never-failing support.

For Marian W., without whom, quite literally, this book would never have been written.

For the friends I made while traveling in Vietnam:

Anne Convery
Ling and Mike Clatterbuck
Debbie and Jim Fallows
Genevieve and Guy Caufriez
Franz Pitzal
Jean Marc Studemann
Steve Turley

In the words of General Giap, they were truly 'unforgettable days'.

And last but not least, for my husband,
Mike, as always.

## Vietnam
## 1954-1975

Names underlined represent fictitious places

One watches things that make one sick at heart.
This is the law: no gain without a loss,
And heaven hurts fair women for sheer spite.

Nguyen Du
(1765–1820)

# *Foreword*

*Unforgettable Days* is the first part of an earlier saga, *White Christmas in Saigon,* which was born one evening at Goldsmith's College, London, a week before Christmas in 1988 when, with Christmas under discussion in a coffee-break, a fellow adult student, an American, said casually, 'When my husband was shot down over North Vietnam and imprisoned in Hanoi, he was there for six Christmases.'

She had been 21 when he was captured and, for four years, hadn't known if he were dead or alive. It was a situation, she said, that many wives of Americans captured in Vietnam faced. Were they wives or were they widows? As the years went by, were they free to enter into other relationships, or, if they did so, were they being unfaithful to men who were enduring the living hell of a prison cell in Hanoi?

By the time our fifteen minute coffee-break was over, Abbra, Serena and Gabrielle were born fully-fledged, as, in my mind's eye, was every detail of *Unforgettable Days*' storyline, along with its conclusion to be told in *The Turbulent Years*. It was a unique experience, one that had never happened before, though I had, at the time, written 20 novels and, though I have now written another 14, one that has never happened since.

# PROLOGUE

The day was cold, the sky leaden, full of the somberness of November. The three women had arrived in Washington separately, on different days during the preceding week. Now they stood, arms linked, on the corner of 7th Street and Constitution Avenue, about to march in one of the most moving and unorthodox parades the city had ever seen.

'Who is up front?' Gabrielle Ryan shouted in a heavy French accent to her companions. All around them people were greeting one another and calling out, struggling to be heard above the deafening sound of a military band gustily playing 'The Girl I Left Behind Me'.

'General Westmoreland!' Abbra Ellis shouted back, glossy black hair skimming her shoulders, her cherry-red wool coat glowing like a jewel in the dull afternoon light.

'You bet he is!' an army veteran in faded fatigues and a boonie hat responded as he squeezed past them. 'The President sure as hell isn't!'

'Is that true?' Serena Anderson's voice was disbelieving. 'Isn't the President leading the procession?'

Abbra shook her head. 'No,' she said, her eyes dark. 'None of those who should be here are here. Not the Vice President, not the Secretary of State, not Richard Nixon, not Henry Kissinger. Only Westmoreland.' She slipped her hand into Serena's and gave it a tight squeeze. 'Nothing really changes, Serena. You should know that.'

Serena, tall and elegant and stunningly beautiful, nodded. Twenty-four hours earlier she had been working with the refugees in the Nong Samet refugee camp in Hong Kong. Now here she was in Washington again and, as Abbra had said, despite the parade and the reason for it, nothing had really changed. Not where it mattered. Not on Capitol Hill.

'We're moving!' Gabrielle cried as the crowd around them began to edge forward into the avenue and the strains of 'The Girl I Left Behind Me' were replaced by a thunderous rendering of 'God Bless America.'

'This is it!' a long-haired, bearded middle-aged man in jeans shouted exultantly. 'Jesus Christ! I've waited nine years for this!'

A lump rose high in Abbra's throat. She, too, had waited nine years. As they turned into the broad sweep of the avenue, she looked around her, laughter and tears vying for expression. She had been in many marches but never one as ragtag yet as splendid as this one.

General Westmoreland, silver-haired and wearing a trench coat, had led it off over two hours earlier, marching alongside a group of veterans from Alabama. Other veterans had followed, marching under the name of their state: New York, Montana, Maryland, Kansas. Some men wore battle fatigues. Some were resplendent in full dress uniform. Some marched, some walked, some hobbled with the aid of canes. Others pushed themselves along in wheelchairs, or were pushed by a buddy or a wife, a son or a daughter.

As the contingent from each state passed, the crowd lining the sidewalks called out its name and clapped and cheered. The last state represented in the parade was Wyoming; Abbra and Serena and Gabrielle marched along in the center of the crowd following the delegation, and Abbra felt tears sting her cheeks. The men around her had been too busy reuniting to have marched off under the name of their state. Some sported flags; others carried bottles of beer; many walked, arms around each other's shoulders; some laughed exuberantly, cracking jokes with their companions; others wept. They had come together to remember their shared past and to honor their dead, and the occasion had turned into an emotional homecoming that had been long denied them.

The three women walked among the men, their arms linked, feeling natural. On this day, November 13, 1982, they belonged in the parade, just as the men around them belonged. They, too, had paid their dues. Abbra, in the center, hugged her friends' arms, looking first at Serena and then at Gabrielle.

Serena's fragile-boned face was pale, her mouth set firm. Despite the bitter wind she wore no coat. She wore her gray flannel slacks, white cashmere turtleneck, and black velvet blazer with cool, understated English elegance. Her blond hair was pulled away from her face, coiled in a loose knot at the nape of her neck, revealing clearly the thin white scar that ran from high on her temple to the corner of her left eye which marred her otherwise flawless beauty. Another woman might have cut her hair into bangs and a bob, disguising it. It was typical of Serena that she had done no such thing, wearing her hair as she had always worn it.

Gabrielle was typically fully protected against physical discomfort. Her snakeskin boots were high, teeteringly heeled to compensate for her diminutive height. A pale champagne suede coat was belted at her waist, a huge lynx collar soft against her face, a matching hat tilted rakishly on top of impossibly red hair. Looking across at her, Abbra could see that tears were glittering on her lashes. She hugged her friend's arm tighter and Gabrielle turned toward her, flashing her a dazzling smile, saying, 'It is all right, *chérie*. I was remembering. That is all.'

They were reaching the long end of the avenue. To the left of them was the Lincoln Memorial; a little farther away was the Jefferson Memorial. And now, as they crowded down on to a leafy, two-acre site, the memorial they had honored with their parade, and which was to be dedicated, came into view.

Abbra caught her breath. This was why the three of them had returned to Washington. She from San Francisco; Gabrielle from Paris; Serena from Hong Kong. The memorial, two huge, tapering walls of shiny black granite forming a wide V and bearing 57,939 names, was simple and elegant and dignified, everything that the war in which the men had died was not. For the memorial had been erected by veterans of one of the ugliest wars that had ever taken place. The war in Vietnam.

Al Keller, national commander of the American Legion, addressed the packed throng stretching far back along Constitution Avenue. 'Today we dedicate a memorial to a generation of Americans who fought a lonely battle,' he began ringingly.

Abbra's eyes were not on him but on the wall. The names had been engraved in chronological order of death, beginning with army major Dale R. Buis, who had been killed on July 8, 1959, and culminating with air force second lieutenant Richard Vane Geer, who had died on May 15, 1975. So many names, so much heartbreak.

The crowd was packed with women, many, like herself, in their late thirties, teenage children alongside them. Others were much older, their faces harrowed with lines of grief and loss, their husbands at their sides, their mouths grim as they surveyed the huge black wall bearing the names of their sons.

*Curtis Richard, Titus Epps, Dan Stuber, Richard H. Davies*

Abbra's throat tightened as she looked at them, remembering the other marches that had taken place in Washington, the demonstrations and speeches protesting the very death of the men now immortalized.

*Glenn Rethington, Richard Salmond, Robert G. Drapp*

She remembered the doors of the Justice Department being barricaded against them, the injured who had lain helplessly on the ground as the police had broken up the demonstrations with water from hoses and with tear gas; and she remembered the singing and the chanting and the folk songs.

*Gerald Aadland, Craig Reska, Perry Mitchell*

Thirteen years before to the month, at the antiwar March Against Death, the demonstrators had recited, one at a time, the names of the 40,000 Americans who had been killed up to then. The past Wednesday morning, in a chapel at Washington's National Cathedral, the bleak recitation had begun again, and she had been one of those taking part. It had been almost more thanshe could bear.

A letter from the Secretary of Defense, Caspar Weinberger, was read; Wayne Newton sang; General Westmoreland spoke. The cold stung their cheeks and she felt Serena shiver.

'We are here to remember the suffering and endurance of those who fought in Southeast Asia...'

Abbra slipped her hands into Serena's and

Gabrielle's.

'We suffered, and we endured as well,' she said passionately, her eyes fiercely bright, and all of a sudden it was as if she had finally reached the end of a long, lonely journey. 'Hell! We did more than that!' She was filled with overwhelming emotion. 'We survived, goddammit! We survived!'

# CHAPTER ONE

'But it's going to be a perfectly respectable party, Mom,' Abbra Daley protested, half amused and half exasperated by her mother's low opinion of her friends and her social life. 'Nearly everyone there will be from Stanford and—'

'And the others?' her mother interrupted crisply as she began to take heavy silver cutlery from a velvet-lined mahogany box. 'The ones who will be there and who aren't from your University? Will that offensive young man you are so obsessed with be there?'

Abbra pushed a fall of silky shoulder-length hair away from her face. 'No,' she said, her eyes clouding slightly, her amusement waning. 'He won't be there.'

Her mother put the silver she had selected to one side and closed the box. 'How can you be so sure? Beatniks don't have to be invited to a party to attend it, do they? They just turn up and make a nuisance of themselves.'

'Jerry is in New York,' Abbra said briefly, keeping a tight rein on her impatience. 'An underground newspaper there is interested in publishing some of his poems and—'

Her mother gave an unladylike snort. 'Poems! Anything that young man writes will be gutter trash. How a girl of your upbringing can be so taken with such an unsavory specimen I can't begin to imagine. Nor do I understand why his kind finds it so necessary to flock like lemmings to San Francisco. Why can't they stay in their hometowns?'

It wasn't a question that she expected an answer to. She carried the silver across to the large dining table, smoothing an imaginary crease from the handmade lace tablecloth, every line of her body registering outrage.

'Who is coming to dinner?' Abbrra asked, realizing that the subject had to be turned away from Jerry. And quickly.

'Tom Ellis is visiting from New York. His son is going to be here as well. And the Parkers.'

Abbra tried to look interested, but it was difficult. Colonel Tom Ellis was an old family friend with a distinguished war record not only in the Second World War but in Korea as well. His conversation – all his conversation, Abbra recalled, centered around things military. His wife had been her mother's childhood friend, and though she had died tragically of cancer shortly after her younger son's birth, the friendship between her parents and the colonel had continued.

'Which son?' she asked, taking a handful of silver and beginning to lay it.

'Older one of course!' her mother said, her tone of voice indicating that the fact should have been self-evident. 'I would hardly invite a *football* player as a dinner guest, would I? The Parkers would think I had taken leave of my senses!'

Sam Parker was an eminent neurologist, as was Abbra's father.

'What's so socially acceptable about the older son's career?' Abbra asked, amusement at her mother's snobbishness restoring her good humor.

'Lewis is an army officer.' Her mother examined a silver candelabrum carefully to make sure that the maid had cleaned it to her satisfaction. 'West Point. Surely you remember that your father and I attended his graduation?'

Abbra shook her head. She had met the colonel on numerous occasions but had only a shadowy recollection of seeing Lewis when she was eight or nine. He had been a teenager in an army cadet uniform, and because she had expected someone her own age she had been intensely disappointed, and too shy to exchange more than half a dozen words with him.

'Tell me about the younger brother,' she said as her mother handed her a clean cloth with which to polish already sparkling wineglasses. 'Is he really a football player?'

Her mother nodded, stepping back from the immaculately laid table and regarding it critically. 'Unfortunately, yes. He's causing his father a great deal of anxiety. If you're here when Tom arrives, I would appreciate it if you wouldn't mention Scott's name.'

Abbra didn't have the slightest intention of being there when the dinner guests arrived. She said again, as she had at the beginning of the conversation, 'Since my car is being serviced, can I borrow yours to go to the party tonight? I promise I won't be back too late.'

Her mother's eyes held hers. 'Do you promise that Jerry Littler will *not* be there?'

'Mom, I'm *eighteen* for goodness' sake!' Abbra said, unable to hold back her impatience any longer. 'This kind of cross-examination is ridiculous!'

'No, it isn't. If I had been more vigilant a few months ago, you would never have become acquainted with a beatnik. Now, for the last time. Will the person I am referring to be there?'

Abbra closed her eyes and prayed for strength. 'No,' she said when she could at last trust herself to speak. 'I've told you. He's in New York.'

'Then you can borrow the car on one condition: Lewis picks you up at midnight.'

Abbra stared at her incredulously. 'You can't mean that, Mom! It's absurd! It's, it's—' She struggled for a word that would do justice to it—' It's *humiliating*.'

'No, it isn't.' Having laid and decorated the dining table to her satisfaction, Mrs. Daley now turned her attention towards the flower arrangements. Both were tasks that she never delegated. 'It's sensible,' she continued, removing a Lalique vase from a display cabinet.

'Lewis won't mind, not in the least, and I'll be able to enjoy the evening with an easy mind. Now, do you think I should use this vase for the roses, or would they look better in the Tiffany?'

Abbra drew in a deep, steadying breath. There were times when her mother's over-protectiveness had to be challenged, but the present issue was too trivial to be one of them. It was also farcical.

'The Tiffany,' she said, her good humor returning.

Her mother caught the new inflection in her voice and looked across at her, a vase in either hand. 'I don't see what's so funny,' she said reprovingly. 'You should be glad that you have parents who care about you.'

'I am,' Abbra said as contritely as her amusement would allow. She made a strategic retreat toward the door before adding mischievously, 'But isn't it just my bad luck that the never-do-anything-wrong older brother is your dinner guest this evening? Being picked up by the football-playing black sheep of the family would have been much more fun!'

The party was being held in a house high on Telegraph Hill. From the bare windows a thousand lights could be seen glittering along the Embarcadero and Fisherman's Wharf.

'Crowded as hell, isn't it?' a friend from her English class at Stanford shouted to Abbra.

Before she could answer, the music changed from the Beach Boys to the Supremes. Abbra merely nodded. It was so crowded it was almost impossible to move. Her cornflower-blue mini-skirt was twisted and riding too high on her thighs. Her shining black hair held away from her face with two heavy tortoiseshell combs was damp with perspiration. 'I hardly know anyone,' she shouted to her friend.

A blond giant moved skillfully between them and grinned down on her. 'I'm your hostess's brother's buddy,' he said, steering her toward a set of French doors. 'Let's go onto the terrace. There should be room to dance there.'

There was. The Supremes gave way to the Beatles, to the Stones, to Sonny and Cher.

'...And so I go to L.A. next week to try out for the Rams.'

'I got you babe,' Sonny and Cher sang out. 'I got you babe.'

'You mean you're going to be a football player?' Abbra asked, grateful for the cooling night breeze that was blowing in from the Bay.

'You bet your sweet life I am. If Scott Ellis can make it professionally, I sure as hell can make it.'

She stopped dancing. 'Scott Ellis?' she said incredulously. 'You did say *Scott Ellis*?'

He nodded. 'He's my buddy. He's here somewhere.' From his advantageous height he scanned the heads of the other dancers.

'There he is, over near the doorway.'

Abbra turned to look. The figure he was pointing to had his back toward them and was surrounded by a bevy of admiring girls. He was tall, easily six feet three or four, with magnificently broad shoulders and a thatch of sun-bleached hair.

'Oh boy!' she said, her voice thick with laughter, feeling no twinge of destiny, no intimation of fate. 'My mother is never going to believe this! I wonder if his father knows he's here in San Francisco? If his brother knows?'

The giant shrugged uncomprehendingly. 'Why should anyone know?' he asked as they began to dance again, this time to the Kinks. 'Scott doesn't have to check in with anyone. He never has. He never will.'

When 'Set Me Free' came to an end, she declined another dance with a smile and a shake of her head, knowing that if she stayed any longer, he would consider her his personal property. She didn't seek out Scott Ellis. He had enough adoring females around him without another one swelling the ranks. Instead, she danced with her friend's brother, and then with some of the guys from Stanford, and then with her friend's brother again.

'Someone's come to get you!' a classmate shouted across to her.

Abbra glanced down at her watch, said an exasperated 'damn' beneath her breath, and began to ease her way through the crowd and out of the room.

'Abbra?' He was twenty-eight or twenty-nine and bore no resemblance at all to the slightly awkward teenager she remembered. He was in uniform, and beneath the porch-light lieutenant's pips gleamed dully.

She nodded, stepping out onto the porch, saying with an apologetic smile, 'I'm sorry about this. I'm afraid there are times when my mother behaves as if I were twelve years old!'

'It's no trouble.' His voice was deep-timbred. 'Your mother said for you to leave her car here. She'll have her chauffeur pick it up in the morning.'

There was no easy affability about him. His mouth was intimidatingly uncompromising, and he was obviously a man who smiled neither easily nor often. Yet she was suddenly sure that she was going to like him. Beneath his peaked cap his hair was thick and curly, and his face was hard-boned and abrasively masculine. He wasn't tall, not nearly as tall as the blond giant she had danced with, but he was toughly built and held himself well, with a muscular coordination that spoke of hard training and perfect physical fitness.

'I suppose you're wondering why my mother didn't ask her chauffeur to pick me up this evening,' she said with friendly ease as they began to walk down the lamplit drive toward his car. 'He *could* have, but you see, if the party had proved to be wild, she wouldn't be able to rely on him to inform her. She thinks you'll be braver.'

'And was it wild?'

There was the merest touch of a smile at the corners of his mouth.

'No. Just the opposite.' She suddenly remembered Scott. 'Your brother was there. Probably still is.'

His car was a two-seater MG. 'That doesn't prove that the party was respectable,' he said dryly, opening the door for her. 'More the opposite.'

She giggled, glad that a sense of humor lurked beneath his somewhat forbidding manner. 'Don't you want to go back to the party and say hi to him?'

'No.' He flinched slightly as someone in the house turned the volume on the record player up. 'Parties are Scott's scene, not mine.'

Her amusement deepened. She believed him. It was impossible to imagine him at a party like the one she had just left. He was far too staid and serious-minded to let his hair down dancing to the Beach Boys.

'I love parties,' she said as he slipped into the seat beside her and slid the MG into gear, 'and I hate leaving them just when they're catching their second breath.'

'We could go back if you want.'

He was a man who rarely acted on impulse, and his suggestion surprised him almost as much as it surprised her. He swung the MG out of the drive and into the street, wondering why he had made it. The answer wasn't hard to find. From the instant she had stepped from the lighted hall onto the porch he had been attracted to her. Because he found her radiant wholesomeness, and her vibrancy and vitality, immensely appealing.

She was staring at him. 'But you don't like parties,' she protested, uncertain about whether or not he was joking. 'And I thought you promised my mother to have me home before the clock strikes twelve and I turn into a pumpkin.'

'I promised to pick you up,' he said, the breeze from the Bay tugging at their hair. 'I didn't say anything at all about the time I would get you home. What do you want to do? Go back to the party or go for a hamburger?'

There was an almost overpowering quality about him that she was beginning to find very interesting.

'A hamburger,' she said, knowing that if they returned to the party, he would immediately become the center of female attention and she would lose the opportunity to get to know him better.

He drove down to a hamburger joint on the Embarcadero and they sat at a table overlooking the ink-black bay.

'Your mother tells me you're at Stanford,' he said when he had given the waitress their order. 'What's your major?'

She suppressed a grin. This was a little like being taken out by a diligent uncle. 'I haven't decided yet. Political science perhaps, or literature.' She remembered her dim memory of Lewis as a teenager in an army cadet uniform. 'Have you always been decisive about what you want to do?' she asked curiously. 'Have you always wanted to be in the military?'

'Always. We're a military family. Apart from Scott, that is. All Scott's ever wanted to do is kick a ball around a field.'

The disapproval in his tone was so intense that Abbra had to struggle to keep her eyebrows from arching in reaction. 'I've never been friends with anyone from a military family,' she said, discounting his father, who was her parents' friend, not hers. 'Is it as restricted and dutiful a way of life as it sounds?'

'No,' he said firmly, and she could see tiny flecks of gold in the brown of his eyes. 'It's fun.'

The waitress delivered their hamburgers and french fries and Cokes. He waited until she had gone and then said, 'I guess you know that my father was a battalion commander in the Second World War?'

Abbra nodded, wishing she had paid more attention whenever the conversation at home had included Colonel Ellis.

'When the war was over he continued to serve in Europe and we were posted to twelve or thirteen different countries. I loved every minute of it and I knew at a very early age what it was that I wanted to do when I grew up. Later, when we returned to the States, I went to West Point and Scott went to Michigan State. It took my father quite a while to adjust to the idea that Scott wasn't going to follow in his footsteps as well.'

'But you did. That must have pleased him.'

Lewis's hard-boned face softened slightly. 'It did. When I graduated from West Point he was as pleased as hell.'

He was silent for a moment. A deeply reserved man, he couldn't remember the last time he had spoken with such ease about himself. Aware that Mrs Daley had cast him in the role of an older brother, and not wanting to abuse her trust, he asked hesitantly, 'I'm on three days leave at the moment. Could we meet again and spend the day in Sausalito or Carmel?'

Her first reaction was pleasure at the inherent flattery in his question. All her previous dates had been with young men close to her own age. Lewis was worlds removed from them. Tough and mature and sophisticated. Then she remembered Jerry.

'I'd like to,' she said truthfully, 'but it's a little awkward.'

'You mean that you're already dating somebody?'

'Not exactly.' She folded her arms on the table and leaned slightly on them, her hair falling forward softly at either side of her face. 'But I do have a kind of an understanding with someone.'

'Tell me,' he said, already determined that whatever kind of understanding it was, it wasn't one that was going to stand in his way.

'Jerry is a poet.' Her eyes took on an

impassioned glow. 'At the moment he is in New York, but he'll be coming back to San Francisco and when he does...' She couldn't finish the sentence as she would have liked to because she and Jerry hadn't made any commitments. Instead, she gave an expressive lift of her shoulders, intimating that no more need be said, that when he returned they would be together.

'Poets are pretty unconventional,' Lewis said, giving no indication that he already knew all about Jerry Littler.

Her mother had told him at dinner how distressed she was by Abbra's infatuation with him. How Littler wasn't a legitimate poet but a long-haired, work-shy beatnik who attached himself like a parasite to anyone foolish enough to fund him.

'He isn't going to hit the roof simply because you have a day out with a family friend,' Lewis continued, determined that Littler was never again going to surface in Abbra's life. 'I'll pick you up at ten tomorrow morning and we'll go to the beach.'

'Do you always make people's decisions for them?' She tried to sound indignant but was too pleased to pull it off.

He rose to his feet, knowing that if he didn't take her home soon her mother would no more allow her to spend the day with him than she would allow her to spend the day with Jerry Littler. 'Always,' he said, flashing her a smile that completely transformed his serious face. 'It's my military training.'

* * *

'Well, I have to admit that I'm surprised by this turn of events,' her mother said doubtfully when Abbra told her the next morning that she was going out with Lewis for the day. 'I approve of Lewis, of course, but he *is* ten years older than you—'

'It isn't a date, Mom,' Abbra said. 'He's on leave and I have nothing else planned for today, and so we're going to the beach together. As friends. There's no romance in the air, so please don't behave towards Lewis as if there were.'

'Nevertheless it would be extremely *suitable*,' her mother said musingly. 'Military weddings are so attractive, and Lewis is obviously destined to become a colonel, perhaps even a general.'

From beyond the front door there came the sound of a car drawing to a halt.

'Well, I am not destined to become an army wife,' Abbra said deflatingly. 'Lewis is a conformist. He's simply not my type.' It was true. Although he was undeniably attractive, he was also staid and predictable. Unlike Jerry.

She didn't wait for him to ring the doorbell because she didn't want her mother to waylay him. She hurried out of the house, her hair swinging glossily, her fashionably short lemon sundress revealing long, suntanned legs. Although it was true that he was not her type, she knew that she was his. She had seen it in his eyes the previous night, and she saw it now as she strode across the gravel toward him.

He wasn't in uniform and he looked different, far more relaxed. His cream-colored slacks were snug on his hips and his short-sleeved cotton shirt was open at the throat, revealing a hint of tightly curling, crisp dark hair.

'I've brought a picnic,' he said, sliding the MG into gear.

She was just about to say how impressed she was when she saw bruising on his right temple that had not been obvious the previous evening. 'What on earth did you do to your head?' she asked, staring at a painful-looking swollen place an inch or two into his hairline. 'Walk into a door?'

He gave a sheepish grin, 'I got thwacked on the head a few days ago on a training maneuver.'

'It looks nasty.' She was suddenly very much her father's daughter. 'What did your medic say about it?'

'You don't run to a medic with every little bump and bruise,' he said, amused and more than a little pleased by her concern. 'The last thing a career soldier needs is a long medical record.'

She frowned slightly. She could understand that. Peak physical fitness was obviously the first requisite for a soldier. Nevertheless, she knew enough about neurology to appreciate that any head injury, however slight, justified medical attention.

'Your commanding officer should have *ordered* you to go to a medic.'

He smiled. 'My commanding officer hadn't the slightest idea that I'd been hit,' he said, dismissing the subject and pressing his foot down harder on the accelerator, heading south, toward Carmel.

They spent the morning strolling along Main Street, browsing in the little shops and boutiques, pausing at a café to sip margaritas, walking barefoot along the beach.

'Let's drive out of town and picnic up on the cliffs,' he suggested as they began to walk back to the car.

She nodded agreeably, happy in his company, enjoying herself hugely.

'What are you going to do with this bachelor's degree of yours when you get it,' he asked suddenly.

She knew very well what she wanted to do, but she had never told anyone. Not even Jerry. *Especially* Jerry.

She said now, unselfconsciously, 'I want to write.'

'You mean you want to be a journalist?'

'No.' A wide smile curved her mouth, dimpling her cheeks. 'I want to write fiction.'

His brows rose slightly. 'Wouldn't journalism be more sensible?' he asked, opening the car door for her.

Her smile deepened. It was impossible to imagine Lewis doing anything that wasn't sensible. 'It would, but I don't want to be sensible. I want to be a novelist.'

He began to laugh but she didn't mind. She began to laugh with him. 'I want to be a world-famous, best-selling, *superstar* novelist!'

They were still laughing when he parked the MG high on the cliffs and retrieved the picnic basket from the backseat.

'What have you got in there?' she asked, the ocean breeze blowing her hair around her face as they walked over the springy turf.

'Thinly-sliced ham and melon and roast chicken,' he said, setting the basket down and sitting cross-legged beside it. 'And peaches and strawberries and watermelon.' He pulled her down beside him. 'And French bread and whipped butter and pastries...'

She was on her knees, sitting back on her heels. He forgot about the picnic. Just looking at her high-cheek boned face and her wide-set blue, heavily lashed eyes, brought a lump into his throat. She was very beautiful. The most beautiful girl he had ever seen. But he couldn't tell her so. Not so soon. She didn't yet feel about him as he was beginning to feel about her, and to say anything now would jeopardize the intimacy developing between them.

'I have another weekend leave at the end of the month,' he said lightly, lifting a bottle of Chablis from the basket. 'Why don't we do this again? We could go to Sausalito or to the zoo.'

'Let's go to the zoo.' She helped herself to a slice of melon. 'I haven't been there for years. Not since I was a child.'

He smiled. She made it sound as if her childhood were light-years behind her.

He raised his glass toward hers. 'To the zoo,' he said, suddenly so sure that they were on the verge of a very special and precious relationship, that he had to resist the temptation of leaping to his feet and whooping out loud.

'Where are you stationed?' Abbra asked three weeks later as they strolled past the koala bear enclosure.

'Fort Bragg, North Carolina.'

She halted in stunned surprise, staring at him. 'But I thought you were stationed somewhere near San Francisco. Do you mean you've come all the way from North Carolina just so that we could go to the zoo?'

'I came all the way from North Carolina to have a pleasant weekend away from school.'

'School?' she asked curiously, beginning to walk along beside him once again. 'If you're a lieutenant, what are you doing in school again? I don't understand.'

'I'm at Fort Bragg, at the Special Warfare School, taking courses in counter-insurgency, counter-guerrilla operations, and military assistance operations with foreign governments.'

This time she not only stood still. The blood drained from her face. 'You mean you're going to Vietnam?'

'I hope so,' he said with dry humor, 'or the months I've spent studying Vietnamese history and customs and language will be a waste!'

'But I thought only marines were going out there. To guard the air bases.'

In February there had been a devastating Viet Cong attack on a U.S. base near South Vietnamese Army headquarters at Pleiku. American special forces and military advisers had been billeted at the camp, and eight of them had died and a little over a hundred and twenty others had been wounded. Almost immediately President Johnson had ordered retaliatory air strikes against the north. Abbra remembered clearly the disbelief she had felt at his action when she had seen the newspaper headlines. A month later American marines had splashed ashore at Da Nang to guard the nearby airfield from Viet Cong attack. They had been the first U.S. combat troops to land on the Asian mainland since the Korean conflict.

'But they won't be the last,' her father had said grimly. 'There's going to be no backing down now. We're committed whether we like it or not.'

'What will you be doing out there?' she asked, not sure that she really wanted to know.

'I'm going to be a military adviser to the South Vietnamese Army.'

'So you will be helping the Vietnamese fight their own war?'

'What a nice, simplistic way of putting it. Yes, Abbra, when it comes down to the bottom line, that is what I'll be doing.'

It was as they were leaving the zoo that she thought she must have inadvertently said something that had shocked him, just as much as his conversation about Vietnam had shocked her.

He stopped short suddenly, his eyes blank, as if in stunned surprise.

She turned toward him questioningly. 'What is it? What did I say?'

For a second she thought he wasn't going to answer her, and then he said vaguely, 'I'm sorry ... just a minute...' He raised his hand as if to ward her off.

He looked a little as if he were going to faint. She frowned, stepping toward him, saying in sudden deep concern, 'Lewis! What is it? Are you sick?'

'No...' He still didn't move, although the color had begun to come back into his face. He shook his head as if to clear it. 'That was the damnedest thing.' There was a park bench a few yards away from them and he walked across to it, sitting down, beginning to laugh a little. 'Hell! I suddenly felt as if I'd gone down the biggest roller-coaster in the world!'

'You mean you were dizzy?' She sat beside him, trying to keep the alarm out of her voice.

'Yes. No.' He seemed to have completely recovered. He gave her a slightly abashed grin. '*Giddy* would be a better word. Nothing was going round and round. I just felt as if I'd fallen a hundred floors in an elevator.' He rose to his feet. 'Come on. If we don't leave soon, we'll be locked in for the night with the animals.'

As they began to walk back toward the car, she said curiously, 'Has that ever happened to you before, Lewis?'

'No.' This time his grin was genuinely carefree. 'It must have been the shrimp rolls at lunch.'

She was silent for a minute, and then she said hesitantly, 'You don't think it might have something to do with the blow you received to your head last month?'

His grin vanished. He stared at her. 'No, I don't. That's a ridiculous suggestion.'

'Not really. Daddy has patients who—'

'I had a reaction to something I ate. That's all.'

There was such finality in his voice that she didn't finish the sentence she had begun. She was probably being imaginative anyway. To say anything more to him before she had spoken to her father was pointless.

'Who are we talking about?' Abbra's father asked.

She shrugged vaguely. 'Just a friend. She got hit on the head a few weeks ago and never had it checked out.'

'And what did you say happened to her in class? Did she have a momentary loss of consciousness?'

'Not exactly. It was more as if she just didn't know where she was for a second. She said afterward that she felt as if she had fallen a hundred floors in an elevator.'

'It sounds as if she might be suffering from focal epilepsy. It's quite common when there's been a blow to the head. It results in an underlying structural abnormality being revealed. Natural resistance to epileptic activity is lowered, and mild seizures can occur. Tell her not to worry too much, but it goes without saying that she should report what happened to her doctor at the earliest opportunity.'

'If it *was* a mild epileptic seizure, would she have more and would they be harmful enough that her choice of career might be affected?'

'If what she suffered was a mild epileptic seizure triggered by the injury she received, then it is more than likely that there will be another. There are no hard and fast rules where epilepsy is concerned. And, of course, if that is what it is, then her choice of career may be circumscribed.'

'She wants to go into the army,' Abbra said, her hands behind her back, her fingers crossed.

Her father picked up a copy of the *Chronicle* and shook it open, saying with finality, 'If she has become subject to epileptic seizures she is highly unlikely to be accepted into any profession requiring a stringent physical. Suggest to her that she become a schoolteacher instead.'

Even though she knew Lewis would not want

the subject raised again, she was determined that the next time he flew out to see her, she would do so. Incredibly, because of what happened within minutes of their meeting again, she forgot all about her intention and the subject was never broached.

He had taken hold of her hand, drawing her toward him, and before she could protest, his arms had slid around her and he had lowered his head to hers, kissing her lovingly.

In the first brief second, as his lips touched hers, her every instinct was to push him gently away, and to say that though she was fond of him, she didn't want their easygoing friendship to develop into anything more. She didn't. It was a very pleasant kiss. The nicest she had ever received. Instead of pushing him away her arms slid up and around his neck, her mouth parting softly and warmly beneath his.

'But there is still Jerry,' she had said afterward, not wanting to be guilty of leading him into believing that what was happening between them was serious.

He had shrugged dismissively and she had been unable to see the expression in his dark eyes. 'Jerry is in New York,' he had said, and neither of them had mentioned him again.

In June there were newspaper reports of battalion after battalion of South Vietnamese troops being defeated by the Viet Cong, and Lewis's phone calls to her, and letters, were full of impatience because he still hadn't received orders to leave for Saigon.

It was while he was on the telephone, telling her how President Johnson was going to have to send more combat troops to Vietnam, that she knew he was experiencing another giddy spell.

He broke off speaking in the middle of a sentence.

'Lewis?' she had said. 'Lewis?'

'Yes. Just a minute...'

His voice had the same disoriented quality about it that she had noticed at the zoo.

'Lewis!' she had said again, her voice sharp with anxiety. 'Lewis! Are you all right?'

'Yes.' There had been a moment's hesitation, and she knew that he was lying. There was a note in his voice she had never heard before, a note that seemed incredible in a man so tough and supremely confident. A note of fear.

She said with utter certainty, 'You've just had another giddy spell.'

'Wait a minute, Abbra...' He sounded as if he were gathering his wits with difficulty. After a little while he said, 'I'm okay now. I was just a little light-headed for a second.'

She said carefully, not wanting to arouse the same chill response in him that she had aroused the last time she had tried to talk to him about it, 'When it happened before, at the zoo, were you tired afterward?'

'Yes,' he said, and at the relief in his voice she knew he was assuming she thought his momentary disorientation was merely due to overtiredness.

She said gently, disillusioning him, 'I spoke to Daddy about what happened. I told him it had happened to a university friend. He thinks the giddiness and momentary loss of awareness may be a mild form of epilepsy known as focal epilepsy. And all epilepsy sufferers feel the need to sleep after an attack.'

'Epilepsy?' First there was disbelief in his voice, then anger. '*Epilepsy*? You can't be serious. You can't suggest I'm suffering from *epilepsy*! Christ, Abbra! That's the most ridiculous thing I've ever heard! I'm damned glad you didn't mention my name to your father! A malicious rumor like that could end my career!'

'Not if medical tests proved it *was* only a rumor.'

'There's no need for medical tests! I was a little disorientated for a couple of seconds. I didn't fall down on the ground in a fit, frothing at the mouth and swallowing my tongue!'

'That's grand mal. I never suggested you were suffering from grand mal. All I'm suggesting is that the blow you received on your head has done more damage than you were aware of. Some epileptic seizures are so slight that it's even hard for the sufferer to realize what it is they are experiencing.'

'I couldn't care less whether they know or not! *I* wasn't experiencing a seizure! I've passed medical test after medical test, and for your information, I am one hundred percent physically fit!'

'Go for a complete physical,' she said softly, refusing to give in. 'Then we need never mention it again because there will be no doubt, one way or the other.'

'There's no doubt now!' he said, obviously furious, and hung up on her.

Abbra was sure Lewis would never telephone her or see her again. She was intensely unhappy. Over the last few months he had become a part of her life. She tried to stop thinking about him and to think about Jerry instead. The rumor at Stanford was that he was on his way back to San Francisco. Once she saw Jerry again, she would stop missing Lewis. Lewis had been too old for her anyway. Too endearingly old-fashioned.

It was a Sunday morning, three weeks later, when the telephone calls came. The first had been from Jerry. He had laconically said that he was back in town and at his old apartment in North Beach. He was tied up all day, but if she wanted to see him tomorrow, it was fine by him.

The next telephone call, minutes later, was from Lewis.

'You were right,' he said briefly, his voice oddly flat. 'I've been to a doctor. A neurologist. I have a hairline fracture of the skull, and the blow evidently reduced my resistance to epileptic seizures. What I'm actually suffering from is something called temporal lobe epilepsy, which I think is the same sort of epilepsy your father was referring to. There are a wide range of symptoms that can be experienced and the brief, momentary loss of awareness I've suffered from a time or two, along with that almost pleasant giddy sensation, is the way that I experience it. It may develop and I may, in the future, suffer a full-scale epileptic attack. On the other hand, I may never notice a damn thing wrong with me, ever again.'

'And the army?' she said fearfully. 'What did the doctor say about your career in the army?'

'He didn't know about it. However many army physicals I undergo, I'm unlikely to have a brain scan. And without a brain scan no one can know that there's anything wrong with me. And there isn't really anything wrong. I haven't had another attack, and I personally doubt if I ever will have another.'

'So you're not going to give your army medical officer a copy of the neurologist's report?'

'No.'

'But, Lewis—'

His voice was no longer flat. It was so overwrought it was nearly out of control. 'For Christ's sake, Abbra! The word epilepsy on my army records would finish me! I'd be desk-bound for the rest of my career! And why? Because very occasionally I feel as if I've come down a roller-coaster? No one is ever going to know about this, Abbra. No one! Not ever!'

'Okay.' She didn't know why, but she had begun to cry. 'I'm so sorry about it all, Lewis.'

'Yes. I know.' His voice had softened. He sounded unutterably weary. 'I have a two-day pass, and I have some other news for you as well. I'll see you this evening. We'll go to a movie.'

'A movie would be lovely.'

She had put the telephone receiver back on its rest. She knew that what he was doing was very wrong, but she couldn't think any less of him for doing it. The army was his passion and his life. He always had wanted to be a soldier. She couldn't even begin to imagine him as anything else. And he was right about the epilepsy. Once on his army medical record it would never come off, no matter how mild the form he was suffering from, no matter if he never, ever suffered from another attack again.

He would be here this evening. She would see him then. And though Jerry had said he was tied up all day and couldn't see her until tomorrow, she was going to ignore what he'd told her. After all, she hadn't seen him for nearly six months, so she certainly wasn't going to wait another six hours. She was going to drive over and see him right away.

Half an hour later she parked her Oldsmobile in the street outside his apartment. The apartment was over a liquor store and she ran up the stairs, excitement mounting in her till she could hardly bear it. She had missed Jerry. He was so talented, so outrageous, such wonderful fun. She could smell the sickly sweet aroma of marijuana and was uncaring. Jerry was a poet. All poets smoked pot. And pot was harmless. Nothing more than a stiff drink.

The door at the top of the uncarpeted stairs was closed. She gave only the briefest of knocks before opening it, a wide smile on her face, saying sunnily, 'Hi, Jerry! I thought I'd surprise you!'

He didn't look remotely surprised. Only vastly amused. He was laying naked on unclean, disheveled sheets. The girl beside him, eyebrows raised in surprise, was naked also. As was their sweat-sheened male and obviously mutual friend.

It was the girl who was smoking marijuana. Jerry was snorting coke. Abbra had never seen the white powder before, but she knew what it was.

She stood for a moment, almost too dazed to react, all the anticipated pleasure draining from her. There was a time when she might have thought this kind of a scene was fun, hip. No longer. The semen-stained sheets, and the tangled, perspiring bodies made her feel nauseated. She didn't want any part of this. She didn't want to be even remotely connected to such people.

She turned on her heel, uncaring of the shouts of laughter that followed her down the stairs.

She was crying when she reached the Oldsmobile. Not because she knew that she was never going to see Jerry again, but because she was so ashamed of her own foolishness. How could she not have seen him as her mother had so clearly seen him? As Lewis would no doubt have seen him. How could she have been so stupid for so long? So blind?

She rammed her car key into the ignition, slamming the Oldsmobile into gear. She didn't want to go home. Not yet. Not until it was evening and Lewis would be there.

She drove north, stopping the car in deserted countryside to walk. Walking always calmed her and it calmed her now. She was glad that she had driven down to North Beach so unexpectedly. Glad that she had seen what she had seen. She felt suddenly much more mature, more sure of who she was and of what she wanted in life. As dusk fell she returned to her car, driving back to San Francisco, happy and eager to see Lewis again.

He pulled in the driveway only seconds ahead of her. She was out of her car even before he was, running toward him. 'Oh, Lewis! I'm so glad to see you!' she cried, hurling herself into his welcoming arms.

He held her very close, sensing a momentous change in her. 'What is it?' he demanded gently, and then intuitively, 'Is it Jerry? Have you seen Jerry?'

She nodded, lifting her head to his, her arms still tightly around his waist. 'Yes, and Jerry doesn't matter anymore. I didn't realize it until today, but he never has mattered.'

'I'm going to 'Nam,' he said, not letting go of her. 'I leave at the end of next week. Will you marry me before I go?'

'Oh, yes, Lewis!' She began to laugh and cry simultaneously. 'Yes! Yes! Yes!'

# CHAPTER TWO

Serena Blyth-Templeton woke at dawn to the sound of an army of men hammering tent pegs into the ground to make gigantic marquees. She groaned and rolled over pulling a pillow over her head. It was the longest day of summer. The day Bedingham was to play host to the Rolling Stones, the Animals, a dozen lesser-known bands, and God alone knew how many thousands and thousands of fans.

'Oh hell, oh shit,' she said loudly. 'I should not have driven home last night! I should have stayed in town!'

But she hadn't stayed at her family's town house in Chelsea; she had driven home through the English countryside, intoxicated on champagne and high on marijuana, and the fates had been kind to her, as they always were, and she'd had no accidents and no police cars had come screaming after her. Serena didn't know whether this was a relief or a disappointment. Life was so boring, and a night in a cell sounded as if it might have a certain piquancy about it. It would certainly stir up her father, which was always fun, and it might even impress Lance.

Her twin brother had become obsessed with everything extremely left wing. If it was anti establishment, anti his father, anti his privileged upbringing and expensive education, then Lance was fervently in favor of it. The latest object of his contempt was the police, though Serena privately doubted that Lance had ever had anything to do with them apart from cursing them when they politely asked him to remove his Aston-Martin from the double yellow lines outside the house in Cheyne Walk. Nevertheless, for the past two months Lance had denounced all policemen, even their friendly local police, as 'fascist pigs,' to his mother's bewilderment and his father's irritation.

The hammering continued relentlessly, the goosedown pillow no defense against it. With a groan of despair Serena flung it to one side and with an obscene lack of a hangover, sprang agilely from the bed. It was a day she had been looking forward to for months, though wild horses wouldn't have made her admit it. To do so would have been uncool. She had decided early on in the planning of the concert that the only acceptable reaction to Mick Jagger's presence and performance at Bedingham was to assume an attitude of sophisticated indifference. After all, she wasn't a groupie, queuing all night for the privilege of seeing Mick at a distance of five hundred yards. She was Lady Serena Blyth-Templeton, and as such Jagger was surely *her* guest, just as much as he was her father's.

With long, easy strides she crossed to the window and pulled back the curtains. The greensward that fronted Bedingham and stretched away gently uphill into a three-mile-long avenue of elms was nearly invisible beneath a stage swarming with technicians and groaning under the weight of expensive sound equipment. Seating around the stage was still being erected, though the punters, as Serena's father always referred to those members of the public who paid for the privilege of visiting Bedingham would, for the most part, either sit on the grass or stand.

Serena smiled. Despite her indifference to almost anything and everything, she loved Bedingham passionately. It had been in her family ever since the sixteenth century when Matthew Blyth, an adventurer, had been rewarded by Henry VIII for dubious services rendered, and been given permission to acquire and domesticate the dissolved abbey of Bedingham in Cambridgeshire. He had done so with zest, transforming Bedingham into a house fit for royalty.

Under Mary's reign, when upstart Anglicans were out of favor, Bedingham had suffered and lost the major part of its more glittering trappings, but under Queen Elizabeth I, favor had been restored and more land acquired. Through a satisfactory marriage alliance Blythes became Blyth-Templetons. Under Charles I, the Blyth-Templetons being royalist, Bedingham suffered a minor setback, but after the accession of Charles II, its star entered its zenith. The family was ennobled, an east and west wing were added, and the elaborate formal gardens around the house conceived and executed.

Under the boring rule of the Hanoverians, Bedingham had lost a little of its grandeur, declining to play host to a royal family undeserving of it. Under Queen Victoria it had continued to flourish. A long library had been added to the house, and more avenues and follies added to the grounds. Only in the last century had true difficulties arisen, and these, being financial, Serena's grandfather had sensibly solved by marrying the only daughter of an American railroad king of Swedish descent.

Serena patted the ancient stone sill of the mullioned window. After playing host to Tudors, Stuarts, Saxe-Coburgs, and Edward VII, Bedingham was now going to play host to the Rolling Stones. 'You've seen a lot,' she said affectionately to the ivy-covered bricks and mortar, 'but in four hundred years you won't ever have seen anything quite like this!'

There was a perfunctory knock at the door, and without waiting to be asked to enter, her brother strolled into the bedroom, his thumbs hooked into the pockets of his jeans, his hair shoulder-length. 'Hell of a lot of noise, isn't there?' he asked cheerfully. 'The old man is going to open the gates at eight to relieve the pressure building up in the village. Apparently the local roads are already jammed. Hundreds of those coming to the concert camped in surrounding fields last night. I don't suppose we'll be at all popular with our farmers.'

Serena shrugged, indifferent to the wrath of the farmers who tenanted Bedingham land. 'What time does the concert get under way?'

'Ten o'clock, but what you really mean is what time does Jagger arrive?' Lance flung himself facedown on the rumpled bed and rested his chin in his hands. 'Two o'clock, supposedly. Until then, the fans have to be content with lesser mortals.'

'He is staying on, isn't he?' Serena asked, turning away from the window and rummaging in the drawer of a George III mahogany chest for a pair of jeans and a T-shirt. 'I mean, he is coming to the ball?'

'He's been invited and the word is that he's accepted, but I can't quite see it, can you?' Lance asked, grinning at her speculatively as she pulled the jeans on beneath the discreet cover of her nightgown. Ever since she had returned home on vacation from her Swiss finishing school, she had been at pains to let him know how shockingly sexually experienced and liberated she had become. It amused him that her sexual liberation didn't extend to himself and that, where he was concerned, proper sisterly modesty was still the order of the day.

Serena, aware of his amusement and knowing very well what had caused it, pulled her nightdress defiantly over her head, her breasts gloriously naked as she reached for her T-shirt with a studied lack of hurry, not bothering to keep her back towards him. 'Why shouldn't he accept?' she asked. 'HRH has accepted, hasn't he?'

A flare of shock, like an electric current, had run through him. Her breasts were small and high, her nipples so pale as to be almost invisible. They needed biting into to gain color. He found the mere idea cripplingly erotic. 'Yes,' he said, wondering why incest had never entered his thoughts before. 'Prince Charles is coming.'

The ball that was to follow the concert was to be the kind of ball that Bedingham was accustomed to. Dress would be formal, the young bloods of England's oldest families would be in attendance, a carefully selected sprinkling of stage and screen stars were invited to add glamour to the evening.

Serena pulled her T-shirt down over her head. Wondering why he had never before realized the strength of his sexual feelings for his sister, Lance said, 'Why you should think Charles's presence guarantees a fun evening, I can't imagine.' Lance's views of the Windsors were on a par with his ancestors' views of the Hanoverians. They were bores and he could well do without them.

Serena surveyed her reflection in a walnut-framed cheval glass. 'I like Charles,' she said unexpectedly. 'He might be a stuffed shirt, but he's a sincere stuffed shirt.'

Lance temporarily forgot the fascinating path down which his thoughts were taking him and rolled over on to his back, shouting with laughter. 'Oh, God, Serry! Don't tell me you have ambitions in that direction! I couldn't bear it! Queen Serena! What a hoot!'

'I think I would make a very good queen,' Serena said, sweeping up her long, pale gold mane of hair and piling it experimentally on top of her head. 'A tiara would suit me.'

'Bollocks!' Lance said disrespectfully, 'the days of Blyth-Templetons fawning to royalty are over, thank God. What we need in the family now is some good, unadulterated, revolutionary blood!'

Serena let her hair fall back down to her shoulders. She adored Lance and always had. He was the most important person in her life, but he bored her when he got on his political soapbox. She frowned slightly as she searched in the bottom of her French armoire for a pair of white leather high-heeled boots. Perhaps it wasn't so much boredom as resentment. Until his political involvement with the far left, they had always been in complete agreement about everything.

As children they had often been left for long periods in the care of nannies and au pairs and housekeepers while their parents had cruised the Mediterranean, skied in Switzerland, or shot grouse in the Scottish Highlands. They had been totally dependent on each other for companionship and affection and had grown up with the unswerving attitude that it was the two of them against the rest of the world. The unity that had been forged between them as children was still the most important thing in their lives, and Serena had tried hard to share his left wing passions. She had failed. Politics, even revolutionary politics, bored her.

She found the boots and pulled them on. Except for politics they had always been alike in everything. Both of them were tall and slender, light-skinned and blond-haired. In Lance this had resulted in a certain air of effeminacy, and Serena often thought that one of the reasons for his radical left wing views was that he thought they gave him a harder, more macho image.

There was nothing pale and washed out about the combination of Serena's Nordic and Anglo-Saxon beauty. There was strength as well as delicacy in her fine-boned features, and the Swiss sun had given her skin a luminous honey-gold tone. Her eyes were gray, wide-set, dark-lashed, their smoky depths alight with fiery recklessness. When she moved she did so with utter assurance, carrying her tall, superbly proportioned body with the arrogance and ease of a dancer or athlete.

She lifted the two dresses that had been hanging on the front of her armoire, and that she had moved in her search for her boots, back into position. Both were white. One bore a Mary Quant label and was so minuscule as to border on the indecent; the other bore a Norman Hartnell label and was of heavy satin, ankle-length, and encrusted with thousands of tiny seed pearls. The Mary Quant was the dress she intended to wear for the concert; the Norman Hartnell was the gown she was to wear for the ball. She looked at the dresses in happy anticipation, knowing that they said a lot about her. They were at opposite ends of the fashion spectrum, yet she thought them equally wonderful. She liked extremes. It was safe, middle-of-the-road moderation that she couldn't stand.

'Our house guests, the Andersons, arrived while you were living it up in town last night,' Lance said, wondering if Serena would be disturbed if she knew the way his thoughts were turning, or if she perhaps shared his agonizingly erotic fantasy. 'Pathetically small-town America despite their millions and their boast of being one of Boston's oldest families.'

Since Lance had spent the last few months denouncing America and Americans with the same arbitrary passion he mustered to denounce the British police force, his verdict on their house guests was not surprising.

'Where does their money come from?' Serena asked with interest.

The American ability to rise from pauper to millionaire in a single generation fascinated her. Their own great-grandfather had been a penniless Swedish immigrant when he had arrived in America, yet when he had died he had left his daughter a fortune so large that Bedingham and they were still thriving on it.

'Banking,' Lance replied. He shrugged,

then sat up on the bed, swinging his legs to the floor. 'But the family fortune is bolstered by whisky. The grandfather picked up a whisky franchise in Scotland during the last days of prohibition. When prohibition conveniently ended, he became a millionaire overnight.'

'He was taking a risk,' Serena said, pulling a comb through her slick-straight hair. 'What if prohibition hadn't ended? What would he have done with his whisky franchise then?'

'He was in politics,' Lance said dryly. 'He *knew* prohibition was going to end.'

Serena gave a deep-throated chuckle. 'I think I would have liked the grandfather. What is the grandson like?'

Lance shrugged again, suddenly sure that Serena would also like the grandson. He didn't like the idea. 'He went to Choate, he's at Princeton now and he thinks England is an anachronism.'

'If he's at Princeton, he can't be *that* dumb,' Serena said, tossing her comb down on to the Lalique tray on her dressing-table, 'and if he thinks England an anachronism, I would have thought you would have been in total agreement with him. After all, you're the one who wants to bring the country to its knees and revolution to the streets!'

'Maybe so, but I don't need a bloody American to help me do it!' he said, throwing a pillow at her.

Serena sidestepped the pillow with ease. 'Come on, brother mine,' she said, striding toward the door, her breasts pushing tantalizingly against the thin cotton of her T-shirt. 'Let's make sure Bedingham is ready for its day of glory.'

That Bedingham would be among the first buildings to be put to the torch if Lance and his fellow revolutionaries ever had their way was something never mentioned between them. When Lance was with his left wing friends, he always and loudly disowned Bedingham, vowing that when his father died, he wouldn't accept his hereditary title, and that for all he cared, the house could be reduced to a pile of rubble. It was a statement he never made in front of Serena. He knew how much and how deeply she felt about Bedingham. It was a measure of how deep his feelings were for her that he never talked rashly of Bedingham's future in her presence. They walked down the sweeping staircase, through the large inner hall and then through the entrance hall, its floor tiles emblazoned with the Blyth-Templeton family motto and crest. Even though the concert was not due to start for two hours, they could hear music.

'The music is coming from transistor radios,' Lance said as they stepped out on to the stone steps of the south entrance. 'My God! Look at the crowd pouring down from the gates! What is it going to be like when things really get under way?'

'It's going to be fabulous!' Serena said, her eyes shining as she ran down the steps toward the gravel dividing the house from the lawns fronting it.

The gates that her father had opened at eight o'clock were so far distant they couldn't be seen, but the first of the fans to stream through them were already making their way down through the avenue of elms, toward the lawns and the stage.

'She Loves You' was blaring out from a score of transistor radios, and Roy Orbison blared from dozens more on a different station.

'Hey, want a joint?' the first of the invaders to reach the front of the house, a long-haired individual wearing an Afghan coat and a multicolored headband, shouted across to her.

'I'd love one!' Serena responded enthusiastically, accepting the sweet-smelling marijuana and drawing deeply on it while Lance looked at her, not knowing whether to be amused or annoyed. 'Wouldn't breakfast be more suitable?' he asked. 'It's barely the crack of dawn.'

Serena sucked down another lungful of smoke. 'It may be more sensible, Lance, but it will also be boring and I'm going to do *nothing* today which is boring. Today all I'm going to do is have fun, fun, *fun*!'

At ten o'clock her father announced that the concert was to begin – but he did so, Serena thought, with the air of a drowning man bereft of all help.

Masses of singing, shouting, dancing bodies covered the lawns surrounding the stage, and the grassy hill and avenue beyond. There was tight security around the house. Uniformed police were at every entrance, and there were large No Admittance signs on all the doors. Her father, after his dazed declaration that Bedingham's pop festival was officially under way, had reeled into the house, unable to believe that his simple project for bringing in extra income could have turned into such a monster. Never in a million years had he expected so many thousands of young people to throng to Bedingham. He couldn't even begin to imagine where they had all come from. And never had he imagined that music could be so excruciatingly, so shatteringly, *loud*.

'It's unbelievable!' he said weakly to Serena as they passed on the stairs. 'A sea of unwashed, half-naked humanity stretching as far as the eye can see.'

'It's a hot day,' she said practically, 'and if the new class of punters is beginning to get you down, just think of all the lovely lolly they're bringing in.'

Her father already had. It was his only consolation.

'But the grounds,' he moaned, clinging to the banister. 'There won't be a blade of grass surviving by the time it's over!'

She patted his arm. 'Bedingham survived the Civil War,' she said comfortingly, 'and it will survive the Stones. Stop worrying, Daddy. Enjoy yourself.'

'Serena!' he called out after her as she

continued buoyantly on her way. 'Our house guests! Are you taking care of them?'

'Haven't even seen them,' Serena responded, not halting in her march for the door. 'I should have a whisky if I were you, Daddy,' she added over her shoulder. 'It will steady the nerves.'

Her father groaned and turned toward his study. Serena's was the first sensible suggestion anyone had made since the debacle had begun.

As Serena ran lightly down the sweeping stone steps of the south entrance, past the policeman on duty, she had a bird's eye view of the rear of the stage. It was packed with sound equipment and back-up musicians, and one of them, a tall, languid-looking man about her age was so striking-looking he attracted and held her attention despite the press of people around him.

He was standing at the very edge of the rear of the stage, leaning nonchalantly against an amplifier, his thumbs hooked into the pockets of his jeans, one foot crossed over the other at the ankle.

His negligent stance, and his air of bored indifference in the midst of such fevered excitement, reminded her of Lance, though that was as far as the similarity went. The musician's hair was blue-black, falling low across his brow, and despite his slender build, there was a sense of power under restraint about him, an animal-like magnetism that

Lance conspicuously lacked.

The Animals had just bounded onto the front of the stage; the roar of applause and shouting and stamping was deafening. As Eric Burden's raw, unmistakable voice gave vent to the first line of 'House of the Rising Sun', Serena smiled to herself.

The musician might not be a famous name, but he obviously had other more than compensating qualities. And Serena saw no reason why she shouldn't enjoy them. By the time she had reached the rear of the stage, Burden was reaching the last erotic, skin-tingling stanza of his song.

'I'm Serena Blyth-Templeton,' she shouted to the stewards who blocked her way. 'Let me through!'

They responded to the authority in her voice almost immediately, but even so, by the time she squeezed around to the edge of the stage, her quarry had disappeared.

'There was a musician here a few minutes ago,' she shouted over the roar of applause to a still-perspiring member of the band who had preceded the Animals. 'Do you know where he went?'

'Haven't a clue, love,' he said, looking her up and down appreciatively. 'Will I do instead?'

Beneath his stage makeup he had blemishes and there was a whiff of stale alcohol on his breath. 'No,' she said, softening the blow with a grin. 'I'm sorry, but you won't.'

He shrugged and laughed, and as Burden

began to sing 'Don't Let Me Be Misunderstood' she philosophically abandoned her search and moved to the front of the stage, squeezing into the center of the crush, dancing on the spot to the sound of the music, cheering until she was hoarse when the song came to an end.

As morning edged into afternoon, the heat became almost unbearable. 'I thought it was supposed to rain every day in England,' a powerfully built Australian yelled to her as they stood, arms around each other's waists, swaying to the beat of the music.

'It usually does!' she shouted back. 'But sometimes, just sometimes, we actually have a summer! This is it!'

Some girls had dispensed with their T-shirts altogether, dancing bare-breasted, shrieking with laughter as the occasional cooling bottle of beer was poured over them. Serena was tempted to take off the Quant mini-dress she had changed into just before the start of the concert. If she had been anywhere else, she would have done so. Only respect for Bedingham restrained her.

When the announcement came over the loudspeakers that the Rolling Stones had arrived and would be appearing in approximately twenty minutes, a roar went up and the chant 'We want Mick' began to surge through the vast crowd.

Serena extricated herself from the sweaty hold of the Australian. She needed the bathroom and she had no intention of forcing her way to one of the many portable facilities that had been parked on the grounds. As the female group onstage pounded into a blistering rendition of 'Then He Kissed Me', she pushed and shoved her way out of the throng, running toward the house. She ducked beneath the barriers that had been erected, saying breathlessly to the policeman who ran toward her, 'I'm Serena Blyth-Templeton! I live here.'

The policeman recognized her and lifted the last barrier to allow her through. She ran up the south entrance steps and hammered on the enormous double doors there. The butler ascertained it was a member of the family and not a member of the mob and opened the door. Serena ran past him, saying between gasps for air, 'Thanks, Herricot. Super fun, isn't it?'

The butler didn't demean himself by agreeing with her. Instead, he speedily relocked and bolted the doors and retreated to an inner sanctum where he could lengthen his odds of survival by placing cushions against his ears.

Serena took the steps of the great staircase two at a time. She was dripping with perspiration and she wanted to have a quick, cold shower before she returned to the fray. Even in the house the music was deafening. From her bedroom window she had a spectacular view of the sloping hillside and the avenue of elms, every inch of space packed with dancing, clapping, cheering, applauding fans.

Banners were being waved, some emblazoned with 'We love Mick', others with 'Peace not war', and 'Americans out.'

She giggled as she stepped out of her dress and danced, hips swinging, into her bathroom, hoping that the visiting Andersons wouldn't imagine the banners were personally for them. American involvement in Vietnam had been escalating all summer, and so had the protests against it. Today, at least, Lance was surrounded by thousands of political sympathizers.

She stood, face upturned beneath the shower, the water turned on full blast. For once life wasn't boring. She was blissfully high on a combination of alcohol and generously shared joints. In another few minutes Mick Jagger would be onstage. Later, there would be the ball, and Jagger would be there. She would meet him, and who knew what would happen after she did?

She stepped out of the shower, treading dismissively over the discarded white mini, yanking another dress from her armoire, this time a lemon-colored one, equally short. To the best of her knowledge, the idea of a Bedingham pop festival was the first and only idea that her forty-six-year-old father had ever had. It had been stunningly well worth the wait. There were television cameras recording the event, BBC interviewers roaming through the crowd, and the festival was already being spoken of as if it were an established annual event. As it would be.

'This year the Stones, next year the Beatles!' she said zestfully to the house in general, striding out of the bedroom, slamming the door behind her.

As she hurried down the main staircase, a door in the inner hall below her opened and a tall, dark stranger walked nonchalantly out of the salon and toward the door leading to the drawing room.

'What the devil do you think you're doing?' she shouted indignantly, beginning to run down the remaining stairs toward him. 'The house is closed to visitors! Didn't you see the signs? The barriers?'

He turned unhurriedly, one hand on the knob of the living room door. 'I would have had to be blind not to have seen them,' he said dryly.

She stopped suddenly on the bottom step, her heart beginning to slam. She knew she had been right about his overpowering masculinity when she had seen him from a distance. Now, close up, his sexuality rushed over her in waves. 'The house is closed to visitors,' she repeated, walking toward him.

His eyes weren't dark like his hair; they were a hot electric blue, and there was charm as well as insolence in the lines of his long, mobile mouth.

'I'm not a visitor,' he said, his eyes moving from her hair to her face, to her breasts, to her legs and back again with brazen appreciation.

The minute he spoke she knew that he was

American, but an American with a very generous dash of the Celt. His tall, lean build, and his coloring, were those of a certain type of Irishman and, like them, he had a whippy look to him that said he would be an ugly customer in a fight – and something else about him made Serena believe he wouldn't need much of an excuse to join any fight.

'I know damn well you're not a visitor!' She wanted to sink her teeth into his neck, to lick the perspiration from his skin, to see if he looked as magnificent naked as he did in his open-necked white shirt and his tight-fitting blue jeans. 'You're a musician. I saw you earlier, on the rear of the stage. Now, will you please leave the house? As I have already said, it is not open today to visitors.'

She had walked right up to him, with every intention of physically knocking his hand away from the drawing room doorknob. When he left, she would go with him. She wasn't about to lose him again. But she would be damned to hell before she allowed anyone, even this excessively handsome man, to have the run of Bedingham.

'I am not a visitor,' he said again, leaning back against the door and folding his arms negligently across his chest. 'And I'm certainly not a musician.'

'Then who the devil are you?' she demanded. Suddenly her eyes widened and her voice choked with laughter, she said 'Oh, hell! Don't tell me! I know! You're an Anderson!'

'And you're a Templeton,' he said, eyes

gleaming with answering laughter and with something else, something she knew was naked in her own eyes: unconcealed, instant sexual desire.

'A Blyth-Templeton,' she corrected him, her eyes moving over him with the same blatant appreciation he was showing. At five feet ten, she was nearly as tall as he. Slowly her eyes roved back toward his face, over the bulge in his crotch, the olive flesh tones of his neck and throat, the attractively self-deprecating quirk at the corners of his mouth. Their eyes met and held, and excitement raged through her. This wasn't going to be just good! This was going to be sensational!

'What is it?' he asked. 'Sabrina? Sophie? Selina? I can't remember.'

'Serena. And you?'

'Kyle.'

She nodded. She had been right about the Celtic blood. 'I thought you were supposed to be old Boston, not Boston Irish,' she said, so close to him that she could feel the warmth of his breath on her cheek.

'Our family is like yours,' he answered her, white teeth flashing in a dazzling, down-slanting smile. 'We turn a blind eye – when it suits us.'

She laughed throatily. 'And would it suit you now?' she asked, one hand on her hip, the line of her thigh knowingly provocative.

He grinned. It was very rare for him to meet a girl tall enough to face him eye to eye, and rarer still to be so flagrantly propositioned by one as beautiful. She had come down the broad, sweeping staircase toward him with all the speed and grace of a panther. His grin deepened. With her long mane of gold hair, and her honey-gold skin, she wasn't a panther, she was a puma. Sleek and supple, and wonderfully predatory.

'Why not?' he said, easing himself casually away from the door. 'How about a guided tour?'

Outside, the screams and shouts had reached cataclysmic proportions as the Stones belted out the opening bars of 'It's All Over Now' and Mick Jagger leapt onstage.

Serena's smile widened. Incredibly she no longer gave a damn about Jagger. 'Come this way,' she said, opening the drawing-room door with a flourish. 'It will be my pleasure.'

This room was Bedingham's formal drawing room, used only for receptions and soirées. An eighteenth-century Blyth-Templeton, eager for a room that would serve as a grand reception room for county balls, theatricals, concerts, and other entertainments, had commissioned the leading architect of the day and asked him to create one. He had done so by removing several internal walls and ceilings and the rooms above them, creating a grandiose room that rose the whole height of the house, culminating in a wide skylight dome, ecclesiastical in splendor.

Kyle whistled through his teeth. 'Is the whole house as old as this?'

'This isn't old,' Serena said in amusement, walking across to the white marble and ormolu chimney breast and standing with her back to the sheet of mirror that rose above it, one foot on the fender as Kyle looked around him. 'This room was added in the 1770s, which is late in Bedingham's lifetime. The house was originally built around the remains of a dissolved abbey in 1532.'

'Okay,' Kyle said as she led the way out of the room and through a door in the far corner to an adjoining room. 'I'm impressed. What room is this?'

'It's known as the Red Room because of the color of the walls. We use it as the family dining room.'

Unlike the drawing room, which had been light and airy, the walls covered in panels of yellow silk, the carpet a dove gray bordered in blue and gold, the Red Room's walls and ceilings were painted a deep Pompeian red. The room was dark and oppressive.

'It isn't a color I'd like to live with myself,' he said with blunt frankness.

Serena laughed. 'It wasn't our choice either. It was painted like this in Queen Victoria's reign and hasn't been altered since.'

Kyle shook his head in disbelief. 'My mother has the house painted every year. She'd have a stroke at the thought of eating in a room that hadn't been changed in over a hundred!'

'Oh, we refurbish it a little every now and then,' Serena said, laughing and watching him, wondering where she would take him for the culmination of their tour. Her bedroom or a guest bedroom? She walked across to one of the windows looking out over the north lawns. 'Do you see that yew tree? The one nearest the house? It was already fully grown when Henry VIII gave Matthew Blyth permission to domesticate the abbey. Wood from that tree provided bows for the weapons of the yeomen of England. That is how old Bedingham is.'

He looked across at her curiously. 'You really love this place, don't you?'

She turned away from him, the deafening sound of the concert a little more muted now that they were on the north side of the house. 'Of course,' she said simply. 'It's magnificent. Let me show you upstairs.'

They left the room by an opposite door, climbing the back stairs and coming out in a long gallery, the walls ornately decorated with plaster garlands of fruit and flowers and laurel wreaths.

'I know where we are again,' Kyle said as from outside the thunderous beat of 'Little Red Rooster' was replaced by 'Not Fade Away'. 'My room is the little yellow room, just off the first landing.'

Serena ignored the guest rooms. They weren't splendid enough as a setting for what was about to take place. Only one room was splendid enough.

'This is the Queen's Room,' she said, throwing open a door and entering a large sun-filled room with a four-poster state bed standing in the center on a small dais. 'So called because Queen Elizabeth I is reputed to have slept here, and Queen Anne in 1712 most certainly slept here.'

There was a central canopy, the corona carved with Prince of Wales feathers. The bedposts were painted white and gold and the netted hangings were backed by crimson brocade edged with thick braid and a deep knotted fringe, and held at the corners by elaborate tassels.

'It's impressive, but a little small,' Kyle said, standing at the side of the bed, one hand resting on a white and gold post.

'When Queen Anne slept here, she slept alone,' Serena said, her tongue moistening her lips as she stood at the opposite side of the bed, barely four feet away from him, wanting him so much that she could barely stand.

'Poor Anne.' His glossy blue-black hair was low over his brows, his Celtic blue eyes holding hers. 'Has anyone slept in it since?'

The dark, rich throb of his voice sent shivers down her spine.

'Queen Victoria,' she said, her vulva engorged and aching. 'And one or two lesser notables.'

'But no one recently?'

Her voice was hoarse, her eyes burning. 'No one in living memory,' she said, wondering how long it would take them to scramble out of their clothes, wondering if the state bed was strong enough for the punishment it was about to receive. To a roar of applause that could be heard a county away, 'Not Fade Away' merged into 'I Wanna Be Your Man'.

The light in his eyes was devilish. 'Then let's rectify the situation,' he said, his hands on his belt, his buckle already half undone.

Without a further word of encouragement, without his even laying a finger on her, she pulled off her boots and unzipped her dress, sliding it off her shoulders in feverish haste, kicking it away from her, wrenching her panties down with trembling fingers.

He threw his jeans and shirt away from him, whistling low. 'I knew you'd look fantastic naked,' he said thickly, 'but you look even better than I'd imagined!' Without wasting any more time on words, he reached across the bed for her, pulling her down on it, rolling her beneath him.

Her nails clawed his back, her legs opening wide. She needed no preliminaries, no soft words or caresses. She had been ready for him ever since she had faced him at the foot of the staircase. 'Now!' she demanded fiercely, twining her legs around him, her body straining toward his in primeval need. *'Now, you bastard! Now!'*

His mouth came down hard on hers, and the moment that he mounted her, he entered her, plunging deeply and unhesitatingly into her hot, sweet center. Outside, Mick Jagger blasted into 'Come On', fifty thousand fans screamed and shouted, the ancient bed shook and shuddered, and as Kyle's sperm shot into her like hot gold, Serena reached a climax that left her almost senseless.

For long minutes neither of them even attempted to move or speak. His heart slammed thuddingly against hers, beads of perspiration running down his neck and shoulders.

'That...' he said at last, easing himself away from her and rolling over on to his back, '... was quite ... remarkable.'

Serena let out a long, deep, satisfied sigh, and opened her eyes. 'I knew it would be,' she said composedly. 'I knew the minute I saw you, on the rear of the stage.'

He turned over on his side, resting his weight on his elbow. 'That's quite an ability,' he said, grinning down at her. 'If you could put it in a bottle and market it, you'd make a fortune!'

She giggled and then stretched languorously. 'Before we make love again, I need a drink and a smoke. Stay here and conserve your energy and I'll go on a foraging expedition.'

'If you're intent on making love again in anything like the same fashion as last time, make sure whatever you bring back is strong,' he said teasingly.

She sat up and leaned over him, kissing him full on the mouth, her sheet of pale gold hair swinging down like a curtain around them. 'I will,' she said, her eyes dancing as she drew her mouth away from his. 'Because I am. Again and again and again and again.'

He groaned in mock defeat, and she laughed springing from the bed and stepping back into her lemon mini-dress, saying, 'I'll be back in five minutes. Don't move.'

'I couldn't,' Kyle said, the hot afternoon sun spilling through the leaded windows onto his hard, lean body. 'I doubt I'll ever move again!'

'You will,' she promised, swinging from the room as Jagger launched into 'The Last Time'.

Kyle grinned. He knew he would. His zest and vigor were more than equal to hers. He just didn't see why she should take anything for granted.

By the time she returned, he was already hardening again at the mere thought of her. She was like some magnificent amazon. Beautifully proportioned, totally uninhibited.

'Where did you learn to make love in such a hurry?' he asked as she moved a couple of Staffordshire figurines from a rosewood side table to make room for two bottles of Margaux and two glasses.

'I wasn't in a hurry,' she said impishly, taking off her dress and tossing a joint across to him. 'If I'd been in a hurry, I would have made love to you on the steps of the great staircase!'

He laughed, watching her as she poured out the wine, the tousle of her pubic hair a rich wheat-gold. 'Hurry or not, it was still pretty experienced.' He lit the joint, inhaling deeply. 'How old are you?'

'Eighteen,' she said, walking across to the bed, a full glass of wine in either hand. 'And you?'

'Nineteen.' He didn't want to talk about himself; he wanted to talk about her. 'Where did the expertise come from? Rollicking with the yokels in local haystacks?'

'Certainly not. The expertise is from an *extremely* exclusive Swiss finishing school.'

He arched an eyebrow. 'I thought they were for perfecting French and learning how to play hostess to ambassadors.'

'They are also for learning how to ski,' she said as if explaining everything.

White teeth flashed in a grin. 'Okay. I give up. What has learning to ski to do with sex?'

She laughed huskily at his innocence. 'Skiing itself has nothing to do with it, but oh, those Swiss skiing instructors! Those wonderful, handsome, athletic, adventurous, sex-mad, *virile* Swiss skiing instructors!'

'If Swiss skiing instructors are responsible for the mind-bending experience of a few minutes ago, then I raise my glass to them,' Kyle said, lifting his glass of Margaux high. When he put it down again he said, the mere tone of his voice making her damp with longing, 'Finish your wine. It's my turn to surprise you.'

She did. And he did. 'Oh,' she gasped, her eyes widening, the sensation in her solar plexus like a bomb that had been detonated. 'Oh! *Oh! Oh!*'

They didn't talk again for a long time.

Outside, Mick Jagger was succeeded by Peter and Gordon, and after them Gerry and the Pacemakers.

In the Queen's Bedroom, all through the long afternoon, Serena and Kyle made love with the zestful, undiminished appetite of two healthy young animals. He made love to her slowly, withdrawing whenever she neared satisfaction, teasing and arousing her until she screamed at him to come to a conclusion. He made love to her with his tongue alone, not allowing her to reach out and touch him, forcing her to remain completely and excruciatingly passive. By the time they lay exhausted, sheened with sweat, the ornate brocade covers of the bed half falling on the floor, the sun was sinking in the sky and both bottles of Margaux were empty.

'What is the *wildest* thing you've ever done, Kyle?' she asked, her head on his chest as the sweet smell of marijuana surrounded them.

Kyle squinted up at the canopy above him, and the carvings of the Prince of Wales feathers. 'Making love on a bed Queen Elizabeth I and Queen Anne slept in while Mick Jagger and a score of other pop groups sing a mere fifty yards away comes pretty near to heading the list,' he said dryly.

Serena moved her lips languorously over the smooth, sun-kissed flesh beneath his cheek. 'But what else have you done that is *really* wild?'

He frowned, his head so light with alcohol and marijuana that he could scarcely think straight. 'I once flew my uncle's Piper Twin Comanche under the Brooklyn Bridge.'

She giggled and he carefully killed the cherry in his joint and even more carefully placed it on the table at the side of the bed. 'What about you? Or are your escapades so wild as to be beyond belief?'

'I don't think so,' she said modestly. 'On the last night of term, the school's head girl crept into my bed. She's German and built like a Valkyrie.' She giggled again, moving her hand lower down his abdomen. 'That was pretty wild.'

Kyle would have liked to ask for more details, but he was having difficulty coordinating what he wanted to say with what he was able to say.

'I wish we could do something wild, something really wild, together,' Serena said, bending her head to his penis, her tongue circling it in long, lazy strokes.

'You mean, like *both* of us going to bed with your German friend?' Kyle asked, wondering who the fool had been who had said that English girls were frigid.

Serena paused in her ministrations. 'No, silly. Something momentous and far-reaching and totally, totally shocking.'

'We could always elope,' he said, wondering if he was physically capable of making love one more time, and if he was, whether he could capture a place in the *Guinness Book of World Records*.

'Eloping isn't shocking,' she murmured,

straddling him, holding his penis with one hand and moving herself teasingly and tormentingly back and forth over its engorged tip.

'Believe you me, as far as my parents are concerned, it is,' he said, wondering how long he could bear the pleasure before having to take action. 'In fact, I can't think of anything that would shock them more!'

She slipped the head of his penis into the mouth of her vagina. 'You're quite right,' she said, her voice high and slurred from wine and marijuana. 'My parents would be shocked to death. It would cause the most frightful fuss.' She sank down on him, closing her eyes in ecstasy. 'So why don't we do it? Why don't we elope?'

Kyle tightened his arms around her, deftly rolling her beneath him. 'Because I don't know any blacksmiths,' he said reasonably, driving deep inside her in an agony of relief.

She laughed, twining her legs around him, suddenly sure that she loved him and that she would always love him. 'Silly,' she said, her diction very slurred now. 'Marriages at Gretna Green over the blacksmith's anvil haven't been legal for years and years.'

'Then why do people elope there?' He gasped, his eyes tightly closed, an expression of intense concentration, almost of agony, furrowing his features.

'Because...' Serena struggled for breath. 'Because ... you can be married in Scotland without parental consent as long as you're over sixteen.'

'I'm over sixteen,' he said unnecessarily, knowing that his climax was going to be the most shattering he had ever experienced. 'Let's forget the ball this evening. Let's go to Scotland instead.'

'I'd love to,' she panted, lifting her legs over his shoulders. 'Oh, Kyle! Oh, God! *Oh, Kyle!*'

# CHAPTER THREE

Gabrielle Mercador sat completely immobile, the late afternoon sun streaming through the skylight onto her semi-naked body. One hand was resting on a small table at her right-hand side, and her chin was propped on her other hand while her large, luminous eyes gazed soulfully into the distance.

'That is enough,' said the heavily-built, bearded Frenchman standing a few yards in front of her, wiping his brush on a rag and surveying the painting on the easel before him with satisfaction. 'We are nearly there, *ma petite*. Another three or four sessions and it will be complete.'

Gabrielle happily snapped out of her pose and soulful expression and stretched catlike. 'Good,' she said, not bothering to walk across to survey the result of the three-hour sitting. 'Do you want me back the same time tomorrow, Philippe?'

He nodded, still studying his handiwork. 'Yes, but it is a pity you cannot come in the morning, *ma petite*. The light is so much better. There is a softness about afternoon light that is not compatible with what I am trying to achieve.'

Gabrielle gave a small Gallic shrug of her shoulders as she crossed the studio toward her pile of clothes. *'C'est impossible,'* she said as she reached for her brassiere. 'I am still sitting for Léon Durras in the mornings.'

'Bah!' Philippe uttered expressively, at last looking away from his painting and toward her. 'Durras has never done any decent work, and he's too old to begin doing so now!'

The corners of Gabrielle's generous mouth quirked in amusement. She sat regularly for over a dozen artists and was used to their jealous backbiting and bickering. For a moment she was tempted to remind Philippe of Léon's recent excellently reviewed exhibition but decided against it. Such provocation would result in a harangue from Philippe that could last half an hour, and she hadn't the time to spare to listen to it.

'Tomorrow afternoon, then,' she said, zipping herself into a short, straight black skirt and pulling a thin sizzling pink cotton top down over full, lush breasts.

'Unless that bastard Durras falls down dead, and then I'll see you in the morning,' Philippe said sourly.

Gabrielle grinned. Twenty years before, just after the liberation of Paris, Philippe's wife had been Léon's mistress. It was an insult Philippe had never forgotten, or forgiven.

She slipped her feet into perilously high stiletto-heeled shoes and picked up her straw shopping bag.

'Are you singing at the Black Cat this

evening?' Philippe asked suddenly as she walked across to the spiral staircase that led down from the studio to the ground floor and the street.

She paused, one hand on the metal handrail. 'Yes,' she said coquettishly, 'are you coming?'

He forgot the bad temper that her sitting for Léon Durras had aroused. 'I might,' he said with a grin.

She laughed. 'Then I will see you there,' she said, blowing him a kiss and going carefully down the awkward stairs into the street. Philippe was easily old enough to be her father, and in all the years she had been modeling for him, he had never made an indecent suggestion to her, but he liked to flirt. It made him feel good. And flirting was such second nature to Gabrielle that she wasn't even aware when she was doing it.

She swung out of the darkened vestibule and into the sunlit street, a petite, buoyant figure with a shock of squeaky-clean titian curls, laughter-filled green-gilt eyes, and a wide, generous mouth. Her mother was Vietnamese, her father French, and from her mother she had inherited cheekbones that were Asian and high, like those of a Tartar princess, and a short, straight, perfectly shaped nose. From her father she had inherited a firm chin, an earthy sexuality, and the hard-headed common sense that is every Frenchwoman's birthright. No one knew where her remarkable hair coloring had come from. It was as individualistic, as unique as everything else about her.

'Good afternoon, *chérie*,' the aged flower seller on the corner of the rue de Clignancourt and the boulevard Rochechoart called out to her as she swung past, her capacious straw shopping bag over her shoulder, her bottom bouncing tantalizingly beneath her tight, brief skirt.

'Good afternoon, Helena! It is a lovely day, is it not?'

Helena cackled toothlessly. The little Mercador was always so full of *joie de vivre* that just seeing her made the grayest day seem bright.

*'Oui!'* she shouted back jauntily as Gabrielle brought the Montmartre traffic to a halt by stepping out into the street, crossing over towards the place d'Angers. 'It is when you are young, *chérie!*'

Gabrielle grinned and raised a hand to show old Helena that she had heard, and then she walked across the place and into the avenue Trudaine, humming beneath her breath. She would sing 'Fever' tonight at the club, and 'Lover Man' and 'Fly Me to the Moon', and it was about time she gave 'I Gotta Right to Sing the Blues' a public airing. She had been rehearsing it for weeks now and thought that at last she had personalized it and made it her own.

'Good afternoon, Gabrielle!' the local butcher called out to her as she walked exuberantly past his window.

Gabrielle gave him a wide, dazzling smile and threw him a kiss.

'Good afternoon, Gabrielle!' the old woman selling papers at the corner of the avenue Trudaine and the rue Rodier, said to her. 'How is your mother? Your father?'

'They are both well, thank you, Madame Castries,' Gabrielle replied sunnily, taking a newspaper and tucking it into her bag.

'That is good,' Madame Castries said with a pleased nod of her head. The little Mercador wasn't like some eighteen- and nineteen-year-olds. She looked after her parents. It was a pity that there were not more girls like her.

Gabrielle went into the bakery and bought two loaves of bread, chatting to the baker about his wife's health and the progress his children were making at school. In the maze of streets that lay to the south of Sacré-Coeur, there wasn't a man, woman, or child who didn't know her and didn't greet her with pleasure.

She had lived in Montmartre since she was eight years old. Since the French had been defeated at Dien Bien Phu and her father had circumspectly decided that it was time he and his family left Saigon for good. Her mother had never settled comfortably in Paris, which was so vastly different from Vietnam. The climate was cold and damp instead of hot and humid. Her father, too, though France was his homeland, had never been able to come to terms with the difference in lifestyle between

Saigon and Montmartre. Only Gabrielle, after the first few bewildered days, had adjusted, as happy in the narrow, cobbled streets of Montmartre as she had been in the wide tree-lined boulevards she had left behind her.

She crossed the road to number fourteen. A passing *gendarme* winked at her and told her he would be at the club that evening. A young man on a motor scooter called out to her that he had seen Léon Durras' latest canvas and that, thanks to her, Durras had created a masterpiece. Gabrielle paused at the door that led up to her parents' top floor flat, laughing and shouting back that she was glad he thought so.

Beside her, on the wall, was a bird cage with two canaries in it. As the motor scooter zipped away, Gabrielle put her hand into the bottom of her straw bag and withdrew some birdseed.

'There, *mes petits*,' she said, tossing it into the cage. 'Enjoy your supper.'

The canaries belonged to old Madame Garine, who lived in the ground floor flat. When Gabrielle had first arrived in Paris, only the canaries in their little cage had been familiar to her. In Saigon every house had its cage of brightly fluttering birds, and in those first strange, lonely days, Madame Garine's canaries had been a great comfort.

She stepped into the lobby and hurried up the dark stone steps, a rueful smile on her lips. Her father had promised her mother and her, when they left their large sun-filled house in Saigon, that they would live just as comfortably in Paris. They had not. In Saigon there had been servants and easy luxury. In Montmartre there was only a small flat and penny-pinching economy. Her mother, lonely without her Vietnamese family and friends, had begun to stay more and more indoors so that now, ten years later, she very rarely ventured out. It was Gabrielle who shopped, Gabrielle who brought the gossip of the streets to the dining table, Gabrielle who insured that there was still laughter and gaiety in the Mercador household.

Her father, Étienne, had left his home in a small provincial French town for Saigon in 1932. He had had only a moderate education and could see no great future for himself in France. The colonies promised richer pickings. A family friend, already in Saigon, saw to it that there was work waiting for him when he arrived, and for eight years he was happily and profitably employed as a civil servant in a French government department. In 1938, enjoying the rank and lifestyle of a senior department head, he married Duong Quynh Vanh, a Roman Catholic Annamite of good family. When war broke out in Europe a year later, it made little difference to Étienne and Vanh Mercador. Étienne continued to enjoy the respect and prestige of his government position, and Vanh continued to enjoy the lazy leisurely life-style of a French colonial wife. And then, in 1940, the Japanese swept south.

The French administration in Vietnam was crushed, the French interned as the Japanese surged onward, driving the British from Malaya, the Dutch from Indonesia, and the United States from the Philippines.

Étienne gritted his teeth, proclaimed himself a supporter of the French government in Vichy, and escaped internment by the skin of his teeth. Vanh's brother, Dinh, moved north, seeing in the Japanese invasion of his country hope for a future Vietnam free of *all* invaders. The Japanese would be defeated eventually by the Allies. When they were, Dinh was determined that his country would no longer be governed by the likes of his brother-in-law. Vietnam would become independent and free.

In the North, a middle-aged freedom fighter, Ho Chi Minh, was consolidating nationalist groups under one banner, fighting a guerrilla war against both the Japanese and the French. Dinh said good-bye to his family in the south and went north, on foot, to join him.

When the war ended and the Japanese left, Étienne had looked forward to a period of increased prosperity. But his brother-in-law's belief that native Vietnamese could force the French out was naive. The French had governed the country for a hundred years and, now that the war with the Japanese was over, they intended to govern it for another hundred.

Vanh had kept her thoughts to herself. She loved her husband, and she loved the French way of life. She had been educated in French convents, and she enjoyed the ease and luxury of her husband's French salary. Yet, like her brother, she wanted to see her country independent. As life after the war began slowly to return to normal, she comforted herself with the belief that the French would allow the Vietnamese a greater say in the governing of the country, and in the fact that she was, at last, pregnant.

In 1945 and '46, the French reasserted their authority over Vietnam, but only with difficulty. In the North, Ho Chi Minh proclaimed a provisional Vietnamese government in Hanoi, and in the south, Britain came to France's aid, subduing bitter protests and bloody street fighting, and imposing French rule yet again.

As a child in Saigon, Gabrielle was happily unaware of the tensions surrounding her. The family home was in the avenue Foch, a wide, tree-lined, flower-filled boulevard. She had a Vietnamese nanny to look after her, a monkey for a pet, and a garden crammed with tuberoses and orchids and gardenias to play in.

Fighting continued from 1946 until 1954 when the French met with the forces of General Giap, Ho Chi Minh's right hand man, at a small village on the Lao border, called Dien Bien Phu. All the previous bloody engagements had been running guerrilla battles, in which the Viet Minh had the advantage. At Dien Bien Phu, the French, with superior air power and superior weapons, and fighting the kind of battle that they were accustomed to, were confident that they could thrash the Viet Minh once and for all.

Shortly after French troops were airlifted in to the floor of the steep valley, General Giap moved thirty-three infantry battalions, six artillery regiments, and a regiment of engineers toward Dien Bien Phu. In a tremendous feat of muscle power, soldiers, coolies and cadres dragged artillery to the tops of the surrounding mountains. From then on, the incredulous French were under constant blistering attack. A howitzer was positioned within range of the French airstrip, cutting off flights in and out of the valley and making it almost impossible for them to receive supplies or to evacuate their wounded. Almost from the beginning the French were in a state of siege.

Seven horrific weeks later, in a sea of blood and mud and vomit, the Viet Minh's red flag went up over the French command bunker. The French had been defeated; colonial rule in Vietnam was at an end, and an international conference was set up in Geneva to plan the country's future.

Whatever that future was, as a minor French civil servant, Étienne knew that his good fortune had run out. He packed his bags and returned to the land of his birth with his wife and child. And the three had long since settled in Paris.

Gabrielle climbed the last few steps and opened the door of the apartment. From the kitchen there came the appetizing aroma of shredded pork and rice vermicelli, for her mother still cooked the traditional Vietnamese dishes.

'Hello, *Maman*. Is Papa home?' she asked, putting her straw bag on the kitchen table and removing the two loaves of bread and the newspaper.

'No, he is playing *boules*,' her mother said, kissing her cheek.

When they had first returned from Saigon, her father had been devastated to discover that his government would not employ him. He had found work as a manager of a local garment factory and then the factory had closed. For the past two years he had not worked at all.

Gabrielle looked down at the table. There was a letter from her aunt. Her mother, diminutive and fragile in Vietnamese traditional dress, sat down at the kitchen table, a doubtful frown creasing her brow.

'Nhu says that so many Americans have arrived in Saigon in the last few months, it is as if they are taking over the country. That instead of being a French colony, Vietnam is becoming an American colony.'

Nhu was her mother's sister in Saigon, from whom letters were received regularly.

'Nhu is being ridiculous,' Gabrielle said briskly.

She loved her pretty, decorative mother

dearly, but intelligence and a grasp of current affairs were not her strong points. 'Without American aid, the Viet Cong would be victorious and Nhu would be living under a Communist regime. She doesn't want that, does she?'

'No,' her mother said uncertainly. 'But Dinh believes it is the only way and that communism under Ho will not be as bad as we fear.'

Gabrielle sighed. 'It will still be communism,' she said impatiently. Her mother's trouble was that she wanted to be loyal to all the people that she loved. Whenever she was reminded of Dinh, the dearly loved brother she had not seen for nearly twenty-five years, she wondered if the Communist threat was not as terrible as her sister said it was.

On a dark evening in 1963 he had knocked at Nhu's door and had stayed until the early hours of the morning. It was the only time that any of his family had seen him since he had walked north so many years before. He was now a colonel with the North Vietnamese forces. He had come south on an undercover mission for General Giap. The General intended to infiltrate large numbers of his forces into the south and he wanted the situation in the south assessed before he committed them. Together with a dozen military specialists and a handful of civilian cadres, Dinh had trekked down a jungle trail that threaded its way through southern Laos and north-eastern Cambodia, into the highlands of South Vietnam.

'But how can they sweep south now that the Americans are helping us?' her mother had asked him bewilderedly. 'The North Vietnamese are peasants. They cannot fight America!'

Now she said, still bewildered, 'It is so hard to understand what is happening at home when we are so far away.'

Saigon was still home to her mother, though neither of them knew if she would ever see it again.

Gabrielle finished her glass of kir. 'I want to go over my repertoire for this evening, *Maman*. I don't want anything to eat before I go. Save me something for when I come home.'

Her mother nodded. Gabrielle had been singing in Montmartre nightclubs for over two years now, but it had been two weeks since her last engagement and she had been carefully putting together a whole new selection of songs.

Gabrielle went to her tiny bedroom and picked up her guitar. When she sang in the clubs she sang to piano accompaniment, but there was no room in her parents' flat for a piano, and even if there had been, there was no money for one.

Painstakingly she went over all the songs that she intended to sing. Her musical style was very strongly her own. Although she often sang songs that internationally known stars had made famous, she had the ability to take the most well-known lyric and transform it so that her audience felt as if they were hearing it for the first time.

The club circuit was highly competitive, and though she was not aware of it, her growing success was due to the perfect match between her voice and her personality. She had a husky, knowing voice, with a sensual chuckle deep inside it, the kind of voice that announces its owner loves not always wisely, but too well, and who doesn't give a damn one way or the other. Though she'd become popular singing standard love songs by Irving Berlin, Cole Porter, and Lerner and Loewe, she had begun to write her own songs: committed, passionate love songs that sent tingles down the spines of her audience.

Satisfied with the selection she had made, she bathed in the apartment's ancient, iron-framed bathtub and dressed for the evening's performance.

The fresh skirt that she stepped into was a little longer than her previous one had been, but was still black. The sweater she wore was also black, long-sleeved, and fell low over her hips, the neck high and straight, every inch covered in a mesh of tiny, glittering sequins. She slipped her feet into high-heeled black suede pumps, and dropped her list of songs and the accompanying music into a small black shoulder bag.

*'Au 'voir Maman! Au 'voir, Papa!'* she called out as she walked out of her bedroom and toward the apartment's front door.

*'Au 'voir, chérie!'* her parents called after her from the kitchen, where they were eating their evening meal. 'Good luck!'

Gabrielle closed the door and started down the three flights of stone steps that led to the street. Her parents always wished her luck, and her mother often waited up until the early hours of the morning so that she could make her an omelette and coffee when she returned home, but nothing Gabrielle could do would persuade them to come and watch one of her performances.

She hurried down the last of the steps and walked quickly through the lobby and out into the spangling blue dusk. They never said so, but she knew it was because no matter where she appeared, striptease artistes invariably preceded and followed her act. Girls who took off their clothes before men were, in her parents' eyes, little more than women of the streets, and they did not wish to be reminded of how closely their daughter worked with them.

The dome of the Sacré-Coeur was pale against the evening sky as she hurried past it, toward the Black Cat. She wondered if Philippe would keep his word and visit the club that evening. She doubted it. He would be immersed in work, already making sketches and drawings for whatever his next project was even though his present painting was incomplete.

'Good evening, Gabrielle,' the porter at the Black Cat said to her as she hurried down the steps into the club. 'You're early this evening.'

'I want to run through a couple of songs with Michel,' she said, flashing him a smile that made the bulge in his crotch harden. He knew that his employer had tried hard to persuade her to remove her clothes as she sang; regrettably he'd been unsuccessful. It was a pity. It was a sight he would have given a year's salary to see.

Gabrielle greeted Henri, the barman, as he busily polished glasses. 'Is Michel here yet?' she asked, sitting down on one of the high stools.

Henri paused in what he was doing and poured her an anisette. 'He's in the dressing room, trying to persuade Paulette to sleep with him.'

Gabrielle laughed. Michel was her pianist, a tall, thin, bespectacled youth who could play the piano like an angel, but who enjoyed a spectacular lack of success with women.

'I'll go and rescue her,' she said, draining her glass and pushing it back across the bar toward him.

Henri removed it with a grin. 'It is not Paulette who needs rescuing so much as it is Michel who needs helping!' When she laughed, he added, 'It's nice to have you back, Gabrielle. The last couple of singers have been long-haired beatniks who looked as if they never washed. At least tonight, with you and Paulette on the bill, the club will be full.'

It wasn't hard to fill the Black Cat. Even when packed to capacity the large below-street-level room held only seventy people, and then the tables and chairs were squeezed so closely around the tiny stage that Paulette often complained that she could feel the audience's breath on her flesh.

That evening Paulette performed to a boisterously appreciative audience, coming offstage with the perspiration breaking through her makeup. '*Mon Dieu*, Gabrielle. I should have listened to my mother and become a schoolteacher! It would have been an easier life!'

'You wouldn't have liked it,' Gabrielle said impishly. 'It would have been far too boring!'

When the applause for Paulette began to fade, Michel began to play her introductory music. She waited for a moment, judging her timing, and then walked out on to the stage.

Gavin Ryan was no expert on nightclub singers, especially singers who sang in clubs as small and sleazy as the Black Cat, but he had known the first time he had seen her, nearly three weeks before, that the audience's response to her was unusual.

Singers in Montmartre clubs were given far less attention than the strippers. When the strippers had departed and the singer came on, it was generally the signal for the audience to turn its attention to the bar and order another round of drinks while they discussed the merits or faults of the last stripper.

Gabrielle was different. When she came onstage, she commanded the audience's attention even before she began to sing. After the excess of flesh that had preceded her, and that the patrons were accustomed to, her black skirt and glittering black high-necked, long-sleeved sweater were as stark and uncompromising as a nun's habit, the spicy red flame of her hair almost indecent by contrast.

She made none of the usual efforts to woo her audience with flirtatious words and smiles before she began to sing. Instead, as Michel played the first few bars of her opening song, she stood perfectly still, insolently indifferent to them, and when she sang, it was as though she were singing for herself and herself alone.

Gavin put down his glass of cheap champagne. He had seen her twice before, in a different club, and was as riveted by her now as he had been then. She had the most extraordinary face, both sensuously feline and appealingly, childishly gamine, and there was the merest hint of duskiness in her complexion, as if she were of mixed blood, Moroccan, perhaps, or Algerian.

The fellow Australian he was sitting with the first time they had seen her had said to him, 'I agree with you that she's amazing-looking and that she has a terrific singing voice, but I wouldn't go near her if I were you, cobber. They're all on the game, the lot of them. No telling what you might catch.'

Gavin rather reluctantly agreed with him. At twenty-three, he'd bummed his way from Brisbane halfway round world, and miraculously caught nothing worse than influenza in India. The hostesses in the club were certainly prostitutes. He had already spurned two very definite propositions. It was a pity though. There was something mesmerizing about Gabrielle Mercador. She had the rare capacity to be completely still, and yet to command unwavering attention. When she sang, the emotion in her voice was naked, raising goose pimples on his flesh. Her opening song was followed by one he had never heard before, then she sang '*La demoiselle élue*,' by Debussy, and then the most evocative rendering of 'Fever' that he had ever heard.

When she walked off the stage to enthusiastic applause he felt a devastating sense of loss. Telling himself he was a fool, he rose to his feet. As he did, a young black girl strutted onto the stage dressed in thigh-high black boots, white satin shorts, and a revealing scarlet bolero. He turned away, uninterested, squeezing his way through the crowded room toward the bar.

The bar was deserted. Every back was turned toward it as the black girl divested herself of her bolero, throwing it wide and high into the audience to thunderous wolf whistles and shouts of crude encouragement.

'A beer,' Gavin said to Henri, wondering if he was going to have enough sense and willpower to resist coming to see Gabrielle Mercador the following evening.

He wasn't aware of her approach. One minute he was deep in thought, the next he heard a husky, enticing voice asking the barman for an anisette with water.

He turned his head swiftly, eyes widening in disbelief. She was standing next to him, so near that he could smell her perfume. Her makeup was heavier than he had expected, but almost immediately he realized that that was because of the strong spotlight under which she sang.

'Excuse me,' he said in halting French before he could lose his nerve. 'But could I have the pleasure of buying your drink?'

'*Non, merci*.' Her response was automatic. She never socialized with the patrons. They were nearly always sweaty and lustful and drinking too much.

She hadn't looked at him when he had spoken to her, but now, as she turned to move away, she did so, and she hesitated. He wasn't the usual sort of patron. He was young and clean-cut, with a mop of shaggy, sun-gold hair. His disappointment was obviously so sincere that she said impulsively, trying to soften the blow she had dealt him, 'I'm sorry, but I never drink with the patrons.'

Gavin was nonplussed. In all the other clubs that he had been into, *all* the girls – singers, strippers, and hostesses – touted for laughingly expensive bottles of champagne.

'I'm sorry too,' he said, not wanting her to walk away from him. 'Couldn't you make an exception? Just this once?'

He had strongly marked brows bleached blond by the sun like his hair, and his eyes were a deep, warm gray.

'Yes,' she said, breaking one of her cardinal rules. 'A lemonade please.'

He quirked an eyebrow. 'Not another anisette?'

She laughed. 'No, I have to perform again in half an hour.'

'I saw you last week at the Columbo,' he said, searching for the correct French words with difficulty. 'I thought you were sensational. That's why I came here tonight. I wanted to see you again.'

'Oh, how nice!' Her pleasure was genuine. There was nothing hard or artificial about her. Prostitute or not, she was the nicest girl he had ever met. He cleared his throat.

He was far from sexually inexperienced, but he had never before attempted to do what he was going to do now.

'Are you, er, available later on?'

A small frown creased her brow. '*Pardon*? I'm sorry. I don't understand.'

'Could I see you later on, after the show?' He wondered if his French was totally incomprehensible to her and put his hand inside his breast pocket, withdrawing his wallet, hoping to indicate that he knew what the situation was.

Her eyes widened as she looked at his wallet and realized what he was trying to ask her. If it had been anyone else, she would have walked away indignantly, but he looked so uncomfortable and so agonized that instead of being insulted she began to giggle.

He flushed scarlet, not knowing what he had done or said to make himself ridiculous.

'I'm sorry,' she said, still giggling. 'It's just that you have made a mistake. I am a singer. That is all. Only a singer.'

Relief swamped him, and he didn't care that he had made a first-class fool of himself.

'I'm glad,' he said, grinning. 'My name is Gavin Ryan, and I still want to take you out after the show.'

'I am not sure,' Gabrielle said truthfully. 'I will make up my mind later. Where are you from? New Zealand? Australia?'

'Australia,' he said, wondering how he could have been such a fool and determining to sock his friend on the jaw the next time he saw him.

'And what are you doing in Paris?' she asked as the black girl finally divested herself of her last article of clothing to wild applause.

'I've just gotten myself a job as a reporter with a press agency. What I really want to do is to go out to Vietnam and cover events there, but the agency has a rule that you have to work for three years in one of the European offices before being assigned as a war correspondent.'

Gabrielle's eyebrows rose slightly. 'And what do you know about Vietnam?' she asked teasingly.

'I know there are some big stories brewing there,' he said, loving the way she spoke. 'And there's going to be one hell of a lot of action now that the Americans are beginning to fight.'

A three-piece band had begun to play, and couples were starting to cram the tiny dance floor. She put her glass of lemonade down on the bar. 'I have to go now,' she said regretfully. 'I am onstage again in ten minutes. Good-bye, Mr. Ryan, it has been nice talking to you.'

'But I thought you said I could see you after the show?' His alarm at the prospect of losing her was so naked that she burst out laughing again.

'I said that I would *think* about it,' she said reprovingly.

'And have you?'

His anxiety and urgency were so raw that she couldn't resist teasing him just a little longer.

'I will let you know, when I sing,' she said, moving away from him. 'My first song will be my answer.'

He watched as she moved away from him and then ordered himself another beer. If her song was a refusal, he would come back tomorrow night, and the night after, and the night after that. He would come back every night until she agreed to see him. Until he could talk to her in clean air, and not in a smoke-filled cavern packed with a lecherous audience totally unworthy of her.

When she walked out onstage, his chest physically hurt. She stood for a moment, perfectly poised, effortlessly in command of her audience, her spicy red curls burning like a candle flame. The pianist began to play and a tiny smile quirked the corners of her mouth as she turned toward the bar where he was standing and began to sing, 'I'll Be Seeing You'.

He had his answer. His grin was so wide it split his face. He wanted to shout a loud 'hooray'; to push to the front of the stage and seize her and hug her until she was breathless.

'A bottle of champagne,' he said to Henri. 'A genuine one!'

When the last notes of the song died away, she began to sing Irving Berlin's 'Always'. Though neither of them could possibly have guessed it, it was a song that was appropriate for the long, agony-filled years that lay ahead.

# CHAPTER FOUR

Abbra had never been happier. Lewis was given a special two-day pass and they were married in the military chapel at Fort Bragg. The only thing marring the day was the absence of Scott. He was at football training camp and was unable to be best man though he had sent his congratulations and his apologies. A friend of Lewis's, who had been his classmate at West Point, was best man.

After the wedding her parents returned to San Francisco, and after her one-night honeymoon Abbra had followed them by train.

It was a strange feeling, becoming a married woman with so little warning. A married woman whose husband was, in twenty-four hours time, going overseas to fight in Vietnam.

Once she was back home the feeling of strangeness increased. Outwardly her life was the same. She still lived with her parents in Pacific Heights; she still attended college. Yet inwardly she'd changed. She no longer had any interest in parties or dances. They were for girls who were on the lookout for men, and she was no longer looking; she was married to Lewis and she had no desire to behave as if she were still single.

She began to see less and less of her close friends. After the first heady pleasure of showing off her wedding ring and receiving her friends' squeals of congratulations, she found that she had very little to say to them. The endless talk about who was dating whom was no longer fascinating, and they were not interested in the things that preoccupied her: the military situation in Southeast Asia and her fears for Lewis's safety.

As September merged into October, she wondered if returning to San Francisco had been a mistake. If she had moved into quarters on an army base, then at least she would have had other married women to talk to, women who would understand her position and who perhaps also had husbands serving overseas. As it was, she felt oddly isolated and increasingly lonely. After six months in Vietnam, Lewis would have five days leave. He had already written to her and suggested they spend his leave together in Hawaii. There was hardly a waking moment when she wasn't thinking about it, looking forward to it, but there was another three months before the dream would become reality, and the three months stretched ahead of her as if they were three hundred.

On the second Thursday in October a ring at the front door put an end to her growing worries. She was in her bedroom, writing the daily portion of her weekly letter to Lewis, when her mother knocked and entered, saying in a voice that indicated she wasn't very pleased by the event, 'You have a visitor, Abbra. Scott.'

Abbra put her pen down immediately, rising to her feet in happy anticipation.

'I appreciate the fact that as he is now your brother-in-law a certain courtesy is due him, but I don't approve of him, Abbra. He is so unlike Lewis. Why any well-educated young man should opt out of his responsibilities in the way that Scott has done is completely beyond me. With all his opportunities he should have become a lawyer or a stockbroker. Or followed his father and Lewis into the army.'

'Playing professional football *isn't* opting out of responsibilities, Mom,' Abbra said patiently, sliding the half-written letter into the top drawer of her desk. 'It's a career, just like any other career, and it's a tough and competitive one.'

Her mother shook her head, unconvinced. 'I'm sorry, Abbra, but I can't possibly agree with you. Professional football players are not the sort of people that we would normally mix with.'

'Well, we're mixing with one now, so everyone had better start getting used to the idea!' Abbra said with asperity. 'Where is he? In the living room?'

Her mother nodded, her lips tightening. Even though she had approved of Lewis, she had not approved of the indecently quick wedding. It had not been at all the kind of wedding she had pictured for her daughter. And now this. A football player in her house. She didn't like it, and she had no intention of allowing it to become a regular event.

Abbra ran quickly down the stairs, hoping that her father wasn't being as cold to Scott as her mother had obviously been. When she went into the living room and found him standing by the window in an otherwise empty room, her reaction was one of relief.

'Hello,' she said with a welcoming smile. 'I'm Abbra.'

Scott had been looking out over the bay and turned quickly, shocked amazement flaring in his eyes. He strode to meet her, suppressing his emotion almost immediately. 'I'm glad to meet you, Abbra,' he said, taking her hand. 'Sorry I wasn't able to make the wedding. It was my first training camp and there was no way I could break loose, even for a day.'

'It's all right,' she said truthfully, 'I understood.'

He grinned down at her. 'That's good. My father certainly didn't. When I was injured in the first game of the season, he said it was God's punishment for my putting training before family commitments!'

Her eyes darkened with concern. 'I'm sorry. I didn't know you had been injured. What happened? What did you do?' As she asked, she wondered why he'd looked shocked when she walked into the room. What had he been expecting? Someone far more glamorous and sophisticated? He had known she was still at college. Surely he couldn't have expected her to be much older?

'I made a seventy-five-yard touchdown interception which won the game, but I was hit after the whistle and the ligaments in my ankle were badly torn. I've been having physical therapy on them now for six weeks, and it will take another three or four weeks before I can play again.'

He was taller than Lewis, six feet three or perhaps six feet four, and he was as powerfully built as the genial giant she had been dancing with the night she had met Lewis. Scott's hair was nearly as blond as the genial giant's had been. It grew low into the nape of his neck, a rich barley-gold, and thick and curly.

'So while I'm resting up and having treatment on it, I thought I'd catch up on my family obligations.' He grinned again. 'Which in this case means getting to know my new sister-in-law. I wondered if you'd have an early dinner with me, to help the process along?'

'I'd love to!' she said immediately. It was deeply important to Abbra that she get on well with Lewis's family. Though she had met his father as a child, the wedding was their first real opportunity to talk. She'd liked him and been fairly sure that the feeling was mutual. Now she had a chance to get to know Scott and she would also, at long last, be able to talk to someone about Lewis.

'I'll just put some shoes on and let my

mother know I'm going out,' she said.

Incredibly, he hadn't realized she was barefoot. He and Lewis were so dissimilar in taste and temperament that he had never in a million years imagined Lewis would have married any girl he, Scott, thought halfway passable. When Abbra had walked gaily into the room in jeans and an open-neck cotton shirt, glossy dark hair swinging silkily around a square-jawed, high-cheekboned face, he had been so stunned that he could hardly speak. He had known that she was still at college, but had never for a moment imagined she would be so young and glowingly vital.

He looked down at her feet. They were narrow and well-shaped, the nails painted a pale, pearly pink. He wanted to tell her not to put on anything too stylish in the hope that after they ate they would be able to go down to the beach and walk. Almost as soon as the thought entered his head he cursed himself for a fool. He was taking her out for a meal, but it wasn't a date. It couldn't end on the beach or anywhere even remotely similar. She was his sister-in-law, not a prospective girlfriend, and the sooner he realized it, the better.

Her mother was crossing the hall as they left the house. He said goodbye with friendly politeness, and she responded with chilly formality.

'Was it something I said?' he said half jokingly to Abbra as they walked across the gravel drive toward a gleaming new Ford Mustang.

When she had left the room for her shoes, she had also changed out of her jeans and cotton shirt, and was now wearing a turquoise skirt that swirled around her legs, a pale mauve silk shirt, and high-heeled, delicately strapped sandals. Her eyes, as they met his, were agonizingly apologetic.

'I'm sorry, Scott. It's just that my mother doesn't approve of professional football players. She's convinced that all they do is hang around bars and get into drunken fights.'

He opened the car door, the grin back on his face.

'It could be your mother is right,' he teased.

She gurgled with laughter, the sound carrying back to the house. In the luxuriously furnished living room, Mrs. Daley sat down on a sofa, her back straight, her lips tight. When her husband came home she was going to have a very serious talk with him. Scott Ellis was nowhere near as socially acceptable as Lewis and, brother-in-law or not, she didn't like his free and easy attitude toward Abbra. This initial excursion could not be allowed to develop into a habit. If it did, goodness only knew what the gossips would make of it.

It was early evening and the light was soft over the Bay and the bridge and the cliffs beyond. Scott drove down Broadway, leaving the opulence of Pacific Heights behind him, maneuvering deftly through the Chinatown traffic and on to Columbus Avenue toward her favorite Italian restaurant.

'Hi,' one of Luigi's chefs called out to her from the open-plan kitchen. 'Long time no see!'

'I've been busy getting married,' Abbra responded as Scott ignored the formality of the booths and led the way to the counter, where they could sit and eat and watch the chefs as they worked. She held up the third finger of her left hand so the chef could see her gleaming new wedding ring.

'Congratulations,' he said, beaming at both of them, and then, to Scott, 'You're a lucky guy.'

Scott's eyes danced in amusement and Abbra flushed rosily, saying quickly, 'This isn't my husband. My husband is serving overseas. This is Scott Ellis, my brother-in-law.'

The chef paused in what he was doing and looked at Scott with fresh interest. 'Say, aren't you the guy who was injured scoring during the Rams' season opener?'

Scott nodded, and admitted modestly that he was.

The chef shook his head sympathetically. 'That was pretty bad luck. I saw the game on TV. It was a pretty mean late tackle. The guy should have been suspended. I wish to God you were playing for the 49ers. We could use you!'

Scott accepted the compliment with easy

grace and returned his attention to Abbra. 'I'm glad to see that you don't talk about football *all* the time,' she said teasingly as they ate perfectly cooked fettuccine with a delicious white sauce, and talked about books and writers, discovering a shared passion for Dashiell Hammett.

'Did Lewis tell you I did?' he asked, topping up her glass of burgundy.

There was something in his voice that reminded her that Lewis had been disapproving of Scott's choice of career. The flush that had touched her cheeks when the chef had mistaken him for her husband edged back. 'No, of course not,' she said, uncomfortably aware that if Lewis hadn't actually said so, he had certainly hinted at it. 'It's just that I imagined professional football players would talk about football and nothing else.'

'Well, this one doesn't,' he said good-naturedly, knowing that she was being tactful and that Lewis had most certainly been speaking disparagingly about him. 'The problem is, when I'm with Lewis, I don't know what the hell else to talk about!'

She stared at him, wondering if he was joking, and then realized with amazement that he wasn't. 'But how can you not have anything to talk to him about?' she asked bewilderedly. 'He's your brother!'

He grinned. 'And you're an only child, right?'

She nodded.

'Believe me, Abbra, being a sibling doesn't

automatically mean that you have everything in common. Most brothers that I know have very different interests. Where Lewis and I are concerned, the differences are pretty big. Dad has lived his life for the army. He loves it passionately and I don't think it ever occurred to him that Lewis and I wouldn't follow in his footsteps. With Lewis he was lucky. As a child all Lewis wanted to do was play soldiers. Me? I was sick to death of soldiers and army life. All I wanted to do was play football, and that's exactly what I've done. I don't have any regrets, but it hasn't exactly brought me and Lewis very close.'

'You make it sound as if you're not even friends.' Her voice was heavy with disappointment.

He resisted the urge to cover her hand comfortingly with his. 'In a lot of ways we're not. We don't hang around together and we never have. But what we have is deeper than friendship, so don't worry about us, Abbra. We're brothers. We annoy and infuriate each other, but when it comes to the bottom line, we care about each other more than we care about anyone else. And that's all that matters.'

'Doesn't he write to you from Vietnam?' she asked, her dismay ebbing.

'I had a brief note from him at the end of July, shortly after he arrived. He sounded as if he was in his element, though how anyone could actually *enjoy* living out in the jungle and facing sniper fire twenty-four hours a day, I can't imagine.'

As soon as he said it he regretted it. Her face had paled, her eyes darkening until they were a deep-drowned purple. 'Did he tell you that he was under constant sniper fire?'

He shook his head. 'No, don't worry, Abbra. That's just my own idea of what life out there must be like. He told me he was serving as an adviser to a Vietnamese infantry battalion, but to tell the truth, I don't have an idea of what that means.'

Zabaglione had followed the pasta and wine, and coffee had followed the zabaglione.

'He's part of a five-man American advisory team,' Abbra said, her voice warming as she was at last able to talk about the subject closest to her heart. 'It's composed of a captain, a first lieutenant, and three non-commissioned officers.'

'And Lewis is the first lieutenant?' Scott asked, already knowing the answer to his question.

'Yes.' There was such quiet pride in her voice that his heart felt as if it were being squeezed tight. 'They are operating in the southernmost part of Vietnam, in the Ca Mau peninsula. Lewis says that the Vietnamese battalion commander has been fighting the Communists for over six years, and that several of the other Vietnamese officers have been fighting for just as long.'

'And before that they were fighting the French,' Scott said, sliding his coffee cup away from him and signaling for another. 'It isn't worth thinking about, is it?'

'No,' she agreed, bleakly trying to imagine what it must be like for Lewis, rarely seeing another American apart from the four in his team; spending days, sometimes weeks at a time hunting through the U Minh or Nam Can forests for reinforced Viet Cong regiments; never knowing when they would stumble into an ambush or meet with enemy fire.

He saw the troubled expression in her eyes, and this time he did reach out and comfortingly cover her hand with his. 'Don't worry about him, Abbra. Lewis is a professional soldier. This is what he's been trained for; he's looked forward to it his whole life.'

She stared at him, appalled. 'He isn't *enjoying* it out there! He couldn't be! No one could!'

'Well, perhaps *enjoying* is the wrong word,' Scott said, not truly believing that it was. 'I guess I should have said that he would be satisfied that he was doing the job he was trained for and doing it well.'

'Yes,' she said slowly. 'The area where he's operating is one that the Viet Cong have been trying hard to control for several years. He told me that hundreds of teachers and village chiefs had been assassinated for refusing to cooperate with them. If the area is more stable now that he and his Vietnamese battalion are operating there, and if the people in the villages are suffering less, then he *will* be gaining satisfaction from what he's doing.'

Scott wasn't sure whether the area would be more stable or not, but obviously thinking that it would be was the only way Abbra could come to terms with Lewis being there. He wondered how she would get along with the wives of Lewis's fellow officers, and remembering the wives of his father's fellow officers felt a surge of pity for her. He couldn't imagine her as a typical army wife, her only interest her husband's career, living for him and through him, with no real interests or life of her own.

'We'd better go,' he said gently. 'Your mother will think I've run off with you.' It was nearly ten-thirty and they had been talking for over three hours.

She rose regretfully. It had been the nicest evening she could remember since parting from Lewis.

'Are you going back to Los Angeles tonight?' she asked, wondering when she would see him again.

He shook his head. 'I'm not really supposed to be driving at all, not until the physical therapist gives me the all-clear. I've arranged to stay over at a friend's house and then I'll drive leisurely back to L.A. tomorrow morning ready for my afternoon appointment with the therapist.'

She nodded understandingly, saying nothing as they walked out into the street, but he noticed that her shoulders were drooping very slightly and it occurred to him that she had enjoyed the evening just as much as he had. He opened the car door for her. None of Lewis's friends or their wives were living in San Francisco, and he couldn't imagine that her mother encouraged much conversation about Lewis, or about anything else that interested her.

'I'm coming up again next weekend,' he said casually. 'It would be nice if you could take pity on me again and have dinner with me. Being a semi-cripple, I'm not exactly in great social demand at the moment.'

It was a lie. As an up-and-coming star with the Rams, his social life had never been more hectic and his injury had made not the slightest bit of difference to that part of his life.

Her face lit up, and he slid his arm around her shoulders, hugging her tight. He had driven to San Francisco on a duty visit to meet a sister-in-law he had expected to have nothing in common with. Instead, he had found a woman he knew was going to be a great friend and that he loved as family already.

Abbra happily accepted the crushing hug in the manner that it was given. She had never had any brothers or sisters, and she was overjoyed at the immediate closeness that had sprung up between her and Scott.

'We nearly met once before, on the night that I first met Lewis.' Her face softened, her eyes glowing as she remembered. 'It was at a party given by a friend of mine in San Francisco at the end of May. Her brother had invited lots of his friends, and you were among them. I danced with another friend of yours. He pointed you out to me because he was telling me how he hoped to be drafted by the Rams, and of how you had already signed with them.'

They were at the car now, and he had released her shoulders, and was staring down at her. 'You mean we were both in the same room and I didn't notice you?' he said incredulously. 'It isn't possible!'

She laughed affectionately. 'Oh, but it is. You were surrounded by admiring females.'

He continued to look down at her, still puzzled. 'I don't remember Lewis being at any party that I was at. In fact, come to think of it, I can't remember Lewis being at *any* party.'

He opened the door for her and she slid into the seat. 'I'm surprised he didn't tell you. He was on leave and had had dinner with my parents. He came to pick me up.'

He quickly came around the car and eased himself behind the steering wheel. 'And he never came in and joined the party?'

She shook her head and he could smell the faint lingering perfume of her shampoo. 'No. We left together and went out for a hamburger and a Coke.'

He sat in the dark car, not moving as the enormity of her words sank in. Then he switched on the engine and slammed it into gear. Jesus. He'd been as near as *that* to meeting her first; to asking her out; to falling in love with her.

'What's the matter?' she asked in concern as he slewed out of Columbus Avenue and into Broadway, his brows drawn together in a savage frown. 'Have I said something to upset you?' She couldn't, for the life of her, think what it could have been.

'No.' He looked toward her, forcing the frown away, giving her a lighthearted grin that was far from what he was feeling. 'I was just thinking how the course of our lives can be altered by small acts. Entering or not entering a room; being somewhere five minutes early or five minutes late. That sort of thing.'

She nodded. 'I know. I go cold with fright when I think of how I might have refused to let my mother send Lewis instead of our driver, and how, if I had, I would never have met Lewis.'

It hadn't been exactly what he was thinking, but he could scarcely tell her that. He drove her home, still appalled at his instant reaction to knowing that they had been in the same room together before she had met Lewis. If he had seen her, would he have noticed her? The answer was a thundering yes. And would he have asked her out on a date? He couldn't imagine himself meeting her and not asking. But would he have fallen in love with her? That was a question he couldn't answer.

He had never in his life been seriously in love, and he didn't expect he ever would be. Long-standing commitments were not his style. Lewis was the one who was always serious about any emotional involvement he might enter into, and it was typical of Lewis that after meeting Abbra and falling in love with her, he had seen marriage as the next logical step. Scott had enough self-awareness to know that if it had been him, he would never in a million years have thought of anything other than having an intensely passionate and enjoyable love affair.

As he swung the car into her parents' drive, he smiled ruefully. He hated to admit it, but Abbra had been far better off falling in love with Lewis than she would have been falling in love with him. The smile deepened into a self-deprecating grin. Hell, how had he the arrogance to even imagine that she *would* have fallen in love with him? He was a football player, and in the world that Abbra and her parents inhabited, a football player came pretty low in the potential-husband stakes.

'Why are you smiling?' she asked curiously as he braked to a halt.

He laughed, wondering what on earth she would say if he told her. 'I was just thinking how damned lucky Lewis is to have you as a wife,' he said tactfully, 'and of how damned lucky I am to have you as a sister-in-law.'

He walked around and opened the car door, resisting the urge to kiss her on the cheek. 'I won't come into the house with you. I have a feeling your mother has seen enough of me for one day.'

She stepped out of the car, the night breeze blowing her hair softly across her face. 'And

I'll see you next week?'

He nodded. 'I'll pick you up about seven. We'll go somewhere a little more upbeat than Luigi's. The Golden Eagle or the Kichihei. Somewhere that Lewis will approve of.'

As she walked away from him into the house, she wondered if, subconsciously, he often tried to do things that would gain Lewis's approval. Perhaps, when Lewis's tour of duty in Vietnam was over, they could go together and see Scott play. She was sure Lewis had never done so, and she knew that though he wouldn't admit it, Scott would be as pleased as hell to know his elder brother was cheering him on.

Although it was after eleven by the time she reached her room, she didn't immediately begin to get ready for bed. Instead, she sat down at her desk, taking her half-finished letter to Lewis out of the drawer. She wanted to tell him all about Scott's visit and, as usual when a pen was in her hands, she became unaware of time, and it was well after midnight before she eased her chair away from the desk.

Talking to Scott about Lewis had somehow made Lewis seem much nearer. The three months until she'd see him again no longer seemed like three hundred, but more like thirty. She undressed and slipped on her nightdress. The following week, when she'd see Scott again, would make the time seem even closer. With a happy smile she climbed into bed and turned off the light, closing her eyes, imagining that Lewis was with her, holding her, loving her.

'But you can't possibly intend to go out with him again!' her mother said, horrified. 'You're a married woman, Abbra! You can't still go out with young men as if you were single!'

'I'm not, Mom,' Abbra said, quickly losing her patience. 'Scott is my *brother-in-law*, not a date. There's a whole world of difference.'

Mrs. Daley was not sure that there was, but she could hardly say so without sounding crude. Her husband had not agreed that Abbra's friendship with Scott Ellis was undesirable, and to her dismay Abbra had gone out with him again. The following week he had driven up to San Francisco and they had gone to the zoo and on a ferry ride, and for a fish supper at Sausalito.

'I really don't like it,' she had said to her husband. 'How do we know that Lewis will approve of all the time Abbra is spending with his brother? I was under the distinct impression that Lewis did not think very highly of Scott!'

'He doesn't think very highly of Scott's choice of career,' her husband corrected her. 'Their father told me that. But I'm sure it's just Scott's age. I'm sure he'll come around.'

Mrs. Daley pursed her lips. There was nothing for her to do but make sure that Abbra continued to be aware of her disapproval, and to hope that the day would never come when her nameless fears would take on substance.

* * *

In November, Scott was pronounced fit and was in the roster to play in a home game against the Cleveland Browns.

'Why don't you drive down and watch the game?' he suggested to Abbra. 'You could be the first member of my family to see me play.'

'I'll be there,' she promised. Lewis had written to her, telling her how pleased he was that she and Scott had become friends, and in his last letter he had teasingly asked if she was now a fan and attended games.

Her mother had shaken her head in disbelief when Abbra had told her of her plans. 'You are going to get yourself a reputation for being one of those girls who follow football players from city to city!'

'Oh, Mom! You're being ridiculous,' Abbra said in affectionate irritation. 'Everyone knows that Scott is my brother-in-law. No one is going to think that I'm a fan who has latched on to him!'

'They will,' her mother insisted. 'And almost as bad is the amount of time you're spending away from your school work. You have exams to think about and you should be home studying, not driving down to Los Angeles to watch the Rams play the Browns!'

Abbra sighed, feeling a twinge of guilt. She hadn't told her parents yet, but she had already made up her mind to leave college at the end of the semester. She would be leaving when Lewis returned anyway, and college was no longer what she wanted. She wanted to write, and she had already begun, showing Scott her first tentative stories, encouraged by his enthusiasm.

'You should send them off to one of the women's magazines,' he had said when he had read them. 'They're much better than most of the stuff they publish.'

She had laughed. 'And when was the last time you read any stories in a woman's magazine, Scott Ellis?' she asked teasingly.

He had grinned, his wide-set eyes and thick curly hair reminding her of a painting she had seen of a medieval Medici princeling. 'Perhaps it wasn't very recently,' he admitted, unabashed, 'but I'm damned sure that what you've written is worthy of publication, and they certainly won't be published if all you do is put them away in a drawer. The British Special Air Service has a motto, "Who dares, wins." Remember that and send them off. Nothing ventured, nothing gained, and all that jazz.'

She had laughed again and told him that he was an idiot, but a few weeks later, when she had gone over the stories for the twentieth time, she plucked up her nerve and sent one of them to the fiction editor of a leading women's magazine.

Despite her mother's continued disapproval, she drove down to Los Angeles to watch the Rams play the Browns and enjoyed herself thoroughly. It was the first time she had seen Scott in his own environment, and she was surprised by the amount of attention he attracted from fans and the media.

'You've been playing for the Rams only a few weeks. How come you're such a big star?' she asked teasingly.

'I don't know,' he replied with his easy, self-mocking grin. 'It must be the way I comb my hair!'

She had laughed, but the time that she spent with him when he was Scott Ellis, professional football player, only increased her deep affection for him. He had such an open and honest air that she knew no amount of flattery would corrupt him. Despite his media appeal and his veritable army of fans, there was a total lack of pretence or show about him. He was, quite simply, always himself. And even though he was far more of an extrovert than Lewis, underneath his easygoing affability there was the same kind of attractive solidity and inner strength.

At the end of the month, when the team was playing in Denver, he asked her if she would like to fly out and watch the game with the team wives and girlfriends. She had already met and made friends with quite a few of them, and when one of the girls suggested that she share a room with her, there seemed to be no reason why she shouldn't go.

'A *weekend*?' her mother had shrieked. 'It's absolutely impossible! Totally unthinkable!'

This time even her father agreed.

'I'm a married woman, Daddy,' she said, knowing that her mistake had been in returning home after her marriage as if she were still a schoolgirl. 'I'll be with other women I know and with my brother-in-law. Morally and physically I shall be utterly safe, and there is no reason at all why I shouldn't go.'

Her father was not swayed by her argument, and only a timely telephone call from her father-in-law prevented her from either having to cancel her plans or face an all-out fight with her parents.

'It's Colonel Ellis,' her mother said, the telephone receiver in her hand, a hint of respect in her voice. 'He wants to speak to you, Abbra.'

Ever since the wedding her father-in-law had courteously telephoned her once a month. Usually he merely asked her how she was; if she had heard from Lewis; and reminded her that she was welcome to spend a few days in New York at the family home whenever she felt like doing so. This time he was telephoning to say that he had business in Pueblo, so he was going to drive to nearby Denver to watch the Rams play the Broncos. He had spoken to Scott to tell him he would be there, and Scott had told him that she was also going. He was telephoning to tell her he was looking forward to seeing her.

From then on she knew that the battle was won. After she had finished speaking to him, he spoke with her father. Abbra heard her father agreeing with the colonel that it was a pity he and her mother couldn't accompany Abbra for the weekend and make a real reunion of it, but that they would, no doubt, meet up again next year to celebrate Lewis's return home.

Her father-in-law's attitude toward the President's buildup of forces in Vietnam was predictably enthusiastic.

'It's the only way to show those bas—' He corrected himself quickly. '—To show the Communists that we mean business,' he said as they ate dinner in a small restaurant he had taken them to after the game. 'Leave them to their own devices and they'll be swarming up Waikiki Beach before we've had time to blink!'

'Isn't that a little bit of an exaggeration?' Scott asked idly, spearing a forkful of broccoli. 'The Communist aim is to unite North and South Vietnam under Ho Chi Minh, not invade America.'

Abbra saw an angry flush stain her father-in-law's neck and knew that he was controlling his temper only with difficulty. 'The Communist aim is world domination!' he said, forcefully, leaning across the table toward his son and stabbing his finger on the tablecloth to emphasize his point. 'If Vietnam falls to the Communists, then the entire region, the whole of Southeast Asia, will collapse too, and when that happens, the United States will find itself surrendering the Pacific and having to defend our own shores!'

'And if we continue to send in more troops, and the conflict continues to escalate, then the end of the road is going to be the direct intervention of China and nuclear war,' Scott said, provoking his father even more.

The colonel's nostrils flared, the red flush staining and spreading. 'How the hell have you become such an expert on what will or will not happen?' he bellowed, oblivious of Abbra and the other diners. 'You haven't been to West Point! You're a ball player, not a general!'

'I'm just giving my opinion,' Scott said tightly.

His father was about to say that his opinion wasn't worth a shit, when he became aware of Abbra's agonized expression and of other diners turning their heads toward their table with prurient curiosity.

He clamped his mouth tight shut, took a deep, steadying breath, and then gave Abbra an apologetic smile. 'I'm sorry, Abbra. I should have warned you that my opinions and Scott's differ widely. But the lessons from World War Two are too easily forgotten. If we and our allies had moved earlier than we did to stop the Nazis, then that war could have been averted. The same rules apply to the Communists. We need a strong display of muscle to make sure that they know we mean business. Then, and only then, will they back down and allow the South its freedom.'

He glared coldly at Scott as he spoke, daring him to contradict. Scott, tempted almost past endurance, resisted the urge for Abbra's sake. He knew she had been thrilled that at last his father had attended a game and watched him play. And that the flare of disagreement which had erupted between them had distressed her.

'Okay,' he said, suppressing his irritation and forcing a smile. '*Pax*. Let's talk about something a little less emotive. Let's talk about the Rams' chances next week when they play the Chicago Bears.'

The conversation turned to smoother waters, and the evening had ended amicably but from then on Abbra was aware of the great difference between Scott's uneasy relationship with his father, and Lewis's relationship with him.

In December, President Johnson announced that the bombing of North Vietnam would be halted on Christmas morning for an indefinite period. In the first week of January she received a letter from Lewis describing a Christmas Day dinner of locally caught duck embellished with *nuoc mam* sauce, and an afternoon spent treating the village children to candy from his SP rations, and in the same week Scott decked a fellow player in the dressing room for making off-color remarks about his relationship with her.

It was an ugly incident and one she was not aware of. It had been a home game against the Chargers and the Rams had lost miserably. Tempers had been short in the locker room and someone had savagely made an accusation that there was too much partying going on between games and not enough hard training.

One of the veteran players on the team, who had been receiving bad coverage in the press with veiled hints that he had peaked and was now past his prime, had looked viciously across at Scott and said loudly, 'That goes *especially* for guys who can only get it up with their brothers' wives. What do the two of you do every night, Ellis? Pray that some accommodating Viet Cong puts a hole in big brother?'

Scott's fist sent him flying backward even before the word *brother* was out of his mouth. The brawl that followed was the worst to take place in a locker room that anyone could remember.

When they had finally been separated, and when their furious coach had warned them that if there was a repetition of the incident, both of them would be suspended for a week without pay, Scott had stormed into the club bar, where Abbra was waiting for him, saying tersely to her, 'Come on, we're leaving.'

'What on earth is the matter? What's happened to your face? What...?'

'Come on,' he had repeated taking her by the arm and steering her toward the door. In another few seconds the club room would be full of differing reports of what had happened, but all the reports would be unanimous on what the remark was that had triggered the fight. It made him sick just to remember it, and the thought of her overhearing it made him feel murderous. 'I had a disagreement with another player in the locker room,' he said to her when they were safely outside. 'It was no big deal, but I don't want to find myself drinking with him this evening. Let's go to Yesterdays for a beer and a sandwich.'

He had been so obviously reluctant to talk about the incident that she hadn't asked any further questions. At the end of the week she was flying out to Hawaii to join Lewis, and she could scarcely think of or talk about anything else.

'Hawaii's going to be a big change for him after Vietnam,' Scott said, driving downtown, the filthy words of his fellow player ringing in his ears.

Abbra had begun to tell him that it would not be quite so bad as perhaps they imagined, because Lewis had already enjoyed a three-day rest and recuperation break at Vung Tau, an in-country beach resort, but Scott was no longer listening to her. In the three months since he had met her, he hadn't looked up any of his old girlfriends, and he hadn't once dated any new ones. In fact, incredibly, for the last four months he had been totally celibate. It was quite a thought, and so was the reason for it.

She was talking happily about the presents she had bought for Lewis and jealousy, hot and hard, twisted his gut. He hadn't been dating because he had been happier with Abbra than he could possibly be with anyone else. He hadn't been screwing around because the only girl he wanted to screw was Abbra. His brother's wife. His hands tightened on the steering wheel until the knuckles were white. Jesus. Why hadn't he seen the truth before? Why had it taken the ugly words of a team mate, jealous of his prowess on the field, to make him see the blindingly obvious? And now that he had seen, what in the name of all that was holy could he do about it?

'I never thought the time would pass,' she was saying to him, her eyes glowing, her face radiant. 'In three days we'll be together again. Have you ever had something happen to you that is so momentous you can hardly believe it's true?'

'Yeah,' he said grimly, turning the car into Westwood Drive, feeling as if a knife were twisting in his heart. 'I have, Abbra. I most certainly have.'

# CHAPTER FIVE

For the next forty-eight hours Lewis filled every one of Abbra's waking thoughts. On the morning that she was to fly out to meet him she could hardly breathe for physical excitement.

'There's some mail for you, darling,' her mother said as they sat at breakfast. 'I've left it on the hall table.'

'Thanks, Mom.' Abbra pushed a plate of barely touched scrambled eggs away from her and rose to her feet, her voice breathless.

'I have to leave now, or I'll miss the eight-thirty airport bus.'

'They run every fifteen minutes,' her father said in fond amusement. 'Why not let me or our driver give you a lift out to the airport? What's so special about traveling there by bus?'

'Nothing, Daddy.' She slipped her arm around his neck and kissed him on the cheek. 'It's just easy, that's all.'

'And it's just another little gesture of independence,' her mother said, the distress behind the pleasantly uttered words unmistakable.

Abbra refused to respond and to be drawn

into another tense conversation with her mother about the way she was leading her life. These conversations had become increasingly frequent. She knew that the real cause was that her mother was unable to accept that Abbra was no longer a child. She hadn't anticipated the change in her that marriage would bring. The wedding had been too sudden for her mother to be able to truly adjust to it, and not for the first time Abbra wished that Lewis hadn't been sent overseas immediately after their marriage. If only they'd been able to start their married life together in America. The transition, then, from a daughter to a daughter who was also a wife would have been more clearly marked and one her mother could have coped with.

'Come on, then,' her father said, picking up her suitcase. 'It's eight-fifteen now. If you want to catch the eight-thirty bus, we'll have to move.'

'Bye, Mom.' Abbra kissed her mother's cheek, following her father out into the hall, grabbing the mail from the hall table as she did so and stuffing it into her shoulder bag.

It would take an hour to get to the airport and to check in. The flight to Honolulu would take approximately another five and a half hours, and the connecting flight between Honolulu on Cahu and Lihue on Kauai, where she was to meet Lewis, would take another twenty or thirty minutes. Seven hours. In seven hours time they would be together again. It still seemed to her too wonderful to be true.

Her father dropped her off at the bus terminal at the corner of O'Farrell and Taylor streets near Union Square, and kissed her good-bye.

'Give Lewis my best,' he said, taking her suitcase out of the Cadillac's trunk. 'And tell him to make sure he comes home all in one piece in six months.'

'I will,' she promised fervently. The thought that at this very moment Lewis was no longer in danger on Vietnamese soil, but was winging his way across the Pacific in a Boeing 707 was exhilarating. For the next five days no bullets would mow him down; no bombs would blow him up. He would be deliciously safe, safe, *safe*.

She stepped onto the already full bus. She was on her way. Every minute that passed was one that was bringing them closer together. His flight from Saigon was due to land in Honolulu three hours before hers, and he was going to fly straight on to Lihue and would be waiting for her when she arrived.

As she checked her baggage in at the airport she was almost sure that some of the other women traveling on her flight were also army wives. One or two of them seemed to know each other, and she wished she had the nerve to approach them and to ask if they were joining husbands on leave. Too shy to do so, she bought herself a paperback book and glanced down at her wristwatch. Only six hours to go. Lewis's flight would now be two thirds over. At this very moment he would be thinking about her as she was thinking about him.

'Soon, my love,' she whispered to herself as her flight was called. 'Soon!'

All through the flight the book lay unopened on her lap. Their reunion would be the first they had ever had as husband and wife. She wondered if such reunions were something she would eventually get used to and become blasé about, and smiled at her idiocy. How could she ever become blasé about meeting Lewis? It wasn't possible. Even if they were married for fifty years, she would still feel the same hungry excitement at the prospect of meeting him again after an absence, whether the absence was one of days, or one of months, as it was now.

As the plane flew high over the searing blue of the Pacific, she looked frequently down at her wristwatch. Five hours. Four hours. Mentally she was with Lewis as his flight landed at Honolulu and as he transferred to his Kauai flight. She couldn't even begin to imagine what Hawaii would seem like to him after the horrors he had been living with.

His letters home, though scrupulously regular and reassuringly loving, had told her very little about his actual day-to-day existence. She knew only what she had told Scott. That he was part of a five-man advisory team assigned to an ARVN battalion; that they operated in the Ca Mau peninsula, rarely seeing other South Vietnamese units;

and that most of their time was spent in hunting down the Viet Cong regiments that used the Nam Can and U Minh forests as a base.

One of the things she was most looking forward to was hearing about his experiences. She wanted to know what his life in Vietnam was like, every possible detail. She wanted to share it mentally and be a part of it. His reticence on paper had disappointed her at first but then she had realized that putting emotions down on paper didn't come as easily to most people as it did to her. Lewis was obviously one of those. When they were together, and when at last they could talk, it would be different. Then there would be no reticence, only a total union of their hearts and minds.

The pilot's voice came over the intercom with matter-of-fact prosaicness. 'In ten minutes we will be landing at Honolulu Airport. I hope that you have had a pleasant flight and that you will fly with us again. Thank you.'

Excitement spiraled through her. In about an hour, she would be in Lewis's arms. The 707 dipped to the right, circling in to land, and far beneath her she could see Pearl Harbor and the silver-tawny flanks of Diamond Head and the great golden curve that was Waikiki Beach.

'Have a pleasant stay,' the stewardess said, smiling at her as she stepped out into brilliant sunshine and balmy heat.

A Hawaiian band was at the edge of the

runway playing traditional music. Hula girls, laden with flowered leis, stepped smilingly forward to greet them, laughingly placing the leis around their necks.

As Abbra felt the flower petals brush her skin, and as she inhaled their perfume, happiness struck through her so pure and hard that she could barely contain it. Lewis had served over half his tour of duty in Vietnam and he had not been injured. In another six months time she would be meeting him again, and when she did, it would be for a far longer reunion. From then on their married life together would truly start. They would have a home on an army base and she would be what she longed to be – a full-fledged army wife.

She had a ten-minute walk before reaching the terminal for the interconnecting island flights and the small plane that was to take her to Kauai. For the hundredth time she looked down at her watch. In half an hour's time she would be with him. He would already be at Lihue waiting for her, she thought as she boarded. As the plane gathered speed and left the ground, she clenched her fingers into the palms of her hands, hardly able to bear the joyous anticipation flooding through her.

Abbra stepped out into the brilliant sunshine, her eyes feverishly scanning the low, white airport buildings. The only waiting figures were some distance away, and none of them was in army uniform. For one terrible, terrifying moment, as she descended the steps, she thought that he wasn't there. That something had gone horribly wrong; that his flight had been delayed; that perhaps he hadn't even left Saigon. Or even that his leave had been cancelled. And then she saw him, broad-shouldered and auburn-haired, dressed in white flannels and a light blue cotton shirt and loafers.

'Lewis!' she cried, oblivious to the crush of passengers round her. '*Lewis*!'

She was running toward him, her arms wide. A waist-high barrier separated arriving passengers from those who had come to meet them, but she didn't notice it. She raced toward him, entering his arms.

'Oh, Lewis!' she gasped joyously. 'Oh, darling, *darling*.'

His mouth came down hard on hers, and the months of separation slid away from her as if they had never existed.

'Oh, God, I missed you!' he groaned, burying his head in her hair, holding her so close to him that she thought her ribs would crack. 'You wouldn't believe how much I've missed you, Abbra!'

'Oh, but I would,' she said fiercely, raising her face to his. 'Because I've missed you every single minute of every single day!'

The grin that only she could conjure from him split his face. 'Then let's make up for lost time.' He relaxed his hold and took her hand in his. 'And the first thing is for you to come to this side of the damned barrier!'

With their hands still tightly clasped they walked the length of the barrier, and when she rounded it he folded her against him once again, oblivious to the indulgent glances of the people around them.

'I thought today would never come,' he said huskily when at last he lifted his head from hers. 'I knew I loved you when I married you, Abbra. But only now do I know how very, very much.'

She raised her hand, touching his face gently with the tips of her fingers, all the love she felt for him shining in her eyes. 'I love you with all my heart,' she said softly. 'I couldn't live if you didn't love me, Lewis. I wouldn't know how.'

He hugged her against him again, his throat so tight he was robbed of speech, and then, sliding his arm around her waist, he led her out to where her luggage was waiting.

'Where are we staying?' she asked as they stepped out of the airport toward the waiting line of orange taxicabs. 'In a hotel or an apartment?'

'An apartment.' Sudden doubt flared through his eyes. 'That's okay, isn't it? If you'd prefer a hotel, I can always cancel the apartment.'

'No.' She shook her head firmly. 'An apartment will be wonderful.'

It would be a place of their own, even if it was for only a few days. She didn't want them to spend their time together in the impersonal atmosphere of a hotel. The scent from the flowers around her neck, as Lewis gave the taxi driver the address of their Poipu Beach apartment, was as thick as smoke in the sunlight, the heat beating up from the ground in waves. Their fingers were still intertwined, and she gave his hand a squeeze, hardly able to believe that after all the long months of waiting, he was, at last, beside her.

'Happy, sweetheart?' he asked as he opened the rear door of the taxi for her.

'Oh, yes!' She was so happy that it hurt. He slid into the seat beside her, and she looked across at him. He had changed in the six months they had been apart. He had lost a little weight. Her heart twisted in her breast. If he had lost weight, it was not surprising. The surprise was that he had not lost far more.

'Were there many fellow officers with you on your flights?' she asked, hugging his arm. 'There were quite a few women on my flight to Honolulu, and I'm sure they were army wives flying out to join their husbands.'

'A couple,' he said, covering her hand with his. 'Not many. Taipei and Bangkok are more popular destinations than Hawaii.'

'But why?' Her brow creased in bewilderment. 'Hawaii is at least *American*. I would have thought they would far rather spend their R&R on American soil than in Taipei or Bangkok!'

'Taipei and Bangkok are closer to 'Nam, and I guess most of the men don't want to be hassled with a long flight.'

'But it's not closer for their wives!' she protested.

He grinned. 'Not many wives fly out to share R&R. You're in the minority, Mrs. Ellis.'

'But why not? I don't understand. I could not bear to think of you on leave and so near home and not being with you.'

There was no way he could explain to her that for most men serving in 'Nam, R&R was an opportunity for a week-long orgy of screwing and drinking, and that the last thing they wanted was a wife. Instead, he said, 'Hawaii isn't close to home for most wives. From New York, which is where Des Cawthorn's wife comes from, for instance, Hawaii is as far away as Italy and Switzerland.'

'Who is Des Cawthorn?' she asked with avid interest, wondering if he was perhaps a member of Lewis's team.

'A fellow officer who was on my flight,' he said, shrugging dismissively. He had no desire to talk about Cawthorn, or the way other officers spent their leaves. 'Do you see that mountain over there?' he asked, changing the subject as their taxicab hurtled across the southeast corner of the island. 'That's Mount Waialeale, and believe it or not, it's the wettest place on earth.'

'You're kidding,' she said disbelievingly. 'In *Hawaii*?'

He nodded, the naturally hard line of his mouth softened by a smile. 'I know because all I had to read while I was waiting for your plane were tourist brochures. It rains an average 500 inches a year; that's a lot of rain!'

'As long as it doesn't rain on the beach, I don't care,' she said, resting her cheek against his sturdy shoulder, savoring the sight, sound, and cologne-fresh smell of him.

It was still only mid-afternoon when they reached their apartment, and though the beach shimmered and shone only yards away, neither of them was even remotely tempted by it.

'The beach can wait,' Lewis said in a voice that expected no contradictions and received none. He deposited the luggage in the cane-furnished living room and turned toward her, his eyes so hot and dark she could barely tell iris from pupil.

For one sudden spellbinding moment she felt actually shy, and then his arms closed around her and her shyness vanished. In one easy movement he lifted her off her feet, carrying her into the sun-dappled bedroom as if she were a new bride.

'It's been so long,' he said hoarsely, lowering her to the bed, his mouth on her hair and her eyelids and the corners of her lips, his fingers gently and purposefully undoing the little pearl buttons on her blouse. 'I love you, Abbra. Only you. Forever.'

Her arms were around his neck, her body seeming to melt boneless into his. 'Ah, Lewis,' she whispered, shivering in pleasure as his hands found her flesh and touched and explored. 'I love you ... I love you ... I love you...'

He slid her arms out of her blouse and her breasts were pale in the sunlight that spilled across the bed, the nipples silkily rosy. With powerful yet careful hands he lifted her up beneath him, sliding her skirt down, his fingers brushing lightly over the wisp of cream lace that encased the dark spring of her pubic hair.

'Please love me,' she whispered, breathless and panting, shocked by the shameless depth of her hunger and need. 'Now, Lewis! Oh, please! Quickly!'

The slow deliberation of his lovemaking was one of the things that most aroused and excited her. Even now, when they had been separated for six long months, he did not take her in haste. He shed his clothing, drawing her toward him, reveling in the sight of her nakedness and then, when she thought she couldn't endure another moment of waiting, he rolled across her, closing his mouth over hers, reaching for her body with his hands.

The next morning they hired a jeep and set off toward the Hanalei Valley. The roadsides and fields were a mass of color. Poinsettias bloomed wild in scarlet profusion; Judas trees lifted their clouds of scented flowers the color of purple daphne; bougainvillea ran riot, blossoms of magenta and pink and foaming cream vying for supremacy.

'Oh, it's wonderful,' Abbra sighed, leaning close to Lewis as he circled her shoulder with one arm, driving the jeep with single-handed expertise. 'I never want to leave. Never.'

At Nawili wili they parked the jeep and swam in a tiny cove to the north of the bay; and at Kapaa they paused again, strolling the streets, admiring the wooden nineteenth-century buildings and the balconies that bellied out over the shop fronts, crammed with terracotta pots of narcissus and iris.

'Where to now?' Lewis asked. 'Another beach? Lunch somewhere? Or a walk out on one of the headlands?'

His heart seemed to leap in his chest as he looked down at her. She was wearing a white silk blouse, open at the throat, a red cotton skirt that swirled around her legs just short of her knees, and delicate sandals so insubstantial he wondered how she could possibly walk in them. Her hair was a little longer than it had been on their wedding day. It skimmed her shoulders glossily, pushed away from her face with delicately carved ivory combs.

'Has anyone ever told you that you're the most beautiful woman in the world?' he asked, wishing that he hadn't suggested the beach or a walk, but bed.

'No.' Her eyes danced with happiness. 'I don't think they have, Lieutenant.'

'Then let me rectify the omission.' He put his hands around her waist, swinging her up into the jeep. 'You, Abbra Ellis, are without doubt the most beautiful woman in the whole wide world!'

'Why, thank you,' she laughed, kissing the

tip of his nose. 'I was hoping you would think so!'

'Abbra...' His voice had deepened and he was about to suggest that they drive straight back to the apartment, but before he could she said, 'I think I'd prefer a walk out on one of the headlands, to the beach or to lunch. Where have we to go? Kilauea Point or Makeheuna Point?'

Makeheuna Point was back the way they had come, and only a few short miles from Poipu Beach. 'Makeheuna,' he said unhesitatingly, knowing that from there they could very quickly get back to the apartment and bed.

Not until they were out on the Point, the grass rough beneath their feet, an indigo sea creaming at the base of sandstone cliffs, did she say at last, 'Tell me everything you couldn't tell me in your letters, Lewis.'

He looked down at her, an eyebrow quirking. 'Such as?'

Her arm was around his waist, her head leaning against his shoulder. 'You know what I mean.' Her voice was low and soft and full of love.

He hadn't the faintest idea. He sat down on the coarse grass and pulled her down beside him. 'You're not worrying about my fidelity, are you?' His brows pulled together in sudden concern. 'Because if you are, there's no need.'

She stared at him in astonishment. It had no more occurred to her that he would be unfaithful than it had that she would be unfaithful to him. 'No, of course not,' she said indignantly. 'I'm talking about your life in Vietnam. What it is that you're doing. What it's like for you living with the ARVN, under constant fear of enemy attack?'

The rare grin that other people seldom saw creased his hard-boned face. 'You sound like a newspaper reporter,' he teased, pulling her so that her back was resting against his chest. 'I've told you what I'm doing. I'm a military adviser to an ARVN battalion. What more can I possibly tell you?'

She pulled free of his arms, turning to face him, sitting back on her heels. His reply was so unexpected, so staggeringly unlike anything she had even remotely imagined, she could only say unsteadily, 'You are kidding, Lewis, aren't you?'

He shook his head, his brows pulling together again slightly. 'No, I'm not, Abbra. There's very little else to tell you. Most of our time is spent out on patrol, hunting down Viet Cong. It's hot and it's wet and the insects are hell. What more can you possibly want to know?'

'But I want to know everything! I want to know how it feels to march for hour after hour through flooded paddy fields; I want to know what it's like to be surrounded by South Vietnamese – any one of whom could be Viet Cong; I want to know how it feels when you go into battle or are ambushed, knowing that any moment you might be killed!'

He stared at her as though she had taken leave of her senses. 'But for God's sake, why?' There was more than just bewilderment in his voice. There was revulsion.

Despite the midday heat she felt suddenly chilled. Surely he understood? How could he *not* understand? She was seized with the crazy notion that she was talking to a stranger. A stranger who was being polite, but who had no insight into her heart and mind.

'Because I love you!' she said desperately, leaning toward him and taking his hands in hers, holding them tight. 'Because I want to share *everything* with you! I want to share your experiences in Vietnam so that while you are there I can feel closer to you!'

His rising irritation ebbed. She was still scarcely more than a child and had no idea how ghoulish her request had sounded. He drew her toward him, saying gently, 'Vietnam is a million miles from anything you could ever imagine, Abbra. There's no way that I can share my experiences there with you. Hell, I wouldn't want to, even if I could!'

'But what about your fellow officers? The ones in the ARVN? Can't you tell me a little something about them?' she asked, unable to believe that he meant what he said.

He sighed, running a hand through the close-cropped curly thickness of his hair. 'Okay,' he said at last, humoring her with deep reluctance. 'My fellow officers in the ARVN have been fighting nearly all their lives. First the French, now the Communists.

Trung, our battalion commander, fought under General Giap at Dien Bien Phu, and over the years he must have been wounded more times than he, or anyone else, can count.'

'I thought General Giap was a Communist?' she interrupted, confused.

'He is. He's Ho Chi Minh's right-hand man. But when the Vietnamese were trying to free themselves from colonial rule, Communists and non-Communists fought together. After the French conceded defeat, Trung crossed to the government side. He hadn't fought to free himself of French domination in order to exchange it for life under the Communists. Many of the men in the battalion have a similar history. It's the experience of the older officers, under Giap, that makes them so tenacious in battle.'

She was silent for a moment, wondering how it must feel for them to be fighting against a general they had once fought for and who, if the tone of Lewis's voice was anything to go by, they still admired.

'Have there been many battles?' she asked apprehensively, at last bringing the subject around to the one that preoccupied her.

'A few,' he said, the grin back on his face as he rose to his feet and stretched down a hand toward her. 'Those are the best times, when the adrenaline begins to surge...'

She stumbled as he drew her to her feet, her eyes wide and horrified. Her earlier shock at his amazement that she would want to know about his life in Vietnam was nothing to the shock she felt now. She felt as if a huge weight were on her chest, crushing her.

'—but for most of the time it's just tedious monotony,' he continued, assuming the horror in her dark eyes to be fear for his safety. 'Most of our time is spent in arduous day-long searches for Viet Cong we never locate. We find their campfires, but ninety times out of a hundred we don't find them. They vanish. God alone knows where.' Her hand was in his, and they were walking back to the jeep. 'Happier now?' he asked, smiling down at her, feeling that he had indulged her enough.

She opened her mouth and tried to tell him that she had never felt less happy in her life; that she couldn't believe that his reaction to battle, and to death and killing, were so many light-years removed from her own. As her gaze met his, the words died in her throat and she felt dizzy, as if an abyss were opening at her feet and yawning wide. He was a professional soldier. His attitude to war was never going to be the same as hers. Her horror at his words, if he knew of them, would only drive a wedge between them. The feeling of perfect unity, so important to her, would be lost forever.

'Yes,' she lied, her voice little more than a croak. She forced a smile. 'Yes, of course.'

They had driven back to the apartment and made violent love, but that night, as she lay sleepless in the circle of his arms, his words repeated themselves time and time again. 'Those are the best times, when the adrenaline begins to surge...'

Scott had been right after all. In some way that she couldn't possibly understand, Lewis was *enjoying* his time in Vietnam. It was as if the war between North and South Vietnam, in a country half a world away from his home, was *his* war, just as World War II had been his father's war. She closed her eyes and tried to sleep, but sleep was a long time in coming, and when it did come, her dreams were disturbed and restless and full of horrifying imagery.

They didn't talk about Vietnam again. The next morning, when he woke her by kissing her gently on the mouth, she forced all visions of him as a soldier and in uniform to the farthest corner of her brain. The adjustment she knew she would have to make could not be made now. It would have to be made when she was back in San Francisco. Now was the time for loving and closeness. She had to forget about Vietnam, as Lewis was apparently forgetting about it. All that mattered was that they were together and that they loved each other and always would love each other. Not until the day before the end of his leave did reality intrude upon them again.

They had driven up to Waimen Canyon for the day and were walking back to where they had parked the jeep when an open-topped

Chevrolet pulled up near them with a screech of tires and a chunkily built man, his hair as closely cropped as Lewis's, vaulted out of the car, yelling 'Whoa, Lew! So this is where you're hiding! I thought you'd be on Waikiki, soaking up the sun!'

There was a pretty Hawaiian girl in the Chevrolet's passenger seat, but though her smile was friendly, she made no attempt to walk across and join them. Her dress was low-cut and clinging, her nails, as they drummed idly on the Chevrolet's door, vividly scarlet.

'Abbra, I'd like you to meet Des Cawthorn,' Lewis was saying, and Abbra could tell from the underlying tautness in his voice that he was annoyed by the accidental meeting. 'Des spent two months on our team at the end of the year. Since then he's been sitting pretty at staff headquarters in Saigon.'

'*No one* sits pretty in Saigon,' Des Cawthorn said cheerfully, shaking Abbra's hand. 'Relax for just a minute and some damned terrorist will lob a bomb through the window. How are you enjoying Hawaii, Mrs Ellis?'

Abbra didn't know if he was joking about the bombs in Saigon or not. She hoped he was. She had spent the last few months praying that Lewis would be transferred to a desk job at staff headquarters.

'I think it's wonderful,' she said truthfully, her eyes drawn against their will back to his waiting companion, a sudden frown marring her brow.

Des saw the direction of her thoughts and had the grace to look slightly abashed. 'Well, I guess I'll be getting along and let the two of you enjoy your last day together,' he said, taking a step or two backward. 'Nice meeting you, Mrs Ellis. See you on the plane in the morning, Lew.' With a grin and wink he turned on his heel, striding back toward the Chevy. As he slid behind the wheel, the Hawaiian girl circled his neck with her arm and Abbra said uncertainly, 'That was the Des Cawthorn who flew with you from Saigon, wasn't it?'

Lewis nodded, turning and walking in the direction of their jeep. She hurried after him, slipping her hand into his. 'Didn't you say that he was married?'

'Yes, his wife is a high school principal in Pittsburgh.'

'But that *wasn't* his wife, was it?' she persisted, distressed.

'No,' he said tersely, wishing fervently that the encounter had never taken place.

She climbed into the jeep silently, and then said in a small, bewildered voice, 'Is that why so many men choose Taipei and Bangkok? Because of the girls and ... and things?'

He sighed, running a hand through his tight, short curls. 'I guess so, Abbra. It's hard to explain, but five days isn't long enough for most men to unwind from 'Nam. They have to use girls and booze and dope. The way they spend their leave is as far removed from their real lives as the rest of their time in

'Nam is.'

She wanted to say to him that if he would only *talk* about Vietnam to her, then she might very well understand. And she wanted to ask him if he, too, sometimes sought release in girls and booze and dope. The words remained strangled in her throat, but he saw the agony in her eyes and took her hands in his, saying fiercely, 'For Christ's sake, Abbra! I'm not Des Cawthorn! I'm not a grunt in 'Nam against my will! I'm a professional soldier, carrying out a job I've been trained for! I don't need to seek oblivion in sex or drink or drugs, and if I did, I sure as hell wouldn't choose to find it with a whore!'

His voice was raw, his gold-flecked eyes dark with urgency. 'I love you, Abbra. Don't you understand that? Don't you know what it means? I don't want other women, and I don't make love to them. There's only you, Abbra. Only you. Always.'

Tears of shame for even allowing such thoughts to enter her head glittered on her eyelashes. 'I'm sorry,' she whispered contritely. 'I didn't really believe ... it was just seeing Des Cawthorn with his Hawaiian girl ... Knowing that his wife was probably missing him and longing to be with him just as much as I missed and longed to be with you. I know you're not like him, Lewis. You're honorable and true and I will never doubt you again. Not for a moment.'

Gently he wiped the tears away from her face. 'That's good,' he said huskily. 'Let's cut this trip to the canyon short and go back to the apartment.'

She nodded, too full of emotion to speak without bursting into tears.

He rammed the jeep into gear, speeding away from the canyon, on to the route south. She hugged his arm, leaning against him, terrifyingly aware of how little time was left to them. When she remembered how she had allowed his remarks about battle to come between them, the shame she felt at having even imagined he would be unfaithful to her deepened. What did it matter how he felt when he was in battle? How could she possibly understand something so removed from her own experience? What mattered was that he loved her in a way few women were fortunate enough to be loved. She was lucky. Lucky. And she would never allow anything to come between them ever again.

The sun was still high in the sky when they returned to their apartment, but they closed the shutters and retired to bed, showing each other in every way they knew how, just how much they loved each other, and how much they would miss each other during the coming six months.

When she awoke among the crumpled sheets, the knowledge that time had nearly run out on them engulfed her and filled her with a panic she could scarcely control. For the first time she understood why some wives preferred not to have a reunion until their husbands' time in Vietnam was completely over. To have been together again, only to be parted so swiftly, was almost unbearable. He turned toward her, opening his eyes sleepily, and she fought down the panic, afraid that he would see it and that it would spoil their remaining few hours.

Right from the start they had agreed that she would not drive with him to the airport to see him off on his flight back to Saigon. Her own flight did not leave until six hours later, and she was going to tidy up the apartment, return the key, and hire a taxi for her own trip to Lihue. Not until then was she even going to admit to herself that their idyll was at an end. She was going to imagine that he was leaving on a fishing trip, a golf trip. Anything that would allow her to enjoy every second of their time together.

She made a special breakfast of papaya and mangoes, smoked salmon and scrambled eggs, champagne and freshly squeezed orange juice.

'Abbra,' he said thickly, stretching a hand out to her across the flower-decked table, and for a moment the tears she was holding in check nearly overwhelmed her.

'No,' she said, smiling fiercely, 'please don't say it, Lewis! Please don't say anything! Please let's pretend for just a little longer.'

It wasn't until she was searching her shoulder bag for her flight ticket that she found the unopened envelopes she had scooped up so hurriedly from the hall table the morning she had left San Francisco.

'What are those?' he asked teasingly, circling her waist with his arms. 'Letters from admirers? Movie offers from Hollywood?'

She laughed, leaning back against him, grateful for the fleeting sensation of normality that the unopened mail had given. 'Whatever they are, I hope they aren't important. I've been carrying them around all week.'

The first letter was from a book club; the second was from an aunt in Nebraska; the third was a letter of acceptance from the fiction editor of the magazine to which she had sent her short story so many months before.

She stared down at it incredulously. 'Oh, my goodness! I've done it! I'm going to be published! Oh, Lewis!' She twisted around in his arms, hugging him tight. 'I can't believe it! I'm an author! Isn't it great?'

Still holding her with one arm, he took the letter from her. 'What on earth did you write that they would want to publish?' he asked, amusement in his voice. She was about to say that she had written about an army wife, apart from her husband, but in a moment of blinding revelation, as instantaneous as Paul's on the road to Damascus, realized if she did so, his reaction would be horror, not pride.

'I wrote a ... a love story,' she said weakly, disappointment rushing so hard on the heels of elation that she felt physically light-headed.

'Just as long as no one knows about it,' he

said easily, pulling her toward him again, his mouth hot and sweet against her temples.

She swallowed, unable to think clearly. Surely other people would know of it? Surely her name would be beneath the title in the magazine? Surely he *wanted* other people to know of it? To admire her? Damn it. *She* wanted other people to know of it! She said fiercely, 'It was a very *well-written* love story, Lewis. Otherwise the magazine that I sent it to wouldn't publish it. They have millions of subscribers and...'

His amusement deepened at her indignation. 'Okay, okay,' he said, conciliating, rocking her against him. 'I didn't mean to sound insulting. It's just that as an army wife you have to be a little careful, Abbra.'

'But why on earth...' she began, and then she remembered the precious minutes ticking away, and horror at how near they were to spending them arguing stopped her short.

'Yes?' He tilted her face toward him, his warm brown eyes alight with the love he felt for her.

'Nothing,' she whispered. 'Oh, hold me, Lewis! Tell me that nothing is going to go wrong between us. Not ever!'

'Nothing will ever go wrong between us, sweetheart,' he said, his voice so full of certainty that her fears died as quickly as they had arisen. For a long time he held her against him, feeling the slamming of her heart against his, the softness of her hair against his cheek. At last, his voice suspiciously hoarse, he said gently, ‘It’s ten-thirty, Abbra. I have to go.’

The floor seemed to tip and tilt beneath her feet. She took a deep, steadying breath, reminding herself that she was an army wife; that partings such as these were a part of their life together; that the last thing he needed was for her to be upset.

‘Yes,’ she said unsteadily. ‘Please go quickly. Please go quickly and stay safe.’

He kissed her one last time, hard and hungrily, and then he turned on his heel, striding from the room, slamming the door behind him.

She stood where he had left her, listening as he pulled away from the front of the apartment, listening as the sound faded into the distance.

He had gone. The coming six months would pass just as the previous six months had passed. All she had to do was endure them.

‘I love you, Lewis,’ she whispered aloud. ‘Oh, God, I love you so much!’ And then, forgetting all about her determination to be brave, she flung herself facedown on the crumpled sheets of the bed and cried.

# CHAPTER SIX

'You're what?' Serena's father said incredulously, lowering his shotgun to his side.

The last remains of the debris from the concert had been removed finally and for the first time since the event had taken place, he was enjoying a morning walk in his grounds, his two aging cocker spaniels at his heels.

'We're married,' Serena said composedly. She held out her hand for his inspection and the plain narrow wedding ring, all they had been able to purchase in their haste, glittered corroboratingly.

'You're *what*?' her father repeated, staring disbelievingly first at Serena and then at Kyle, who he couldn't quite place, and then back at Serena again.

'We're married,' Serena repeated obligingly. 'It was all rather sudden, Daddy, and—'

'You're *what*?'

Kyle sighed. Serena had been adamant that it was up to her to break the news to her father, but it was obvious that she wasn't doing a very good job of it, or his new father-in-law was stone deaf. 'We're married, sir,' he said, his careless stance and the rather bored tone of his voice taking away any respect there might have been in the word *sir.*

'The devil you are!' the earl spluttered, the dogs looking mournfully up at him, aggrieved at the interruption to their walk. 'What sort of silly statement is that? Married indeed! Take your cock-and-bull stories somewhere else and leave me in peace!'

This time it was Serena's turn to sigh. Her father really was an ass at times. 'We're married,' she said for the fourth time. 'Married as in Darby and Joan, trouble and strife...'

'Marriages are made in heaven,' suggested Kyle helpfully.

'Marry in haste, repent at leisure,' Serena finished, a little insensitively.

'If this is a new parlor game, now is neither the time nor the place for it!' her father said.

They were standing on the crown of the hill looking down toward the house. It had taken Serena and Kyle a good ten minutes from the point where they had parked the car to walk up through the avenue of elms and waylay him, and in Kyle's opinion it had been a wasted exercise.

'For the love of God,' Kyle muttered beneath his breath, and then, louder, 'Serena and I were married yesterday. If you don't choose to believe us, there's nothing we can do about it. We've told you, and as far as I'm concerned, that's where our responsibility ends.'

The earl glared at him, his hand tightening on his shotgun, and Kyle backed away a foot or two. 'How dare you, you insolent young pup! You've no business on my land! Remove yourself immediately!'

'Kyle is a house guest, Daddy,' Serena said with admirable patience. 'He's Royd Anderson's son. They've been staying with us since the end of last month, remember?'

Her father peered at Kyle, vaguely recognized him, and slackened his hold on the shotgun. 'So he is. Stupid of me. Now, whatever it is you want, leave it to later, there's a good girl. I haven't had a day of peace since that wretched concert. Men were still moving litter at six o'clock yesterday morning, and some damn fool of a fellow has been on the telephone all morning insisting the event has to be repeated next year!'

Kyle turned toward Serena and said in weary disbelief, 'We're wasting our time. You've told him four times, I've told him twice.'

'Told me what?' the earl asked with absent-minded interest, wondering if they had perhaps interrupted him on his walk because they wanted to join him. Americans often liked a little shooting, and the Anderson boy looked as if he might be handy with a gun. He wasn't dressed for it though. A button-down shirt and tight jeans and crepe-soled suede shoes. Serena was no better. Her minidress barely skimmed her bottom, and her thigh-high white boots had heels on them that made walking over rough ground virtually impossible.

'Wellingtons,' he said forthrightly. 'Much

more sensible.'

Kyle raised his eyes to heaven, wondering if insanity ran in the family and if perhaps marrying Serena in haste, without a medical check beforehand, had been wise.

'We haven't come to help you decimate the local wildlife,' Serena said, long practice enabling her to follow her father's often tortured thought processes. 'We've come to tell you that we've been away for a few days. In Scotland.'

'Hadn't missed you,' her father said truthfully. 'Were you here for the concert? Shocking row. Couldn't hear myself think. Shall never have another.'

Serena refused to be deflected into talking about the concert. 'We went to Scotland to get married,' she persisted, speaking slowly and clearly, as if to a child. Her father continued to stare at her in blank incomprehension, and she abandoned patience, saying exasperatedly, 'For Christ's sake, Daddy! We *eloped*!'

'You *what*?' he expostulated for the fourth time, understanding at last beginning to dawn. 'You can't be married! You're too young. Need consent.'

'That's why we eloped,' Serena said with remarkable restraint. 'You don't need consent in Scotland, Daddy. Not if you're over sixteen.'

She held her left hand out toward him again. He looked down at the shining new wedding ring and said with commendable brevity, 'Your mother won't like it. There's going to be a devil of a fuss.' He peered long and hard at Kyle, and then said with brutal candor, 'Come to think of it, I don't like it much either. Needs some thinking about.' And he turned on his heel, stalking away. The spaniels spoiled the effect somewhat. They had fallen asleep and he had to return for them, prodding them awake with the butt of his shotgun.

'I suppose it could have been worse,' Kyle said as he and Serena began to walk back toward the house.

'Oh, yes, and it will be! Poor daddy. He really did make hard work of it, didn't he? I wonder what conclusion he will come to after his walk and his think?'

'God only knows.' At the prospect of Serena's father thinking, Kyle's imagination failed him. For the past four days he had been permanently high on alcohol or marijuana or both, and he was finding his present sobriety something of a strain.

'Who do we tell next?' he asked, determined that whoever it was, he would fortify himself with a joint or a stiff whisky beforehand.

'What about your father? He's the one who holds the purse strings, isn't he? Might as well find out if you're to be cut off without a dollar to your name,' Serena suggested.

'If I am, I shall divorce you,' he threatened in perfect seriousness.

Serena grinned and pushed her long mane

of pale gold hair away from her face. 'Don't worry. If you and your money are parted, I shall *beg* for a divorce!'

The earl's reaction to news of the marriage was mild in comparison with Kyle's father's. 'Of all the stupid, crass, *inane* things to have done!' he thundered. 'We're *guests* here, for Christ's sake! Don't you realize he's a peer of the realm? How many millions of...'

He was about to ask how many million dollars the whole fiasco was going to cost, before it was over, in alimony and settlements, when the peer in question ambled into the room. He bit the words back with difficulty, contenting himself with a strangled, 'You need horsewhipping, for Christ's sake!'

Kyle stood nonchalantly in the center of the yellow-walled room, his hands in the pockets of his jeans, Serena at his side. His father, mindful of his host's presence, sucked in his breath. 'Just answer me one question,' he demanded unsteadily, 'in the name of God, *why*?'

Kyle shrugged. 'It seemed like a good idea at the time,' he said truthfully, a lock of blue-black hair falling Byronically low across his brow.

His father choked, Serena giggled, and the earl said in obvious puzzlement, 'There's half a dozen newspaper reporters at the gates, clamoring for admittance. Wouldn't be fobbed off. Said they knew the story of the elopement was genuine. Said someone had telephoned them anonymously from here with the news.'

Royd Anderson suppressed a groan and tried to look as baffled by the information as the bearer of it. He knew damned well who had leaked the news to the press, sabotaging any hopes of a quiet annulment. His wife had stared at him for only the briefest of seconds after he had broken the news to her, then said unequivocally, 'Good, it couldn't be better.'

'What do you mean, it couldn't be better?' he had yelled. 'Don't you realize what this marriage is going to cost us? This isn't a marriage that is going to *last*! This is a joke! You can bet your life both of them were stoned out of their minds when they said "I will" or "I do" or whatever the hell it was that they said. When it comes to the divorce, and the Blyth-Templeton lawyers get to work, they'll be talking in seven-digit telephone numbers! Christ!' He ran his hand through his thick thatch of grizzled hair. 'The only reason for that awful pop concert was to get some cash to fill the family coffers! By marrying Kyle, that girl has set herself up financially for the rest of her life! And on *my* money, goddammit!'

'You're being extremely shortsighted!' his wife had said with composure. 'Think of the social advantages. Serena's name has been linked romantically with that of Prince Charles. She could probably have been the future queen of England if he'd put her mind to it.'

'The future king of England could probably

have afforded the divorce! I can't!'

They were in their bedroom and she was sitting at the dressing table. Until now she had been talking to his reflection in the mirror, but now she turned to face him, saying chidingly, 'You're being ridiculous, Royd. Look at things sensibly for a minute. The way Kyle has been behaving these past two years, he could have eloped with a barfly, a two-bit actress, a flagrant fortune hunter...'

'She *is* a fortune hunter!'

'But she's *not* a two-bit actress! She is *Lady* Serena. She is the only daughter of one of England's oldest and most respected aristocratic families. The Blyth-Templetons can trace their family tree right back to Henry VIII. Think of the social contacts we will gain. Serena is still close friends with Prince Charles. He will attend the wedding, he will probably be godfather to their first child...'

'Have you completely lost your mind? The wedding is over! In the past! History!'

'*That* wedding may be over,' his wife agreed, undeterred, 'but the *real* wedding is still to come. I believe St. Margaret's, Westminster, is the church for high society weddings. We shall have to hire a couple of private planes to ensure that our side of the family is represented. *The Boston Globe* and the society editors of *The Washington Post* and *The New York Times* will have to be informed.'

Royd chewed his bottom lip. 'You really think this could be to our advantage?' he asked, frowning.

'Of *course* it is!' She rose to her feet, crossing the room toward him, removing a speck of fluff from the shoulder of his jacket. 'Think of some of the girls Kyle *might* have eloped with. Think of the *prestige* of him marrying a girl whose name has been romantically linked with that of England's future king. Think of the social advantages of our being related by marriage to leading members of the British aristocracy. The only thing is, we mustn't seem *too* pleased by it. We don't want the Blyth-Templetons thinking that we *planned* it. They must be absolutely furious. By marrying Kyle, Serena has ruined any hopes they might have had where Prince Charles was concerned. They are probably scheming how to have it speedily annulled right this very moment.'

Royd had muttered darkly that he wouldn't blame them if they were, and had marched off in the direction of the yellow room, where he had been informed that the newlyweds were awaiting him. He still hadn't spoken to Kyle face to face. News of the wedding had been telephoned to him earlier in the day, when he had been enjoying a lavish business lunch in London. He had promptly abandoned his steak tartare and driven back to Bedingham at high speed.

His host had greeted him and had unhappily confirmed that their respective children had, indeed, eloped to Gretna Green and had now returned to Bedingham as man and wife.

Royd still couldn't believe it. Kyle was suicidally hotheaded, but for him to get *married*, and at *nineteen*, made no sense whatsoever. He had already discounted the fact that Serena might be pregnant. Hell, they'd been in England only three weeks! Even if Kyle had knocked her up the moment he had met her, she still couldn't know if she was pregnant or not. Besides, he was damned sure that neither Kyle nor Serena possessed a shred of the kind of responsibility that might have prompted a quick marriage if she had been.

His anger, which had been white hot, had ebbed a little since his conversation with his wife. She had been right. There *were* advantages to the marriage. As he strode along the long portrait-lined corridor and down the main staircase, his remaining fury was tempered by embarrassment. Kyle was a *guest* at Bedingham, for Christ's sake, and as a guest he had transgressed every rule in the book. He slammed into the drawing room, intending to give his son the lecture of his life, only to be stopped dead in his tracks by his host walking in on them.

'Newspaper reporters are a bloody tenacious breed,' the earl was saying glumly. 'Won't leave until they get a story. One of them even had the effrontery to ask if he could come in and take a photograph of the happy couple!'

'Well, he can't!' Kyle snapped, his amusement at the consternation he and Serena had caused beginning to wane.

His father-in-law eyed him unlovingly. He couldn't imagine what Serena saw in him. He looked more Irish than American. All quick temper and damn-your-eyes. 'It's not what I would have wanted,' he said with unhappy bluntness, 'but now that it's happened, there's nothing to do but live with it.'

Royd, once he was sure that it was the marriage that was being referred to and not the presence of the newspaper reporters, breathed an infinitesimal sigh of relief. Now that news of the elopement had been leaked to the press, any steps his host might have taken in order to terminate the marriage would have been seen only as an insult to Kyle and to himself. 'How did Serena's mother take the news?' he asked in awkward concern.

He had been friends with the earl for nearly five years, ever since they had been guests on a Mediterranean yachting cruise hosted by a mutual friend, but he still found it difficult to think of the countess by her Christian name, and virtually impossible to address her by it. To address her by her title, when he was her guest, went against his democratic principles. So 'Serena's mother' helped him get around the situation.

The earl pondered the question. He was physically unable to tell a lie, and he was dimly aware that to tell the truth might be a little tactless. 'Emotionally,' he said at last, rather pleased with his choice of word. 'She took the news very emotionally.'

The stark truth was that his wife had shocked him by being, not outraged at the news, but overjoyed. 'Oh, it's a *wonderful* marriage! How clever of Serena! There will have to be another wedding, of course. A proper one at Bedingham. We'll have the reception out of doors on the front lawn, with a few marquees in case of rain.'

'Can't see what you're so pleased about,' he had protested, baffled. 'The child is only eighteen. The whole affair is damned ridiculous.'

'No, it isn't,' his wife had said practically. 'The Andersons are one of Boston's oldest families *and* they are extremely wealthy. As the only son, Kyle will eventually inherit. I couldn't be more pleased at the way things have worked out if I'd arranged it all myself.'

'Well, *I'm* not pleased,' he said stubbornly. 'If there's going to be a proper wedding at Bedingham, it means there will be caterers all over the place and hundreds of people littering the grounds with their vile cocktail sticks and cherry stones. It will be nearly as bad as the concert and I'm not having another of those, no matter *how* financially successful you say that it was!'

He said now, reluctantly, 'There'll have to be another wedding, of course. Families present. All that sort of thing.'

Kyle groaned and Serena looked across at him in amusement. 'It's beginning to get a teeny bit boring, isn't it? Shall we drive up to

London and celebrate our nuptials with champagne at the Ritz?'

'No! I've just driven all night from Scotland! I'm sure as hell not going to drive all the way to London!' the groom said unequivocally.

The earl waited with interest for his daughter's reply. When Serena suggested doing something, she was accustomed to people falling in with her plans. It became obvious, almost immediately, that she had no intention of having them thwarted now.

'Then I'll go by myself,' she said, unperturbed, holding out her hand for the car keys.

The earl's interest deepened. Kyle's father held his breath. The groom was being faced with an ultimatum, and both of them knew it. The groom knew it, too, and was blissfully indifferent.

'She's getting low on gasoline,' he said, speaking of Serena's Porsche as if it were a ship at sea and sliding his hand into his hip pocket for the car keys. 'You'd better put some in at the first gas station you come to.'

'Thanks,' Serena said coolly, taking the keys from him. 'See you. Bye,' she added and turning on her heel, she strode nonchalantly from the room.

The earl was aware of a grudging surge of respect for his new son-in-law. He had called Serena's bluff and seemed unconcerned about the outcome. Perhaps there was more to him than he had first thought. 'Have a whisky,' he said to him companionably.

'Devilish long drive, Scotland to Bedingham. Wouldn't fancy it myself.'

Royd was unable to share the earl's apparent calm at the turn events had taken. Before he had even spoken to Kyle he had been ninety-nine per cent certain that the marriage hadn't a hope in hell of surviving. Now he was a hundred per cent sure, and he knew who was going to have to foot the bill. He glared in impotent fury at his son, unable to gain even the slightest grain of comfort from the fact that his soon to be ex-daughter-in-law was also the ex-close friend of the future king of England.

Serena was surprised at the depth of her disappointment as she drove at high speed past the gaggle of reporters at the gates. Damn Kyle. If he hadn't wanted to drive, he could at least have been happy for *her* to drive! The news of their elopement would soon be in all the national papers, and being in town with him, receiving the congratulations of all her friends and endlessly celebrating would have been fun. As would a continuation of the glorious, almost nonstop sex they had been enjoying. She swung out of Bedingham Village and onto the main road south, pressing her foot down hard on the accelerator. Damn Kyle. Damn him, damn him, damn him!

As far as the press were concerned, her arrival in London, and her presence at the more exclusive discos and nightclubs without her spouse only served to elevate a minor society story into a major one. 'Runaway Lady Serena Parties Without Groom' was one headline and 'Anderson Heir Stays Home While Bride Cavorts' was another. Serena did not care. The elopement, and her subsequent discarding of her groom, had only added luster to her already wild and reckless reputation.

On her first night in town, after a party at Annabel's that had gone until dawn, she had been escorted back to the Chelsea house by a long-standing male friend, and had shocked both him and herself by saying on the doorstep, a note of surprise in her voice, 'You can't stay the night, Toby. I'm a married lady now. Adultery after forty-eight hours of wedded bliss is a little steep, even for me.'

'But I thought the elopement was just a joke,' Toby Langton-Green protested, piqued.

'Well, it was,' Serena said, her thought processes slightly dulled by the amount of champagne that she had consumed. 'But it's not a *complete* joke, if you see what I mean.'

'Dashed if I do,' Toby said, swaying unsteadily on his feet. 'Not as if the fellow would know, is it?'

'No,' Serena agreed. 'But *I* would know.'

Toby hiccuped, not relishing the thought of a drive back to his own bed in Hampstead. 'And does that matter?'

'Yes,' Serena said, intrigued at the discovery. 'I'm afraid it does, Toby. Strange, isn't it?'

'Bloody peculiar,' Toby agreed. 'If I can't

sleep in the marriage bed, or what will be the marriage bed if the groom ever deigns to put in an appearance, can I at least sleep on the sofa?'

'Yes.' She yawned. 'But don't wake me when you leave, Toby. I haven't slept for forty-eight hours, and I won't want to get out of bed until the end of the week.'

She staggered exhaustedly across the threshold, heading unhesitatingly for the bedroom. Toby remained in the minuscule living room for a minute or two, eyeing the sofa with reluctance. It really did look damned uncomfortable. He removed his evening jacket, extricating his arms from the sleeves with difficulty, and went in search of Serena. The very least she could do was to loan him a pillow for the night. She lay on the bed, facedown and fully clothed, snoring softly, and he was able to flop thankfully down next to her without her giving any protest.

Serena remained in town all week. The newspapers continued to avidly follow the story of her elopement, fueled not only by her own fevered party-going, but by that of her groom's.

Twenty-four hours after Serena had driven away from Bedingham, Kyle had also left his father-in-law's roof, whether amicably or not, the press were unable to decide. They had scrambled into cars and followed him, certain that he was driving to London in order to reclaim his erring bride. They were wrong.

His destination was not Chelsea but the Dorchester, where two of his cousins and a mutual friend from college had just checked in. Within hours the groom and his cronies were out on the town, painting it red. For five newsworthy nights, Serena could be found dancing with Toby Langton-Green or a dozen other old admirers at Annabel's and the Cromwellian, and Kyle could be found squiring any one of a number of debutantes to the Claremont and to Ronnie Scott's. Flocks of photographers followed in both their wakes, eager for the moment when the paths of bride and groom would cross. Against impossible odds, they did not do so.

Serena and her entourage would abandon the hexagonal-sided dance floor at Annabel's for the slightly larger one at The 400 only to miss a full-scale confrontation with Kyle and his cronies by seconds as they boisterously left The 400 for the Ad Lib.

Media interest mounted when the earl announced that following the elopement and civil wedding of his daughter and Mr. Kyle Anderson of Boston, a church wedding was to take place at Bedingham's fourteenth-century parish church.

Serena read the news with interest. There were times when she had to admire her father. To have made such an announcement, and gone ahead with all the plans necessary for such a wedding – when she and Kyle were hitting the headlines daily and separately – showed breathtaking aplomb. She wondered if arrangements for her wedding dress and her bridesmaids' were also being made in her absence. And if Kyle was as bemused by the situation as she was.

At the thought of Kyle, her bemusement vanished. That morning the William Hickey column had published a photograph of him dancing with one of her old school chums at The Darkroom. She had been there herself earlier in the evening, with Toby, and was not sure if her fury was because she had been cheated out of confronting him, and freezingly ignoring him, or of confronting him and being rapturously reunited with him. One thing was certain. *She* wasn't going to be the one to contact him! *He* would have to contact her!

He didn't do so, and the date of the wedding drew closer. When his cousins returned to the States, Kyle returned with them, and while his parents remained at Bedingham, announcing that they would not be returning to Boston until after the wedding ceremony, Kyle was photographed wining and dining young women in New York.

Serena didn't know whether to be amused or outraged. The date was set, and it had not been an easy wedding to arrange. The bishop, whom her father had approached for permission, had agreed that a church wedding was desirable even though a civil ceremony had already been conducted. He was not so sympathetic, however, when it came to his attention that the bride and groom were no longer on speaking terms and not even on the same side of the Atlantic. It had taken all her father's considerable charm to persuade the bishop to allow the second ceremony to take place.

'Don't worry about your dress, darling,' her mother had said to her airily over the telephone. 'Mary has all your measurements and is going ahead with the most *wonderful* design...'

'Mary?' Serena had asked, mystified.

'Quant. Sweet girl. I've invited her and her husband to the wedding, of course, and Mr. Jagger and the Animal man.'

By Animal man, Serena assumed her mother was referring to Eric Burden. 'What about the groom?' she asked, intrigued. 'Have you invited him as well? And has he accepted?'

'I'm not sure I like your sense of humor, darling,' her mother had replied crisply. 'Of course Kyle will be there. How could he not be?'

'Very easily. According to this morning's newspapers, he's still in New York.'

'New York isn't far away these days.' Her mother's voice was bland. 'Why, even Socialists go there for holidays now.'

At the mention of Socialists, Serena was reminded of Lance. She hadn't seen him since the day of the concert and was missing his companionship and acerbic remarks almost as much as she was missing Kyle's lovemaking. 'Where's Lance?' she asked, a small frown furrowing her brow. 'Is he back at Bedingham yet?'

Lance had removed himself from Bedingham the weekend that she and Kyle had eloped, informing his mother that he was about to take part in an antiwar vigil outside the American Embassy. Serena had watched the television news attentively, but though the demonstration had been reported at length, she had seen no sign of Lance's distinctively tall, slender figure and silky pale hair.

'No, darling,' her mother said without apparent concern. 'These demonstrations of his go on for weeks sometimes. Was Kyle hoping he would be best man?'

'Kyle and Lance barely know each other,' Serena responded dryly. 'And I'm quite sure that Lance is the last person on earth Kyle would invite to be his best man. *If* Kyle is going to turn up at the church, and *if* he's had the forethought to ask someone to be his best man, both of which events I think highly unlikely, then he will ask one of his innumerable cousins or a buddy from Princeton.'

When she had replaced the telephone receiver on its rest she had gazed long and hard in a nearby mirror. Kyle could easily have gotten in touch with her if he had wanted to. The address of her mother's Chelsea house was hardly a secret, nor was the telephone number.

She tilted her head thoughtfully. Neither, of course, was the address and telephone number of the Dorchester, which was where

Kyle had been staying until his departure for the States. *She* could have gotten in touch with *him* if she had wanted to. And she was honest enough to admit that she *had* wanted to. After all, it wasn't as if they had quarreled bitterly. The few days they had spent together had been unbelievably wonderful. Yet she hadn't telephoned the Dorchester, and now the wedding that had been arranged for them was only three days away.

The frown that had creased her brow when she had been talking to her mother deepened. An army of Blyth-Templetons was due to descend on Bedingham in droves; flocks of Andersons were about to depart from Boston at any moment aboard a private plane chartered by her father-in-law. And she still hadn't decided what she herself was going to do.

Was she going to be there? Was she going to walk down the aisle on her father's arm, in her Mary Quant wedding dress? And if she was, would Kyle be there at the altar, waiting for her? The newspapers were already running bets on the outcome, and the odds were heavily against either her or Kyle being at the church for what was being termed the non-wedding of the year.

She turned away from the mirror abruptly. If only Lance hadn't left in such an annoying way, then she would at least have had someone to share the ridiculousness of the situation with. As it was, there were times when she was beginning to find it extremely boring.

Moodily she turned on the bath faucets and

emptied half a bottle of Chanel No. 5 into the steaming water. But she wasn't bored with Kyle. If the truth were known, she was missing him dreadfully.

When there was only twenty-four hours to go before the ceremony, her father finally telephoned her with what he seemed to regard as a minor query. 'Wondered if you'd seen Kyle lately?' he asked pleasantly. 'His parents haven't. They're at Bedingham again. Until the wedding.'

'There isn't going to be a wedding, Daddy. Or, rather, there isn't going to be *another* wedding. One's obviously quite enough.'

'Poppycock. Has to be another wedding. Your mother wouldn't like it if there wasn't. You should be here by now. Rehearsal at the church and all that sort of thing. I'll tell your mother that you are on your way. Don't want her getting into a state over everything. Kyle's mother isn't being much of a help. She was quite hysterical at breakfast. Has some fool notion young Kyle is going to make a mess of everything.'

'Well, he probably is,' Serena said, wondering how on earth she could have let such a farcical situation arise. 'He's obviously not going to be there, and neither am I.'

'Don't be a silly girl,' her father said lovingly. 'Wouldn't be cricket if you didn't turn up. Bad for the family name and all that,' and he severed the connection, leaving her standing there, the telephone receiver in her hand, tears glittering on her eyelashes.

There were no signs of tears when Toby Langton-Green picked her up that evening in his MG.

'The papers are doing you proud,' he said, dropping a copy of the *Evening Standard*. 'The latest odds on a complete debacle at the church tomorrow are fifty to one. If only one of you turned up, I'd stand to win a quite tidy little sum. I don't suppose you're thinking of doing so, are you?' he asked hopefully.

Serena glared at him. 'Don't be an ass, Toby. Do I look like a bride on the eve of her wedding?' She was wearing over-the-knee derring-do snakeskin boots and a shocking pink, breathtakingly short minidress, the material glittering and shimmering and clinging to her curves as though it were a second skin.

'No,' he said frankly, putting the MG into gear and pulling away from the curb. 'Can't say you do.'

He turned into the King's Road, heading west toward Chiswick. 'I thought we were going for drinks at the Peppermint Lounge and then on to White's?'

'We are.' Toby was elegant in a lace-frilled evening shirt and blue velvet dinner jacket. 'But there's a party I'd like to drop in on for a few minutes.'

Serena looked across at him doubtfully. Toby was looking extremely pleased with himself. As if he knew something that she didn't know and it amused him.

'If you've arranged for newsmen to be

there, so that you can hit tomorrow's headlines as "The Man who Escorted the Bride who Never Was" then you're going to be very disappointed, Toby. I'm not playing.'

'Of course you're not, dear girl,' Toby said understandingly, patting her knee as he rounded Fulham Palace Road. 'Wouldn't dream of it. Nasty things, reporters. Avoid 'em like the plague myself.'

The party was in a towering block of luxury flats overlooking the Thames.

'Toby!' squealed their hostess, pushing through the crush to greet them. 'Serena, *darling*!'

Serena stared beyond her to where Kyle was lounging against a far wall, one foot crossed over the other at the ankle, a whisky glass in his hand. Their eyes met as streamers flew and champagne corks popped. 'Toby!' Serena admonished. But she was elated as the corners of Kyle's mouth twitched and broke into a dazzling grin. 'Toby! You *devil*!'

'Had to do something, old girl,' he said, his grin nearly as wide as Kyle's. 'Stand to make a tidy sum if one of you turns up tomorrow. If you both turn up, I stand to make a bloody fortune!'

Kyle eased himself carelessly away from the wall and crossed the room toward her. 'Long time no see,' he said affably, reaching out for her with a strong hand and drawing her close. 'Don't we have a date somewhere tomorrow?'

'Oh, you bastard!' she sobbed, her arms sliding around him, her body fitting in perfect familiarity against his. 'You unbelievable, impossible, evil-natured, *wonderful* bastard!'

As far as media attention went, it was without doubt the wedding of the year. The elopement and then the bizarre separation and subsequent behavior of the bride and groom had aroused prurient interest. The presence of pop stars such as Mick Jagger and Eric Burden, and personalities such as Mary Quant, insured that there was a full complement of reporters and photographers present when the bride and her father arrived at Bedingham's ancient ivy-covered church.

Her dress was of white lace, miniskirted and daringly low-necked. Instead of the usual white satin pumps, she wore knee-high white kid boots, and her veil was the length of her dress, billowing around her and held in place by a single, lush white Bedingham rose.

She was followed down the aisle by two of her friends from finishing school, who had been delighted by the countess's suggestion that they would surprise Serena by being her bridesmaids, and their dresses, too, in lemon silk, were knee-skimmingly short.

The only blight on the ceremony was the mysterious absence of the bride's twin brother.

'I don't understand it,' Serena said, turning to her mother as they posed for photographs before leaving the church for the reception. 'Where on earth can he be? Do you think we should report him to the police as missing?'

'Oh, I don't think Lance would like that at

all,' her mother said. 'You know how he feels about the police.'

Serena knew how Lance felt, but she was becoming so worried that she was beginning not to care.

'It's been four weeks,' she said to Kyle as they were driven the short distance back to the house in her father's Silver Shadow Rolls-Royce. 'He's *never* disappeared for so long at a stretch before. Not even when he was taking part in the vigil outside South Africa House.'

'For goodness sake, forget about him,' Kyle said equably. 'He's not a child. The only people who could be excused for worrying about him are your parents, and neither of them seem even faintly upset.'

'Neither of my parents are what you might call obsessively *caring*,' Serena said, twisting her new diamond-encrusted wedding ring around her finger. It lay snugly next to the cheap, shiny ring she had originally been married with and which she had adamantly refused to remove. 'In fact, they can't even be described as normal.'

For once Kyle agreed with her. 'But whereas Lance would know they wouldn't be worrying about him, he would certainly know that *I* would be worrying.'

Kyle looked across at her, one eyebrow rising slightly. It wasn't the first time he had noticed the throb of emotion in her voice whenever she spoke of her brother. He had met him only briefly, when he and his parents had first arrived at Bedingham, he hadn't been overly impressed. There was something weak, almost effeminate about Lance Blyth-Templeton, and from what he had heard of his political affiliations, he doubted if they would ever have much in common.

'He's probably at Bedingham,' he said, not caring much whether he was or he wasn't. 'The wedding was a bit of a free-for-all. You can't blame him for skipping it.'

The reception was already under way as their Rolls slid to a halt outside the south entrance. Eric Burden performed a rendition of 'House of the Rising Sun' without the benefit of his group, Mick Jagger sang 'Come On', and Kyle and Serena, remembering the circumstances under which they had previously heard him sing it, exchanged hot looks and then burst into shouts of uncontrollable laughter. When old Herricot eased himself through the crush to her side and whispered to her that Master Lance had arrived and was in the old nursery and wanting to have a few words with her, Serena's happiness was complete.

'Lance has arrived,' she said exuberantly to Kyle. 'I'm just going to find out where he's been. I won't be five minutes.'

She had hurried off, still in her wedding dress and veil, and Kyle had frowned in annoyance and then had his attention taken by an Anderson aunt, eager to give him her congratulations.

Serena rushed into the room that had been the nursery. He was standing with his back toward her, staring down onto the grounds and the giant marquee and the milling guests.

'Lance!' she cried joyfully, running toward him. 'Where on *earth* have you been?'

He spun toward her, his face a white, contorted mask.

'You bitch!' he snarled, seizing her wrist. 'You stupid, *whoring* little bitch!' And raising his free hand, he slapped her open-palmed across her face with all the force he was capable of.

# CHAPTER SEVEN

Gavin wanted his date with Gabrielle to be special. He didn't want to sit with her in a smoke-filled bar. He wanted a whole day with her, and he wanted the day to be spent far away from Montmartre's steeply narrow streets and shabby nightclubs.

'I'll pick you up at ten on Monday,' he said to her when she told him that Monday was her first day off.

*'Ça va,'* she said agreeably, hiding the disappointment she felt. 'Okay. But I am not singing anywhere on Monday. I could meet you a little earlier if you wish.'

He had chuckled and hugged her, aware that for the first time he had met a woman who not only filled him with raging desire, but who also aroused in him the laughing affection that he had previously reserved only for his younger sisters. He was well aware that it was a lethal combination.

'Ten in the morning,' he said, grinning down at her. Even in her stiletto-heeled shoes she still barely reached his shoulder.

She groaned, affecting horror at the thought of facing the day at such an ungodly hour, but her eyes were sparkling and he knew that she was pleased.

'We'll go to Versailles or Fontainebleau or Chartres,' he said, not really caring where they went, just as long as they were together and away from the pimps and prostitutes who thronged the area around the Black Cat.

They went to Fontainebleau. He had bought a battered old Citroën the second week after he had arrived in Paris, and as he swung out of Montmartre and on to the many-laned *boulevard périphérique*, Gabrielle noted with amusement that he drove with the panache of a native Parisian, blissfully unintimidated by the suicidally inclined drivers hurtling along on either side of them.

The leather of the Citroën seats was cracked and disintegrating and reeked of Gauloises and stale perfume. Gabrielle settled herself comfortably in the front passenger seat, aware that her own distinctive perfume was already mingling with the exotic odor left by past occupants.

Gavin headed south for Fontainebleau via the small town of Évry, and the villages of Fleury-en-Bière and Barbizon. The day was already hot, only the merest wisp of cirrus trailing across the brassy blue bowl of the sky as they skimmed down the white, tree-lined roads.

They lunched in Fontainebleau at a small hotel of the same name, and it wasn't until the wine had been poured and the first course served that he asked the question he had been longing to ask from the moment he had first set eyes on her. 'What nationality are you, Gabrielle?'

'French,' she said, and then, knowing that she hadn't answered the question he had been trying to ask, she added, 'But though I'm a French citizen, I'm only half French. My mother is Vietnamese.'

He had expected her to say that she was French-Moroccan or French-Algerian. He stared at her, his sunbleached brows rising comically. 'No wonder you asked me what I knew about Vietnam when I said that I was eager to be sent there.' He looked touchingly discomfited. 'Do you know the country? Have you been there?'

'I was born there,' she said, taking a sip of her wine. 'It was my home until I was eight.'

Mentally, he figured out that she'd left the country shortly after Dien Bien Phu. He looked slightly disappointed. 'Then you were too young to have any real memories of it. I don't suppose you know any more about the situation out there than anyone else does,' he said regretfully, about to abandon the subject.

Gabrielle laid down her fork and leaned her elbows on the table, clasping her hands and resting her chin on them. 'No,' she said slowly. 'No, I was not too young.'

The years rolled away; the memories were so vivid that she could almost hear the clicking of Mah-Jongg tiles; see the wide, lush avenues and the white stuccoed house with the many verandas that had been her home; smell the aroma of exotic spices, the fragrance of carefully tended tuberoses and gardenias, the dark, pungent scents of the encroaching bush. Homesickness, harsh and raw, swept over her. She had known, ever since he had told her he wanted to be sent to Vietnam to cover the war, where their conversation would inevitably lead. What she hadn't known was the depth of longing such a conversation would unleash.

She had been looking beyond him, her eyes unfocused, registering nothing of her present surroundings, seeing only the past. Now she gave her head a tiny shake, the sun that streamed through the restaurant's windows gilding her spicy red curls a burnished gold.

'My mother's family still lives in Saigon, and they write to us regularly.' She paused for a moment. She had never spoken to anyone before of her Vietnamese aunt, and her uncles and cousins. Now she heard herself saying prosaically, 'And one of my uncles, my mother's youngest brother, is Viet Cong.'

If she had said that her uncle was Ho Chi Minh, Gavin could not have looked more stunned. He blinked and said unsteadily, 'And are you in touch with him as well?'

'No.' She paused again and speared a button mushroom with her fork. 'But my aunt is. Irregularly.'

Gavin signaled the waiter over and ordered a beer. He had been enjoying the wine, but if he wanted to think clearly, and assess what

Gabrielle's information might mean to him once he was in Vietnam, he needed the familiarity of a beer to help the process along.

'How irregularly?' he asked when his beer had been poured and he had taken a fortifying drink.

'He left home in 1940 to join the Communists in Hanoi. For twenty-five years no one heard anything from him and then, two years ago, he visited my mother's oldest sister, Nhu, who is living in Saigon.' She paused again. Her uncle Dinh's activities were something she and her mother never discussed with anyone, not even her father.

Her eyes met Gavin's across the white tablecloth. She had known him for only three short days, and out of that time had spent only a few hours in his company, yet she knew instinctively that he would never betray her trust. 'He had come south on an undercover mission for General Giap...'

*'Giap!'* At the mention of the man who had led the Viet Minh forces to victory at Dien Bien Phu, every journalistic nerve that Gavin possessed screamed to life.

Gabrielle nodded. 'He is now a colonel in the North Vietnamese Army, though Nhu said that he did not look like a colonel. He and his men had traveled every inch of the way south on foot, treking through Laos and northeastern Cambodia and entering the South through the highlands. Nhu said that she scarcely recognized him, he had changed so much.'

Gavin's breathing had become light and shallow. 'And why had he come south?' he asked, already seeing the headlines such a story would make.

She tilted her head slightly to one side. 'General Giap wanted to infiltrate large numbers of his men into the south, and he wanted the situation assessed first, by someone he trusted.'

Gavin let out his breath slowly. The story she had told him, if corroborated by names and dates, would sell like hotcakes to *Time* or *Newsweek* or *Le Monde*. But if any of those magazines did publish the story, Gabrielle's family in Saigon would suffer. Nhu, and Nhu's children, would be considered Viet Cong. He would have his story and they would face interrogation and possibly even death. He wondered if Gabrielle realized how grave the consequences of trusting him could be.

'You know what could happen if I sell this story, don't you, Gaby?'

It was the first time he had affectionately shortened her name.

She nodded, her eyes holding his steadily. 'But you will not sell it, will you, Gavin?'

They had been speaking in English, and her heavy accent, as she pronounced his name, sent shivers of pleasure down his spine. He reached across the table for her hands, trapping them in his. 'No,' he said huskily, knowing what her act of trust symbolized for them. 'No, I shall never write anything that could harm you or your family. Not ever.'

'That is good, *mon ami,*' she whispered softly, and from that moment on both of them knew that they were going to be lovers for life.

They spent the afternoon hand in hand, wandering the great gardens of the palace of Fontainebleau.

'Why did you leave Australia?' she asked as they stood in the Jardin de Diana before the bronze statue of the goddess.

The crowds of sightseers who had crowded the gardens at the weekend had now gone. Only a few stray tourists remained, cameras slung over their shoulders, guidebooks in hand.

As a middle-aged American couple approached, intent on photographing the fountain-figure of Diana, Gavin gently steered Gabrielle away, walking in the direction of the old moat that rounded the north wing of the palace.

'Restlessness,' he said with a grin. 'I was eighteen when I left and it seemed to me that London was where everything was happening, and London was where I wanted to be.' His grin deepened. 'I still haven't gotten there!'

Gabrielle gave a little Gallic shrug. 'There is only La Manche to cross. It is only a narrow ribbon of water. You could be in London by this evening if you truly wanted to be.'

'It isn't so easy,' he said without regret. 'Somewhere on the way between Brisbane and Paris, I discovered I really wanted to be a war correspondent. Landing my job at the press bureau is a major step toward that goal. I don't want to hurt my chances by whining for a transfer to London when things are going so well here.'

'*Je comprends*,' Gabrielle said as they rounded the north wing and began to stroll, their arms around each other's waists, toward the formal garden known as the parterre. 'I understand.'

It was now mid-afternoon and behind them the sun-steeped stone of the palace glowed like gold, heat coming out of the ground in waves.

'And then there is also the question of a certain nightclub singer,' he said, pausing beside an ornamental pond and turning her around to face him. 'She may not go with me if I go to England.'

Gabrielle looked up into his boyish, almost vulnerable face. He was not at all the sort of man she had envisaged herself falling in love with. He was ridiculously young, only four years older than herself, and she doubted if he owned much more than the clothes he had on and the battered old Citroën that had brought them to Fontainebleau.

A smile tugged at the corners of her mouth. She knew that she was not being sensible and French. She was, instead, succumbing to a sense of destiny that was wholly Vietnamese.

'I think your nightclub singer may very well go with you wherever you want her to, *chéri*,' she said, and sliding her arms up and around his neck, she raised herself onto her toes and pressed her mouth softly, yet ardently, against his.

His response was immediate. His arms tightened around her and his mouth opened, his tongue sliding deeply and fully past hers.

The hair on the nape of his neck was crisp against her palms, his body hard and urgent as he pressed her into him.

'Let's go back to the town,' he rasped hoarsely, 'and see if the hotel has a room for the night.'

Gabrielle gave a deep-throated chuckle. She knew very well that they would have, as she had prudently reserved one while he had been paying the bill for their lunch. '*Bien*,' she said, agreeing. She was happy for him to think that he was taking the initiative and knowing that as the patron was a Frenchman, her secret would be safe.

It was like being in bed with a good-natured and overeager young bear, Gabrielle reflected as Gavin collapsed, exhausted, beside her. She ruffled his tousled hair with her hand. Whatever sexual experience he had gained on the long trip from Brisbane to Paris, it had been neither expert nor profound. In her widely experienced past she had met men who had a lot to learn, but she had never before met one who had everything to learn.

Gavin heaved himself up onto one elbow. 'Are you all right?' he asked, looking down into her dazed, disbelieving face, the concern in his voice indicating that he believed his enthusiastic and criminally swift act of copulation had caused the earth to move for her, and that she was still in the throes of recovery.

'*Oui*,' said Gabrielle lovingly, wondering which was the best way to handle a rather delicate situation. 'That was—' She paused, searching for a word that would do the experience justice. 'That was *incroyable, mon amour*.' She pulled him down toward her, the corners of her wide, generous mouth quirking into a smile. 'As it is still only six o'clock, let us have a little sleep and then, afterwards...' She settled his head comfortably on her breast. 'Afterward I will explain something to you, *chéri*.'

The task of explaining was a deeply enjoyable one, and one that was carried out with such skill that Gavin was happily convinced that most of what he had learned was his own idea.

Gabrielle surveyed the vast double bed and its crumpled sheets late the next afternoon and gave a little sigh. 'Things will not be so easy to arrange when we are back in Paris, *mon amour*,' she said regretfully, leaning back against the pillows. Her previous lovers had either been artists with their own studios or businessmen with their own apartments. Gavin shared decidedly basic accommodation in Montmartre with three fellow Australians.

'Do you always have Monday night off?' he asked her, an edge of panic in his voice as she glanced at the wristwatch that lay on the bedside table and then slid reluctantly from the bed.

She nodded, knowing very well the direction his thoughts were taking. Before he could suggest that they stay every Monday night at the hotel, she said apologetically, reaching for the wisp of black lace that served her as a bra, 'But I cannot stay away from home all night, every Monday night, *chéri*. My parents would worry.'

For a moment he wondered if she was teasing him and then, with a mixture of amusement and incredulity, realized that she was telling him the simple truth. 'But you're a *nightclub* singer!' he protested, laughing despite his disappointment.

'But a nightclub singer with a *very* protective *maman* and *papa*,' she said, laughing with him as she fastened her bra and reached for her panties.

He watched her in rapt fascination, intrigued by the combination of wanton and innocent that coexisted so happily in her sunny, uncomplicated nature.

'Then we'll drive out here every Monday morning and spend the day in bed,' he said, solving the problem with devastating ease. 'And in the evening, after a leisurely early dinner in the hotel restaurant, I will return you at a dutifully early hour to *Maman* and *Papa*.'

*'Bien,'* she said, her eyes dancing as she stepped into her skirt, 'but next Monday I think we will have to forgo our dinner in the restaurant, *chéri.*'

'Why?' His face fell. He didn't want to forgo one minute of the time they would have together.

She pulled her sweater down over full, lush breasts. 'Because we shall be dining *en famille, mon amour,*' and then, in case he had not understood her, she said with unmistakable clarity, 'We shall be having dinner with my parents. *Tu comprends?*'

*'Je comprends,'* Gavin said with a broad grin and in execrable French accent. She hadn't said so, but he was fairly sure that the invitation was a rare honor and one that very few of her previous boyfriends, if any, had received.

That there had been previous boyfriends – a lot of them – he did not doubt. Even taking into account an inborn capacity for sexual enjoyment, her expertise and virtuosity could have been gained only through practice. Strangely enough, the knowledge did not disturb him. Whatever the number of her previous lovers, there was something so pure and unsullied about her, something so joyous and generous, it made them unimportant. What mattered were the qualities he knew he could stake his life on. Her honesty and her loyalty and her greatness of heart. And for him, that was more than enough.

He had been correct to assume that few previous boyfriends had ever found themselves sitting at the Mercador dining table. In actual fact, none had.

Her mother had stared at her, her eyes widening, when Gabrielle had told her that she had invited Gavin to dine with them the following Monday.

'But who is this ... this Gavin?' she had asked apprehensively. 'Is he a new artist you are sitting for, *chérie*? Is he—' She had hesitated, her apprehension deepening. 'Is he a ... a gentleman you have met at the club?'

'Strictly speaking, I suppose that he is,' Gabrielle replied truthfully, 'but he isn't remotely like the usual kind of patron. He's Australian,' she added as if Gavin's nationality explained all.

Her mother sat down weakly. She had envisaged all kinds of horrors. An impoverished artist, a married businessman, the middle-aged patron of one of the clubs, but at least all her imaginings had been Frenchmen. An Australian was so foreign to her as to be almost beyond belief.

'You will like him, *Maman*,' Gabrielle said confidently. 'He is one of life's innocents.'

*'C'est impossible,'* her mother said faintly, imagination failing her altogether.

When Gavin entered the small top floor apartment, Gabrielle's father regarded him dubiously. He had never had any dealings with Australians, and had never wished to. To him they were a breed stranger even than

Americans, and that was saying a lot.

*'Bonsoir,'* he said stiffly, making no attempt to speak in his extremely creditable English.

'Would you like a drink?' Gabrielle asked, helpfully speaking in English. 'A kir?'

'A kir would be fine,' Gavin lied, thirsting for the fortifying alcohol content of a beer. Gabrielle, knowing very well that a kir was the last thing on earth Gavin would normally choose to drink, grinned and disappeared into the kitchen, leaving him to his fate.

*'Êtes-vous à Paris longtemps*?' Gabrielle's mother asked, good manners overcoming her prejudice at his nationality.

*'Deux ou trois mois,'* he replied manfully, deciding that if French was to be the name of the game, the sooner he launched himself into it, the better.

Both Mercadors flinched at his accent. 'Perhaps—' Gabrielle's father said when he had recovered his power of speech, '—perhaps it would be better if we spoke English.'

'That's fine by me,' Gavin said with disarming relief. 'French is a great language, but it can be a little tricky.' A slight smile twitched at the corners of Vanh Mercador's mouth. Gabrielle had been right. There was something innocent and charmingly vulnerable about the open-faced young man she had brought home.

She had thought that all Australians were enormously tall and powerfully built with loud voices and intimidatingly rough manners. The young man before her, though far taller than Gabrielle, was still only five foot eight or nine, and was slim and supple in a crisp white shirt and close-fitting blue jeans. Only his hair, bleached gold by the sun, seemed to her typically Australian, but he did not wear it cropped short, as she had imagined Australians wore their hair. Instead, it was long, as if he were a student, dark blond curls twisting indecently low on the nape of his neck.

'Gabrielle tells me that you are a journalist,' she said haltingly, her English only a little better than his French, 'and that you wish to go to Vietnam?'

Gavin saw a slight frown crease Mr Mercador's forehead and realized that the subject was not one that he encouraged. It was, however, a subject that dominated the evening.

'And will your country, too, become involved in Vietnam, as the Americans have become involved?' Etienne asked him as Gabrielle cleared away the soup plates and her mother placed a large, steaming casserole dish in the center of the table.

'Southeast Asia is our neck of the woods,' Gavin said, and Gabrielle, seeing the look of mystification on her father's face, interrupted, saying, 'Gavin means that Southeast Asia is geographically very close to Australia, Papa.'

Her father nodded comprehendingly. 'And?' he prompted Gavin.

'And anything that happens there is automatically of great interest to us.'

'Will Australia be sending troops to Vietnam, as America has?' Vanh Mercador asked, presiding over the dinner table in a traditional silk *ao dai*, the pastel-colored costume fitting tight from throat to hip, the side-split skirt billowing softly over loose black trousers.

'Last year the Australian government introduced a form of national service,' Gavin said, wondering from where Gabrielle had inherited her startling titian hair. 'It isn't a blanket call-up, it's a selective system in which those who have birthdays on certain randomly drawn dates are required to make themselves available for two years national service. The service was for both the defense of Australia and military purposes beyond Australia.'

The casserole was beef accompanied by mushrooms and freshly made noodles.

'Which will be Vietnam,' Etienne said prophetically, spearing a mushroom with his fork. 'But what the French failed to achieve in Vietnam, no amount of Americans or Australians will be able to achieve.'

Gavin was just about to say that the situation wasn't quite the same, as neither America nor Australia had colonial intentions toward Vietnam, but Gabrielle gave him a warning little shake of her head. 'Perhaps you could tell me what it was like living in Saigon in the thirties and forties,' he said instead. 'I'd be grateful for any background information that you can give me.'

Etienne, when the casserole and the dessert that had followed it had been removed, was only too happy to oblige.

By the end of the evening no remnant of his original hostility toward Gavin remained. True, he was an Australian, which was a pity, but he was also presentable and intelligent and it was better that Gabrielle had brought an Australian home than one of the pimps or the con men who abounded in the area.

The Monday evening dinners *en famille* became a weekly event. Gavin swiftly discovered that where Vietnam was concerned, the tenor of the conversation was far different when Gabrielle's father was not present. Vanh would reminisce about her childhood home in Hue, unwittingly revealing her deep homesickness.

'When you go to Saigon, you must visit my sister, Nhu,' she said repeatedly, her eyes overly bright. 'You must try to persuade her to leave Vietnam and to settle near us, in Paris.'

He had promised faithfully, but he had begun to wonder if he was ever going to step foot on Vietnamese soil.

All through the summer he had bombarded his superiors with requests that he be sent to Saigon to cover the war. The reply was always the same: he was too junior a member of the staff to be sent on such a coveted assignment. Journalists were required to work for at least three years in the head office before aspiring to become correspondents.

Without Gabrielle he knew he would have

succumbed to frustration and restlessness, and that he would have abandoned his ambition and moved on. To America perhaps, or to Canada. As it was, he remained in Paris, becoming as familiar with the narrow cobbled streets of Montmartre as Gabrielle was. Every flower vendor and paper seller knew him by name, as did every barman and doorman. The prostitutes knew him, too, cheekily soliciting him whenever Gabrielle was not at his side. Gavin's reply was always an amused grin and a shake of his head, his amusement caused by the knowledge that if he had ever accepted an offer, the girl in question would have immediately withdrawn it, and indignantly reported his faithlessness to Gabrielle.

It was October and he was at his desk, reading a report that had just come in from Stockholm, where a large meeting had been held protesting against American policy in Vietnam.

'Looks like it's your lucky day,' his immediate boss said as he strolled into the office. 'The agency's manager for Asia is in the building and he wants to see you.'

Gavin had given a quick thanks to heaven, and had taken the stairs leading to the executive offices two at a time.

'If Vietnam is what you want, Vietnam is what you've got,' a laconic Englishman said to him, the top two buttons of his shirt undone and the knot of his tie pulled loose. 'You'll be in Singapore for a few weeks first, until we get your visa sorted out. After that I'd like to see some real reporting from you. I don't want you to just sit on a hill and watch a battle and then report what the Americans say has happened at it. I want you to ignore the Follies and find out what is *really* happening.'

'The Follies?' Gavin asked, wondering if he was being given a caution against the night-clubs and bars of Saigon.

'The Americans give a press conference every afternoon at five, at the United States Public Affairs Office. It's known as the Five O'Clock Follies. You'll soon find out why.'

'Yes, sir,' Gavin said exuberantly, hardly able to contain the excitement surging along his veins. 'And thank you!'

The Englishman looked at him pityingly. 'Don't thank me now,' he said dourly. 'Thank me when you get back. If you still want to. Which you won't,' and he reached for one of the box files on his desk, indicating that the interview was over.

Gabrielle tilted her head slightly to one side. 'Are you quite sure?' she asked.

The elderly doctor rested his clasped hands on the surface of the mahogany desk that lay between them. 'But certainly. There can be no mistake.'

A small smile touched the corners of Gabrielle's mouth. 'Thank you, Doctor,' she said, rising to her feet.

His brows drew together in a concerned

frown. 'And what are you going to do about it?' he asked bluntly.

Gabrielle's smile deepened. 'Why, nothing. Nothing at all.' And with a happy, husky laugh she walked out of his office and down the narrow, winding stairs that led to the street.

She had arranged to meet Gavin at a sidewalk café on the corner of the rue des Martyrs and the rue le Tac, and she quickened her step, not wanting to be late. The October sun was still warm, and she raised her face toward it, her own reaction to the doctor's news so immediate and uncomplicated that it did not occur to her to wonder if Gavin's reaction would be different.

She turned into the rue le Tac and with a leap of joy saw that he was sitting at one of the café tables, waiting for her. There was a cup of coffee on the checked cloth in front of him and a folded newspaper.

'Gavin!' she called out, breaking into a run. 'Gavin!'

He turned his head toward her, rising instantly to his feet, a welcoming grin splitting his face.

'I have some great news!' he said buoyantly as she hurtled into his arms and he hugged her close.

Her eyes laughed up into his. *'Alors, chéri!* I too, have news *incroyable*!'

'Then ladies first,' he said gallantly, reluctantly releasing his hold of her and pulling out one of the cane chairs so that she could sit at the table.

She waited until he had sat down beside her and took his hands, imprisoning them in hers, her eyes shining. 'Are you sure that you do not want to tell me your good news first?'

He laughed and kissed the tip of her nose. 'My news will wait,' he said, exercising superhuman restraint, his head whirling with the hundred and one things he had to do, the arrangements he had to make. 'What do you have to tell me, Gaby?'

She leaned forward and kissed him full on the lips and then, as she drew her mouth lovingly away from his, she said softly, 'I'm having a baby, *mon amour*. Isn't that the most wonderful news you can imagine?'

# CHAPTER EIGHT

Abbra had a window seat on the flight back to San Francisco, and she sat gazing down into the shimmering blue haze of the Pacific. Her reunion with Lewis had been wonderful. The memory of their lovemaking warmed her like a glowing fire and would, she knew, continue to warm her through the months of waiting that lay ahead. And yet ... And yet...

Far below her the blue haze eddied into shades of aquamarine and jade. A small frown creased her brow and her dark-lashed eyes were somber. She knew very well what it was that was troubling her, and she also knew that she could no longer put off confronting it. Her husband was a complete stranger. The man who had said of battle that those were the best times, when the adrenaline begins to surge, had not been a man she had even remotely known. Neither had the man who couldn't understand her desire to know of the life he led when he was away from her. Yet that man, that stranger, was the man she loved and the man she had pledged to share her life with.

The public address system hummed into life and the captain informed them that they were approaching the California coastline and would shortly be landing at San Francisco International Airport. She fastened her seat belt, aware that there were no easy answers. They were married and they loved each other, yet they had not lived together in the day-to-day intimacy of husband and wife. When they did, then they would learn to understand each other. The prospect reassured her, and her frown cleared and a small smile touched the corners of her mouth. In a little less than six months time they would be together again and their married life would truly begin.

'I love you, Lewis,' she whispered as the tone of the engines changed and the plane prepared to land. 'Just come safely home to me. That's all that matters.'

When she walked out into the arrival area, the first thing she saw was Scott's tall, powerful figure. Her eyes lit up and her smile deepened as she began to walk quickly toward him, the skirt of her white linen suit skimming her knees, her long, suntanned legs seemingly endless.

The breath slammed hard in Scott's chest. Ever since he had said good-bye to her he had been determined that he would not drive up from Los Angeles to meet her when she returned. But all his resolutions had been in vain. He had procrastinated to the last possible moment, trying to convince himself that he was not going to weaken, and had then been obliged to drive like a maniac up

Highway One, praying that he wouldn't be stopped by a vigilant patrolman.

Now, seeing her stride gaily toward him, her smoke-black hair falling glossily to her shoulders, her pansy-dark eyes dancing with innocent pleasure at the sight of him, he knew he had been a fool to think he could stay away.

'It's good to have you back,' he said, making sure that there was only affection in his voice as he took her luggage and kissed her with light brotherliness on the temple.

'If only Lewis had been able to come back with me, then I could truthfully say that it's nice to be back,' she said, smiling up at him in a manner that nearly undid him.

Abruptly he began to forge a way through the press of people around them toward an exit. God in heaven, but it was even worse than he had imagined it would be. He had known that meeting her again, after admitting to himself his feelings for her were not in the least brotherly, but flagrantly carnal, would be difficult. But he had not expected it to be near impossible. He had imagined he would be able to simulate the easy camaraderie that had always existed between them, and she would be unaware of any difference in their relationship. Now he was not so sure. The urge to drop her luggage to the ground and to seize her, crush her against him, was almost more than he could endure. Beads of perspiration broke out on his forehead. Hell, it was even worse than making a twenty-five-yard touchdown with only ten seconds left to play.

'How was Lewis?' he asked, struggling to keep his eyes ahead of him, terrified of what would happen to his willpower if he looked down into her face.

'He was fine,' she said, and though the words were studiedly casual, there was so much love in her voice that he felt his shoulder and arm muscles harden into knots. 'He hasn't even had a stomach ache.'

'That's good,' Scott said, leading the way out of the airport terminal into brilliant sunshine. 'So what is he doing over there?'

They were approaching his car, and it was a second or two before he realized that his question was causing her some difficulty.

'Oh, he's still serving as part of a five-man advisory team,' she said at last, her voice so oddly vague that he swiveled his head toward her, his eyebrows rising.

A slight touch of color flushed her cheeks, and she didn't hold his glance; instead, she walked away from him and toward the car. 'He's still in the Ca Mau peninsula,' she said, opening the car door. 'I imagine he'll be there until his tour of duty is over.'

'Yes,' Scott agreed, wondering what on earth was troubling her. 'Sure.' He slid into the seat next to her, turning the key in the ignition, gunning the engine into life. 'You'd think that as his second six months is voluntary, they'd post him somewhere a little easier. Saigon, for instance.'

They were driving out of the airport and on to the freeway. Abbra looked across at him, puzzled. 'What on earth do you mean, voluntary?'

'Well, combat officers usually do only a six-month stint in 'Nam. Lewis must have angled for this second six months. He wouldn't have been given it if he hadn't.' He looked across at her, about to say that it was typical of Lewis to be such a glutton for punishment, and then he saw the expression on her face. His hands slid on the wheel, the car swerving as he said in stunned incredulity, 'But you must have known, Abbra! He must have told you! Christ, I thought *everyone* knew combat officers served only six-month stints!'

'No.' The word was strangled in her throat. She looked deathly pale. 'I hadn't known ... I didn't realize...' She saw the way he was looking at her and forced an unsteady smile. 'Lewis is a military adviser. Perhaps that doesn't come under the classification of being a combat officer. But if it does, you're right, it *is* typical of him to go the extra mile.'

Her eyes were overly bright and her voice was tremulous. For one terrible moment he thought she was going to cry.

'Abbra...' he began, slowing the car down, reaching out to her with his right hand.

'Don't,' she said thickly, pushing his hand away. 'I'm all right and I think you're wrong, Scott. I don't think he volunteered for this second six months of duty. It's obligatory, I'm sure of it.'

Scott said nothing. There was nothing he could say. Even if it hadn't been obligatory, Lewis would have volunteered for it, and both of them knew it.

There was a letter waiting for her when she arrived home. It was from the editor who had accepted her short story, and it suggested that, as she apparently had no literary agent, she might like to contact one. Three names were listed, but one, Patti Maine, was located in Los Angeles. As Abbra stared down at the address, the shocked sense of betrayal she had been feeling at Lewis's act of deceit eased. She had another focus for her thoughts now, and she found shelter in it. Without even pausing to unpack her suitcase, she telephoned Patti Maine's number and asked the secretary who answered it if she could please speak to Miss Maine.

'Who is calling?' a crisp voice asked, and as she gave her name Abbra accepted the fact that she was unlikely to be connected and that she would have to introduce herself by letter.

'Patti Maine speaking,' an unexpectedly young voice said, 'I was hoping you would give me a call, Abbra. Bernadette Lawler wrote me, telling me that she had given you my number.'

Abbra was so taken by surprise at Patti Maine accepting her call, and at being addressed by her first name that for a second she could only say, 'Oh,' and then, gathering her scattered wits, she said with a rush, 'It's very kind of you to speak to me.'

'It isn't kindness at all,' Patti Maine said dismissively. 'If Bernadette's hunch about your work is correct, and Bernadette's hunches usually are, then it's you who will be doing me a favor, not the other way round. When can you come and see me?'

'Tomorrow,' Abbra said instantly, and then apologized for her foolishness. 'I'm sorry, I wasn't thinking. You're obviously very busy. I can come and see you whenever it is convenient for you.'

'You're right, I am very busy,' Patti Maine said briskly, 'but as it happens, my lunch date for tomorrow has just cancelled. If you get to the office by twelve-thirty, we can have a chat and then go on to the Beverly Wilshire. It means I won't have to cancel the table.'

Abbra felt disoriented. 'Thank you,' she said breathlessly. 'Thank you very much. I look forward to seeing you. Thank you. Good-bye.' By the time she had uttered her last thankyou she was speaking into thin air.

'That's terrific!' Scott said when she telephoned him with the news. He had driven straight back to Los Angeles after dropping her off at her home, his thoughts and emotions in turmoil.

He couldn't go on seeing her. It would lead to disaster. Sooner or later, he was bound to reveal his true feelings for her and at the thought of her horrified reaction when he did so, he felt sick. There was only one sensible course of action to take, and he had already taken it. He had a date for that evening and the following one.

'Patti Maine is a big name,' he said, his pulse rate increasing at the mere sound of her voice. 'Hell, even I've heard of her! Your lady editor in New York has certainly done you a big favor, sweetheart.'

The minute he uttered the endearment he could have bitten his tongue, but she seemed not to notice it, saying nervously, 'We're having lunch at the Beverly Wilshire. I haven't a clue what I should wear. Do you think my white linen suit will be okay? Or should I wear something more sophisticated? Like black?'

'Good God, no!' he said, laughing. 'Wear the white linen. You look sensational in it.' It was true, and he found some relief in being able to tell her so in a way that would cause her no unease.

'What will she want to talk to me about?' There was a note of panic in her voice. 'I've only written a few short stories!'

'One of which a leading women's magazine is about to publish,' he finished for her. 'Don't be so modest, Abbra. Your editor wouldn't be introducing you to an agent of Patti Maine's stature if she weren't sure you had something to offer. Enjoy the lunch and don't worry. Patti Maine will do the talking. All you have to do is tell her what she wants to know and be your bright natural self.'

'I'll try,' she said, feeling slightly reassured.

'I think our lunch will be over by three. Probably long before if Miss Maine discovers I'm not the literary sensation she expected! Can you meet me around three-fifteen, or three-thirty? Or will you be at practice?'

'It might be a little difficult,' he said resolutely. 'I have a date tomorrow.'

'Oh!' Abbra was momentarily taken aback. For a highly eligible bachelor, Scott rarely dated. In fact, she couldn't remember his ever having dated all the months she had known him.

'That's great,' she said a trifle uncertainly. 'She must be very special.'

'Oh, she is,' Scott agreed, unable to remember what the woman looked like. Underneath Abbra's congratulations, he could sense her disappointment. She had been looking forward to telling him everything about her meeting with Patti Maine. He wasn't picking up his date until seven o'clock. There was no reason why he couldn't see Abbra first. No reason except that he would be breaking his hard-won resolution even before he had had a chance to put it into practice.

'I'll meet you at three-fifteen,' he said, despising himself for his weakness. 'In the Polo Lounge.'

It was their usual rendezvous whenever she came down to see him.

'Are you sure it won't make things difficult for you?' There was sisterly concern in her voice.

He grinned wryly. 'No,' he said, knowing

that every time he met her it made things more difficult than she could possibly imagine. 'See you tomorrow, Abbra. Drive safe.'

She had worn her linen suit, white kid sling-back shoes, and small pearl stud earrings. Patti Maine's office was in a luxury apartment block just off Highland Avenue. The walls of the entrance hall were pale magnolia, the ankle-deep carpet was magnolia, and pale, creamy out-of-season magnolias were massed in a tall cut-glass vase. A smiling secretary ushered Abbra through a large, similarly decorated room that obviously served as an office, and into a smaller, even more luxuriously furnished inner sanctum. 'Mrs. Ellis,' she announced, discreetly withdrawing.

The woman who rose from the small satinwood desk to greet Abbra was slightly older than her voice had indicated, but not much. 'Hello, Abbra. I'm very pleased to meet you,' she said with a wide, easy smile. Her hair was blond and fashionably bouffant, her short skirt was of pale champagne suede, her shirt blouse was of barely-colored silk, the top two buttons left provocatively undone. 'What will you have to drink? White wine? A spritzer?'

'A white wine, please,' Abbra said, immediately responding to Patti's straightforward friendliness.

Patti gestured her toward a deep-seated cream sofa and poured out two glasses of ice-cold Chablis. 'Now,' she said, handing Abbra her drink and perching on the arm of a nearby chair, 'tell me all about yourself.'

Abbra had never been to a psychiatrist, but she imagined that the experience would be very similar to the one she was now undergoing.

'I'm nineteen, I live in San Francisco, and I'm married to an army officer who is serving overseas in Vietnam.'

Patti Maine cocked her head slightly to one side. 'And you write...' It wasn't a question, simply a statement of fact.

'Yes,' Abbra said, her confidence growing. 'I write.' She hesitated a moment and then added, 'I've brought some of my short stories with me. I left the box in my car—'

'They're probably very good, but they're not what I want from you. Nor do I want the kind of thing that you submitted to Bernadette.'

'Then what *do* you want from me?' Abbra asked, beginning to rise to her feet, not at all surprised and sure that there had been a big misunderstanding.

Patti motioned her to sit down again. 'I want something different from you. Something I have a gut feeling about. Something I feel sure you can do.' She paused for a moment and then said as if it were the most reasonable thing in the world, 'I want you to write a book.'

Abbra stared at her and Patti laughed. 'You write, don't you? Why not go for the big one?

A book that could become a best seller.'

'But I wouldn't know what to write about!' Abbra protested, wondering if Patti was a little unbalanced, or if, perhaps, it was she herself who was unbalanced and imagining the whole conversation.

Patti put down her glass and rose to her feet. 'That,' she replied calmly, 'is a minor problem and one that we are going to resolve over lunch.'

As they picked leisurely at their salads, Patti asked Abbra to tell her all about her childhood and her upbringing.

'No,' she agreed as the waiter poured wine for them, 'I quite agree with you, there's nothing in your personal history that would serve as a springboard for a novel. What about your husband? How did you meet him? What sort of a man is he?'

'Oh, there's nothing there,' Abbra said quickly, so quickly that Patti Maine's intelligent eyes flared with interest. 'I wouldn't want to use anything in my private life as a basis for a novel.' She paused, her eyes suddenly becoming unfocused, seeing something that wasn't visible. 'But there is something...'

'Yes?' Patti prompted her, recognizing the creative light in Abbra's eyes.

'I just came back from Hawaii,' Abbra said, 'and something happened while I was there. Something that I can't quite put out of my mind.'

She took a sip of wine and then began to tell Patti about her meeting with Des Cawthorn.

* * *

For the next two weeks Abbra barely moved away from her desk. She wrote and rewrote, and as she did so, the characters she was creating took on shape and substance, developing a life of their own. There were times when she stared down in surprise at what she had just written, amazed at how one idea sparked off another, and at how her originally simple story line was taking on twists and turns she had never thought possible. Her novel even had a title now: *A Woman Alone.*

Scott had enjoyed his date with Rosalie Bryansten. She had been as unblushingly eager to share his bed as he had been eager to have her share it, and he had found the sexual release of their lovemaking cataclysmic. He was not a man to whom celibacy came easily, and for the first time he realized the incredible strain he had been living under. It was a strain he was determined that he would not subject himself to again. His belief that he could live without seeing or hearing from Abbra lasted all of ten days. By the time the end of the second week was drawing near, he ached for her.

'We're playing the Chargers on Saturday,' he said to her on the telephone. 'Why don't you fly down to San Diego? We could drive back to San Francisco on Sunday and stop by Carmel.'

Abbra was about to ask whether the woman he had dated the previous week would be going down to watch the game as well, and if so, whether a sister-in-law might be an awkward third. She decided against it. For some reason she found it hard to speak to him about the unknown woman he was presumably still dating.

'I don't think I can, Scott,' she said a little wistfully. 'I still haven't finished the outline for the book, though it's taking shape far better than I ever thought possible.'

'It will take shape even better when you've had a rest for a couple of days,' Scott said encouragingly. 'Make a reservation for an early Saturday morning flight to San Diego, and I'll meet you there.'

Abbra felt herself weaken. It would be fun to watch Scott play and to spend the Sunday with him and talk to him about the book. 'Okay.' She laughed. 'You win.'

Scott was exuberant. 'Great! It's going to be a hard game. The Chargers have always been tough on defense, and we're going to need all the support we can get!'

It had been a happy, carefree weekend. The Rams had won and Abbra had been blissfully unaware of the speculative expressions in Scott's teammates' eyes as they asked about Rosalie.

'Rosalie?' she had asked Scott.

'The girl I've been dating.' His voice was casually dismissive and he did not mention her again.

After the game they had gone out on the

town with a crowd of Scott's fellow players and their wives and girlfriends, staying overnight in primly proper separate rooms at the Ramada Inn. The next morning, instead of flying back, Scott had rented a car and they had driven via San Clemente toward Carmel.

'The first place Lewis and I ever went together was Carmel,' Abbra said as the car sped into the little town's outskirts.

Scott grunted noncommittally, but when they reached the turnoff for the main street and the beach, he continued straight on.

She looked toward him, surprised. 'You've missed the exit, Scott.'

'No, I haven't.' His voice was light and easy, betraying none of the dark emotions that he was battling with. 'There's a restaurant near Sausalito that I've been meaning to take you to for a long time.'

She suppressed her disappointment. Perhaps, after all, it was best that they didn't go to Carmel. Memories of Lewis would be so strong that they would be nearly impossible for her to bear.

Scott had looked tense and drawn for the past five days and she wondered if his new girlfriend was causing him problems. She said suddenly, caring for him so much that it was a physical pain, 'Are you happy, Scott? Is there anything troubling you?'

He looked down at her, a smile she didn't understand crooking the corner of his mouth. 'I'm fine, Abbra, just fine,' he said thickly, and she had not pursued the subject. But she had not believed him.

By the end of February her synopsis was finished. She placed the twenty cleanly typed pages into a manilla envelope and addressed it to Patti Maine in a bold, firm hand. 'Please like it, Patti,' she whispered to herself as she drove down to the post office. 'Please God, let Patti like it!'

Lewis's letters to her, since his return, had been slightly more informative than his earlier ones, but not much. He had been given another assignment, still in the deep south of the country, but this time a little nearer to the Cambodian border. Although he was still part of the five-man American advisory team, the team was no longer working with a large South Vietnamese infantry battalion. Instead, they had been posted to a small village, Van Binh. Their task was to assist the villagers with rural development projects and to help the villagers protect Van Binh, and the surrounding villages, from the Communists.

*And these people need all the help they can get*, Lewis had written to her. *The area south of Saigon is so heavily infiltrated by Viet Cong that as far as the government troops are concerned, it's practically a no-go area. A situation we intended to change!*

There was a postscript, written in a hurried scrawl. *My commanding officer has been taken ill and flown out. For the moment I'm in tempor-*

*ary command. Long may it last!*

The situation was the same at the end of March, when his next letter reached her. *The local district chief is a fine man, doing a very difficult job as best he can. Together I think we can make Van Binh and the surrounding villages secure from both Viet Cong infiltration and Viet Cong aggression.*

It was obvious that he was relishing his new responsibilities. *As a co van truong, senior adviser to district chief, I'm in a position to make requests to Saigon for school supplies and building and agricultural development assistance, and you can bet your life I'm taking advantage of the opportunity.*

The letters cheered her up. Although she knew that his primary task was to flush out the Viet Cong operating in his area, he very rarely mentioned them, and never described any encounters with them. Instead, his letters continued to be full of heady exhilaration at being in a position to help the people he had begun to identify with.

All through spring and early summer the letters continued, and she took great comfort from them, happy to think of him as a benefactor, winning hearts and minds. Not wanting to think of him as a warrior.

# CHAPTER NINE

For a moment after Lance struck her Serena was too stunned to react. She staggered backward under the force of the blow, her eyes wide, her mouth open, gasping in disbelief and pain.

'An American, for Christ's sake! *You have to throw yourself away on a stupid, fucking AMERICAN!*' His face was scarcely recognizable, twisted with revulsion.

'But, Lance...' She had regained her balance and she stepped toward him, ugly scarlet weals rising across her face.

*'Christ, don't you understand?'* His voice was a sob. *'It was just beginning for us, Serry, and now it's all over!'*

Bewilderment overrode her anguish. 'What was just beginning? What is all over, Lance?'

*'This, for Christ's sake!'* and he seized her shoulders, his fingers bruising her flesh, his head swooping down to hers, kissing her open-mouthed with demented violence.

Serena could taste blood on her lips. Vainly she twisted her head, trying to free her mouth of his invading tongue, trying to speak to him, to reason with him. But Lance was beyond reason. Serena was the most important creature in the world to him, and he knew that he had lost her for good. She would leave Bedingham, leave England. She would live in a country he hated with a man he had hated on sight. And his sexual desire for her, previously properly held in check and causing him only bemusement, was now unleashed and out of control. There could be no going back now. And he had no wish to go back.

'Serry! Darling!' His hands were on the white silk of her wedding dress; her veil billowed around them.

'Lance! Please!'

He was deaf to the horror in her voice. She was his. She had always been his. There had always been just the two of them. He and Serena against the world. His mouth silenced her protests, his hands slid down from her shoulders, cupping her breasts, squeezing and kneading.

She raised her hands to his hair, grasping its silky fineness, pulling his head savagely backwards, freeing her mouth. 'No, Lance! This is crazy! No! Please!'

She tried to wrench away from him and he flung her back against a wall, panting for breath as the petals from the rose in her hair scattered around his head and shoulders. *'You feel the same way!'* he shouted. *'We've always felt the same way!'*

'Lance! Listen to me—'

His hands seized the delicate white silk and ripped it wide, exposing her small, high, brassiered breasts and the ugly marks on her shoulders where his fingers had dug into her flesh.

'Christ, Serry! We must have been mad not to have realized long ago!' he sobbed, bending his head to her rosy nipples, sucking and biting in an agony of need.

'This is insane, Lance!' Her voice was strangled with conflicting emotions. Lascivious desire was raging through her, as was horror and anguish. Small beads of blood were dripping from her mouth onto her torn dress, spreading and staining. 'Please stop, Lance,' she begged. *'Please!'*

However erotic the experience, it was one that she wished to bring to an end. She couldn't become her brother's lover. It would be an act that would irrevocably drive them apart. 'Lance, *please*!' Her voice was no longer panic-stricken but was calm and loving, deeply urgent.

Her dress slithered down to her hips and he groaned, sliding down onto his knees, still crushing her toward him, his face pressed against the soft flesh of her stomach, his mouth only centimeters above her brief panties and the springy blond bush of her pubic hair.

'Oh, Christ, Serry, I need you!' He was crying now, his tears damp against her skin. Relief surged through her. It had come to an end. She knew by the agonized defeat in his voice that he had come to his senses, that he would not take her by force.

'I love you, Serry. I've always loved you,' he said thickly, his arms still around her, his mouth hot against her naked flesh.

'And I love you,' Serena said softly. 'I shall never feel as close to anyone else. Not ever.' And she stroked his hair gently, knowing that in a moment he would release her, and that in another few seconds they would be laughing shakily at the Greek drama of their passions.

It never occurred to Kyle that he should knock at the nursery door before entering. It wasn't a bedroom, for God's sake. Annoyed by the length of her absence, not wishing to continue standing alone in the yellow drawing room, receiving guests on her behalf, he had excused himself and had asked Herricot where the hell she was. The butler, not accustomed to being spoken to in such a direct manner, had frigidly replied that Lady Serena was in the old nursery and had reluctantly given him the directions so that he could join her there.

As he strode along the upper corridor he heard Serena's voice cry out loudly, *'Lance! Please!'* and then, as he approached the nursery door, he heard, quite unmistakably, Lance Blyth-Templeton saying in an agonized voice, 'I love you, Serry! I've always loved you!'

He froze, one hand on the doorknob, pausing just long enough to hear Serena's reply, and then, without a second's hesitation, he flung open the door, striding into the room, horrified at the scene that met his eyes.

Serena was half naked, her dress lying in a white pool around her feet, her veil still billowing around her. Blyth-Templeton was on his knees before her, clasping her toward him, his face pressed ardently against the white lace of her brief panties. Serena was cradling his head, looking down at him with an expression of unmistakable love, tears of anguish streaking her face.

Not for one fraction of a second did Kyle believe that her tears were those of distress for Lance's obvious sexual advances toward her. He had heard no words of protest, had heard only their mutual confessions of love for each other. And one glance at the wanton intimacy of their embrace left him in no doubt as to the context in which the words had been spoken.

The depth of his revulsion stunned him. He had thought himself way out, liberated, wild. Now, faced with a wife who really *was* way out and wild, his reaction was one of traditional moral outrage.

'Jesus!' he said, his nostrils flaring, the color draining from his face. 'Jesus *God!*'

Serena turned her head swiftly toward him, her eyes flying wide with alarm. 'Kyle! Please! You don't understand!'

Lance was still on his knees, his arms holding her tight, uncaring of Kyle's presence.

'I sure as hell do understand! If I'd had any brains I would have understood a damned lot sooner! I knew there was something wrong about the relationship between you two! I heard it in your voice every time you spoke his name!' White lines etched his mouth, and a nerve jumped convulsively at the corner of his jaw. 'But I never imagined...' His hands had balled into fists. He wanted to kill the bastard, and he wanted to kill Serena too. The marriage service in Bedingham's village church had affected him more deeply than he had ever thought possible. Hell, he had been *happy* to be marrying her again! He had meant the vows he had exchanged with her! But she hadn't meant them. For Serena it had been just another joke, another outrageous experience to add to her long list of outrageous experiences.

'You're being ridiculous!' Serena snapped, her voice edged with panic. She tried to pull herself free of Lance's grasp, but Lance was laughing now, clinging to her as if he never, ever, meant to let her go.

'No! I'm through being ridiculous,' he said savagely, knowing that he couldn't physically assault Blyth-Templeton, that he couldn't bear to have any physical contact with him, not even a blow. 'I'll tell my lawyers to start divorce proceedings immediately!' Unable to bear the sight of Serena's nakedness and Lance's hands on her flesh a moment longer, Kyle slammed the door.

*'Kyle!'* Serena's voice was an anguished shriek. She seized Lance's hands, struggling to break their hold, but Lance was laughing uproariously, hugging her to him, saying jubilantly, 'Let him go! You're free, Serry!

Your marriage was a practical joke. Nothing more.'

*'Let me go, Lance!'* she shouted desperately. 'For God's sake...' She struck out at him with a white-booted foot and he fell sideways, a look of astonishment on his face. Free of his hands, she snatched at her wedding dress, lifting it up and around her hips, struggling to slip her arms into the sleeves of the tattered bodice as she ran for the door. The corridor was empty. Hysteria rose up inside her. He would go. He had meant every word he had said. He would go, and this time he would not return. 'Oh shit, oh fuck, oh hell!' she sobbed, racing for the stairs.

As she reached them, the chatter and laughter of the wedding guests rose to meet her. There were photographers. Journalists. To race down there, her dress savagely torn and half off her shoulders, would cause a sensation that she, and Bedingham, would never live down. She hesitated only a second.

In another few seconds Kyle would be driving away from her at a criminal hundred miles an hour. There wasn't time for her to go to her room and change her dress; to put on a wrap; to make herself decent. 'Oh, damn you, Lance!' she sobbed, beginning to run down the stairs.

It was her father-in-law who averted a further scandal. Aware that both the bride and groom had deserted their guests, he had walked angrily out of the yellow drawing room in search of them. As he paused in the marble-floored entrance hall to speak to Herricot and to ask if the butler knew where they were, Kyle came leaping down the grand staircase, taking the steps two at a time, his eyes blazing like live coals, his face ashen.

'What the hell...' his father began as Kyle forced his way through the wedding guests milling in the entrance, sprinting for the doors and the flight of stone steps leading down to the drive.

Herricot closed his eyes, rallying his strength. There would be worse to come, he was sure of it.

Royd Anderson was just about to set off in pursuit of his son when he heard the sound of Serena's running feet. He turned his head swiftly back in the direction of the staircase and sucked in his breath on a gasp of horror. The bride was hurtling down the stairs toward him, the bodice of her wedding gown ripped, her breasts, in their delicate white lace, half-cup brassiere, exposed.

He heard a cry of incredulity from first one guest and then another, and before every head was turned upward, he sprang for the stairs, racing up them, shielding her from view.

'Let me pass!' Serena shrieked, beginning to push him desperately out of her way.

There was no time for reason. No time for anything but swift restraining action. His fist shot out so swiftly that even Herricot wasn't sure if he had seen right. What he did see, and what the vast majority of guests with a view of the proceedings saw, was the bride crumple and her father-in-law sweep her up into his arms.

'Mrs. Anderson has fainted!' he shouted back over his shoulder to the reluctantly admiring Herricot. 'Ask if there is a doctor among the guests, and if not, please telephone for one.'

Herricot's position at the foot of the stairs hadn't been quite as advantageous as Mr. Anderson's had been, but he had received the distinct impression, before Mr. Anderson had shielded her so masterfully from view, that the bride's clothing had been in a state of alarming disorder. He had also received the impression that Mr. Anderson would prefer it if a doctor were not found too speedily. Not, in fact, until the bride could be made presentable.

Kyle never returned to Bedingham. He did exactly what Serena had known he would do. He vaulted into his father's car and drove like a maniac back to London. Four hours later, still glittery eyed and ashen-faced, he was aboard a plane bound for Boston, Massachusetts.

Lance was only a half hour later in following him down the London–Cambridge road. Serena's demented dash in pursuit of Kyle had brought him numbly to his senses. Both his parents and Anderson's would demand an explanation for the abrupt collapse of the marriage, and the disappearance of the groom. There would also be Serry's torn and bloodstained gown to explain away, and the weals on her face and the bruises on her shoulders and breasts.

He didn't for one moment imagine that Serry would tell them the truth, but he was damned sure that Anderson would. He would telephone his father, or his lawyers would make contact. Whichever method he used, Lance knew that he and Serry would be accused of having an incestuous relationship, and that there was a more than likely chance that the accusation would be believed. He had tried to speak to Serena and had failed. A doctor was with her, their parents and Royd Anderson were with her. In a very short while old Herricot would be questioned, and when he was, it would be quickly discovered that Serena had left the yellow drawing room to meet him. Lance had no intention of still being at Bedingham when that moment arrived.

He packed a suitcase swiftly and hurried out of the house, amused to realize that the guests were still apparently unaware of the bride and groom's absence. The giant marquee was still packed with laughing, chattering relations, a band was playing, champagne-laden waitresses were circulating among the groups strolling the lawns, and every inch of carefully maintained grass was covered in a pastel-pink drift of confetti.

Lance gave the scene one last, hate-filled look and then hoisted his suitcase into the rear of his MG. He drove off without a backward glance.

When the doctor arrived, Royd Anderson had persuaded him to sedate Serena heavily. He didn't know what the hell had happened between her and Kyle, but he was determined to try to find out a few hard facts before she gave out any story that would discredit his son or his family. As it was, when she regained consciousness, she steadfastly refused to say anything. Her mother pleaded with her, certain that Kyle Anderson had raped and beaten her. Her father tried to reason with her. Royd, when he finally managed to speak to her alone, flagrantly threatened her. All to no avail. Whatever had happened between her and Kyle remained a mystery, a mystery that wasn't cleared up when, three days later, Kyle telephoned his father from the States.

'I'm at Fort Dix,' he said blandly.

'You're *where*?'

'Fort Dix, New Jersey. It's an army base.'

'I know what the fuck it is!' his father shouted. 'What I want to know is what the fuck are *you* doing there?'

'I've applied to be a pilot candidate in the army. I'm here for basic training, then I go to Fort Polk for a month of advanced infantry training...'

'Like hell you do!' Royd thundered. 'What about Princeton? What about your marriage? What about...'

'After Fort Polk I'll be sent to Fort Wolters

for four months of primary flight training,' Kyle continued, unperturbed.

'No you won't!' The veins in Royd's neck stood out in knots. 'If you want to go into the army, you go in the right way!'

'Which is?' Kyle sounded amused.

'Christ, you're an Anderson! You know damn well which way you go into the army. You go through West Point!'

'No. I'm going in the fastest, easiest way I can, and that means the warrant officer aviation program.'

Royd felt sick. There were beads of sweat on his forehead and his heart was pumping crazily. 'You can't,' he repeated helplessly. 'That program is nothing more than a conveyor belt for Vietnam!'

'By the time my training is finished, 'Nam will be old hat.'

'No, it won't be, and you know it!' In his anger and terror Royd had almost forgotten Serena and the fiasco of the marriage. Now he said suddenly, 'What the hell happened here, Kyle? That crazy wife of yours isn't talking. Her brother has taken off again, no one knows the hell where. Her mother's distraught, and old Blyth-Templeton is even more vague and confused than ever.'

There was a slight pause at the other end of the telephone, and then Kyle said tightly, 'She'll be served with divorce papers. That's all anyone needs to know.'

*'Like hell it is!'* Royd bellowed, dollar signs spiraling crazily through his head. 'I want to

know *exactly* what happened, exactly what I'm—'

'Bye, Dad.' Kyle said, a rare note of affection in his voice. Then the line went dead.

Royd looked at Serena with loathing. From the moment she had woken from her sedated sleep, she had shown no visible sign of distress, only an icy calm. She faced him now, pale gold hair hanging waterfall straight down her back, the skirt of her minidress barely skimming her buttocks, her fashionable thigh-high boots giving her the appearance of a female Gulliver.

'He joined the army, goddamn you! He's at Fort Dix.'

For a second he had the pleasure of seeing utter horror flash through her eyes and then she was utterly composed again, saying coolly, 'I can imagine Kyle as a lot of things, but not as a run-of-the-mill soldier.'

'He won't be a run-of-the-mill soldier,' Royd snarled. 'He's training to be a helicopter pilot.'

Serena returned his glare with composure, tilting her head slightly to one side. 'Yes,' she said thoughtfully, 'it's easier to imagine him as a pilot. He'll enjoy it.'

'He won't damned well enjoy it when he's flying under fire in 'Nam! If he's killed, you'll be responsible! If he comes back with two stumps for legs, you'll be the one to blame!' He saw her flinch and continued viciously. 'He wouldn't be there if you hadn't driven him away! He'd be on his honeymoon, for Christ's sake! He's done this because of you! What the hell happened between the two of you? It was all lovey-dovey when you were receiving the guests. I know *when* the shit hit the fan! I just want to know *why*.'

'The shit hit the fan, as you so graphically put it, when your dumb-brained son put two and two together and came up with a hundred and five.' Despite her outwardly cool appearance, her voice was unsteady and Royd looked at her in astonishment. She looked as if she were about to burst into tears.

'You mean there was a misunderstanding? You mean the whole thing could blow over?' His voice was incredulous.

'Yes, there was a misunderstanding, and no, it won't blow over,' she said, her voice once again under tight control.

'What about the divorce?' he asked bluntly. 'Are you going to contest it?'

He saw her eyes widen fractionally, their smoked-crystal depths darkening. 'No,' she said after a slight pause. 'No, I don't suppose so.'

The fleeting compassion he had felt for her when her voice had trembled vanished. 'You can forget any ideas of a huge settlement,' he said savagely.

She held his gaze steadily, looking vaguely surprised. 'I hadn't thought about the money,' she said truthfully, 'but you've no need to worry. I don't want any.'

Royd sucked in his breath and then turned

on his heel, striding away from her. He had no intention of ever seeing her again. He was leaving Bedingham, leaving England. He could not communicate with a woman who said she didn't want any money. Especially one who obviously meant what she said.

Serena was deeply relieved when the Andersons finally left Bedingham. The day after they did, her mother flew down to join friends at Cowes, and her father took off for Scotland, a mound of fishing gear in the rear of his Land-Rover. At long last she had Bedingham to herself, and it offered her a measure of comfort.

That she needed comfort came as a surprise. Their elopement had, after all, been nothing more than a ridiculous joke. But the wedding at Bedingham hadn't been a joke. It had been a profoundly moving experience. And she was sure that she was not alone in that feeling. Though he hadn't said so, she was almost certain that Kyle had been as deeply affected by it as she had been. And now, thanks to Lance's idiocy, it was all over.

She stayed at Bedingham until the end of August and then, when her mother returned from Cowes and her father returned from Scotland, she drove with uncharacteristic soberness back to London. There seemed no fun left in her life now that Kyle had gone. Toby and her host of other friends no longer amused her. By the end of September she had come to the startling conclusion that she was so bored there was nothing to do but look for a job.

'Rupert Carrington is looking for someone to manage his antique shop in Kensington,' Toby said to her helpfully. 'Why not give him a call?'

'I don't know the first thing about antiques.'

'Rubbish, darling,' Toby said, amused. 'You live among antiques at Bedingham. A knowledge of them must be in your blood and in your bones.'

Serena nodded thoughtfully. He was probably right. She certainly didn't know much about anything else, and her only other option would be a boutique.

'Right,' she said purposefully, 'selling antiques has to be a more intelligent proposition than selling clothes. I'll give him a call.'

Her call was successful. Rupert's only stipulations were that she should be known by her maiden name and title. As Lady Serena Blyth-Templeton she would, he explained, have decidely more clout where clients were concerned than she would have as plain Mrs. Anderson.

By Christmas Serena's life had settled into a moderately satisfactory pattern. She worked three, sometimes four days a week in Rupert's exclusive antique shop, her newfound interest in what she was doing prompting her to enroll in a Sotheby's 'Works of Art' course. She lived her private life as though she were still single, dining with well-born escorts at the Ritz and the Savoy, and dancing until the small hours at Regine's and Annabel's.

Annabel's was her favorite nightspot, and she began to go there with Rupert, sharing late suppers with him, never much before midnight, and always ending with a dish of the club's famous marmalade icecream and a glass of exquisitely sweet Château d'Yquem.

But behind her laughter she was not the same person she had been before her marriage. There were times when Toby caught a look of pensiveness in her eyes. Certainly the old Serena would never have taken her job with Rupert seriously, and not even Rupert had expected her to remain once the initial novelty of being a working girl had worn off.

Her reunion with Lance had been surprisingly easy. He had strolled carelessly into the Chelsea house, his hands in his jeans pockets, his negligent stance and the way he held himself reminding her so much of Kyle that her throat had ached.

'Sorry for being such a stupid fucker,' he had said with a sheepish grin. 'I was a bit over the top, wasn't I? Am I forgiven?'

'Oh, Lance, you *are* a fool!' she had said, walking quickly toward him and hugging him tight, too relieved that everything was once again normal between them to feel angry or bitter.

At the start of the New Year the long-expected divorce papers were served on her, and she was intrigued to discover that the grounds on which Kyle was seeking the divorce were desertion on her part. There was no mention of adultery. No mention of incest. The papers only needed her signature, but she stared down at them for several minutes and then put them, unsigned, in her bureau drawer.

Through February and March she didn't hear a word from Kyle or his lawyers. It was as if he were too involved in his new life to pay enough attention to free himself from her.

'Where is he now?' she had asked her father. 'Still at that revolting-sounding training camp?'

The earl, who was still in contact with Royd, said, 'No, he's just finished his primary flight training at Fort Wolter and now he's at a place called Rucker, or Pucker, or something similar, in Alabama. He'll be there for another three months.'

'And after that he'll go to Vietnam?'

'Yes,' her father replied, looking at her over the top of his glasses in a way that made her deeply uncomfortable. 'After that he'll be in Vietnam.'

At the end of March, 4,400 protestors marched in New York City in an antiwar demonstration. In April Lance was arrested when a demonstration outside the American Embassy in London had broken up in wild disorder. In May he was arrested again. The war had become impossible to ignore. It dominated the front pages of both national and regional newspapers, and every evening the television news was full of scenes of bombing and carnage, carnage that Kyle would soon be experiencing firsthand. At the beginning of June; Serena told Rupert, 'I think I may take off for a week or two. You'll be able to manage if I do, won't you?'

Rupert raised an eyebrow slightly. He rarely set foot in the shop now. Serena handled both sales and buying with such cool panache that he'd left the shop completely to her. They had also begun to sleep together on an increasingly regular basis, and he wondered if she would invite him to accompany her wherever it was she intended to go.

'Yes, sweetie,' he said, and then, as the expected invitation wasn't forthcoming, he added, 'Where will you go? France? Italy?'

'Alabama,' Serena said, enjoying his look of stunned surprise. 'To attend to some unfinished business.'

She booked herself into a hotel in Daleville, which was the closest town to the army base. She had brought the divorce papers with her, signed. If he refused to see her, then she would mail them to his lawyers. But she hoped passionately that he would not refuse.

Contacting Kyle had been difficult. The first morning she had telephoned the base and asked to speak to Mr Kyle Anderson.

'This is the army, ma'am,' a voice had said dryly. 'We have lieutenants and warrant officers, but we don't have misters.'

'Well, he'll hardly be a lieutenant,' Serena said tightly, 'he joined the army only ten months ago.'

'Then it wouldn't be likely, ma'am, would it? May I ask if you are a wife or a girlfriend?'

'Wife,' Serena said succinctly.

It took over half an hour before she was finally told that Warrant Officer Anderson had been contacted and another ten minutes before she heard his voice on the other end of the line.

Shock rippled through her. She had thought herself completely in control of the situation, but at the sound of his voice she knew that where Kyle was concerned, she would never be completely in control.

'Hello there, Warrant Officer,' she said, adopting an exaggeratedly careless tone in order to mask the nervousness she was feeling. 'I was just passing through Alabama and wondered if you'd like to help me break my journey.'

There was a long silence at the other end of the line, during which she died a thousand deaths. Then, to her overwhelming relief, he said, a slight hint of amusement in his voice, 'No one passes through Alabama on their way to anywhere. What are you doing here?'

'I've told you, I'm just passing through.'

'On the week I'm due to leave for 'Nam? A bit coincidental, don't you think?'

Serena felt suddenly sick. 'I didn't know you were due to leave so soon. When do you go?'

'Thursday.'

'Oh!' She gripped the telephone receiver tightly. Today was Monday, or was it Tuesday? She wasn't sure. Transatlantic flights always confused her timewise. 'Does that mean you won't be able to see me?'

This time the silence at the other end of the telephone stretched out. 'I hadn't planned on seeing you ever again,' he said at last. This time there was no amusement in his voice.

'Nor me you,' Serena snapped. 'But 'Nam is 'Nam, and a wife is a wife, and I rather fancied the idea of bidding the warrior good-bye. With your shield or on it, and all that.'

'You mean that the thought of my perhaps not coming back would be a sexual turn-on for you?' he asked with lazy curiosity.

'No! That isn't what I meant at all!' She was so indignant that her pose of careless indifference slipped, and before she could stop herself she was saying, 'I've missed you, goddammit! I want to sleep with you again!'

'Then why didn't you say so?' This time all the old amusement was back, and though she couldn't see him she knew that his eyes were full of laughter and that his mouth was crooked in a smile. 'You called just as I was about to leave camp on a twenty-four-hour pass. Where do you suggest we spend it?'

'Here,' Serena said promptly. 'In bed.'

'Where's here?'

'The Daleview Motel.'

'Okay,' he said with military efficiency. 'I'll be there in forty minutes.'

* * *

He was with her in thirty-five. When she opened the door of her room she gasped, her eyes widening. He was in uniform, warrant officer bars and silver wings emblazoning his immaculately cut jacket, his cap worn at a rakish angle. 'Kyle! My God! You look incredible!' She wanted him so much she could barely stand.

Hot, electric-blue eyes met hers, the lazy grin that turned her heart over touching the corners of his mouth. 'You're looking pretty good yourself,' he said, and as he moved forward to enter the room she stepped toward him, her arms slipping up and around his neck.

His arms closed around her, both the rift and the hideous reason for it temporarily forgotten. God, but she was beautiful he thought. He had forgotten how beautiful. She reminded him of a picture he had seen in a gallery somewhere. It had been of Diana the Huntress, and she had been tall and beautifully boned and splendidly half naked with a look of fearless, wanton daring in her eyes. It was a look he had never seen in the eyes of a flesh and blood woman. Until he had met Serena.

His hands slid down, cupping her buttocks, pressing her in against the rocklike bulge in his pants. She had more style in her little finger than other women had in their entire bodies, and he wasn't going to forgo the pleasure of this unexpected reunion, no matter how loud the voice of common sense yelled that he should.

'Oh, Kyle, I've missed you!' Her voice was low and husky, breaking with need. 'I've missed the sight and smell and the taste of you!'

'How the hell do I smell? You make me sound like a hog,' he said as he lifted her off her feet, striding toward the large double bed in the room.

She giggled throatily, her mouth on his neck, her tongue licking and tasting. 'You smell of soap and sun-ripened lemons and newly baked bread, and you taste ... Oh, God!' Her teeth gently bit his flesh. 'You taste *wonderful*!'

'Let me taste you,' he said thickly, lowering her to the bed, pushing her brief skirt waist high.

She trembled in delicious anticipation, closing her eyes, winding her fingers through the black silkiness of his hair. She had been faithless scores of times over the past ten months but never once had she experienced the total abandonment that Kyle aroused in her. He confounded her with desire. Convulsed her. Crucified her.

'I love you, Kyle,' she whispered in shocked acceptance of the truth. 'Love you! Love you! Love you!'

Afterward, their bodies slaked and sheened with sweat, he leaned against the pillows and said, as if their lovemaking had not taken place, 'Have you signed the divorce papers yet?'

She had been lying beside him, her head resting on the taut flatness of his stomach, her arm flung across his hips. She moved slowly, pushing herself into a sitting position, her hair spilling down over her firm, high breasts. 'No,' she said, 'but I will if you want me to.'

He was looking at her through half-closed lids, remembering. 'Yes,' he said. 'I think it would be best, don't you?'

She pushed her hair back over her shoulder and said hesitantly, 'You were wrong in what you thought, Kyle. There has never been anything unnatural in my relationship with Lance. What you walked in on was an isolated occurrence. And one that I was not a willing partner to.'

He swung his legs from the bed, walking in splendid nakedness to his discarded jacket, searching in the pockets for cigarettes and a lighter. It was a subject he had vowed not to raise. He had seen what he had seen and he had no desire to have his feelings of revulsion reawakened by useless protestations of innocence. He found his cigarettes and tossed one across to her. 'You weren't exactly crying "Rape" or "Help me!" were you?'

'No, but I had been crying out for him to stop,' Serena said, the throb of truth in her voice. 'And he had stopped. He had come to his senses and he was desperately sorry and ashamed of what had happened and I was comforting him. That was when you walked in on us.'

'Christ! How could you comfort a pervert?' Kyle spat out, lighting his cigarette and drawing hard on it. 'He's your brother, for Christ's sake! How could you even bear to let him touch you after what he had done and tried to do?'

Serena's eyes held his, crystal clear and utterly without guile. 'Because I love him. Not in the way that you assumed. I love him because up till then he'd been the most important person in my life. I love him because in some way that I can't explain there's something vulnerable about him, something that arouses my protective instincts. He doesn't like you and he never will, and he was shocked and distressed by our marriage. What happened between us in the nursery was as much a storm of anger on his part as it was forbidden passion. He apologized to me the very next time he saw me. It was a crazy incident that has been forgotten. I'd like it to be forgotten between us as well.'

Evening sunlight seeped through the drapes into the room. Her fragile-boned, beautiful face was somber, her hair tumbling down to her waist like a golden, silken curtain. He wanted to believe her. Hell, he almost *did* believe her.

'If you're telling me the truth, why didn't you write me, telephone me, get in touch with me?'

'Would you have listened to me if I had?'

'No,' he said honestly. 'No, I wouldn't.'

'But you believe me now?'

Her eyes held his in perfect steadiness. 'Yes,' he said slowly. 'Yes, I believe you.'

A wide smile curved her mouth. 'Then put your cigarette out,' she said, sliding voluptuously down the pillows onto her back, one leg bent at the knee, the other sprawling wide, 'and come and make up for a stupidly wasted ten months!'

He had done as she had bid, and divorce had not been mentioned again. Four days later, as she sat aboard a plane, bracing herself for takeoff, she opened her handbag in search of a mint and found instead the divorce papers in their battered envelope.

She took them out of her bag, looking at them as the plane screamed down the runway and began to climb.

Kyle would be aboard a troop carrier heading west toward Vietnam. She pressed the tips of two fingers to her mouth, blowing a small, loving kiss in the direction that she fondly imagined the Pacific to lie, and then she tore the envelope in half and in half again and again, letting the small pieces of paper flutter down on to her lap like so many pieces of confetti.

# CHAPTER TEN

For a long time Gavin could only stare into Gabrielle's radiant, glowing face.

'A baby?' he said at last, desperately playing for time. Christ. What was he going to say to her? What in hell was he going to do?

*'Oui, mon amour.'* She slid her hand into his, squeezing it tight. 'I have had my suspicions for a few weeks now, but I am so irregular and I have felt so well. However...' She shrugged, grinning impishly. 'Today I thought I would make quite sure.'

'And there's no doubt?'

'No, none at all.' She drew away from him a little, looking at him curiously, aware for the first time that his reaction was not quite what she had expected. 'What is the matter, Gavin? You are not annoyed, are you?' The joy in her eyes had died, and her kittenlike face was suddenly wary. 'You do not wish me to get rid of it, do you, *mon amour*?' she asked, tilting her head a little to one side, the October sun gilding her sumptuous curls.

'No!' His reply was so outraged and emphatic that her eyes lit with laughter again. *'Très bien,'* she said, a husky chuckle deep in her voice. 'Because I would not have done so, even if you had wanted me to. So ... as you have no objection to me having our baby, perhaps you would tell me why you are looking so unhappy about news that I thought would delight you?'

'I *am* delighted,' he said, wishing that he could take her in his arms and pull her on to his knee. 'Except—' he hesitated awkwardly— 'except I have news as well.'

'Oh!' She looked into his face and then slowly leaned back in her cane chair. '*Je comprends*. I understand. You are to go to Saigon?'

He nodded. 'Almost immediately.' He leaned across the metal-topped table, taking both her hands in his. 'Gaby, I...'

He wanted to tell her that her news changed everything. That he would no longer be going. But he couldn't. Vietnam was too important. As a journalist he was sickened by reading reports of fighting that had been filed by newsmen who had never left the comparative safety of Saigon, newsmen who did little more than repeat, verbatim, whatever statements were issued to them by the American command.

He wanted to do more. He wanted to get out into the countryside and to report on what he himself saw. He wanted to report the war from the Vietnamese standpoint as well as from the American. He wanted to discover for himself if the American view – that the war was essentially a conflict between Vietnamese and Vietnamese and that America was merely coming to the aid of a democratic government fighting to hold off the forces of communism – was accurate.

The letters he had seen from Nhu to Gabrielle's mother had made him doubt the American argument. If the South Vietnamese government was a democracy, then it was not what he or many other westerners, would recognize as a democracy. And if westerners were being misled about the true nature of the South Vietnamese government, then what other deceptions were being perpetrated? Whatever they were, he wanted the chance to discover them for himself. And to make them public.

'Gaby, I...' he began again, his eyes agonized.

She leaned toward him, silencing him with a kiss. 'I know, *mon amour*,' she said gently as she drew her mouth away from his. 'You must go.' Her eyes were bright with intensity. 'And I want you to go. Talking about Vietnam with you these past few months has made me realize how very Vietnamese *I* am. When I think of home, I think of Saigon, not Montmartre. When I think of my relations, I think of Aunt Nhu and Dinh and my Vietnamese cousins, not of the distant members of my father's family who never visit us or ask us to visit them.'

Grateful for her understanding, love for her swept over him like a tidal wave. For a brief, crazy second he was tempted to tell her that wild horses couldn't drag him from her side, and then she said, her voice unexpectedly fierce, 'Go to Vietnam for me, Gavin. Visit Nhu. Find out if what we are reading in the newspapers and seeing on the television is truth or propaganda. Write about things as they are, not as the Americans would like us to believe they are.'

'There's one thing we must do before I go,' he said, knowing now that he would go. She looked at him questioningly, and he was amazed that the idea had never occurred to him before.

'We have to get married,' he said, enjoying the look of astonishment on her face.

'But it is not necessary, *mon amour*,' she protested. 'Just because there is going to be a baby does not mean that—'

'It is very necessary,' he said firmly, rising to his feet and pulling her up. 'And not because of the baby.' He drew her into his arms, oblivious of the waiter who had come out to clear their table and of the indulgent glances of passersby. 'It's necessary because I love you, Gaby,' he said thickly. 'Because I could never live with anyone else. Because I want you to be my wife.'

She laughed up at him. 'I have never thought of myself as a wife,' she said teasingly but with truth. 'But if you think I'll make a good wife...'

'You'll make a wonderful wife,' he said hoarsely, lowering his head to hers, kissing her passionately.

There was not enough time to arrange a

church wedding. Gavin was to leave for Saigon on the following Friday and only with extreme difficulty was a wedding arranged at all.

The bride wore a simple, hastily bought cream satin dress. It was demurely mid-calf length with short cap sleeves and a satin jacket to match. She wore cream stiletto-heel satin pumps and carried a small bouquet of mixed roses – Gloire de Dijon and pale, flushed Ophelias and tiny, pink-budded Michelle Meillands. There were no guests; her parents served as witnesses and after the ceremony the small wedding party repaired to La Closérie des Lilas in the boulevard Montparnasse for a celebratory champagne lunch.

When they were leaving the restaurant, disaster struck. Gavin, happily intoxicated, turned round to speak to his father-in-law, who was walking a yard or so behind him, lost his footing, and fell awkwardly down the short flight of steps leading to the street.

Gabrielle's first reaction was to burst into laughter, and then she saw his face whiten and tense against the pain, and the ugly angle of his leg as it lay buckled beneath him.

'Gavin! What have you done? Are you all right?' She ran down the steps, kneeling at his side. *'Merde alors!'* she muttered, pressing her gloved hand to her mouth, seeing only too clearly what he had done and knowing that his leg was either fractured or broken. She turned to her father, who was hurrying down the steps toward them. 'An ambulance, Papa! Quickly!'

Turning her head back to Gavin, she saw that the whiteness of his face and the tight, clenched lines of his mouth were occassioned as much by fury as by pain.

'Of all the stupid, fucking *idiotic* things to have done!' he said as she slid her arms comfortingly around him. 'There'll be no Vietnam now! Not with a stupid, fucking broken leg!'

Despite the anguish she felt for his disappointment, she had to repress a smile. It was so unlike Gavin to swear, and his Australian accent, usually so faint that it was mistaken for American or Canadian, was now comically pronounced. 'There will be, *chéri*.' There was such fierce confidence in her voice that despite his pain and disappointment he gave a shadow of a grin.

'Maybe,' he said, wondering who the agency would send in his place. How long would his leg take to heal? And would the agency still consider him as a war correspondent when it was?

'Do you think you can brush some of this confetti out of my hair before the ambulance arrives?' he gasped as the maître d'hôtel and a couple of waiters ran out of the restaurant toward them, uttering cries of concern. 'There'll be so many bad jokes if people realize it's my wedding day.'

She lovingly did as he asked, knowing that as she was still wearing her cream satin wedding dress, everyone would know that it was his wedding day even if she removed every speck of confetti from his hair.

'*Je m'excuse*,' she whispered to him as the ambulance screeched to a halt and her father and the maître d'hôtel shooed away the curious group of onlookers. 'I am so sorry, *mon amour*.'

He clenched his hands and his jaw against the pain as the ambulance driver lifted him onto a stretcher. 'Phone the office,' he said to her tightely. 'Speak to Marsden. Tell him what an ass I've been.'

She carried out his instructions and listened first to an expletive even more colorful than Gavin's had been, and then to a hasty apology. 'How long is he going to be laid up?' Marsden had asked her.

'I don't know,' she said truthfully. 'Perhaps five to six weeks. It might be much longer.'

It was two months.

Gavin devoted most of the time to learning Vietnamese, insisting that when his mother-in-law visited him in the hospital, she speak to him only in her native tongue. In the few days prior to their wedding neither he nor Gabrielle had seen any point in looking for a place of their own, and there seemed no reason to do so now, not until Gavin was discharged from the hospital and knew what the future held for him.

In November, a U.S. airborne division crushed three North Vietnamese regiments in the la Drang Valley. Though the engagement cost the Communists nearly two thousand men, and was regarded as a victory by General Westmoreland, more than three hundred Americans died, the majority of them in a single ambush.

'Does this mean that the Americans have gained the upper hand, that the end may be in sight?' Vanh asked bewilderedly. Gavin, still hospitalized, and with his leg in a cast held in traction, shook his head. 'No. No matter how much Westmoreland insists that it was a victory, American parents won't consider it one, not with an entire company of American boys virtually decimated.' His voice was cynical. 'The ratio of a couple of thousand to three hundred might seem to be in America's favor, but American parents aren't going to equate their boys' lives to those of the enemy. The end isn't in sight yet, Vanh.'

He wasn't the only one who thought so. Later that month, Robert McNamara, President Johnson's Defense Secretary, a man who had previously been firmly optimistic about America's role in Vietnam, visited Saigon and was visibly shaken by what he found. The North Vietnamese had begun to infiltrate the south, there was no sign of them halting, or of General Westmoreland being able to curb them. 'The war is going to be a long one,' McNamara bleakly told the reporters covering his visit. 'There is no guarantee of U.S. military success,' and, even more bleakly, he admitted that U.S. troops killed in action were expected to be in excess of a thousand a month.

In December, Marsden promised Gavin that he could expect to be sent to Saigon in June or July, when the reporter who had gone in his place returned.

Cheered by this news, Gavin applied himself to his study of Vietnamese with fresh enthusiasm. He was discharged from the hospital at the beginning of December, returning on crutches to the Mercador apartment, and whenever his father-in-law was absent, he and Vanh and Gabrielle spoke nothing but Vietnamese. His accent was nearly as execrable as his French one, but Vanh assured him that this did not matter. He could now make himself understood in her native language and he could read and write it with passable fluency.

'Which is more than the majority of reporters stationed there can do,' Gabrielle said with satisfaction.

Her stomach had begun to round now, and she was no longer sitting for any artists. She was still singing, though, and Gavin would walk with her to whichever club she was appearing in. He still couldn't walk without a cane, and his persistently heavy limp worried him far more than he dared admit. If he was not one hundred percent fit by the summer, he knew that the agency would not send him to Vietnam.

At Christmas there had been a faint flicker of hope that the war might end in a negotiated peace. President Johnson had announced a halt to the bombing of the North, a halt that began on Christmas morning. Although the war on the ground continued with as much ferocity as ever, the bombing freeze lasted thirty-seven days. President Johnson sent emissaries to more than forty countries, trying to assure them he was willing to come to terms with the Communists.

The Communists remained unconvinced. A Radio Hanoi broadcast denounced the bombing halt as 'a trick' and said no political settlement was possible until the Johnson administration halted the air raids 'unconditionally and for good'. They did not. On January 31 the bombing raids over the North resumed, and hope for a negotiated peace died. In response, anti-war demonstrations in America and Europe increased in both number and participants.

'Have you been given a firm departure date for Saigon?' Gabrielle asked Gavin one evening as he walked her through the cobbled streets toward the club where she was to sing. His editor had said June or July and it was now the end of March.

He shook his head, his shock of dark gold hair tumbling low over his brow. 'No.' His arm tightened around her shoulders. He knew what she was thinking. The baby had become more active, disturbing not only her sleep but, as he held her close in his arms at night, his as well. The birth no longer seemed an abstract event. The baby was already a little person who was somehow manifesting its own personality. It was due the second or third week of June, and Gavin desperately wanted to be there when it was born.

In April he was told officially that he was to fly out to Vietnam on June 1st. Relief and dismay hit him in equal amounts. Relief that though he still had a pronounced limp, he had not been replaced, and dismay that he would not be with Gaby for the baby's birth. He knew he would not see his son or daughter for a year, or perhaps even eighteen months.

'Never mind, *chéri*,' Gabrielle said, gallantly hiding her own fierce disappointment. 'We will still be here when you return. And babies are not very interesting creatures. All they do is sleep and eat.'

Her careless dismissal did not deceive him in the slightest. He hugged her tight, determining to speak to Marsden to request that his departure be delayed by at least a month. Gabrielle, sensing his thoughts, pulled away from him, looking up at him with an unusually serious light in her eyes. '*Non, chéri*,' she said firmly, 'you must not do what you are thinking of. They might very well change their minds and send someone else. You have been given the opportunity, and you must take it. *C'est compris?*'

'*Oui*,' he had said, knowing that his French always amused her. '*Je comprends*.' He had pulled her gently against him, kissing her hairline, her temples, the corners of her eyes. '*Je t'adore, ma chérie*,' he had said huskily, lowering his mouth to hers. '*Je t'adore.*'

By May the situation in Southeast Asia was worse than it had ever been. The continual heavy bombing raids over the North had failed to quell the resistance of the North or to bring the North Vietnamese to the conference table.

U.S. Defense Secretary Robert McNamara reported that despite the efforts of American troops patrolling the border areas, North Vietnamese were infiltrating the South at a rate of four thousand five hundred men a month, three times the 1965 level. Because of the savage fighting taking place in the border areas, Vietnam's neighbors, Laos and Cambodia, were finding themselves increasingly in the firing line. Even more ominously, China's border territory was being threatened. The war was escalating.

'It does not help that America has no real understanding of Vietnam or the Vietnamese,' Gabrielle had said bitterly. 'Look at this report in today's *Le Monde*. We are not Vietnamese, we are gooks. That is not just American terminology for the North Vietnamese. It is the way they speak of the South Vietnamese as well. How can there be success when the Americans speak with so little respect of the people they are fighting with and for?'

The most recent letter from Nhu was equally disconcerting. 'The present government no longer has the support that America would like to believe it has,' Nhu had written to Gabrielle. 'Premier Ky may seem to be popular, but his popularity does not run deep. The Buddhists hate him and are doing everything possible to remove him from power.'

She was right. French newspapers were full of reports of fighting in Da Nang and Hue between troops loyal to Ky and other South Vietnamese troops loyal to the Buddhists.

'It is crazy,' Gabrielle had said disbelievingly. 'Not only is the South fighting a war with the North, it's beginning to fight a war against itself as well!'

As Gavin packed his capacious nylon bag, there were reports of Buddhist parades, hunger strikes, and other demonstrations taking place in the city, demonstrations that degenerated into riots as government troops ruthlessly dispersed them with tear gas and bayonets.

Gabrielle wrapped her arms around her now-enormous stomach, despising herself for her sudden cow-hearted desire to plead with Gavin not to go. 'If he is brave enough to go, then I must be brave enough to allow him to go,' she scolded herself. She decided not to read any more newspapers or listen to the radio news broadcasts until Gavin boarded his plane.

The day before his flight he drove her down to Fontainebleau for a last, sentimental lunch at the Hôtel Fontainebleau.

'Take care of yourself, Gaby,' he said, his gray eyes dark with anxiety as their dessert plates were cleared away and the coffee cups were placed on the table.

She nodded and then winced, sucking in her breath sharply. It wasn't the first time that she had seemed to be in discomfort, and he said in deepening concern, 'What is it, sweetheart? Heartburn again?'

'No, I do not think so, *chéri*.'

He took her hand across the table and squeezed it tight. 'I wish to God I could stay with you and be here when the baby comes.'

Gabrielle winced again, and when the spasm of pain had passed, she gave him a small, satisfied smile. 'I think that you are about to have your wish, *mon amour*.'

He stared at her, a comprehension dawning, his eyes widening in disbelief and horror. 'But you can't ... It isn't due for another two or three weeks ... We're over an hour's drive from Paris.'

'That doesn't matter, silly,' she said, rising to her feet with difficulty. 'Babies don't come so quickly. Not first babies anyway. We have plenty of time.'

He pushed his chair away from the table, grabbing his jacket. 'Let's go now! Quickly! Can you walk to the car?' He ran his hand distractedly through his hair. Christ! His flight left in seventeen hours. What if the baby hadn't been born by then? He couldn't leave her in the middle of childbirth. It wasn't humanly possible.

The waiter was hurrying toward them and Gavin grabbed a handful of notes from his pocket. 'We have to leave,' he said, thrusting the notes into the waiter's hand, uncounted. 'My wife has been taken ill ... The baby is coming.'

Gabrielle was grasping the back of the dining chair, her knuckles white.

'Ready, sweetheart?' he asked, sliding his arm around her.

'Yes,' she said as he began to lead her from the room, and then, almost immediately, she stopped, leaning her weight against him. 'No.' She sucked in a deep breath, her hands splayed across the hard, swollen magnificence of her stomach. Her eyes met his, bright with laughter and nervous anticipation. 'I was wrong when I said that first babies don't come quickly, *chéri*. This baby is. It is coming very quickly.' A spasm of pain crossed her face, so intense that he did not need to ask if she was sure.

'Oh God!' he said, looking round wildly for the waiter. 'Oh hell!'

The waiter's eyes were nearly as alarmed as his own. 'A chair, monsieur!' he said, thrusting one of the dining chairs toward Gavin, presumably for Gabrielle's use. 'I will get the proprietor!'

'Get a doctor, for Christ's sake!' Gavin shouted as the laughter left Gabrielle's eyes and she gasped in pain, her face ashen.

The waiter fled and Gabrielle panted. 'My waters have broken. I'm all wet. Can you help me up the stairs? To our usual room?'

He nodded, praying that the room was unoccupied; that a doctor could be found in time; that the baby would be healthy; that Gabrielle would be safe.

They were nearly at the top of the stairs by the time the proprietor came running up to them. He took one look at the size of Gabrielle's stomach and at her face, and squeezed past them, running ahead and flinging open the door of the room they had so often reserved in the past.

'A doctor has been called! Is there anything I can do? Hot water? Extra blankets?'

Gavin looked at him helplessly. He knew that hot water and blankets were customarily called for whenever a birth was imminent but he hadn't the faintest idea why, or what they were used for, and there was already a wash basin and water in the room and plenty of blankets on the carefully made bed. 'Yes. No. I don't know,' he said as Gabrielle seized the door jamb and leaned heavily against it, sucking in short, sharp breaths.

'Lean your weight on me, Gaby,' he said urgently. 'Let me help you to the bed.'

She did as he said, and to his amazement gave a little giggle. 'Oh, *chérie*! I should have known that I would not have a boring, routine labor!' She broke off, sitting on the edge of the bed, once again panting deeply. When the pain had passed, he lifted her legs onto the bed and she said with impish amusement, 'Do your realize that this is the bed where we first made love, *chérie*? It is possibly even the bed where the baby was conceived. It feels very right that it should be born here.'

She broke off again, closing her eyes and clenching her fists.

'Tell me what to do, Gaby,' he said urgently, wondering where the hell the proprietor had fled to; where the doctor was; where anybody was.

'Oh!' She gave a low, deep cry, twisting her head sharply to one side. When she could speak again she gasped, 'Take my panties off for me, *chéri*. Put towels on the bed. The baby is coming. I can feel it!'

He stared down at her, panic racing through him. 'It can't! The doctor isn't here...'

She gave a deep, anguished grunt of pain. The sound was primeval and unmistakable: a sound he had never heard before. 'Oh God,' he whispered, knowing that his child was about to be born. The panic faded. Suddenly he felt calm and perfectly in control. Babies that came as speedily as this one was weren't babies who would experience any difficulties at birth. It was going to be all right. It was going to be more than all right. It was going to be wonderful.

'Breathe deeply, Gaby,' he instructed as he pulled her panties down and removed her stockings and garter belt. 'Breathe deeply. The baby is coming! I can see it!'

Her legs were wide, her knees drawn high. There was a sheen of sweat of her face, a look of total, intense concentration.

'Don't push anymore!' Gavin commanded as he saw the crown of the baby's head pulsing inside her vagina. 'Don't push! Pant!'

He didn't know where his knowledge came from. But it didn't matter. All that mattered was that he knew that he was right.

'Try to relax, Gaby!' he urged, squatting down at the end of the bed. Nothing mattered in the whole world but what was taking place between her legs, the awe-inspiring, unbelievable miracle of that pulsing head covered with gleaming dark-gold hair.

Gabrielle gave another deep, primitive groan of pain. She felt as if she were being torn apart, as if the baby were splitting her wide open, wrenching her impossibly wide. 'No!' she cried, and then, as the head crowned, she screamed.

Gavin didn't hear her. He had no sense for anything except the child he was easing into the world. The baby's head was in his hands now, warm and damp. There was a pause. Nothing happened. Gabrielle was silent, panting for breath.

'I think it's time to push again,' he said, not lifting his gaze from the dark gold head he held with infinite care. 'Push for the shoulders to come out, Gaby. But don't push too hard. Gently. Gently.'

The pressure was building up in her again, and nothing in the world could have prevented her from pushing. She was bathed in sweat, almost mesmerized by pain, but above everything she was exultant. The baby was nearly born. It was nearly over. Her sense of triumph was ecstatic. Every muscle in her body bore down. There was a great rush of water between her legs, a slithering sensation and then an overwhelming nothingness. The rock-hard bulge that had been splitting her in two was no longer there. She was free of pain, free of the child that had inhabited her body for nine long months.

'Oh, God,' she sobbed, trying to push herself up against the pillows, trying to see. 'Is it all right? Why doesn't it cry, Gavin? Why doesn't it cry?'

He wasn't listening to her. He was carefully and gently wiping mucus away from the baby's nose and mouth. The umbilical cord was thick and blue, unbelievably knotted. Still the baby didn't cry, and he blew gently on its face. There was a little shudder from the slippery wet body in his hands, and then a little cry.

'Oh, God,' she sobbed again, this time in relief. 'Is it all right? Is it a boy? Is it a girl? Oh, let me hold it, Gavin, please let me hold it!'

For the first time since the baby's head had begun to crown, he looked toward her. 'It's a boy,' he said with a wide, triumphant grin. 'It's a boy, Gaby, and he's perfect!'

There was nothing to wrap the baby in, and he placed it in her eager arms, the wrinkled red flesh still smeared with blood and mucus, the umbilical cord springing from its tummy, its eyes closed, its tiny hands balled into fists as it squalled lustily.

'What do I do now?' he asked, grinning

down at them both, tears of joy and relief streaming his face. 'Do I cut the umbilical cord? Tie it off?'

'No,' Gabrielle said firmly. 'You have been magnificent, *mon amour*, but there is no need for you to do anything else. The doctor will be here soon. The only thing I need is something to wrap the baby in so that he does not catch cold.'

He handed her one of the hotel's towels, and together they wrapped it gently around their son. He stopped crying as they did so, snuffling a little and pursing his mouth hungrily.

'This is what he wants,' Gabrielle said with deep satisfaction, baring her breasts and lifting the baby toward them. She guided a nipple into the hungry little mouth and the baby immediately began to suck.

'Clever little thing, isn't he?' Gavin said in wonder.

Gabrielle laughed, her eyes shining joyously as they met his. 'I think the afterbirth is coming away,' she said. 'Have another towel ready. Where is that doctor? It must be hours since he was called.'

Gavin crossed to the wash basin for another towel and looked down at his wristwatch. 'It isn't,' he said, his voice full of disbelief. 'It's only been twenty minutes.'

Gabrielle looked lovingly down at her suckling son. 'What are we going to call him?' They had thought of several names, some French, some Australian, even some Vietnamese, and decided on none of them.

'Whatever you want to call him,' Gavin said, returning to the bed with the towel and spreading it beneath her.

'Then I would like to call him after you, and after my father, and, if you do not mind, after my mother's brother and her father.'

'I don't mind,' he said truthfully, 'but Gavin Étienne Dinh is going to be quite a mouthful. What name will we use?'

'Gavin,' she said unhesitantly. *'Mon petit* Gavin.'

There came the sound of footsteps hurrying up the stairs.

'The doctor,' Gavin said with relief. He looked at his watch again. 'I'm going to have to leave you both in another few hours,' he said awkwardly.

'I know.' Her spicy red curls were tousled and damp with sweat. Except for a smudge of mascara below her eyes, no makeup remained on her face. She looked unbelievably beautiful.

'I love you, Gaby,' he said, knowing that as long as he lived, he would never forget how she looked at that moment, cradling their newborn son. He would remember *always*.

There was a peremptory knock at the door and the doctor strode into the room. Sixteen hours later, as Gabrielle lay in the small, sun-filled bedroom at Fontainebleau, their son in a hastily acquired crib at her side, Gavin sat aboard an Air France 707, flying up and over Paris, heading for Saigon.

# CHAPTER ELEVEN

Lewis had several distinct advantages over the majority of his peers serving in Vietnam. He was there because he wanted to be, not because he had been drafted. And he believed that America's presence in Vietnam was both justified and honorable.

In Lewis's eyes, any country fighting for freedom against the threat of Communist domination deserved financial and military assistance. After serving six months he no longer believed that South Vietnam was the shining democracy that America's propaganda machine liked to depict, but he was damned sure that dictatorial and repressive and full of faults as it was, it was still a hell of a lot better than the government in the North.

Unlike Hanoi, whose avowed aim was the invasion of the South, Saigon had never announced any intention of invading the North, nor had it tried to impose its system of government onto an unwilling people.

In his six months in the peninsula he had witnessed enough acts of barbarism perpetrated by the Viet cong and the North Vietnamese Army to know exactly why he and his countrymen were in Vietnam. They were there because the South Vietnam government had invited and welcomed them there; they were there because they were helping the South Vietnamese fight for their freedom; and they were there to stem the expansion of world communism.

Besides the advantage of total commitment, he also had other, less obvious advantages. Unlike many of the draftees, he did at least know where Vietnam was, geographically. He also had a good understanding of the country's history and customs and language. Even rarer, he didn't loathe the country on sight; he didn't regard South Vietnamese civilians with contempt; and he didn't despise the South Vietnamese who fought at his side.

He knew he was lucky. The majority of the Army of the Republic of South Vietnam was poorly trained and poorly motivated. His fellow officers' bitter complaint that the ARVN did not want American help in fighting, but wanted them to fight the war *for* them, was often justified.

His own experience as a military adviser had been a good one. His first assignment had been with the 21st ARVN Division. By the time his six months with them had come to an end, and he had gone on leave in Hawaii, he had nothing but respect for both the South Vietnamese officers of the battalion and the men. They were hard, dedicated fighters it had been a privilege to serve with. On his return from leave, he had learned that he was not returning to the 21st, but instead was being assigned to a MAT team in An Xuyen province.

MAT was short for Mobile Advisory Team. Each of South Vietnam's forty-two provinces had a large American advisory team assigned to it, and, as each province was divided up into several districts, each of these teams was assigned several smaller MAT teams. The teams were based in remote hamlets and villages, and the men assigned to them lived alongside the villagers and rarely came into contact with other army personnel – Vietnamese or American.

Lewis had been specifically trained for this type of environment and he adapted rapidly. He was promoted to the rank of captain and posted to Van Binh as team leader and district senior adviser. His wide-ranging responsibilities for the welfare and military security of the villages and hamlets in his district sat easily on him.

The village where his team was based was deep in the delta, as far south as it was possible to go in Vietnam. The whole area was criss-crossed with canals and ditches, the water gleaming glossily against the dark green foliage of reeds and vines and waist-high elephant grass.

Lewis was glad that his assignment was not the usual GI troop duty. Here in Van Binh he was the most senior officer. There was no one he had to ask permission of before his orders could be implemented. With his four fellow

Americans, and with the help of the local Popular Forces platoons, forces made up of trained and armed local villagers, he was able to wage his own private war against the Viet Cong units who used the area as their sanctuary.

Lewis and his men found themselves up against more than just Viet Cong. Although An Xuyen province was eighty miles from the Cambodian border, the North Vietnamese Army regiments operating out of Cambodian sanctuaries used the Delta's vast network of canals to their advantage.

Nearly all the patrols and ambush operations that Lewis and his men undertook were carried out in or on water. Water dominated their lives, although the rainy season, with its nightmare of ceaseless rain and ankle-deep mud, and its attendant miseries of mildewed clothing, damp bedding, sodden cigarettes, foot rot and a dozen other forms of fungicidal infection were now behind them. Lewis came to hate the long hours spent negotiating the canals by sampan, but he never, unlike some of the men under his command, prayed for a posting to Saigon. He had spent three weeks in Saigon at the beginning of his tour of duty, and he had no desire to spend even another hour there.

One of his lecturers at West Point, a man who had spent many years in Vietnam, both before and after the defeat of the French, had told him how beautiful Saigon was, likening it to an elegant French provincial town. By July

’66, when Lewis arrived in Saigon, all traces of elegance were fast disappearing.

Tu Do Street, the main thoroughfare that had reminded Lewis’s lecturer of a boulevard in Avignon, was now littered with blatantly seedy girlie bars and brothels and massage parlors. American dollars flooded the city, bringing instant wealth to some, and increasing the poverty of others. The number of prostitutes in the city doubled and then quadrupled as girls flocked in from outlying villages, eager for a share of American wealth.

It was the sight of these girls more than anything else that sickened Lewis. The city-born whores were easy to ignore. They were like whores anywhere, tough and professional and more than capable of taking care of themselves. But the eager young girls swarming in from the countryside, lured by the knowledge that a prostitute in Saigon could now make more in a week than her father could in a year, was a different matter. Their delicate-boned faces were still innocent and fresh, their eyes full of nervous appeal as they solicited outside the restaurants and bars and the Continental Palace Hotel and the Majestic and the Caravelle.

Lewis had been approached repeatedly, and each time had vehemently told the girl in question to pack her bags and hightail it back to her village. The only response had been a look of blank bewilderment and then a repeated honeyed request that he take advantage of the services she was offering. After half a dozen such encounters, he had stopped trying, knowing that nothing he could say or do would make the slightest bit of difference.

Whenever he saw one of his fellow countrymen taking advantages of prostitutes' services, Lewis was disgusted. The massage parlors and clubs in Tu Do Street were full of Americans. In some clubs, such as The Sporting Bar and La Bohème, dope as well as sex was freely for sale, and the air was thick with Cambodian red marijuana as fourteen- and fifteen-year-olds draped themselves, topless, around the necks of relaxing servicemen.

Despite the other problems in the countryside, the atmosphere of mercenary depravity was blessedly absent. The village girls dressed and behaved with traditional modesty; there were no small boys busily trying to sell the sexual services of their still smaller sisters and though Lewis knew no one should be trusted absolutely, since there was a great deal of Viet Cong infiltration in the area, he found the village men both courteous and helpful.

Most of the residents were farmers or fishermen. They grew rice in the paddy fields that surrounded the village and they caught fish in the many canals. Apart from this they had very little. There was no running water in the village, no electricity, no sewerage; none of the things that Lewis and his men had always taken for granted. As an adviser it was part of Lewis's responsibility to help the people with development projects. Aid was available, if only people knew how to apply for it. As all the villagers were virtually illiterate, no one had.

Within hours of his arrival Lewis had requested medical aid and educational aid and had asked for everything that there was the faintest hope of getting.

His assistant team leader was a young Texan who was as eager as he was to improve the primitive conditions.

Apart from Lieutenant Grainger there were three northerners in his team. His light weapons specialist, Sergeant Drayton, was from New York State, and his heavy weapons specialist, Sergeant Pennington, and the team medic, Master Sergeant Duxbery, were both from Massachusetts.

As a team they worked well together. The only short-time man, with an eye on his flight home, was Drayton, but even he was committed.

It was while he was with Drayton in the palm-thatched hut that served as their team house that he heard the shouts and screams that introduced him to Tam.

'What the devil's going on out there, *Trung uy?*' he snapped, looking up from the map he had been studying and addressing Drayton by his Vietnamese rank, as was customary.

'Christ knows,' Drayton said, hoping to God they hadn't been hit, and striding quickly toward the open doorway.

There was no smoke and no sign of an explosion. The ruckus was coming from the perimeter of the village, some one hundred yards away from the fortified team house and the huts that served as troop barracks. 'It's nothing, *Dai uy*,' he said, turning back to Lewis with relief. 'Just a local disagreement.'

The screaming had continued, unmistakably female, and furious and raging rather than being full of fear or pain. Village life was as full of marital discord as any American army base for marrieds, but the village women were usually too indoctrinated by the Buddhist precepts of female docility and obedience to protest too strenuously at mistreatment.

'For Christ's sake, can't someone shut that woman up?' he said bad-temperedly, throwing down the pen he had been marking the map with and striding across to the doorway to join Drayton.

'I think some of them are trying to bring her up here, *Dai uy*, and some of them are trying to hustle her into one of the village huts,' Drayton said, leaning against the bamboo frame of the doorway and watching with amused interest.

'I don't want her in here,' Lewis said decisively, knowing that once the villagers milled into the team house there was no telling when he would be rid of them. The agitated group was beginning to move slowly toward them, despite the furiously resisting girl in its midst and the several dissenters viciously tugging her in the opposite direction.

'Looks like someone's wife has been up to a bit of no good,' Drayton said, taking a box of matches and a pack of Camels out of his pocket and settling himself to enjoy the entertainment.

'We're here to fight a war, goddammit, not act as marriage counselors!' Lewis abandoned all hope of finishing the job he had in hand until the fighting, kicking, and screaming group had been dispersed. 'Come on.' He began to walk across the beaten earth to the approaching melee. 'Let's settle this fracas with a little American common sense.'

Drayton sighed and ground his freshly lit cigarette out under his rubber-soled sandals. They had been up half the night hoping to ambush a squad of Viet Cong rumored to be bringing supplies in to the local units. Lewis was now mapping out the site for an ambush that he hoped would be more successful.

As soon as the quarreling villagers saw the two Americans they halted in their tracks, still holding on tightly to the kicking, screaming girl.

Lewis strode up to them. He was wearing only a pair of black pajama pants and rubber sandals, as he had found the loose cotton clothing that the villagers wore was more comfortable and practical than standard army issue.

'What the hell is going on here, *Em*?' he asked the village headman, addressing him as a brother and a good friend.

The village headman looked unusually

nervous. 'This girl crazy, *Dai uy*. That is why we bring her to you. So that you know we do not sympathize with her, or help her. That there are no more crazy girls in our village.'

A slight frown creased Lewis's brow. He had anticipated a marital or parental dispute. The nervous expression in the old man's eyes indicated that there was more to the disturbance than he had originally thought.

Immediately after the old man had spoken, a storm of protest had broken out from the men still trying to tug the protesting girl in the opposite direction. Yes, the girl was crazy, they confirmed, but she didn't need to be brought before the *Co Van*. She needed only a whipping.

Lewis raised his voice over the conflicting shouts, demanding that the girl's father step forward. A man even older than the village headman reluctantly did so, dragging the girl behind him.

'Is this your daughter?' Lewis demanded. The girl was now on the beaten ground, still struggling to free herself of her father's grasp, and of the dozens of other pairs of hands helpfully restraining her.

'Yes, *Dai uy*.' The old man looked as nervous as the headman, and there was something else in his eyes as well. Fear.

He looked swiftly from the girl's father to the headman. In the months he had been in Van Binh he had forged a good relationship with the old man, a relationship that he believed had been founded on guarded mutual trust.

'Why is this girl crazy, *Em*? Why does she need to be whipped?' There was steel in his voice, and the conflicting shouts from the men around them died down. Everyone was waiting and listening. Only the girl seemed unaware of the new tension, continuing to kick and struggle against her captors.

'This girl's brother-in-law is a Viet Cong, *Dai uy*,' the old headman said at last, reluctantly. 'He is not from Van Binh. He is nothing to do with Van Binh. The girl's sister has shamed her family and has run off to join her husband in the jungle. This girl, who is crazy in the head, was trying to follow her.'

Lewis understood the villagers' agitation. Their village was designated as one that was free from Viet Cong control. As such it received special privileges. If it was suspected that there was a Viet Cong infrastructure at work, life would become more difficult for both the villagers and the team.

'Truly, *Dai uy*,' the headman said, his eyes pleading for Lewis to believe him. 'The girl's brother-in-law is not from Van Binh. No one in Van Binh knows him. He sent message to his wife and his wife go into the jungle to join him. No one knows where. Even this stupid girl does not know where.'

Lewis's instincts were to believe him, but he had no intention of relying on instinct alone. There was a good deal of questioning to be done before the matter was closed, but he had no intention of conducting questioning out in the open on the village perimeter.

'You take the girl, *Dai uy*,' the headman continued. 'You punish her. Then you know that our village does not sympathize with Cong.'

Lewis had no intention of doing any such thing. For the first time he turned his attention to the panting, breathless girl. Despite the tangled mat of hair half covering her face, he was surprised to see that she was far younger than he had anticipated, fifteen or sixteen.

'Let her father punish her,' he said, determined to keep the incident on a domestic level if possible.

There was a general murmur of relief from the crowd of interested villagers, and the girl's father beamed toothlessly at him. 'That is what I say in the beginning, *Dai uy*,' he said with a look of defiance toward the headman.

His daughter didn't share in the general relief. Still with her rump on the beaten earth, her knees bent and her bare feet planted firmly in the dust, she glared up at Lewis, her delicate-boned face filthy, her sloe eyes sparking venomously. Then, to the horror of the bystanders, she spat at him.

Lewis's jaw hardened fractionally, and then he gave a nod of dismissal to the headman and turned, striding back toward the team house. Sergeant Drayton remained just long enough to see the girl's father clump her energetically around the head and then, as she was dragged off to her family hut, this time with the full support of the headman, he turned and followed Lewis.

'You shouldn't have let her get away with it, *Dai uy*,' he said, referring to her contemptuous spit. 'Not responding to such an insult will be seen by the villagers as a weakness.'

'Did you get a close look at her?' Lewis asked wearily, hoping to God that there weren't more village women in contact with lovers or husbands who were Viet Cong. 'She's little more than a child.'

'Not in Vietnamese eyes,' Drayton said truthfully. 'Under all that dirt and that mat of hair she was quite a looker. The only wonder is that she isn't married and hauling a couple of kids around with her.'

Lewis grunted, knowing that Drayton was right. She had probably been of marriageable age in Vietnamese eyes for over a year. 'Tell the headman and the girl's father that I want to see them both.' He still believed that his indifferent reaction to her gesture had been the only one possible; any other reaction would simply have made matters worse.

Drayton left again, and spotted Pennington, who was returning to camp after a training session with one of the Popular Forces units. 'Hey, Pennington,' he said, when he reached the other man, 'looks as if Charlie is more welcome in Van Binh that we thought.'

'What the shit is that supposed to mean?' Pennington said after him as Drayton continued to stride away toward the village.

'It means that one of the local belles has a

VC for a husband,' Drayton yelled back, turning his head around but not bothering to halt. 'And she wasn't alone in thinking he was the local hero. Her sister wanted to follow the pair of them into the jungle and share in the action as well!'

Richard Pennington stared after him and then shrugged and continued on his way to the team house. It wouldn't have surprised him if the whole damn village was Cong. The villagers smiled, agreed with everything that was said to them, took every dollar that was offered, and left him with the uncomfortable sensation that none of their real feelings had been revealed. Whoever had coined the word *inscrutable* for Orientals hadn't been exaggerating. They were so damned inscrutable that most of the time, at least for a boy from rural Massachusetts, they were incomprehensible.

By the time Lewis finished questioning the headman and the girl's father, he was nearly a hundred percent convinced that the girl's marriage to a Viet Cong was an isolated instance.

That night he took Sergeant Drayton and Sergeant Pennington and five of the village men out on another attempt to ambush the Viet Cong supply squad rumored to be trying to make its way through their area.

Lewis was almost certain he'd picked the correct trail, and for seven long, tedious, damp hours they lay in wait at a strategic point along it, tortured by leeches, ants, mosquitos, and a hundred and one other nameless tormentors, and by the constant drip, drip, drip of the tropical moisture seeping down from the foliage above them.

It wasn't until the first hint of gray touched the night sky, that Lewis began to think that another night's efforts had proved fruitless. Then he heard faint sounds of stealthy movement coming down the track toward them.

'*Cong lai!*' one of the village militiamen whispered urgently. 'The Communists are coming!'

Lewis nodded, pressing his cheek against the stock of his M-16, his finger tightening around the trigger. There was no need for him to give any orders. Each man knew exactly what to do and when to do it. It was going to be a textbook operation.

The slightly built, black-pajama-clad figures took on shadowy shape and substance. Lewis could hear their labored breathing, smell their body odors. His excitement grew to fever pitch, he could hear his own heartbeat slamming, could feel his pulse racing. It was an exultancy that he could never in a million years have explained to Abbra, an exultancy that would only increase if the unsuspecting Cong engaged them in a fierce firefight.

'Any minute now, you bastards!' he whispered to himself. 'Any minute now!'

The first of the Cong was now nearly level with him, and he hoped to God that he had judged the positioning of Drayton, Pennington, and the militiamen correctly. If he had, then by now all the Cong trudging in their leader's wake would be in a rifle sight. If he hadn't, then when he opened fire, and the others followed suit, they would come under answering fire from Viet Cong at the rear of the column. He took a deep breath. The barely visible, dark-clad figure leading the column was now abreast of him. Zero hour had arrived.

'Okay, Charlie,' he thought as he positioned the M-16's sight onto the leader's chest. 'It's bye-bye world time.'

His finger tightened on the trigger, and the instant his own volley of shots blasted the man into eternity, Pennington and Drayton and the militiamen opened up on his followers.

It was all over in under a minute. A short and bloody operation that wiped out the unsuspecting Cong while resulting in no injuries to themselves.

'For fuck's sake, *Dai uy*! They really walked into that one!' Richard Pennington whooped triumphantly as they speedily searched the pockets and packs of the dead Cong. 'Bam! Bam! Bam! One after the other. Not even one round of retaliatory fire! Grainger is going to shit himself with envy when he hears about it!'

Lewis grinned, still on an adrenaline high as he sifted through the packs of provisions that the Cong had been carrying. Pennington was right. It had been a dream of an operation.

'He sure as hell is,' he said, knowing that his lieutenant was going to be apoplectic with fury at having missed out on such a trouble-free confrontation.

Fatigue was beginning to set in as the nervous energy of the long wait and the resulting action began to ebb. He distributed the supplies among his men and then ordered them to head back to Van Binh, assigning himself the task of bringing up the rear. There was a slight chance that they hadn't accounted for all the Viet Cong in the supply squad. A chance that, tired and triumphant, they could come under unexpected sniper fire. And if they did, Lewis wanted to be in the position to handle it.

He slept the next day until noon. During the afternoon he made out his report on the night's action, and it never occurred to him to wonder what had happened to the girl who had caused the disturbance the previous day.

During the next two days he sent out a platoon of local men, under Lieutenant Grainger's command, to make a thorough sweep of the area where the ambush had taken place, while he supervised a full-scale medical check of the women and children in the village that his medic, Master Sergeant Duxbery, had been planning.

The operation met with great success. Women and children from nearby villages swelled the ranks of Van Binh's population, all of them queuing patiently in the sweltering heat until it was their turn for Duxbery to examine them.

It was only as Duxbery was coming toward the end of his task that Lewis remembered the kicking, screaming girl who had put the village's loyalty to the South Vietnamese government in doubt.

'Was the sister of the Viet Cong bride a genuine head case?' he asked, not really believing for a moment that she had been, but idly curious.

Duxbery sat in one of the bamboo and thatch village houses that he had turned into a temporary clinic. He looked up at Lewis, his eyes red-rimmed and tired. 'What was the name?' he asked, pulling a sheaf of paper toward him.

'Tam. Nguyen Van Tam.'

Duxbery looked through his list of names and shook his head. 'She's not down here, and the only women still to be seen are the ones who are too old or too sick to make it to the clinic. She wasn't sick, was she?'

Lewis remembered the girl's fierce and energetic struggles. 'No, she wasn't sick,' he said, his brows drawing together as inner alarm bells began to ring furiously. Had he been too complacent about the incident? Too quick to believe that the girl didn't know the whereabouts of her sister and her brother-in-law? The thought that there might be more than one village girl with knowledge of the local Viet Cong's whereabouts, and who was more than willing to keep slipping away from the village with information for them, was not a pleasant one. Still frowning, he strode quickly out of the makeshift clinic and went in search of the headman.

The headman was beamingly reassuring. 'The girl is still in the village. How could she run away when neither she nor anyone else knows where the local Viet Cong camps are?'

'If she's in the village, why didn't she attend the medical inspection?' Lewis demanded.

'She is still being punished, of course.'

'Let me see her,' Lewis demanded suspiciously, no longer trusting a word that was being said to him.

The headman nodded obligingly, leading the way down the single village street toward one of the closely packed bamboo and thatch houses that backed out onto a canal.

'She is there, *Dai uy*,' he said with flourish of pride, indicating a darkened doorway. 'Her father punish her very, very good.'

Lewis bent his head down to enter the house, and was almost immediately overcome by the stench of stale sweat and vomit. A middle-aged female figure sitting just inside the doorway rose with a cry of alarm as he entered.

'It all right,' Lewis heard the headman saying to her as she fled outside, 'the *dai uy* just wants to see how your foolish daughter has been punished.'

The interior of the hut was so dark that for a few seconds Lewis could see nothing. When his eyes adjusted to the dim light he saw only too well, and what he saw he didn't believe.

The girl was lying, half-naked, on the floor, her wrists manacled together with bamboo and secured to a stake driven in the ground. But it wasn't the sight of her bound wrists that filled him with horror. It was the blood-encrusted weals that scored her back and buttocks.

'Jesus!' he spat out, sucking in his breath and striding quickly across to her. She was barely conscious. Her lips were dried and cracked and he could see no sign of a water jar.

*'Can you hear me?'* he asked urgently. *'Can you speak?'*

A swollen eyelid flickered open. The tangled mat of her hair was even thicker now, stiff with dried sweat and flecks of blood.

*'Di di mau,'* she whispered hoarsely. Added to Lewis's feelings of horror and revulsion and concern, was a tug of amused admiration. Loosely translated, what she had said was, 'Get the hell out of here.' It was a strong language for any rural Vietnamese girl, and unheard of language for anyone to be using to an American who was not only a *dai uy*, but a *co van* possessing life-and-death powers.

'I'm going to take you to the *bac-si*,' he said, taking a knife from his belt and slicing through the bamboo. *Bac-si* was the Vietnamese word for doctor and the title that the villagers gave to Master Sergeant Duxbery. The girl closed her eyes again, muttering a word that was barely intelligible but which

Lewis was certain was grossly insulting.

Arranging the scrap of dirty blanket that covered her as strategically as possible, he lifted her up in his arms, carrying her out into the fierce sunlight.

When he emerged, the expression on the headman's face changed from one of beaming complacency to one of alarmed concern.

'What is the matter, *Dai uy*?' he asked anxiously. 'Why do you look so angry?'

'Did you know what had been done to her?' Lewis asked, white-lipped. 'Was it on your orders?'

'No, no, *Dai uy*.' The headman hurried at his side as Lewis made his way up the village street toward the hut where Master Sergeant Duxbery was seeing the last of his patients. 'Your orders. The girl was to be punished by her father. You said so.'

Lewis swore viciously. 'For Christ's sake! I didn't mean she was to be beaten to death!'

The headman gave a slight shrug. The *dai uy* had chosen not to punish the girl himself. No one could be blamed if the girl's father had punished her in a way that displeased the *dai uy*. It was the *dai uy*'s fault. He should have carried out the punishment himself.

'Bring her father to me!' Lewis ordered, hating himself for not foreseeing what would happen; hating the primitiveness of the society that allowed such things to happen; hating, for the first time since he had set foot in it, the whole damned fucking country.

'You found her,' Jim Duxbery said

unnecessarily as Lewis entered the hut. He eyed the savage whip marks on the girl's back as Lewis laid her as gently as he could on the table. 'It appears that parental discipline is a little heavy-handed in these parts,' he said dryly, reaching for a bottle of hydrogen peroxide.

'You're fucking right it is!'

Jim Duxbery looked across at Lewis with interest. Ellis was that rarest of breeds, a professional soldier who very rarely resorted to foul language.

He saturated a swab with the peroxide and said briefly, 'This is going to sting like the devil, but it's the only antiseptic I have.'

As the peroxide touched her flesh, beginning to bubble, the girl let out an agonized cry, her eyes flying open.

'It's to stop the cuts on your back from becoming infected,' Lewis said to her, taking hold of her hands and gripping them hard. 'Hold on to me. It won't hurt for long.'

For a minute he thought she was going to drag her hands contemptuously from his grasp, and then Duxbery began to swab the weals in earnest and she moaned, digging her nails into his palms.

'When this is over, I want you to come up to the team house,' Lewis said to her in Vietnamese. 'I want you to be our cleaning girl.'

Jim Duxbery looked at him, his eyebrows rising slightly. They already had a cleaning woman. She wasn't a day under fifty and her teeth were blackened with betelnut. It had long been a source of contention with the team that Ellis had hired such a crone when there were lots of pretty village girls that he could have chosen.

'No,' the girl whispered hoarsely, shaking her head vehemently.

Lewis dismissed her refusal. 'It wasn't a request, it was an order,' he said brusquely. He knew that if she came up to the team house every day, no one would dare to lift a hand to her.

'No!' Vainly the girl tried to pull her hands free of Lewis's comforting grasp. 'No, no, never!'

Lewis swore. He was sure that if he returned her to her home, another beating, this time to punish her for attracting the *dai uy*'s attention in such a way, would soon follow. He explained all this to her, but her only response was a sullen silence and a firm shake of her head.

'She won't come,' Jim Duxbery said, cleaning the last of the hideous blood-encrusted cuts. 'If gentle docility is a natural characteristic of Vietnamese women, then this girl is the most uncharacteristic Vietnamese girl I've ever met.'

'She'll come,' Lewis said grimly. As the peroxide bottle was put away and Jim began to apply salve to the festering weals, the girl determinedly pulled her hands free of his.

Reluctantly, he did not restrain her. There was something about her that intrigued him, something that attracted him as he had been instantly attracted to Abbra. He wondered if it was because, in some curious way that he couldn't define, she reminded him of Abbra. As soon as the thought came into his head, he dismissed it as ridiculous. How could she remind him of Abbra? She was an illiterate, dirty Vietnamese peasant. And yet there was something about her ... the defiant tilt of her jaw and the uncompromising light in her eyes.

'*Dai uy*.' It was the first time she had addressed him with any semblance of politeness. She had pushed herself up on one elbow, facing him, her dark eyes suddenly speculative. '*Dai uy*, I will come to the team house as a cleaning girl on one condition.'

It was going to be money, of course. A spurt of disappointment surged through him. For some insane reason he had been sure that the girl, despite her obvious hatred toward Americans, was not mercenary.

'What is the condition?' he asked, wearily taking a pack of Winstons from the pocket of his tiger-stripe fatigues. 'That you teach me English,' she said. As her eyes fearlessly met his, he knew what it was about her that reminded him of Abbra. She was not only vital and strong-willed. She was also, beneath the grime of sweat and dried tears, exceptionally beautiful.

He knew damned well why she wanted him to teach her English. She would be of great value to the Cong if she could serve them as an interpreter.

*'Khong xau,'* he said, determining to so successfully win her heart and mind for the South Vietnamese government that she would forget all ideas of running away and joining the Cong. 'Okay. No sweat.'

He grinned suddenly. Not only was it going to be easy. It was also going to be fun.

# CHAPTER TWELVE

Kyle was on the longest, most mind-bending high he had ever experienced. It was better than alcohol, better than drugs, better than sex. It was combat high, and after six weeks in 'Nam he was drunk on it.

He had been assigned to a company of the Assault Helicopter Battalion, 1st Cavalry Division (Airmobile). Their base was on the perimeter of the Central Highlands, where there had been heavy fighting ever since the vicious Ia Drang Valley battle, six months before.

For the first two weeks he flew only routine flights, ferrying commanding officers to neighboring units in Pleiku and Qui Nhon. Nothing he saw or experienced made him sorry he'd volunteered. The countryside was lush and dramatic, dense jungle interspersed with soaring, gleaming ridges of rock. He loved skimming low over them, clearing them with only feet to spare, flying the Huey over the jungle canopy with the same measured recklessness with which he had driven his Ferrari.

The women were another reason for signing up. They were all beauties, slender and fragile-boned and, according to his buddies who had been in 'Nam for a while, universally willing. Regrettably, he had not put the truth of their statements to the test. Saigon, with its bars and clubs, was 260 miles away to the south, and though some lucky bastards had been detailed to fly down there on administration flights, and had enjoyed overnight stays there, Kyle had pulled nothing more exotic than quick, celibate daytime trips to Pleiku and Qui Nhon.

On his third week in-country he had his first taste of flying troops in to a landing zone. He and Chuck Wilson, his copilot, were to fly to Yan Len in formation with sixteen other Hueys and four gunships. When they had dropped the troops at the scheduled landing zone, they were to fly back to a cold landing zone some distance away and stand by until radio contact instructed them to make a pickup.

'It's going to be a walkover,' the experienced Chuck said nonchalantly.

Kyle grinned, a flicker of excitement twisting deep in his gut. He didn't want it to be a walkover. He wanted it to be adrenaline-packed hassle. After all, that was what he was here for. To walk on the wild side and to live dangerously. Anything else just plain sucked.

The early morning sun was fierce in his eyes, sweat already staining his fatigues as the signal to crank up was given. He slipped on his sunglasses and clicked on the intercom.

'Ready?' he asked the crew chief and the

gunner, and on receiving their affirmatives he rolled the throttle open. The starter motor whined, the rotor blades began to accelerate, and then the turbine caught. Slowly Kyle pulled the collective up, and the heavily burdened Huey rose, climbing laboriously above tree level as it closed up in formation with the other three ships in the squad.

The elation he experienced at being airborne surged through him. Flying in close formation, he would have no opportunity to do any of the acrobatics that he loved, flying fast and close to the ground with only a couple of feet between the treads and the treetops, or executing wild, ship-shaking U-turns that terrified whoever he was flying with half to death, but there would be compensations.

Although Chuck had predicted the mission would be a walkover, it was more than likely that they would meet with enemy fire when approaching the landing zone. And it would be Kyle's first time. His heart began to race, his nerve ends tingled with anticipation. For the first time since he had been in 'Nam, he found himself thinking of Serena. It was a crazy time to be thinking of anyone or anything besides the job at hand, but he knew why she had suddenly sprung into his thoughts. Her heedless, reckless nature would have responded to the dangers of 'Nam just as hungrily as his own.

He grinned to himself as they neared the landing zone, and he slowed the Huey down from 100 knots to 80 knots so the gunships could fly ahead. Hell, but she would have made a great chopper jock. She was certainly a great lay. It was even possible, when his tour of duty was over and if she didn't send back the divorce papers, she would make a great wife.

White smoke streamed behind the gunships ahead of them as they peppered the landing zone with flex gun and rocket fire. He hoped she wouldn't return the divorce papers. The fun they had together was too mind-blowing to be thrown away. His grin deepened. Christ, if he wasn't careful, he would be metamorphozing into an adoring husband!

'Close up,' Chuck said tersely over the intercom, breaking into his thoughts.

Kyle acknowledged, closing the distance between the Huey and the gunships, and dropped lower.

'Clear to use gun doors! Clear to use gun doors!' his flight leader radioed from the leading Huey.

As the Huey lost height, the rotor pitch changed and the noise deepened to an ear-splitting whine. They were only three hundred feet from the ground now, and a bare quarter of a mile from the landing zone. Kyle felt his stomach muscles tighten. The landing zone was hot. There was enemy fire as well as the blasting fire from the gunships.

'When do our gunners get the okay to fire?' he yelled across to his twenty-three-year-old senior.

'Now ought to be about the right time,' he said laconically, flicking on his intercom.

They were only a hundred yards from the landing zone. Kyle could see the gunners in the Hueys ahead of him, blasting down into thick bush. He wondered how the hell they could see what they were firing at. Rockets were pounding the ground, shooting earth scores of feet into the air. The white smoke from the gunships was barely discernible now among the swirling colored smoke that identified the center of the landing zone, and the dense black and gray plumes of artillery and rocket fire.

'It's a hot LZ, guys,' Chuck said unnecessarily over the intercom to the troops about to disembark, and then, to the door gunners, 'Fire at will.'

Kyle's hands were slippery with sweat on the control stick. The pilots of the Hueys ahead of him were reporting that they were taking enemy fire. He knew it hadn't been expected. The operation had changed character. They were flying into enemy fire, and he didn't envy the troops about to disembark one little bit.

They were losing height rapidly now, the tail rotor spinning just a few yards from the ground. Chuck's hands joined his on the control stick, army regulations in case one of them was hit. The door gunners behind them were giving it all they'd got, the noise from their guns deafening, the reverberation decidedly disconcerting.

'Jeez!' Kyle exclaimed beneath his breath, the blood hammering in his temples as bullets smashed into the Huey's airframe. He began to decelerate rapidly, the Huey's nose rising steeply to slow its forward motion. As he hovered some three feet from the ground, about to land vertically, the troops began to leap to the ground, racing for cover, firing as they went.

Sniper fire was raining in on them, a pilot in one of the other Hueys was hit, and the last of the troops had sprung to mother earth before the skids had even made contact with it. Fear and exhilaration, equally mixed, surged through Kyle's veins. This was reality. This was the big time. At any second the ground fire could blast the Plexiglas chin bubble under the Huey's nose, or destroy the instrument panel or slam into his own unprotected body, winging him on his way to eternity.

Over the intercom the order came for him to go. He didn't need telling twice. The other choppers around him were all dipping their noses in unison as they picked up airspeed, the gunships still darting and swooping above them as they gave covering fire. The downdraft from the rotors riffled the tall grass beneath them; the air was heavy with the smell of cordite, thick with smoke.

The Huey gained height, whirring up above the tree line, the door gunners still blasting away into the bush beneath them. Kyle pressed back on the control stick and began to climb to cruising height and the chatter,

chatter, chatter of the guns ceased.

It was over. They were flying to a standoff position and they hadn't been hit. He hadn't screwed up. Wilson hadn't had to take over.

He did so now. 'I got it,' he said over the intercom and then, dryly, 'I told you it would be a walkover.'

Kyle clicked off his intercom and let out an exultant whoop. It hadn't been a walkover, but it had been the most mind-blowing few minutes of his life. He was drenched with sweat, bathed in it. He clicked on his intercom again, so keyed up with adrenaline that he couldn't wait for the moment when they flew back in. 'For a walkover, it was pretty hip,' he said with a grin.

Chuck banked to the left to keep in formation and shot him a pitying look. 'You won't think so in another few weeks,' he prophesied darkly, 'not after you've flown a few dust-off missions.'

'How did the medical rescue missions get the name dust off?' Kyle asked curiously.

'Rumor has it that it was the call sign of one of the first medevac pilots to be killed,' Chuck replied, leveling out and cruising at twelve hundred feet, high enough to be out of the way of any stray ground fire but low enough for a quick descent to the cold landing zone they were fast approaching – where they were to laager, or stand by.

They didn't have to wait long before they received a radio call instructing them to return and pick up. This time Chuck took the controls, Kyle assisting him when tracer fire streamed past them and the Hueys descended to the landing zone, door gunners firing like a swarm of predatory dragonflies.

It was hairier picking the troops up than it had been disgorging them. This time the Huey had to make a firm landing, its rotor blades beating the air as men raced across the clearing to scramble aboard.

Kyle could see one running figure fall, and then another, both of them hauled to their feet by their companions and half dragged, half carried to the Huey's open doors.

Over the radio came the order to power up, and Chuck rotated the throttle, watching the gauges, then the order came to lift off, and as Kyle watched a black-pajama-clad figure burst from the bush, racing toward them, a grenade in his hand, the order came to go.

As they did so, picking up airspeed, one of the door gunners hit the figure running in their wake. There was a violent explosion, a billow of dust, and then the Huey swung up and over the trees edging the clearing, and the black-pajama-clad figure was no longer discernible. All he could see were scraps of black cloth blowing in the downdraft.

During the next few weeks such missions became routine though not all of them were into hot landing zones. Many were straight forward drop and extraction missions, as unexacting as a courier or an administration flight. Others were not so pleasant.

The first time he had had to fly back to base with a load of bloodstained canvas body bags aboard he had nearly puked. Unseen arms and legs poked stiffly and grotesquely at their coverings. Even worse were the bags that looked half empty. Just a trunk being delivered back to base for shipment home. He remembered the army's proud boast that any man wounded would be hospitalized, by chopper, within twenty minutes, and the promise that serious injuries would be flown to Japan within twelve hours. He gagged at the stench rising from the bags. The army had forgotten to add that any man killed would be home in a week.

A month after his arrival he finally drew a coveted three-day stop-over in Saigon. It was a maintenance trip and he was to fly his Huey down to Tan Son Nhut air base so that it could be overhauled at the big depot there. His copilot was Chuck Wilson.

'Seems like the army doesn't want you out of my sight, Anderson,' he had said with affected weariness.

Kyle had grinned. He liked Chuck Wilson. He had a sophisticated, laid-back, world-weary attitude to the war that he himself liked to assume. At twenty-three Chuck was the old man of the outfit, a possessor of three Purple Hearts, and on his second tour of duty. Kyle couldn't help wondering what he had been like before 'Nam. When he had been young.

'Maybe they figure you're too old to totter

around the big city by yourself,' he said, itching to be in the Huey's cockpit, winging his way south.

'And maybe they figure that you're not going to live too long unless you start treating your seniors with a little more respect,' Chuck said, cuffing his ear.

The flight down to Saigon was great. The country they were flying over was mainly Viet Cong territory, so they flew high, at a cool five thousand feet.

'What made you up for another tour of duty?' Kyle asked curiously over the intercom as the coast flashed into view and they neared the city.

He knew that Chuck must have volunteered. With three Purple Hearts, he never had to serve in 'Nam again.

A faint smile tugged at the corners of Chuck's mouth. He had wondered when Kyle would ask. 'Because if you're sane, you hate the 'Nam with every single cell that's in your body, and if you're insane, you get hooked on it.'

They were over the city now, and it looked as if it was going to live up to all the names it had been given in the past. Pearl of the East. Paris of the Orient. It lay beneath them, a panorama of long, wide avenues flanked by tamarind and lime trees; spacious, lushly green parks, delicate, pink-stuccoed houses; the Saigon River winding its way sensuously through its center.

Chuck's smile broadened. 'I got hooked.'

Kyle began to decelerate as they approached Tan Son Nhut and the rotor pitch changed, the noise deepening as they lost airspeed. 'I know,' he yelled back, the Huey responding beneath his hands as smoothly as pure silk. 'I'm hooked as well!'

'There's a word for it,' Chuck said, and this time he wasn't smiling. The tone of his voice made the hair on the nape of Kyle's neck stand on end. 'It's psychotic.'

From the ground Saigon was not the flawlessly elegant city it had appeared from the air. It was still possible to see how graciously French it had once been, before the hundreds of bars and clubs and strip-joints had opened. But the freshness and charm it had once possessed had been destroyed forever.

'You're the one who knows his way around,' Kyle said exuberantly, relishing the sensation of being let loose after a month's captivity. 'Where do we hit first?'

They had left the Huey at the maintenance base and hopped a cab to the central square, two blocks down Tu Do Street. 'We check into somewhere decent,' Chuck said, paying the driver off and leading the way across the square. 'Somewhere with hot baths, clean beds, and a decent bar.'

'And that is?'

'Here.'

They were outside the four-storied European splendor of the Continental Hotel.

Kyle gave a whistle of appreciation. He

liked the way Chuck did things. It was the way he had always done things himself.

'Isn't this where Graham Greene is supposed to have written *The Quiet American*?'

'The very place,' Chuck said as they strolled across the lobby to the reception desk. 'He wrote it on the terrace, and there's always a hyped-up journalist sitting there, reading it.'

The room they were given was enormous. 'How come we get the VIP treatment?' he asked, impressed.

'The proprietor is a personal friend,' Chuck said, strolling across to the windows and looking down into the square. 'And for a friend he'll always find a room, even if it means throwing someone else out!'

Kyle began to take off his sweat-soaked shirt, making a beeline for the shower. 'Give me five minutes and then I want a tour of Tu Do from beginning to end!' he shouted, turning the water on full blast.

It was a tour that was still only half completed nine hours later, when the city's curfew forcibly curtailed it. First they had descended on the bars. In the Sporting Bar, packed with Green Berets, Kyle had become happily drunk. In the Bluebird he had been delighted to find that ready-rolled joints were easily available, being dispensed on demand from a jar beneath the counter.

Weaving their way out of the Bluebird, they had made their way to La Bohème, where the girls paraded in see-through dresses and descended on them like a flock of vultures, taking their hands and thrusting them strategically down their dresses and up their dresses, cooing, 'You buy me Saigon tea?'

Kyle had grinned. If Saigon tea was what it took to get on even friendlier terms with the ladies of the town, then he was quite prepared to buy it until it ran out of their ears.

'I think this is where we split for half an hour,' Chuck had said with a wink, a golden-skinned beauty draped around his neck.

Kyle had been only too happy to agree. His only sexual outlet since he had arrived in the country six weeks earlier had been the near orgasm he experienced when flying the Huey fast and low in and out of combat zones. 'Come on, baby,' he said to the girl who had claimed him by the simple and effective expedient of clutching his balls. 'You've got a customer. Lead the way.'

Half an hour later he and Chuck had staggered into the nearby Melody for a reviving bourbon.

'This is a journalists' bar,' Chuck had said, heaving himself onto a bar stool. 'It's a good place to come if you don't want to be harangued by Green Berets telling you how they could win the war single-handed if it wasn't for the ARVN.'

'Lucky journalists,' Kyle said, looking around him. The girls were prettier and fresher-looking than the girls in La Bohème, and he was beginning to wish that he had saved his strength.

'Stop crying into your bourbon,' Chuck

said, reading his mind. 'We'll call back here later on. After we've eaten.'

It was dark now and Tu Do was packed with off-duty servicemen looking for a little recreation. Neon lights glittered out the names of the bars and clubs. Denver, Cincinnati, Arcen Ciel, Maximos, La Pagoda, Joe Marcel's, Bong Lai, Chicago. The music reverberating out of the ultraviolet-lit depths was a pulsating cacophony of Jimi Hendrix, James Brown, Wilson Pickett, and the Temptations.

They dined at the Blue Diamond, ordering sweet and sour pork and drinking more bourbon. Afterward they strolled unsteadily across to the Maximos, avoiding the heavily congested traffic with difficulty. It seemed to Kyle that every South Vietnamese in the country was the proud owner of a Honda or a Yamaha or a 50cc Suzuki, and that all were intent on mowing down anyone or anything that got in their way. Cabs fought for road space, horns blaring. Jeeps blasted their way through, seeming to care even less for the rules of the road than the cyclo riders. There was not the slightest attempt to control traffic. It was every man for himself, and the devil take the hindmost.

The next morning Kyle couldn't remember whether they had returned to the Melody or not. Chuck assured him that they had, and that they had bought enough Saigon tea to float a tanker.

They breakfasted at the Continental, huge

ceiling fans creaking noisily above their heads, the heat already oppressive.

'Well, we hit half of Tu Do Street pretty thoroughly last night,' Chuck said, drinking his third cup of black coffee. 'What does the little tourist boy want to do today?'

'Hit the other half.'

Even at eleven in the morning Tu Do was crammed with streetwalkers, pimps, children selling cigarettes, and trucks and jeeps and a thousand bikes.

'Christ!' Kyle yelled, leaping to safety as a little four-door Renault taxicab nearly mowed him down. 'I was told this city was the Avignon of the East! Avignon, my ass! It's more like New York City when there's a subway strike!'

They had begun drinking in the Sporting Bar. 'These guys are a gas,' Chuck had said, referring to the Green Berets. 'To hear them talk, you'd think they were God's own!'

The ceiling fans above the bar were more efficient than the ones at the Continental, and Kyle began to feel relatively comfortable. It was impossible to feel cool. That morning sweat began to darken his fatigues before he had even finished putting them on, and he had long ago vowed that no matter how bleak a Boston winter, he would never crave the sun again. He downed his third beer, his sense of well-being increasing.

'You guys Air Cav?' a powerfully built Green Beret asked, peering at the horse patch on Kyle's fatigues.

Kyle nodded, draining his glass.

'What's the matter with you guys, don't you have no bar of your own to go to?' the Green Beret grumbled.

Kyle grinned. 'If we do, I haven't found it yet.'

The Green Beret belched, 'Jeez. You a new guy? How many days you got left in 'Nam? Three fifty-eight? Three fifty-seven?'

'Three twenty-three,' Kyle said, unperturbed.

'Jeez,' the Green Beret repeated sympathetically. 'Your poor mother. I'm short. I've got nineteen days left. Nineteen and then I'm on that big silver bird back to the world!'

'Air Cav,' the guy sitting next to them said derisively. 'What do the fucking Air Cav know. You two chopper jocks?'

Kyle nodded while Chuck continued to drink his beer as if no conversation were taking place.

'What the hell! Fly in, fly out. Hot showers at night, clean sheets, orange juice, Coke, and American apple pie. What the fuck do you guys know about sleeping in the jungle with a million bugs for weeks on end, about having your feet in paddy fields so long they begin to rot, about not being able to take a step without wondering if you're going to set off a booby trap that will blow your legs in front of your face, or a hole in your chest they could drive a truck through. What the fuck–' he was yelling now '–do you guys know about fighting a cocksucking war?'

Kyle didn't answer. Watching from the Huey as he offloaded troops into jungle scores of miles from the nearest base camp, knowing that they were setting off on patrols into Viet Cong territory that would possibly last for days on end, he had often wondered the same thing.

His war bore no relation to their war. His war was flying hundreds of thousands of dollars of steel and Plexiglas with all the skill and recklessness and panache of a World War I flying ace. It was the sexiest thing he had ever experienced. To Kyle, a Huey was the last word in glamour. He loved to see them flocking back to base like great, silk-black birds of prey. He loved their speed, their maneuverability, their sheer, goddammed eroticism. Chuck answered the savage questioner for him.

'I know that statistically one in five of us is going to end up dead,' he said conversationally, still hunched over his drink and not bothering to turn his head.

There was a slight, ominous silence. Although neither Chuck nor Kyle were built on the bull-like lines of the men on either side of them, they both possessed the air of dudes who, in Green Beret parlance, definitely had their shit together.

'Let's give the guys a break,' the first Green Beret said magnanimously, too hot to want to brawl with the Air Cav. 'What are you drinking? Jeez. Why don't we make a party of it?'

They did so, spilling drunkenly out from the Sporting Club two hours later, arms around each other's shoulders as if they'd all been buddies since first grade.

'How about a little fem-i-nine company?' The Green Beret who had initially been belligerent was now as friendly as a pussycat.

'I need to stop by the International and pick up some more dough.' His buddy hiccuped. He turned unsteadily toward Chuck and Kyle. 'You staying at the International too? The officers' club at the International serves the best rare sirloin and baked potatoes with sour cream this side of the Brooklyn Bridge.'

Kyle had long ago guessed that the Continental's fading splendor catered mainly to journalists and civilians, and that staying there wasn't normal for U.S. military personnel. 'Sure,' he said agreeably, 'wouldn't think of bunking down anywhere else.'

By the time they reached the International, Kyle was so affected by the numberless beers and bourbons he had drunk that he could hardly stand. He staggered past the military police at the door, wishing to God that the jerk they were with would hurry up and pocket his dough so that they could hit the street again and find themselves some girls.

The guys back at camp had been right when they said that all Vietnamese girls were more than willing. Christ, he'd enjoyed himself last night almost as much as he had with Serena.

There was a girl behind the desk in the

lobby. The prettiest, sweetest girl he'd ever seen in his life. Jet-black hair flowed straight down her back. Her sloe eyes were thick-lashed and lustrous, her nose as cute as a kitten's, her mouth smiling and inviting. She wasn't wearing one of the short, ill-fitting miniskirts that the girls he had seen the previous night had worn. She wore the most feminine dress he had ever laid eyes on. It was a high-necked ankle-length tunic slit to the waist over loose silk pantaloons. There wasn't an inch of flesh showing, and yet it was a hundred times more arousing than the see-through dresses that the girls had worn in the La Bohème.

'Oh, boy,' he said beneath his breath to Chuck. 'Am I going to get me some of that!'

Chuck said something back to him, but Kyle wasn't listening. He was already weaving his way to the desk and the smiling vision beckoning him onward.

'Shaigon tea?' he queried leeringly, leaning his weight on the desk as the room spun around him. 'How much Shaigon tea for a nice, friendly fuck?'

He was too drunk to see that the smile had frozen on her face and that her eyes had filled with sudden alarm. He reached out for her, grasping hold of her arm and pulling her toward him. 'You wanna feel my dick?' he asked, remembering the free-for-all there had been for such a privilege in La Bohème. 'You wanna feel a real, big, hard American dick?'

Chuck and his newfound buddies, hooting

with laughter, reached him seconds before the military police did.

'Come on, lover boy,' Chuck said as the three of them hauled him away from the desk and began to drag him in the direction of the doors. 'If you want to get your rocks off, you're going to have to learn to do it in the right place!'

They found so many other places during the rest of the day that Kyle was unsure how many of them were right and how many were wrong. One thing he was sure of, though, and that was that none of them contained the dream in flowing traditional dress who had smiled so sweetly at him.

When he awoke next morning in his room at the Continental he was suffering from the worst hangover of his life.

'Can't take the pace?' Chuck asked teasingly as Kyle groped his way into the bathroom and vomited into the john.

It was fifteen minutes before he returned, white-faced, to the bedroom. 'It must have been the dope we were given at the Bluebird,' he said weakly. 'It must have been spiked.'

'Spiked, my ass,' Chuck said. 'You were just out of your league, that's all.' He began to laugh as he slicked his short fair hair down in front of a smoky mirror. 'Christ, you should have heard yourself with the receptionist at the International. "Shaigon tea? How much Shaigon tea for a nice, friendly fuck?"'

Kyle groaned and reached for his pants. 'Don't tell me any more. I don't think I want to remember.'

Chuck, freshly showered and dressed in clean fatigues, leaned against the bathroom door, arms crossed, watching pityingly as Kyle struggled to zip up his pants.

'You were damned lucky not to find yourself in the caring custody of the military police,' he said, grinning. 'There's an army of street-walkers in Tu Do, and you have to proposition the one dink who is definitely out of bounds.' He shook his head in mock despair. 'Christ, don't they teach you guys anything at Princeton?'

Memory was filtering back into Kyle's brain. He pulled on his shirt and said slowly, 'Was that the girl in the long flowing tunic and pants?'

'An *ao dai*,' Chuck said patiently. 'The long flowing silk tunic and pants are called *ao dais*. They're Vietnamese traditional dress.'

Kyle was remembering more than the *ao dai*; he was remembering silk-black hair and soft, gentle eyes, and a sweet, captivating smile. 'Who did you say she was? What did you say I said to her?' he asked, tucking his shirt into his pants. 'I wasn't rude to her, was I?'

Chuck hooted with laughter. 'Depends on what you privileged Princeton guys call rude. How does, "You wanna feel a big, hard American dick," grab you?'

Kyle's lean-angled face tightened. 'Are you shitting me? Is that really what I said?'

'That's really what you said, lover boy.

Didn't seem to impress the lady though. Seemed it was an offer she had no trouble refusing.'

He was still laughing, but Kyle felt even sicker than he had twenty minutes earlier. Christ, had he really said those things? And to a girl who he now remembered clearly had looked as shy and as innocent as a Raphael Madonna.

'Come on,' Chuck said impatiently, dismissing the episode. 'We have only two hours before we have to report to the maintenance depot. Let's get a decent breakfast before we leave.'

Kyle slipped a pack of Winstons into his shirt pocket. 'You go on. I think I ought to make my way over to the International to apologize. Who did you say she was again? The receptionist?'

Chuck nodded. 'But don't bother with any apologies,' he said as they walked out of the room and into the corridor. 'She may be the receptionist, but she's still only a dink. What happened was no big deal, just the sort of thing girls like her have to get used to.'

They walked down the broad sweep of stairs to the Continental's restaurant, the most attractive feature of the hotel. There was only a carved stone fence between the restaurant and the main street. If passers-by saw anyone they recognized dining, they were able to stop and exchange a few words.

Kyle drank his first cup of coffee quickly and then rose to his feet. 'I'm going to split for five minutes,' he said as Chuck looked up at him in surprise. 'I'll be back before you've finished eating.'

Chuck had no time to ask him where the hell he was going as he walked quickly away. He wanted to talk to the girl at the International. He wanted to see her smile again.

When she saw him stride into the lobby, the smile she had been wearing for some departing servicemen died. She took a prudent step or two backward, away from the desk, so that he could not grab hold of her again.

At first Kyle was relieved. She was just as beautiful in the cold light of sobriety as she was when he was drunk. He hadn't made an ass of himself over a girl who wasn't worth it.

'Do you remember me?' he asked, suddenly feeling awkward, as if he were fourteen again and propositioning his first date.

She nodded, remaining a good two feet away from him, her dark eyes wary.

'I was drunk as a skunk,' he said without preamble. 'I understand I said some pretty unforgivable things to you. I've come to say that I'm sorry.'

The expresssion in her eyes had changed from wariness to bewilderment. She hadn't spoken, and he wondered if she understood what he was saying. 'I'm sorry,' he said again, enunciating the words slowly. 'I ... was ... drunk...'

'...as a skunk,' she finished for him, sloe eyes dancing with laughter.

He grinned, no longer feeling awkward.

'And I'm sorry.'

A slight flush of color had touched her pale amber cheeks, and she lowered her eyes from his, saying a little shyly, 'That is all right. I accept your apology.'

Kyle hesitated. He wanted to see her again but was suddenly aware that he had no idea what sort of approach would be acceptable. She was a respectable South Vietnamese girl and he realized with something of a shock that he knew nothing at all about her culture, of what freedoms she enjoyed or didn't enjoy.

'I'm flying back to my base today,' he said, wishing that she would look up again so that he could hold her eyes with his. 'I don't know when I'll be back in Saigon, but when I am, will you have dinner with me?'

She had begun to shake her head, and he said with fierce urgency, 'You can bring along a chaperone if you like. I just want to make amends for my rude behavior. Have dinner with you. Talk.'

This time her silk-dark head rose and her eyes met his, the laughter dancing in them once again. 'You would not mind my elder sister coming with me?'

He shook his head. 'No.' Hell, he didn't care if she brought Ho Chi Minh with her. He just wanted to see her again.

'Then yes, I will have dinner with you the next time you are in Saigon,' she said as a marine walked up to the desk and asked for his room key.

There were more marines entering the

lobby, and as she turned toward them, he said with sudden panic, 'I don't know your name!'

'Trinh,' she said, her voice so lilting that it sounded like a note of music.

He grinned. 'Mine is Kyle.' As the marines descended on the desk, clamoring for attention, he reluctantly turned on his heel, striding buoyantly back out into the searingly hot street.

Three days later the war changed forever for Kyle. He and Chuck had been detailed to fly a search-and-destroy patrol to a village some twenty miles north of their base. There were three other Hueys flying with them, each carrying a full complement of men. Five minutes after they had lifted off, an order came for them to make to an alternative landing zone and to stand by.

'What's the matter?' Kyle had asked Chuck over the intercom. 'Is the original LZ too hot?'

Chuck had shrugged. 'You tell me,' he said disinterestedly.

For four tedious hours they blistered beneath the heat at a landing zone without shade and with no supplies except those they had with them. Chuck settled himself in the Huey's cockpit and managed, with great difficulty, to fall asleep. Most of the men were just sitting miserably in the small amount of shade that the Hueys gave, talking. Kyle was playing poker with a fellow Bostonian who had been in the country even less time than himself.

'Three weeks,' Ricky Skeffington said slightly defensively. 'But don't call me a damned cherry. I hate being called a damned cherry!'

He was a well-built, personable boy with a thatch of bright red hair, a host of freckles, and a cheeky grin that Kyle had liked right away.

For a while, as they played, they talked about football. Ricky had been selected for a draft pick. When his tour of duty was over, he hoped to play pro ball. They talked about the New York Giants and the New England Patriots and what their respective chances were for the next season.

Suddenly Ricky changed the subject. 'A little bird told me you went to Princeton,' he said as he dealt with the flair of a riverboat gambler.

Kyle nodded. Princeton seemed so far in his past that he could barely remember it.

'Okay,' Ricky said, now that he had established Kyle's credentials. 'I did only one year in college, but you're an educated guy. You tell me if it's true what some guy in training camp told me. That the French overran Vietnam and that in the last war America supported Ho Chi Minh against the Japanese?'

Kyle studied his hand and threw away two cards. 'It's true that Vietnam was a French colony and it's also true that America supported Ho Chi Minh in his fight against the

Japanese.' He grinned. 'Hell, the Japs were our enemy too, you know.'

'Yeah, but this guy in training camp said that when the war was over, the Viets didn't want the French back. He said that the British helped the French to regain control and that they did so with American consent.'

Kyle nodded. 'That's more or less what happened.'

'And then what?' Ricky continued doggedly.

'The Vietnamese eventually defeated the French, and it was agreed in Geneva that the country would be temporarily divided at the seventeenth parallel. The idea was that after a year or so, elections would be held for the government of a reunified Vietnam. But the head of the South Vietnamese government was Ngo Dinh Diem, and because he was afraid that an election would put Ho Chi Minh into power, he refused to allow any elections to be held.'

Ricky stared at him in disbelief. 'Jesus H. Christ!' he said at last. 'Someone should tell the fuckers in Washington what the hell's been going on here and get us the hell out! If the South Vietnamese want to vote a Communist government into power, let them. They probably won't like it when they get it, but I sure as hell won't be losing any sleep over it!'

Kyle grinned, amused by the passionate outrage in Ricky's voice. 'Me either,' he said. 'It's your throw, buddy.'

By the time radio instructions were received detailing them to continue to the original landing zone, Ricky had lost his first month's pay.

'I'll get it back, you bastard, next time we meet,' he said good-naturedly as he began to walk toward the Huey's open door. 'I was just lulling you into a sense of false security this time, that's all.'

Kyle had grinned, pulling on his flight helmet and pocketing the bucks. It was okay with him if Ricky wanted to lose a month's pay every time they met. Hell, he was doing him a favor. If he lost all his money at cards, he wouldn't have any to spend on booze and whores!

When they flew into the original landing zone, it was cold and they were given no explanation for their four-hour standoff.

'Have fun!' Kyle yelled to Ricky as he leapt to the ground with his companions. 'Good luck!'

Over the roar of the rotor blades Ricky acknowledged the good wishes, raising his M-16 high into the air and grinning broadly before turning and following his platoon leader into the bush.

They were still in the air, returning to base, when the intercom clicked and they were ordered to fly the hell back. A member of the platoon had been killed and two injured by a Bouncing Betty. Kyle had flinched. Bouncing Bettys were bastards. Land mines that were triggered off by a careless step, and which, when triggered, jumped four or five feet before exploding, spraying down and out, bringing apocalypse not to the guy who had triggered it, but to those ahead of him or behind him.

'They need a dust off, not us,' Chuck had yelled into the intercom. 'We don't have a medic!'

'You're only a minute away from them, and there's a medic with the platoon. He'll fly back with you to the nearest field hospital. Now, git!'

'I hope that fucker Ricky is okay,' Kyle said as they began to bank steeply. 'Did I tell you he's going to play for the Patriots when his tour is over?'

Men were running toward them, carrying the injured in ponchos. Before their skids touched the ground, Kyle caught a glimpse of bright red hair. 'Jesus,' he muttered fiercely. 'Don't let it be him! Don't let it be him!'

As Chuck landed the Huey, Kyle leapt to the ground, running toward the first of the injured men. The bright red hair was plastered dark with blood. His pants had either been blasted off him or had been torn off him by the medic. One leg had been ripped from its socket, leaving a bloody and twitching stump, and where his balls and penis should have been there was nothing but scraps of torn and twisted flesh.

His eyes were wide and frantic as they met Kyle's. 'My legs!' he screamed, stretching his hands out toward him. 'Dear Christ, my legs!'

Kyle was retching, tears pouring down his face as he helped to lift Ricky aboard the Huey.

'Don't leave me!' Ricky screamed at him, and then there was a hideous gurgling sound and his head fell back, blood gushing from his nose and his mouth.

Kyle remembered nothing of the desperate flight to the field hospital. He knew that Ricky was dead, and though the other injured man was still alive, he neither knew what his injuries were nor cared.

For the first time since he had been in 'Nam, the war had reached out and touched him. It had become real. Ricky's blood smeared his hands and his fatigues. There was a scrap of skin on his sleeve. He had been going to play for the Patriots. He was going to be a pro football player. He had promised to win back the money Kyle had won from him the next time they met.

As they lost height and began to descend toward the field hospital, Kyle began to shake. A thousand years ago a numbnut kid with his brain and his body had thought that war was glamorous. He didn't think so now. As the Huey came in to land he leaned out over the ground skimming beneath him and vomited. If he lived to be a hundred, so help him, he would never think so again.

# CHAPTER THIRTEEN

Gavin's emotions were still torn when he landed at Tan Son Nhut airport, countless hours later. He was coiled as tight as a spring with nervous energy and anticipation for the job that lay ahead of him, though he was agonized at leaving Gabrielle behind when she needed him. Most of all he was devastated by the knowledge that he wouldn't see his newborn son again for months, possibly even a year.

A grin of exhilaration touched his mouth as he thought of *le petit* Gavin. It had never occurred to him that when the baby was born it would dive into the world complete with its own little personality, a personality so individual and engaging that Gavin was certain he would be able to single him out even if he were in a room with a score of other, equally newborn babies. He was going to miss *le petit* Gavin. He was going to miss him almost as much as he was going to miss Gabrielle.

A blast of hot air hit his face as he stepped from the plane, so scorching in intensity that it temporarily robbed him of breath. He looked out over a vista of sandbags and barbed wire to where military airplanes shimmered and danced in the heat. There were big-bellied C-130 transports, Phantoms, Air Force 707s, and helicopters and beyond them were long, low buildings that he presumed were also military. After over a year of waiting, he was actually here in Vietnam. He walked down the flight stairs, carrying his only piece of luggage, a nylon zip-up bag, over his shoulder, pinching himself to make sure that he was not dreaming.

The sandbags and barbed wire gave the airport a look of security, but Gavin knew that only two months before the Viet Cong had launched a daring and devastating attack here.

Gavin walked quickly toward the elderly Vietnamese man holding up a sign with the name Gavin Ryan written on it. The heat was suffocating and moist, and in the few seconds since he had left the airplane's air-conditioned interior, he had perspired so much that his shirt was damp beneath the armpits. He followed the Vietnamese across the tarmac toward a battered old Renault, wondering how on earth he was going to survive his cab ride.

The news bureau offices were in Tu Do Street, only a short walk from the Continental, where he intended to stay.

'But no one there now,' the driver said to him, vying for road space amid a battalion of bicycles and pedicabs and tri-Lambrettas. 'Siesta time. When sun so hot, no one works.'

Gavin was relieved to hear it. At least it

indicated that the heat wasn't always so stultifying. 'Then would you mind dropping me off at the Continental?' he asked as they sped over a narrow bridge, narrowly missing a group of laborers in black pajamas and women carrying water on coolie poles.

The driver nodded, entering the city's broad, tree-lined streets. 'Behind those trees is Le Cercle Sportif,' he said informatively. 'Very nice club for Europeans. Very exclusive.' He veered left, the sea of bicycles surrounding them as dense as ever. 'This is Tu Do Street.'

Gavin could see the large red-brick Catholic cathedral that marked its beginning, and, several blocks down on his right-hand side, he could glimpse the gleam of the Saigon River, where it ended.

In front of him, in the square itself, was the shabby grandeur of the Continental, and on the other corner of the square was the taller, more modern facade of the Caravelle Hotel.

'Thanks,' Gavin said as he opened the Renault's door and stepped into the street. He reached for his wallet, but the man shook his head.

'No. The bureau pay me to pick you up. No money, thank you.'

Gavin grinned and hoisted his bag onto his shoulder.

When the sun had lost its ferocity, Gavin walked the short distance from the hotel to the newspaper's office. The bureau chief, Paul Dulles, was a middle-aged and rather elegant Frenchman, and though he was politely welcoming, Gavin sensed that he was dubious about having a suspiciously young-looking twenty-four-year-old Australian on his staff.

'—and so all news is centered on the Buddhists' demands that Premier Ky resign and that a civilian government be elected into power,' he said, thawing a little when he discovered that Gavin's French, though uniquely accented, was fluent enough for them to converse.

He perched on the corner of his desk, one foot swinging negligently. 'It's a lulu of a situation. Ky triggered it off by dismissing one of his former buddies, General Nguyen Chanh Thi. Thi always enjoyed the support of the Buddhists, and within days of his dismissal outraged Buddhists were streaming into the streets of Da Nang and Hue, demanding that Ky resign and that the country return to a civilian government.'

He paused, reaching out for a nearby bottle of Scotch, lifting it queryingly toward Gavin. 'Will join me? There are glasses in the cupboard behind you.'

Gavin did as he was asked, amused to discover that the glasses in question were hand-cut crystal, not the chipped all-purpose glasses usually to be found in bureau offices.

'And it wasn't only Buddhists who took to the streets,' Paul continued, sipping his whisky. 'Government troops who had been under Thi's command joined them. It began to look as if the South was on the verge of civil war, with one half of the South Vietnamese army fighting the other half, and the Buddhist faction growing increasingly hostile toward the Americans.'

His foot continued to swing languidly, revealing striking purple socks. 'Ky dispatched two thousand troops to Da Nang and successfully quelled it, but in the process hundreds of rebel troops and countless Buddhists and civilians were killed. Now he needs to bring Hue to heel. When you've got yourself accredited, I'd like you to go up there. The Buddhist leader is Tri Quang, he's a *bonze*, which is the same thing as being a priest. I'd like to know what sort of a government it is that he wants, and who he would like to see leading it.'

'How do I get to Hue?' Gavin asked.

'With great difficulty!' Paul said with a flash of humor. 'Normally, once you're accredited, you travel by army helicopter. At the moment the Americans are steering clear of Da Nang and Hue, so you'll have to either drive up there or go by local bus.'

Gavin grinned. It was obvious what the setup was going to be. Paul would stay snugly in Saigon while he, Gavin, covered all the assignments in the less comfortable parts of the country. He didn't mind. It was the less comfortable parts of the country that he was interested in.

'Come on,' Paul said, slipping from the desk. 'Let's get you accredited. Until we've done that, you can't go anywhere. Have you got a couple of spare passport photographs with you?'

Gavin nodded, and the two men strolled out into the still-strong sunlight. The square, and the street leading off it, were as crowded and as noisy as they had been when Gavin had arrived.

Paul led the way into JUSPAO, the Joint United States Public Affairs Office. 'All American military announcements are made here,' he said. 'At eight o'clock every morning they put out a three- or four-page press statement, and every afternoon at five they hold a full press conference.'

'The Five O'Clock Follies?' Gavin asked, remembering what he had been told in Paris.

Paul's lopsided grin was in evidence again. 'You've heard about them?' he asked. 'Whenever you're in Saigon, it will be your responsibility to cover them. If a big story breaks, don't waste time by hurrying back to the office with it. Phone it through. In this game, seconds count.'

They walked into one of the countless offices, and a tough-looking marine gunnery sergeant thrust a couple of forms toward them. Minutes later, after handing over his passport photographs, Gavin possessed a little plastic-coated accreditation card that confirmed he was a member of the Vietnam press corps and that his priority for travel aboard U.S. military aircraft was equivalent to that of an American major.

'Phew!' Gavin whistled as they walked back through the maze of corridors to the entrance. 'That's quite impressive, isn't it? I hadn't reckoned on becoming a major overnight!'

'It's nothing,' Paul said dismissively. 'They give journalists the rank of major in case they're captured by the Viet Cong.'

'Why? What difference will being a major make?'

'Very little, I imagine,' Paul said dryly. 'But it is fondly presumed that officers will be treated with more respect than enlisted men. However, as the Viet Cong will also presume that an officer will be in possession of officer-level information, I find it a little disconcerting. Their methods for making people talk are not very refined. Especially if the poor bugger in question has no information to give!'

Gavin grimaced. 'No, it wouldn't be very nice,' he agreed, 'but I wouldn't have thought there was much risk of a journalist being taken prisoner. Surely the only prisoners being taken are pilots who are shot down during bombing raids over the North?'

Paul gave a Gallic shrug of his shoulders. 'They are most at risk, I agree, but American intelligence is pretty sure that some men who are listed as missing in action are being kept prisoner in the U-Minh forest, and in the border areas between South Vietnam and Cambodia and Laos.'

'Where is the U-Minh forest?' Gavin asked curiously as they strolled down a small side street and back into Tu Do Street.

'It's a godforsaken, snake-ridden, Viet Cong controlled tract of land deep in the Delta, where the Saigon military don't venture,' Paul said, waving his hand in greeting as a pretty European girl on a Lambretta called out his name.

'And do you think it's true?' Gavin persisted, intrigued. 'Do you think men are being held prisoner there?'

Again Paul shrugged. 'Who knows? There are certainly enough pilots being held in the North. We received reports of two more who were shot down last month and who have been classified as POWs, a Lieutenant Robert Peel and a Major Lawrence Guarino.'

Gavin was silent for a few minutes as they walked along the crowded street, past sidewalk cafés, where tables and chairs were shaded from the sun by gaily striped awnings. 'It's against the rules of the Geneva Convention,' he said at last.

Paul turned toward him, his brows rising high. '*Merde*! I had no idea you were a lawyer as well as a journalist.'

'I'm not,' Gavin said with a grin. 'I just have a talent for remembering odd nuggets of information. According to Article Nineteen of the Geneva Convention, prisoners of war may not be held in combat zones. And even if the Saigon military don't venture into the U Minh, it's still slap in the middle of a combat zone, isn't it?'

'I take it you've done quite a bit of boning

up on the situation out here?' Paul said, leading the way into a café that was blessedly quiet.

'A little.' Gavin grinned as he thought of the long hours of conversation about Vietnam with Gabrielle and Vanh. He patted his shirt's breast pocket and the piece of paper with Nhu's address on crackled reassuringly. Vanh had insisted that he visit Nhu immediately after he arrived in Saigon, and Gavin had promised that he would do so. However, now that he was here, he felt oddly reluctant to keep his promise.

Even though he had been in the city only a few hours, he realized there was very little fraternization between the Europeans living in the city and the Vietnamese – except for encounters between the bar girls and the soldiers, and between the shoeshine boys and taxi drivers and waiters and their clients. Any visit he made to a non-European part of the city would be glaringly conspicuous and one that might make things difficult for Nhu.

Paul had ordered two beers and Gavin picked up his ice-cold glass, drinking gratefully. He would postpone his visit to Nhu until his return from Hue. By then he would have a better feel for things.

Later that evening he met the other two members of the news bureau's staff. Lestor McDermott was a tall, bespectacled French-Canadian, slightly older than himself, and Jimmy Giddings was an American of unknown age who had been covering wars before either of his colleagues had been born.

'The difficulty with being a news-agency reporter in a war like this,' Jimmy Giddings said to him as the four men sat over drinks on the terrace at the Continental, 'is that ninety-nine percent of the time we're tied to reporting announcements. That is what the powers-that-be want, goddamn them. They don't want opinions and they don't want anything that deviates from what other news agencies are printing.'

'Surely it's different for out-of-town assignments? Situations that we report firsthand?'

Jimmy shook his head cynically. 'If you're thinking that you can trip off to Hue and file a report describing what you've seen there, and then have that report printed verbatim in the newspapers the bureau feeds, you're in for a big disappointment. Only the big guys, guys with regular bylines in *The New York Times* and the *Washington Post* and the *Daily Telegraph* can get away with having what they write treated as holy writ. We lesser mortals have to suffer having firsthand reports emasculated and reworded by our respective world-desk editors.'

'Depressing, huh?' Lestor said to Gavin with a wink. 'But I wouldn't worry about it if I were you. Rolling out of bed each day to attend the Follies is far more comfortable than trawling the countryside, risking your life for a scoop that some pencil-wielding bastard on the world desk will reduce to three lines.'

They all laughed, and Paul, noticing the ring that Gavin wore, asked about his wife.

Gavin had no desire to talk about Gabrielle to men who did not know her and who would not be able to even begin to imagine how wonderful she was. What would their response have been if he'd told them she was half Vietnamese? And that her uncle was a major in the North Vietnamese Army?

Gavin strode into the bureau's office, walking briskly across to Paul's desk. He'd bought khakis, helmet and canteen for himself that morning at the marketplace.

'I'm just about ready to leave,' he said as Paul looked up from the nightlead he was editing. 'I bumped into the Vietnamese who picked me up at the airport. He was able to get hold of a Mini-Moke for me, so I'm driving to Hue.'

Paul nodded, as if the acquisition of a Moke was so commonplace that it was unworthy of comment.

'Do you know the man?' Gavin continued. 'He's volunteered to go with me. Is he safe?'

'As a driver, no. In any other city in the world he would not even be given a license. However, if you mean is he safe from a security point of view, then the answer is unequivocally yes. Just don't let him drive. And Gavin...' He looked up again as another thought struck him. 'Remember you have to be patient when you're telephoning copy back to the office. The American military radiophones link into the old French telephone system, and you have to be connected from exchange to exchange all the way down the country. If you're unlucky, it can take up to two hours.'

'Thanks,' Gavin said dryly, hoping a delay filing copy would be the worst of his problems.

The name of his companion, sitting happily beside him as he drove out of Saigon was Tran Ngoc Huong.

'But all Vietnamese first names, last name,' he said helpfully. 'So my name Huong.'

Gavin nodded. He already knew most of the information that Huong gave him as they drove north in the searing heat of late morning, but he listened patiently, impressed by the fluency of Huong's self-taught English.

Although Hue was less than 500 miles from Saigon, it took them four days to reach it on roads congested with troops and refugees. They arrived to find a city in chaos. Government troops had cut off all essential food supplies in an effort to starve the Buddhists into submission. Rumors about what had happened, or had not happened, when the troops had stormed Da Nang, were rife. On May 26 a group of students and young workers burned down the USIS library; on May 31 they burned the U.S. Consulate.

In the midst of all the mayhem, the mayor of Hue, Lieutenant Colonel Pham Van Khoa, declared that he was no longer going to give the Buddhists his support and moved out of the city, taking the thousand troops under his command with him.

On June 8, when government troops finally entered Hue, the only resistance they encountered was of unarmed civilians. It was a resistance that was soon put down. By the time Gavin returned with Huong to Saigon three weeks later, he had seen Buddhist students forming human roadblocks across the avenues leading into the city, only to be mown down by machine-gun fire. During his stay he had seen women and children brutally manhandled; he had witnessed, in sick disbelief, an aged Buddhist nun burn herself alive before one of the city's central pagodas.

Even though he hadn't managed to interview Tri Quang, who was on a hunger strike, he knew he had achieved a great deal. He had entered Hue under almost impossible conditions, and he had filed copy under atrocious ones. He was so tired he could barely stand, and so hungry that he would have eaten whatever was put in front of him, however dubious. Above all, he was deeply satisfied. He hadn't liked what he had seen in Hue, but he had coped.

As he parked the Moke in front of the bureau's office in Tu Do Street, and as Huong bid him good-bye, he determined that the first thing he would do, after bathing and eating and sleeping, would be to contact Nhu.

Five minutes later he discovered that the

initiative had been taken from him. Her message lay on his desk. She would meet him at seven that evening, on the terrace of the Continental.

# CHAPTER FOURTEEN

Abbra didn't wait for Patti Maine to approve or disapprove of the finished synopsis. The mere act of writing it, of creating the character that had, until then, existed only nebulously in her head, had opened the floodgates of her imagination. She wrote with total, single-minded concentration for eight, and sometimes nine hours a day; she felt as if she'd discovered a whole new world, a world so magical, so absorbing, she didn't want to relinquish it even for a few days. By the time she received Patti's encouraging letter telling her that the synopsis was better than she had hoped and that she now wanted the first three chapters so she could sell the idea to a publisher, Abbra had already completed her second chapter.

'But surely you can take a break for just one weekend?' Scott asked her when he made his regular Thursday night telephone call.

It was the off season now, and Rosalie Bryansten had long ago been relegated to the position of an ex-girlfriend. She had had several successors, all of whose reigns had been equally brief. There was only one person Scott wanted to be with, and that was Abbra.

'I'd like to come down to L.A. for the weekend,' Abbra said truthfully. Scott had tickets for a film premiere, and she knew that if she went she would enjoy herself hugely. 'But I'm just two pages into chapter three, and it's going so well I hate the thought of setting it aside, even for a couple of days.'

Scott was in a telephone booth at the Beverly Hills. He bit his lip, trying hard to curb his disappointment. He had made a pact with himself. Even though he did not have enough willpower to stick to his resolution of never seeing her again, he had promised himself that he would never force the issue. If he tried to override her protestations, he would be doing exactly that.

'Okay,' he said with an easy indifference he was far from feeling. 'We'll make it another time. When chapter three is safely under your belt.'

She gave a little laugh, relief and disappointment inextricably mixed. 'I'll look forward to it,' she said sincerely. 'I'm scared to death about what will happen when chapter three is finished. Patti is sure that she will be able to get a contract on the strength of the synopsis and first three chapters, but what if she can't? What if no one is interested?'

'Patti Maine is a professional,' Scott said, wishing that he could reassure her with more than words. 'If she thinks a publisher will be interested in buying the book, then you can bet your life that they will.'

'But not even Patti has seen the first two

chapters yet. What if they don't live up to her expectations?' she asked, a note of panic creeping into her voice.

Scott chuckled, visualizing the expression on her face, her violet-blue eyes dark with self-doubt. 'You're too hard on yourself,' he said, hoping that she would interpret the love in his voice as brotherly affection. 'You had exactly the same worries over the synopsis. And they were groundless. The book is going to be great. Just try to relax and enjoy yourself while you're writing it.'

She giggled, her doubts fading as they always did in the face of Scott's boundless confidence. 'Okay, professor, I'll do exactly as you say, and I *am* enjoying myself. More than I've ever enjoyed anything before in my life. The minute I sit at the typewriter, and my eyes focus on the paper in front of me, my brain shuts out the rest of the world. I feel like Alice must have felt when she felt through the looking-glass. I just tumble into another world and the hours fly by and it's absolutely terrific.'

Scott's smile faded. He knew that she wasn't exaggerating. Over the last few months she had gained confidence in her talent and she now placed it first, before everything, which was fine by him because he loved and understood her and knew how important her writing was to her. But would it be okay with Lewis? Would Lewis understand, when there were army functions to attend, when she asked if she could be excused because she was in the middle of a chapter? From what he knew of his older brother, Scott doubted it very much.

'Have you written to Lewis about the book yet?' he asked casually, pretty sure that she hadn't.

The pause before she answered was so brief that no one but himself would have been aware of it.

'No.' Her voice was vaguely dismissive. 'I'm going to wait and see if anything comes of it before I do that.'

Scott leaned against the wall of the booth, his sun-bleached eyebrows drawing together in a frown. She had never even hinted that she was anything but deliriously happy and deeply in love with Lewis. Yet she wasn't sharing with him the most important thing that had ever happened to her. He wondered if she was aware that in all likelihood Lewis would disapprove of her writing. And if she was, he wondered what on earth she intended to do when Lewis came home.

It took her a month to finish the third chapter. The original draft had been finished in less than two weeks, but the prospect of mailing it off to Patti and hearing her reaction was so terrifying she wrote and rewrote until she was dizzy.

'Make a copy of it before you send it off,' Scott advised her when she telephoned him with the news that it was finally ready. 'And once you've sent it off, try to forget about it for a few days.' He hesitated for a moment and then said tentatively, 'There's going to be a march this coming weekend in New York. I'm going to fly out there to take part. Would you like to come and keep me company?'

She had no need to ask what the march was for. At Christmas, when President Johnson had ordered a halt to the bombing raids over North Vietnam, there had been a faint glimmer of hope that the war might end through a negotiated peace. That hope had died at the end of January when American jet bombers once again flew north. All through February and March there had hardly been a week when an antiwar demonstration had not taken place in some major American city.

'No,' she said quietly but without the least hesitation. 'You know that I can't, Scott.'

Alone in the apartment he had rented for the summer in Santa Monica, Scott shook his head in despair. The war in Vietnam, and the rights and wrongs of America's participation in it, was the only subject they did not agree on. Scott knew damn well what Abbra's true feelings were about the war. He also knew that if it hadn't been for her marriage to Lewis, and her loyalty to him, she would have participated in any and every peace demonstration. The previous year she had been first in line when students from her college marched in sympathy with the civil rights marchers in Selma. But where Vietnam was concerned, he knew she couldn't be true to her own instincts and judgment.

While antiwar demonstrators protested against the war in Washington, New York, and on campuses across the country, Lewis was risking his life daily and hourly in the cause they derided. For Abbra to march with them would be, for her, the most flagrant act of disloyalty toward Lewis imaginable.

'Then I shall march alone,' he said wryly.

She giggled. 'Hardly. The *Washington Post* predicts there'll be a big turnout.'

Four days later, the morning after the march, she saw that the *Washington Post* had been correct. Protestors jammed the streets of New York, and there was a photograph on one of the inner pages of a young, blond-haired English boy being hauled away by police, a placard declaring 'Johnson for Ex-President' and 'Where Is Lee Harvey Oswald Now That We Really Need Him?' still clutched in his hand. His name was Lance Blyth-Templeton and there was a further photograph of him being escorted to John F. Kennedy International Airport for deportation to England.

She sighed and pushed a silky-dark strand of hair away from her face. It had been two days since she had sent the first three chapters of her novel to Patti. It would be at least a week, possibly longer, before Patti read them and passed judgment on them, and until she did so Abbra knew that she wouldn't be able to concentrate on anything.

During her most recent writing binge, she

had been so immersed in her imaginary world that she hadn't read the newspapers. Now she read the *Washington Post* and the *Los Angeles Times* avidly. Both papers were full of reports of the Buddhist demonstrations taking place in Hue and Da Nang and culminating in grisly photographic coverage of a Buddhist nun immolating herself in the market square in Da Nang.

Lewis's letters did not mention the Buddhist campaign to oust Premier Ky. His initial enthusiasm at being a *co van truong*, and of being in a position to help the living standards of the villagers for the better, continued. At the end of April he wrote to her that a village girl who had been badly mistreated by her family was now working for him as a hooch-maid. 'Her name is Tam,' he wrote in a large, enviably neat hand, 'and she is so quick. I've been teaching her English and in only a few weeks she's become practically colloquial in it!'

It was the kind of letter that Abbra liked to receive. It made no mention of ambushes and search-and-destroy operations and death and killing, and she was able to imagine Lewis as more of a Peace Corps worker, helping the people to improve their harsh living conditions, than as a soldier.

It was several weeks before she received her long awaited telephone call from Patti.

'I'm sorry to have kept you waiting so long, Abbra,' she said cheerily. Abbra's knuckles clutched the receiver so tightly they were white. 'I've been in London and flew back only five days ago. While I was there I showed your synopsis to a publishing friend and he was very interested. He said that if the opening chapters lived up to the promise of the synopsis then he wanted to have first refusal.'

'And do they?' Abbra's voice was a croak.

'The chapters are wonderful!' Patti said, her throaty voice full of laughter at Abbra's barely concealed anxiety. 'Although first novels are usually difficult to place, I'm sure we won't have a problem finding a publisher. I'm sending copies to my London friend immediately, and also to a New York publisher who is building up a new list and who has expressed an interest.'

Abbra leaned her head weakly against the wall. It was all happening just as Patti had said. A publisher was already interested in her novel and it wasn't even finished yet.

'Are you still there?' Patti asked.

Abbra laughed. 'Yes. I'm just trying to believe that all this is actually happening. How long do you think it will be before you hear from the publisher in London?'

'It could be a week, and it could be four,' Patti said practically. 'Leave all the worrying about publishers and contracts to me. Your job, Abbra, is to write the book and to make sure that the remaining twenty or twenty-five chapters are as good as the first three.'

For the next six weeks she didn't see Scott. She didn't see anyone. To her mother's increasing irritation, she stayed almost permanently in her bedroom, her fingers flying over the typewriter keys as she transferred the vivid images in her head onto paper.

'I'm glad it's going so well,' Scott said to her when he made his usual Thursday night call. 'How many chapters have you finished now?'

'Seven?'

'Which is how many pages?'

'A hundred and forty.'

He whistled. 'So you're a third of the way there?'

When she had discussed the book with him in the early stages, she had told him that she thought it would run to about four hundred pages.

'I'm not sure. The more I write, the more I seem to want to write. I think it's going to be longer than I first anticipated. Do you think it will matter?'

She had already signed a contract with the British publisher who had been interested in the synopsis, and a deal had been made with a New York publishing house. The book was going to be published in hardback in Great Britain and in paperback in the United States.

'I don't think so, not unless it's going to be several hundred pages longer than you first projected. Is it in any shape for me to see yet?'

So far she had shown him everything that she had written. The synopsis. The opening chapters.

'Yes.' She wanted Scott to read what she

had written. His remarks were always on target and his boundless enthusiasm bolstered her spirits. 'I would have sent the last few chapters down to you, but I've been so busy writing that I haven't had time to have them copied.'

'Never mind mailing them down,' Scott said firmly. 'Bring them down. It's my birthday on Saturday, and Dad is flying in for a celebration dinner. I've reserved a table at the Polo Lounge for three.'

She could tell by the tone of his voice that to try to refuse would be pointless, and besides, she didn't want to refuse.

'I'll be there,' she promised. 'I'll drive down and stay at the Jamaica Bay.'

The Jamaica Bay, where Abbra had stayed on previous trips to L.A., was on Admiralty Way, just off Marina del Rey and though only four minutes from L.A.X., its beach was superb.

'Okay. I'll pick you up about six and we'll have drinks before meeting up with Dad.'

The days when he would have tried to persuade her to stay at his apartment rather than at a hotel were long gone. That type of arrangement would have been pure torture.

'What do you think?' she asked nervously when he'd finished the last page.

For the past hour he hadn't spoken. They were sitting at table one in the Polo Lounge, and while she had toyed with Pacific bay shrimp and sipped at a glass of Pinot Chardonnay, Scott had been reading the new chapters.

He laid the typewritten pages down on the table and looked across at her, a broad grin on his face. 'I think you're a very clever lady, Mrs Ellis. If you're not careful you're going to be such a huge success that you'll be able to live permanently in the Beverly Hills Hotel!'

She leaned back against the banquette, laughing with relief.

'Do you really think it's good? I've become so involved in the life of the woman I'm writing about that there are times when I feel as if I am her! The next few chapters are set in Boston, and so I'm going there for a few days to walk in her footsteps, so to speak.'

'It sounds like fun.' He hadn't planned anything important for the next few weeks. He could easily fit in a trip to Boston. And if he did, the gossips would have had a field day. He was well aware that his close relationship with his sister-in-law was being commented on, and he lived in dread that the prurient speculation would come to Abbra's attention. He knew her well enough to know gossip might cause her to see far less of him.

He said with forced lightness, overcoming the temptation of Boston with difficulty, 'You haven't wished me a happy birthday yet.'

Her eyes flew wide, a look of horror crossing her face. 'Scott! I'm so sorry! I was so keyed up about your reaction to the book that

I completely forgot!'

He sighed in exaggerated disappointment, shaking his head of curly blond hair in mock despair. 'I don't know, Abbra. I act as a Svengali to you, advising you on every single word you write; I wine and dine you at the most prestigious watering hole in the entire damned country, and what do I get for my pains? Not even a birthday card!'

She had begun to laugh. When she was with Scott, she was always laughing. 'Idiot,' she said affectionately. 'Not only have I brought you a card, I've also brought you a present.'

She reached down into her handbag, which was tucked discreetly beneath the table, and withdrew a card and small gold-wrapped box tied with scarlet ribbon and topped with a scarlet bow.

'Happy birthday,' she said in the soft, low-modulated voice that he loved so much. 'I hope you like them.'

If she had bought him nothing but a ten-cent stick of gum, he would have treasured it for the rest of his life.

The card was a reproduction of Renoir's 'Luncheon of the Boating Party' from the Phillips Collection in the Washington Gallery, and she had signed it simply 'Abbra'. The small box contained a pair of gold, black-faced cameo cuff links.

He kept his head low over the box for a few seconds, knowing that the expression in his eyes was too revealing. When at last he raised his head and looked across at her, his hazel eyes were light and laughing, totally carefree.

'Thank you very much, sister-in-law mine,' he said, resisting the temptation to lean across and kiss her. 'From now on I'll be able to shoot my cuffs with style and panache.'

Style and panache were such an inherent part of his personality that she laughed, her cheeks dimpling. 'I'm glad you like them,' she said, turning her head as her father-in-law's tall shadow fell over them.

'Abbra my dear. You look well. How is Lewis liking his new role as a *co van truong*?' he asked, sitting down next to her. 'Is he making the most of it?'

She nodded. 'Yes. It's given him an opportunity to improve the living standards of the villagers who are living under his jurisdiction.'

Her father-in-law raised his eyebrows. 'He's there to root out Viet Cong, my dear,' he said baldly, 'not play at being a welfare officer.'

Scott raised a hand protestingly. 'No Vietnam,' he said good-naturedly but with steely firmness. 'This is a birthday celebration. *My* birthday celebration, and I don't want it ruined with controversy.'

'There's no controversy between Abbra and myself,' his father said with asperity. 'She understands what the war is about and why Lewis is out there. Which is a damned sight more than those fools who took part in that antiwar demonstration in New York.'

Scott's jawline had tightened and he leaned across the table toward his father, his body taut with tension.

'Listen to me for a moment, Dad. I was—'

Abbra interrupted him with feverish haste. 'You'd better get ready to blow out some candles, Scott. There's a cart heading this way with a cake on it.'

Scott's eyes widened in stunned disbelief.

'Happy birthday, sir,' the waiter said, wheeling the cart to the side of their table.

The cake was iced in lemon, decorated by the figure of a football player wearing a Rams shirt emblazoned with Scott's number, and surrounded by flickering candles.

'Who the devil...' he began, forgetting the fight he was just about to have with his father.

'Everyone should have a cake on their birthday,' Abbra said, wondering for a fleeting moment if she had misjudged his reaction to her surprise.

He began to laugh, taking hold of her hand and squeezing it tight. 'I might have guessed! Hell, I haven't had a birthday cake since I was eight years old!'

'Are you going to blow the candles out, sir?' the waiter asked.

'You have to make a wish,' Abbra reminded him.

He had reluctantly removed his hand from hers, and for a brief moment the smile on his face was rueful. He sure as hell couldn't wish for what he really wanted.

'Come on,' Abbra urged him, laughing. 'You have to blow them all out at once, remember.'

He took a deep breath, blowing them out with ease, not wishing for the thing he really wanted, Abbra's presence at his side as his wife. Instead, he wished that she would be with him on his next birthday, and his next and his next and his next.

'Would your wife like a slice of cake now?' the waiter was asking.

Scott stared at him, momentarily shaken at how the innocent query had dovetailed with his private thoughts.

Abbra had flushed rosily. It was an understandable mistake. She had ordered the cake in her own name, and her name was, after all, Ellis. But she found the assumption that she was Scott's wife strangely disconcerting.

Only Colonel Ellis seemed unperturbed by the waiter's error. 'Mrs Ellis is the wife of my older son, who is serving in Vietnam,' he said, oblivious to the sudden strain on Scott's face. 'Do you want a slice of cake now, Abbra, or when we've finished dinner?'

'When we've finished dinner,' she said, the flush in her cheeks dying slowly.

'I'm sorry, madam,' the waiter said. 'I'm very sorry, sir.'

As he made his apologies and wheeled the trolley and cake away, she tried to catch Scott's eye, wanting to laugh with him over the waiter's mistake, knowing that once they had joked about it, she would feel more comfortable.

'What a silly mistake for anyone to have

made,' Scott said lightly, picking up the leather-bound menu. 'As if I could be so lucky!' And though his voice was light and careless, he didn't laugh, and his eyes didn't meet hers, and her uneasiness was a long time in dying.

Abbra flew to Boston. She had written Lewis about her plans for visiting the East Coast in her regular weekly letter to him, but not the reason behind her trip. She would do that later, she promised herself, when her book was finished. She had two hundred pages finished now, and the book had become such a vital part of her life that she couldn't imagine how she had existed in her non-writing days.

As she strolled the streets, walking in the footsteps of Maddie, her heroine, it was as if Maddie were walking at her side, as if she actually existed. There were times when, if Scott had been with her, she knew she would have been saying, 'That's the corner of the Common where Maddie met Rory,' and 'That's the restaurant where she learned about her son's illness.' It was a strange, beguiling sensation, visiting scenes where events conjured in her imagination had taken place, and where now, as she visited them, it seemed as though they actually had taken place.

'Did you travel to Boston by yourself?' Patti asked her as they lunched in an elegant French restaurant near her office, celebrating the news that Abbra's British publisher was delighted with the first two hundred pages of the novel.

Abbra nodded. 'Yes. I thought that having someone with me would be a distraction, though there were dozens of times when I wanted to show Scott places I had written about.'

Patti laid down her fork and leaned back in her chair. When she had asked if Abbra had traveled to Boston alone, Patti had been wondering if Abbra had taken her mother with her, or a female friend. She hadn't imagined for a moment that she might have taken her brother-in-law.

She asked, intrigued, 'Do you and Scott often take trips together?'

'No,' Abbra said guilelessly, spearing a button mushroom with her fork, two shiny wings of night-black hair swinging forward slightly and brushing her cheeks. 'Not unless you count flying to places like Denver and San Diego to watch him play.'

'But you think he would have enjoyed the Boston trip?' Patti prompted.

Abbra took a sip of her wine and smiled. 'Yes. I think Maddie has become as real to him as she is to me.'

Lunch could wait, Patti decided. She had been curious before about Abbra's relationship with the fabled Scott Ellis. Now she was determined that her curiosity would be satisfied.

'And what about Lewis?' she asked. 'Is

Maddie real to him too?'

Abbra pushed her plate away and leaned back in her chair, but with none of the Patti's sense of leisured ease. 'No,' she said with a slight frown. 'I can't really share the book with Lewis. He has so much on his mind in Vietnam. It would seem—' She hesitated, and then said reluctantly, 'It would seem trivial somehow to be writing to him about a novel.'

Patti's brows rose slightly. 'But it isn't trivial to you, is it?'

'No.' Abbra flashed her a vivid, wide smile. 'It's the most important thing that's ever happened to me. Apart from my marrying Lewis, of course.'

'Of course,' Patti agreed a trifle dryly, her curiosity far from slaked. 'Are Scott and Lewis very much alike? Is that why you spend so much time with Scott? Because it's like being with Lewis?'

Abbra burst into laughter. 'Good heavens, no! They're nothing alike! Lewis is very much a military man. Very correct and precise. Scott is just the opposite, very happy-go-lucky and devil-may-care. I doubt Lewis has ever been to a football game in his life, and Scott's whole existence is focused on the game. I can't truthfully think of any one thing they have in common.'

Patti rested her elbow on the arms of her chair and steepled her fingers together, lowering her chin. Far from being cleared up, the mystery was deepening. 'Then I'm sorry, Abbra,' she said with her usual directness.

'But I really don't know why you and Scott spend so much time together.'

Abbra stared at her. 'But it's very clear,' she said at last, struggling to come to terms with the fact that Patti obviously thought it was strange. 'I mean, we're family. He's my brother-in-law. It's only natural that I go and watch him play, isn't it?'

Patti tilted her head slightly to one side, her blond bouffant hairdo resembling a halo. 'Scott used to be a regular item in the gossip column,' she said musingly. 'Wherever he went, there was always a gorgeous model or movie star clinging to his arm. These last six months there's been no one.' She paused and then said, her voice carefully free of insinuating intonation. 'Apart from yourself, of course.'

Abbra's face had gone white. 'Is that how it looks?' she asked at last, her voice taut. 'As if there were something ... not quite right about our relationship?'

Patti felt a twinge of remorse. She hadn't meant to distress Abbra, just discover exactly what sort of relationship she had with Scott. But if Abbra was unaware of the speculation the two of them were arousing, then she didn't really regret bringing the subject out into the open. It was inevitable that someday, someone would ask, and it was better that the question come from her rather than from a prying journalist.

Abbra had risen to her feet, her hands shaking slightly as she picked up her clutch bag. 'I think I'd better go now, Patti. It's been a lovely lunch, and I'm more excited than I can say about the British deal but I've got a lot of work still to do on the book and I think I should get back to San Francisco and start it.'

Patti nodded. She knew why Abbra was cutting and running, but if it had never occurred to Abbra before that her relationship with Scott was one that was likely to cause gossip, then maybe it was good that she had been made aware of it, and that she give it some thought.

'If you want to talk to me about anything, please don't hesitate to call,' she said, rising to her feet, and kissing Abbra affectionately on the cheek.

Abbra forced a small smile. 'Thanks, Patti. I'll remember. Bye.'

She walked quickly from the restaurant, attracting admiring glances from a group of businessmen at a nearby table. She had driven down to Los Angeles the previous afternoon, and had booked into the Jamaica Bay for two nights. After her lunch with Patti she planned to so some shopping and then, at five o'clock, she had arranged to meet Scott at the Fine Arts Museum. From there they had planned to go to the movies or the theater.

She flagged down a taxi outside the restaurant and asked to be taken, not to Rodeo Drive and the shops, but back to her hotel. She couldn't see Scott. Not now. She sat in the back of the taxi, her knuckles white.

She had met Patti Maine only a half dozen times, but she knew her well enough to know that she didn't speak carelessly. If Patti thought there was something wrong about her relationship with Scott, and had had the honesty to tell her so, then other people must be thinking so too. She remembered the waiter at the Polo Lounge and the innocent mistake that he had made. Major football stars were always targets for gossip, and the press loved nothing better than to insure that the gossip reached as wide an audience as possible. The mere thought of a story insinuating that Scott had abandoned all his previous girlfriends in order to escort his sister-in-law around town made Abbra feel physically ill. No one who knew them would believe the insinuations for a moment, but they would still distress her father-in-law and her own parents.

She stepped out of the taxi at the Jamaica Bay and hurried through the lobby to her room. All sorts of things were suddenly making sense. The speculative expression in some of Scott's teammates' eyes and the quickly suppressed laughter whenever she and Scott joined them for drinks or a meal.

She threw her jacket and her clutch bag on to the bed and reached for the telephone, asking for an outside line. And there had been that odd incident, months ago now, when Scott had been involved in a fight. It had been so unlike him; he was so easygoing and even-tempered. Scott had said merely that the guy he had decked had said something to which he had taken exception. With sudden certainty she now knew what that something had been.

She dialed his number, her fingers still trembling. They couldn't continue seeing each other as they had been doing. Sooner or later a gossip columnist would get hold of the story and milk it for all it was worth. He wouldn't care. She knew that. But she cared *for* him. She didn't want to see ugly speculations being printed about him.

'Scott Ellis's office,' the woman from his service answered.

Her breath was tight in her throat. For a second she was tempted to put the receiver down and to try again later, and then she knew that if she waited, her resolution would fail.

'It's Abbra,' she said, forcing her voice to be steady. 'Please tell Scott I've decided not to stay overnight in L.A. After having lunch with my agent I realized how much work I have to do on the book and I've decided to go away for a while so that I can concentrate.'

As the woman thanked her and hung up, Abbra closed her eyes tight. She wouldn't be seeing him again. Perhaps not for months. There were a hundred and one things she wanted to say to him. She wanted to tell him about the British book deal. She wanted to show him the chapter she had finished writing on Friday.

She wanted, quite simply, to be with him.

The realization was cataclysmic. She stood, still holding the telephone receiver in her hand, staring blindly in front of her. When had it happened? In the name of God, how had it happened?

Clumsily she replaced the telephone receiver.

'Oh, God,' she whispered, not moving, standing as immobile as a pillar of salt. 'Oh, dear, dear God!' And then her tears began to fall, sliding down her cheeks, splashing unrestrainedly onto her hands and her dress.

# CHAPTER FIFTEEN

To Serena's surprise Rupert was waiting for her at Heathrow when she landed.

'In the message you left on my answering machine, you said you would be in the shop on Tuesday morning, so I assumed you would be flying back today.'

'But how did you know which flight I would be on?' she asked as he kissed her chastely on the temple and swung her Louis Vuitton suit-case from the trolley she had been pushing.

'It wasn't exactly a masterpiece of detective work,' he said in his habitual amused drawl. 'Flights aren't pouring in from Alabama on the hour, every hour. This was the only flight you could possibly be on, assuming, of course, that you hadn't fled the wilds of Alabama for the more civilized fleshpots of Los Angeles or New York.'

Despite her fatigue after the long flight, she giggled and tucked her hand affectionately through the crook of his arm. 'It could have been a temptation,' she said dryly. 'Fort Rucker, Alabama, isn't the most alluring place in the world.'

'Fort where?' Rupert asked in deepening amusement as they stepped out of the arrivals bay and into brilliant sunshine.

'Fort Rucker.'

When she saw him waiting to greet her, she had made an instant decision. She wasn't in love with him, not in the way she was in love with Kyle, but over the last few months he had been enormous fun, both as an employer and a lover. It would be a year before she would see Kyle again, and she saw no reason why Rupert shouldn't continue to be enormous fun. And why he shouldn't also become a friend.

'Would it be impertinent of me to ask why anyone in their right mind would wish to leave London and the delights of Annabel's and Regine's, for a place that sounds as if it's straight out of a Civil War novel?'

They had reached his Lagonda and he tossed her suitcase into the trunk, opening the front passenger seat door for her, regarding her quizzically.

Serena stepped into the car, leaning her head comfortably back against the luxurious headrest. It seemed that in her absence Rupert had also come to some decisions about their relationship. Until then he hadn't asked any questions about her private life. He knew about her elopement and the subsequent razzmatazz that had attended her wedding, but he had never questioned her about Kyle and their subsequent, immediate separation. Now, it seemed, he too wanted to take on the role of a friend, in whom confidences could be safely placed.

'Fort Rucker is a U.S. Army Advanced Helicopter Training School.'

Rupert, who had driven the Lagonda smoothly out of the airport parking lot and onto the A4, nearly drove off the side of the road.

A smile curved Serena's mouth. 'Don't worry, Rupert. I'm not thinking of becoming a female air ace. I went there to see Kyle.'

He looked across at her, one eyebrow rising slightly. 'I hadn't realized the two of you were even on speaking terms.'

Serena's smile deepened. 'We haven't been. Which is why I flew to Alabama. I wanted to rectify the situation.'

He was silent for a minute or two, driving at high speed toward the outskirts of Hounslow. 'And did you succeed?' he asked at last, a slight note of tension creeping into his upper-class drawl.

'Oh, yes,' she said, knowing quite well the direction his thoughts were going and enjoying his probing. 'As reunions go, it was definitely eight point nine on the Richter scale.' Her smile faded and she said in sudden seriousness, 'Joking apart, Rupert, it really was the most wonderful reunion. I'm in love with Kyle, heaven only knows why, but I am.'

'And so no divorce?' he asked, keeping his eyes on the road ahead of him.

'No divorce.'

'And no more friendly nights in my company at Annabel's or Regine's?' he asked, taking the turn off for Kew.

'Kyle is going to Vietnam,' she said, a shadow darkening her eyes. 'He's going to be there for a year and I don't imagine for one instant that he's going to spend that year in a state of celibate faithfulness. It wouldn't be in his nature.'

He had turned his head swiftly toward her when she had said the word *Vietnam*, shock flaring across his face. Now he said curiously, 'And is it in yours?'

She pushed a heavy fall of pale blond hair away from her face and over her shoulder. 'No,' she said, unabashed. 'I can't see what difference my going to bed with you makes to my relationship with Kyle. In fact, it's probably beneficial. After all, a steady relationship with one person has to be far preferable than a year-long succession of one-night stands, hasn't it?'

'It's one way of looking at it,' he agreed, both amused at her unsentimental practicality and disturbed by the thought of Kyle Anderson, flying out to South Vietnam and God only knew what kind of a fate.

'It's the way Kyle would look at it,' Serena said with such conviction that he found himself partially believing her. As they sped past the entrance to Kew Gardens, she changed the subject. 'Has Lance got himself into any more scrapes while I've been away?'

'Not that I am aware of.' There was an undertone of indifference in Rupert's voice. At thirty-two, he felt himself too old to be in sympathy with the students who regularly massed outside the American Embassy in Grosvenor Square, chanting antiwar slogans and generally making a confounded nuisance of themselves. If he had any politics at all, they veered toward the right, and he had very little patience with Lance or his revolutionary pretensions.

He turned into King's Road and looked across at her curiously. 'How does Lance feel about having an American for a brother-in-law, especially one who is a member of the armed services?'

She turned her head quickly away from him, before he could see the anguish that had sprung into her eyes. 'He doesn't like it,' she said briefly, with a slight dismissive shrug of her shoulders, as if his not liking it was unimportant. 'You could hardly expect him to, could you?'

'I don't suppose so,' he said easily, heading toward Serena's family home in Cheyne Walk, well aware of the distress his careless question had aroused, and unpleasantly shocked by it. Serena wasn't the kind of girl to become distressed without genuine cause, and he could only imagine that Lance's reaction had been extreme.

'There are a couple of important house sales taking place in Kent this weekend,' he said, making a left-hand turn into an exclusive mews. He drew up before a glossily painted white door flanked by bay trees in terracotta pots and by tubs of geraniums and lobelia and trailing pansies. 'Why don't we both go? We can stay at the Grand at Eastbourne and make a weekend of it.'

'That would be nice,' she said, stepping out of the car, her eyes meeting his, her voice once more perfectly under control. 'What kind of sales are they? Georgian? Regency?'

'Georgian. Primarily glass and silver. There should be some interesting bargains to be had.'

He swung her suitcase out of the trunk and decided not to invite himself in for a drink. She'd had a long flight, and signs of strain and tiredness were beginning to shadow her eyes.

'Don't bother coming in tomorrow,' he said as she searched in her clutch bag for her key. 'Stay in bed all day and have a good rest. Wednesday will be soon enough to be back at the battle stations.'

As she fit her key into the lock she turned toward him with an affectionate smile. 'I might just do that, Rupert. Are you coming in for coffee or a drink of something a little stronger?'

He shook his head. 'No,' he said, and knew that she was relieved. 'I've things to do, people to see. Remember to pack a sensible pair of flat shoes as well as gladrags for our Kent and Sussex trip.'

'Flat shoes?' she asked, laughing despite the strain that thoughts of Lance had aroused. 'What on earth do I need a pair of flat shoes for? I don't think I even possess a pair!'

'Then you should,' Rupert said practically,

gunning the Lagonda's engine into life. 'A walk over Beachy Head before breakfast on Sunday morning is an obligatory part of a weekend in Eastbourne.' He leaned his head out of the window as the car began to pull away. 'And bring a scarf as well!' he called out. 'It can be devilish windy, even in June!'

She raised a hand, waving goodbye, and then stepped into the house with her suitcase, closing the door behind her.

*Lance.* Incredibly, all the time she had been with Kyle, she hadn't given him a single thought. Leaving the suitcase in the tiny hall, she walked through into the sun-filled living room. She hadn't even asked Rupert if Lance had been telephoning the shop, asking where she was. If he had, and if Rupert had told him that she had gone to Alabama, then he would have known why she had gone there. And he would be prepared for the news she was about to break to him.

And if he hadn't telephoned the shop? If he was unaware that she had even left the country? She moved slowly across the room toward the telephone. Then he wouldn't have the slightest inkling that a reunion between herself and Kyle was even a possibility. He, and her parents, and all her friends, believed that her marriage was dead, and that it was only a question of time before a divorce buried it once and for all. The information that her marriage was far from dead, that it was, instead, very much alive and kicking, would devastate Lance, and might destroy the closeness that had been reforged between them. It wasn't the kind of news that could be broken over the telephone, and she didn't even try.

'Would you like to come over for a drink tonight?' she asked, chewing the corner of her lip as she waited for his reply.

'You sound suspiciously formal,' he said cautiously. 'What is this? An invitation to meet a new, godawful boyfriend?'

'No.' She kept her voice light despite her deepening apprehension. 'I've been away for a few days and I'm tired, and I fancy an evening at home. With family.'

By family, Lance correctly assumed that she meant only the two of them.

'Okay,' he said agreeably. 'I'll be there in about an hour and a half, but I shan't be able to stay for very long. I have a meeting to go to at eight.'

She said good-bye to him and walked tiredly upstairs to run herself a bath, wondering whether the purpose of his meeting was the planning of yet another anti-Vietnam war demonstration.

An hour later, feeling marginally refreshed, she switched on the television in order to catch the early evening news. It was dominated, as usual, by the events in Vietnam. Two weeks before, unmoved and uninterested, she would have quickly changed channels. Now, knowing that Kyle was going there, she watched avidly.

There was a clip of film showing helicopters flying through heavy ground fire on an operation named Nathan Hale. According to the news, it was being fought by the 101st Airborne and 1st Cavalry Divisions. She wasn't sure, but she thought Kyle had said he was going to be with the 1st Cav. The idea bothered her even though she knew he hadn't arrived yet. She poured herself a gin and tonic, wincing as one of the helicopters took a direct hit. The film clip ended. The reporter announced in a monotone that Hanoi had rejected the new American proposal for peace talks, and was reiterating its demand that an unconditional bombing halt precede any negotiations.

Premier Ky's jaunty image flashed onto the screen, and the newscaster informed viewers that after smashing anti-government resistance in Saigon, Hue, and other major cities, Premier Ky had applied for conciliation and forgiveness for the 'misunderstandings of the war'.

There was then a short piece of film from Paris, where students were rioting, followed by a brief news item about the Beatles.

She moved away from the television to pour herself another drink, grateful that at least there hadn't been a report of any antiwar demonstrations with protestors being hauled away by the police. Her father still hadn't recovered from the ignominy of Lance's very public deportation from America.

The next program was an inane game show,

and she turned the television off, wishing passionately for the hundredth time that Lance were not so left wing in his views, and so virulently anti-American. She was just about to wander into the kitchen and make herself a sandwich when she heard the unmistakable sound of his MG turning into the mews.

She hadn't bothered to dress, and she pulled the tie belt on her white terry bathrobe a little tighter around her waist, smiling wryly to herself as it occurred to her that she was metaphorically girding up her loins.

'My God! You really *aren't* going anywhere tonight, are you?' he said in amazement as he walked into the room, a bottle of Kahlua in one hand. 'I bought this with me just in case you had nothing else for the vodka but the revolting tonic water you pour in your gin.'

He looked, as he always looked to Serena, heartachingly young, as if he were years her junior and not her twin. His arms seemed to be too long for his jacket, though it had been tailored in Savile Row. With loving amusement Serena reflected that Lance never allowed his left-wing views to deny him the luxuries he had always taken for granted. His wrists protruded from his sleeves bonily, with all the awkwardness of a young adolescent's. Even though his hair was obligatorily shoulder-length, it still didn't look quite as reactionarily unkempt as he no doubt wished it to. Silky-straight and blond, like her own, it served only to make him look more feminine and more touchingly vulnerable.

'You said you'd been away for a few days. Where did you go? Paris? Rome?' Without waiting for an answer, he strolled across to the rosewood cocktail cabinet and poured himself a large vodka. 'I know exactly how you spend your year, and it doesn't include being away in June, when it's the Derby and Ascot and Wimbledon.'

'What does it include?' Serena asked, intrigued, glad of the opportunity to delay breaking her news to him.

He splashed some Kahlua into his vodka, added a generous amount of ice, and said with a grin, 'January in the sun in Cape Town, to the shame of your politically unaware heart. Skiing in Europe in February and March. Home to an English spring at Bedingham in April. Monaco and the Grand Prix in early May, and then on to St. Tropez for the last two weeks of the month. June in England for the aforementioned Derby and Ascot and Wimbledon and, also, as you're a cricket fan, the first and second Tests. A week in Ibiza to break up July, then back to England and Bedingham in August for the beginning of grouse shooting on the glorious twelfth. September is a month-long house party in St. Tropez, October starts in Paris for the Arc de Triomphe and ends in New York, and in November you hare off to the West Indies, coming home to Bedingham, of course, for Christmas.'

'Idiot,' she said, perching on the arm of the

sofa. 'I haven't been to the Arc de Triomphe in years.'

'The rest of it is pretty accurate though,' he said with a grin. 'Or it was until this year and your sudden, inexplicable decision to work for Rupert.'

His brows were raised questioningly. She knew he wanted to know if she was sleeping with Rupert and she decided not to satisfy his curiosity. It would only make what she was going to say to him even more complicated.

'I haven't been to Rome, or Paris,' she said carefully. 'I've been to Alabama.'

'Alabama?' There was blank incomprehension in his eyes. She realized with something of a shock that he knew nothing of Kyle's whereabouts, or what he had been doing for the past ten months.

'There is a United States Army Advanced Helicopter Training School in Alabama,' she said, trying to keep her voice light and easy. 'Since we never talk about Kyle I hadn't realized that you didn't know he had spent nearly all of last year training to be an army helicopter pilot.'

'Training to be a *what*? Christ! I thought he was at fucking Princeton!'

'It shows how long it is since you've spoken to Daddy. I thought he would have told you months ago about Kyle joining the army.'

'Why should anyone in our family talk about Kyle Anderson? Or give a fuck about whatever it is that he's doing? He's history, for Christ's sake! A past event! I didn't think we were even going to celebrate the divorce when it comes through, because doing so would be to acknowledge his existence!'

Her eyes held his. 'Kyle is not a past event,' she said quietly.

He slammed his drink down so hard, vodka and Kahlua splashed onto the cocktail cabinet's rosewood surface. 'No, by God! I don't suppose he is! Not if you've been flying to bloody Alabama to see him!'

They hadn't had a row since the ghastly scene on her wedding day. She said, keeping her voice steady with difficulty, 'I'm in love with Kyle, Lance. It's something you're going to have to accept...'

'I bloody well do not have to accept it!' he shouted, spittle gathered at the corners of his mouth, his fists clenched, his pale face contorted with anger.

He had faced her with exactly the same expression in his voice and eyes when he had been seven and she had ridden his brand new bicycle into Bedingham's lake, and when he had been fifteen and their parents had decreed that she could holiday with friends in the Caribbean, but that he must stay home because his school report had been poor.

In both instances they had fought fiercely, but it had been over within an hour. She had waded waist-deep into the lake, retrieving the bicycle herself, much to her mother's horror. And she had told her parents that if Lance wasn't allowed to go to the Caribbean, then she wasn't going either. And she hadn't. She had spent the holiday in question at Bedingham, with Lance.

She ran a hand through her hair, pushing it away from her face. 'Please be reasonable, Lance. You don't have to speak to Kyle. You don't have to see him. All you have to do is to accept that he's the person I'm married to and...'

'An American army pilot!' he spat out. 'No doubt he joined the bloody army so that he could go to Vietnam and burn babies and rape underage girls and murder old women and bomb the North!'

The tight rein that Serena had been exercising over her patience snapped. 'Don't be so utterly ridiculous!' she flared, jumping to her feet and marching across to the cocktail cabinet. 'I don't know about the babies and the underage girls and the old women, but I do know that he won't be bombing the North! He's flying a helicopter, for Christ's sake! Not a B-52 bomber!'

She poured more tonic into her glass, her hand shaking, appalled at her intense reaction to the hideous images Lance's words had conjured up. Until her reunion with Kyle, she had barely given Vietnam a thought. Now she found herself unable to think of anything else. He would be there soon. Shortly he would be a part of the savagery. When protestors marched through the streets of London and Washington with placards declaring 'Don't turn our sons into killers', it was Kyle, and young men like him, that they were referring to.

Lance was so stunned that she knew the difference between a helicopter and a bomber that he temporarily forgot his rage, and the reason for it. 'It's not only B-52s that are flying over the North, they have F-8 Crusaders and F-2 Phantoms and E-2 radar planes as well. All the poor bloody North Vietnamese have is a handful of MiG fighters.'

For a brief second, thinking of the atrocities that were no doubt taking place in Vietnam, and which might reach out and touch Kyle, Serena had been stunned to find herself near tears. She despised easy emotionalism and she checked herself instantly, telling herself that her transatlantic flight had left her more tired than she had previously supposed.

'Let's call a truce, Lance,' she said wearily. 'If I can forgive you for your demonstrations and marches, and for the unpleasant press attention you attract to yourself, surely you can forgive me for marrying and staying married to Kyle?'

'But your marrying *anyone* is so bloody pointless!' The white heat of his anger had died and his voice was thick with misery and jealous frustration. 'You're not exactly in need of financial protection, are you? And what other reason is there for any woman to marry?'

His bewilderment was so genuine that despite her fatigue there was laughter in her voice. 'Darling brother mine, I can think of one or two reasons, but I doubt if you would regard them as being rational ones.'

'That's your whole bloody trouble,' he said petulantly. 'You never *are* rational! You never think about anything seriously and neither does Kyle bloody Anderson. He's gone out there, quite willing to kill and maim, and I don't suppose he knows any more about Vietnam, or the Vietnamese struggle for liberation, than you do.'

'No,' Serena said agreeably, too relieved that Lance was now being merely sulky, and that they were no longer on the verge of an appalling fight to take exception to his assumption that Kyle would be killing and maiming with impunity. 'I don't suppose he does.'

The last of Lance's anger ebbed away and only irritation remained. 'I don't know how anyone so bright can be so ignorant,' he said.

She grinned. 'I presume you are referring to me, and not Kyle?'

He snorted with derision at the thought of saying anything complimentary, however obliquely, about Kyle.

'Well,' she said, changing the subject, 'at least I don't get myself arrested, brother mine. How many times have you been taken into custody this year for disturbing the peace? Six? Seven times?'

It had been seven times, but the next time a Blyth-Templeton found themselves in the middle of controversy, and consequently in the gossip columns of the nations newspapers, it wasn't Lance who stood there. It was Serena.

She had spent the evening at Annabel's with a party of friends. Toby had been there, and since they hadn't seen each other for quite a while, the champagne had flowed and they had danced on the small, dark dance floor until the early hours of the morning. When the brutal noise of hard rock changed to a slower, smoochier rhythm, she inebriatedly announced that she had had enough, and that she was going home. Alone.

Toby, more than a little drunk himself, knew by now that when she said alone, she meant alone, and he made no attempt to follow her.

As she stepped out of the foyer, two middle-aged men in evening dress alighted from a taxi cab and walked toward the nightclub's entrance.

'Did you hear the late night news?' one of them was asking the other. 'Hanoi Radio has apparently reported that several captured U.S. pilots have been paraded through the city in front of angry crowds.'

'The Americans won't like that,' the other said grimly. 'Too humiliating by half.'

There was a short laugh and then, as the doorman opened the door to them, the words, 'Poor buggers, whoever they are.'

The taxi had moved off, and she stood on the sidewalk, making no attempt to flag one down. *Airmen*. She presumed they had been referring to bomber pilots shot down over the North and captured.

There had been a photograph of one such airman in one of the leading Sunday newspapers a week or so earlier. He had been brought by his captors to stand on what looked to be a small, bare stage, before members of the world press sympathetic to the North Vietnamese cause. His head had been shaved and was lowered, his eyes blinkingly shying away from the fierce light of flashbulbs as he confessed to being a Yankee imperialist aggressor and a war criminal.

Thinking of the conditions under which he was no doubt being imprisoned, and under which his confessions had presumably been extracted, Serena had thought that perhaps his eyes would have shied away from any light. Even daylight.

He had been wearing ill-fitting, coarsely woven prison garments and sandals cut from old rubber tires. His hands had been shackled behind his back and he had looked so prematurely old and stooped, so utterly alone and so abject, her throat had tightened with rage and pity.

Now, as she thought of the young American pilots being paraded through the Hanoi streets so they could be jeered and spat upon, her rage and pity returned tenfold. Kyle could so easily be one of those men, might one day be one of them. She pulled her white mink jacket closer around her shoulders and, abandoning the idea of a taxi, began to walk down Charles Street toward Hyde Park Corner.

In the two months that Kyle had been in Vietnam she had received only two letters. She hadn't been surprised. It was impossible to imagine Kyle as a letter writer, and she herself had written only a couple of times more often. She knew where he was based and had gone to the trouble of looking the area up on a map. She knew the type of missions that he was assigned, and she knew that nearly all of them entailed flying over countryside held by the Viet Cong.

She hadn't yet heard of a helicoper pilot captured and taken north to the infamous prison known as the Hanoi Hilton. But it could happen. And at the thought of Kyle being subjected not only to physical torture but to public humiliation as well, her hands clenched until the knuckles showed white.

It was early August and the night air was warm and balmy. She crossed Hyde Park Corner, which was ethereally quiet apart from a few stray taxicabs, and began to walk down Upper Belgravia toward King's Road. About forty-five minutes later, as she crossed King's Road and entered Chelsea, a crowd of drunken teenagers spilled from a nearby club, chanting riotously, 'Americans out of Vietnam!' and 'Ho-Ho-Ho Chi Minh!'

As they stumbled past Serena, one of them fell against her. *'Ho-Ho-Ho Chi Minh!'* he yelled into her face.

It was the last straw. All the fear and rage

and pity that was burning deep inside her broke free. 'To hell with your bloody Ho Chi Minh!' she shouted back at him, raising her ivory-clasped evening bag and hitting him violently across the face.

The boy staggered backward, falling into the street, and as he did so, and as Serena began to viciously kick out at one of his friends who was trying to seize hold of her, a police car sped into the street, screaming to a halt.

Serena was oblivious. One of the boys had pulled her mink jacket off her shoulders and was trampling on it as he vainly tried to ward off the blows she was raining on him with her evening bag.

'Bastard!' she shrieked at him, her fury at the damage that was being done to her jacket increasing the fury that she felt at their anti-American slogans.

When the two officers intervened, trying to separate the pair of them, Serena hit out at them as viciously as she had hit the boy who was still on his hands and knees in the gutter. The ivory clasp of her evening bag caught one of the officers at the corner of one eye. Blood poured from the cut. Seconds later she was ignominiously bundled into the rear of the police car, still struggling violently.

Her appearance next morning at the Magistrate's Court charged with being drunk and disorderly and having assaulted a member of Her Majesty's Police Force did not go unnoticed by the daily press. By the time the afternoon editions hit the streets, they all contained photographs of Serena, still wearing her knee-skimming, sequin-encrusted, Mary Quant evening dress, a rather grubby white mink jacket slung nonchalantly around her shoulders.

Rupert had bailed her out, ignoring with admirable élan the reporters and photographers who jostled them on their walk from Magistrate's Court to his waiting Lagonda. As they drove into Cheyne Walk, there was an enterprising photographer waiting for them on her doorstep.

Serena stepped out from the Lagonda, sweeping past him, disdaining to shield her face from the flashbulb that went off uncomfortably near her eyes. Her telephone was already ringing, and she knew with wry humor who would be on the other end of the line.

'Well, at least I don't get myself arrested!' Lance said mincingly, mimicking the words she had used to him the night she had told him that she and Kyle had been reunited. He chortled gleefully. 'You have now, sister mine, you have now! Welcome to the club!'

# CHAPTER SIXTEEN

Ten days after the baby's birth, Gabrielle wrapped him snugly in a shawl given to her by the Hôtel Fontainebleau's proprietor's wife, and returned to Paris by public transportation. She felt fit and happy and full of optimism. Gavin was fulfilling the ambition that had brought him to Europe, and in doing so, he was fulfilling her own ambition, an ambition which, until she had met him, she had not even suspected: the deep, burning desire to identify more closely with the country of her birth; to strengthen the links between herself and her Vietnamese aunt and uncle and cousins; to become, after living for more than ten years in France, more Vietnamese than French.

Her father met her at the Gare de Lyon. He pulled the shawl gently away from *le petit* Gavin's face and his own aged and somber face creased into a smile.

'He looks wonderful, *ma chère*. Every inch a Frenchman.'

Gabrielle smiled and retucked the soft wool of the shawl once more around *le petit* Gavin's head. Her son was only one quarter French, and she did not think that he would ever look archetypically French. His hair was the wrong color, for one thing. Like Gavin's, it was a warm honey-gold, but there were hints of auburn among the gold and she knew that as he grew older, the auburn would deepen into a glossy, spicy red.

'*Maman* is thrilled,' her father said, guiding her protectively through the crowds entering and leaving the station. 'She has a crib all ready, and she has ironed and aired all the baby clothes you and she have been so busy sewing and knitting this past few months.'

He had flagged down a taxi and was holding the door open for her. 'The christening is all arranged too,' he said as she stepped inside and sank back against a cracked leather seat reeking of Gauloises. 'I spoke to Father Gerald two days ago, and Gavin Étienne Dinh is to be christened on the first Sunday of next month.'

The taxicab slewed out of the boulevard Diderot and into the avenue Daumesnil. 'It is a pity that his father will not be able to attend the ceremony,' her father said as the taxi swerved violently to avoid a pack of cyclists. 'But...' He shrugged philosophically. 'He is an Australian, and I do not suppose that christenings are as important to Australians as they are to us French.'

Gavin was not a Catholic, and though she knew that he would not mind *le petit* Gavin being baptized a Catholic, she knew that for once her father was right. It was not a ceremony that would have any great meaning for him. She wondered where he was at that precise moment, if he was still in Saigon, or if he had moved north to Hue, or Da Nang. She wondered if he had made contact with Nhu. And she wondered how long it would be before his first letter would reach her.

'Michel came to the house yesterday morning,' her father said as the taxi checked, and then ground to a reluctant halt behind a bus. 'He said he had something very important to talk to you about, and asked that you get in touch with him as soon as possible.'

'Michel?' Gabrielle hadn't given a thought to her young pianist the whole time she had been at Fontainebleau. 'But we had no engagements. We haven't had for nearly two months.'

Gavin had insisted that she accept no offers of work in her last weeks of pregnancy, or for several weeks after the baby was born. Michel had been understanding. He was too good a pianist to be adversely affected by her decision. There were always vocalists looking for good accompanists, and if he didn't wish to form another partnership, however temporary, then there were always clubs who would be only too happy to hire him for his talent alone. And Gabrielle, after years of performing, was glad for the small self-indulgent break.

The taxi driver, running out of patience, accelerated and overtook the bus with a bare three centimeters to spare.

Her father steadied himself with the hand

strap and then said with another of his habitual shrugs, 'He didn't say what it was that he wanted to talk to you about, *ma chère*. But he did seem extremely anxious. He wanted to know where you were so that he could telephone you, but your mother refused to allow me to give him the name of the hotel. She insisted that you needed rest and that today would be quite soon enough for you to be disturbed.'

At the thought of her fragile, gentle mother laying the law down with such unaccustomed fierceness, Gabrielle smiled. No doubt that same fierceness would also be extended to herself, once she arrived home. She knew that her mother would not want her to return to work, either modeling or singing, but would want her to stay home all day, to be company for her. And she knew that she was completely incapable of doing any such thing for an extended period of time. Eventually, the desire to perform, to sing for others, would lead her back to the clubs.

'Philippe also stopped me in the street, asking after you,' her father said as the taxicab swerved across the place d'Angers and into the avenue Trudaire. 'I told him that the baby had been born and he said to give you his congratulations and to tell you that he has work for you if you want it.'

Gabrielle made no comment. It was nice to know that at least one of the artists who had always so regularly commissioned her was prepared to use her again, even after *le petit*

Gavin's birth and the inevitable changes that had taken place to her figure. But she had done less and less modeling in the months that had followed her marriage to Gavin, and now it seemed as if modeling was very much a part of her past.

The taxicab bumped over the Montmartre cobbles and then skidded to a halt outside the shabby entrance to their apartment. She stepped out of the cab into the warm July sunlight and was greeted by the sound of Madame Garine's canaries trilling loudly.

'I'm sorry, *mes petits*,' she said affectionately as she walked past their cage. 'But I have no birdseed with me. I'll bring some down for you in a little while.'

As they entered the lobby she could hear, three floors above them, the door of their apartment open and then the sound of her mother's footsteps hurrying down the stone stairs toward them.

'Gabrielle? Gabrielle? Is that you?'

Gabrielle hurried up the stairs to her mother, *le petit* Gavin stirring restlessly in her arms, his fist pressing against his mouth as he sought hungrily for food.

*'Oh!'* Her mother paused for a moment, overcome with emotion as she rounded the second landing and came face-to-face with Gabrielle and her grandson. 'Oh!' she said again, this time much more softly, running down the last few steps that separated them, the ankle-length tunic of her *ao dai*, split to the waist over loose silk trousers, floating

diaphanously around her. Very, very gently she lifted *le petit* Gavin from Gabrielle's arms. 'Oh!' she said for a third and last time, and this time her voice was unimaginably tender. 'Isn't he absolutely beautiful?'

There were tears of joy in her eyes as she looked down at her now wide-awake grandson. Gabrielle kissed her mother lovingly on her cheek and then, putting a hand beneath her arm in order to steady her, she began to lead her back up the stairs toward the apartment.

'And have you plenty of milk, *ma chère*?' her mother asked concerned, a little while later as Gabrielle sat on the sofa, her blouse undone to the waist, *le petit* Gavin at her breast.

'I have enough milk for a score of babies, *Maman*,' Gabrielle said with unabashed truthfulness.

There was a knock at the door, and her father went to answer it.

'That is good, *ma chère*,' her mother began to say, 'because...'

'Philippe would like a word with you, Gabrielle,' her father said, coming back into the room, Philippe at his heels.

Her mother rose agitatedly to her feet, appalled at her husband inviting a man into the room when Gabrielle was breastfeeding. Gabrielle smiled up at Philippe, completely unperturbed. 'Have you come to congratulate me, Philippe? Or to try to coerce me to sit for you?' she teased.

'Both,' he said, grinning through his beard and sitting his massive figure down in a chair opposite her. 'And I want you to sit for me exactly as you are sitting now. With the baby at your breast, your body lush and ripe and utterly superb.'

Her mother's eyes widened in disbelief. *'Di!'* she said to him furiously, lapsing into Vietnamese, as she always did on the rare occasions when she was overcome by anger. *'Di! Di!'*

Philippe was totally baffled. 'What is the matter?' he asked, rising perplexedly to his feet. 'Have I done something to offend you, Madame? Have I perhaps said something?' If he had, he couldn't for the life of him imagine what on earth it could have been.

Only the anguish in her mother's voice prevented Gabrielle from succumbing to helpless laughter. With great difficulty she suppressed it. 'It's all right, *Maman*,' she said in Vietnamese, 'Philippe is leaving now,' and then, to Philippe, '*Maman* mistook something you said, Philippe.'

Before he could ask what it had been, she rose to her feet, crossing the room toward him and beginning to walk with him to the door. 'I'm not sure that I want to do any more modeling, Philippe, at least not for a little while.'

'You will be a great loss to me, *ma petite*,' he said in his deep rumbling voice, pausing in the doorway and looking down at her with genuine regret. 'Promise me one thing.

Promise me that if you will not model for me, you will not model for anyone else. Especially that bastard Léon Durras.'

The laughter she had been suppressing with such difficulty burst free. 'I promise.' She stood on tiptoe and kissed him on his bearded cheek.

'And the singing?' he asked quizzically, deeply pleased. 'Will I still be able to hear you sing at the Black Cat?'

'I'm not sure,' she said, suddenly thoughtful. 'I shall still sing. I shall always sing. But for some reason that I do not understand, I do not think that I will ever sing again at the Black Cat.'

'You must be telepathic,' Michel said an hour later as she told him about Philippe's visit. He sat across from Gabrielle. 'I've been frantically trying to get in touch with you since yesterday morning to tell you that you've got the chance to do something really different.'

Gabrielle sat in the old, comfortable armchair that dwarfed her, but that had been barely big enough for Philippe. Although she was dressed in a loose black cotton top and a black leather miniskirt, she glowed with color. Her sumptuous red hair had grown longer in the months she had been pregnant, and tumbled around her face in a riot of untamed waves and springing curls. Her green cat eyes danced with happiness. Her suntanned legs and feet were naked, her toenails painted the same vibrant glossy pink as the nails on her fingers.

'And what is that, *chéri*?' she asked affectionately, curling her legs beneath her with restless energy.

Michel grinned at her. Though he was absolutely bewitched by her, he had known from the instant he had met her that his feelings would never be reciprocated. He had learned not to mind. Instead of being her partner in a love affair, he was her musical partner, and he was her friend. And as musical partnerships and friendships often lasted for a lifetime, whereas love affairs seldom did, he had come to terms with the situation. 'Rock and roll,' he said, enjoying the look of incredulity that crossed her face. 'Good old-fashioned, beat-dominated rock and roll.'

She began to laugh so helplessly she could hardly speak. 'I'm a nightclub singer, Michel,' she protested at last, her voice still full of giggles at his idiocy. 'I sing slow, melodic stuff. Torch songs. Committed, passionate love songs. I couldn't become Brenda Lee or Connie Stevens if I tried.'

Michel reached out toward the plate of cookies that her mother had brought in. Like all Gabrielle's friends, he seldom visited her at home, but when he did, Vanh always went out of her way to make him feel welcome. She found his bespectacled, intellectual appearance reassuring. He seemed to her more like a student or a young schoolmaster than a musician.

'No one would want you to,' he said, grinning. 'You're far too sexy to be a teeny-bopper's delight, and an imitative Miss Lee or Miss Stevens isn't at all what Radford has in mind.'

'Radford?' she asked, intrigued despite the fact that rock and roll was not her style.

He finished eating his cookie and leaned toward her, his hands clasped loosely between his knees, his eyes alight with enthusiasm. 'Radford James. He's an American. Black, talented, and very, very ambitious.'

She began to laugh again. 'So what is new, *chéri*?' she asked, leaning over the crib at the side of her chair and tucking the blankets more securely around her sleeping son. 'What is so special about this particular talented, ambitious American?'

'What is special about him is the sound he has come up with,' Michel said in a voice that was so unequivocal that Gabrielle raised her eyebrows slightly. As a musician, Michel was a perfectionist, and he was not impressed easily.

'He had some success with an all-male, all-black group in America in 1964, but they were too like a hundred other groups for them to make any real impression. When the music scene moved to London he followed it, playing the clubs, and at the end of the year he formed a new band. Instrumentally they're great. A hard-edged mixture of black soul and honest-to-goodness rock. More Rolling Stones than Beatles. What he needs now is a lead vocalist. Someone with blatant sex appeal and with the raw-edged quality to their voice that whips up an audience's emotions. He thought he'd found someone. A girl from Liverpool who, like Lennon and Jagger, sounds black when she sings. They played bottom of the bill on a tour in February, and stole the show. Since then they've picked up a record contract and done a month-long tour of the States. Next month they're booked to appear at what is going to be the biggest open-air pop festival ever held in France'.

'And?' Gabrielle prompted impatiently, wondering when he was going to come to the point.

'*And* their lead singer has walked out on them. She's married a South African businessman and returned with him to Johannesburg. Radford needs a female singer. Urgently. A female singer who isn't imitative of any other singer at present on the pop scene. I think that what he needs is you.'

She shook her head, the sun streaming through the window behind her highlighting her titian hair with gold. 'No,' she said, wondering why she found such a ridiculous idea tempting. 'My style is too individualistic for me ever to become a pop singer, Michel.'

'You're wrong!' His voice was vehement. 'I know this could be a turning point for you, Gabrielle! I can feel it in my blood and in my bones! The band is already on the verge of becoming as big as the Stones, or the Beatles or Bob Dylan! When you meet Radford, you'll know why I feel so certain that he's going to be a major star. And when you hear the music, I know you'll want to be a part of it.'

His eyes were so intense, his voice so certain, the laughter that had been rising in her throat died away. To her surprise, she heard herself saying, 'All right, Michel. All right. If you feel so passionately about this American, then I will meet him.'

His grin split his face. 'I knew you would! I knew it was a challenge you wouldn't be able to resist!'

She tilted her head to one side, looking at him curiously. 'Why is this so important to you?' she asked, puzzled. 'After all, if Radford likes my voice, and if I begin to sing with his band, then we will not be working together anymore. And we have worked well together, *chéri*, haven't we?'

She wasn't flirting with him. It was a plain statement of fact.

His grin died and his eyes behind his thick-lensed glasses were embarrassed. 'Yes,' he said awkwardly. 'We have worked well together, Gabrielle. We will still work well together, for I will still arrange the music for the songs that you compose. Only now I shall have another satisfaction as well.'

A flush of color touched his cheeks, and he paused for so long that Gabrielle thought he was never going to find the courage to finish what he had begun to say. At last he said, the color in his face deepening, 'I shall know in the years ahead that it was because you trusted me and acted on my advice that you became a star. And you *will* become a star, Gabrielle. You will become a world-famous star. It is impossible for you to be anything else.'

Gabrielle doubted that Radford James would be interested in hiring her as his lead vocalist. Though part of her success came from her effortlessly erotic stage presence, it was her ability to sing love songs in a husky, knowing voice that made her unique.

'So why go?' Vanh asked bewilderedly. 'There is no need for you to earn money. Gavin has arranged for part of his salary to be paid direct to you, has he not?'

Gabrielle nodded, laying *le petit* Gavin in a Moses basket. 'Yes.' The money that Gavin had arranged to be transferred from his salary to her had been the source of their only argument. In Gabrielle's opinion, the amount was far too much. Gavin had insisted that it wasn't, that he would be living almost exclusively on expenses in Saigon and therefore wouldn't need the greater half of his salary. And that she would.

'Then I don't understand,' Vanh repeated. She was seated at the kitchen table and she looked across the room at Gabrielle forlornly. 'I thought that you would not be working any longer, *ma chère*, that we would be at home together with *le petit* Gavin.'

Gabrielle knew very well that that was what her mother had been hoping for, and she had always known that she would have to disappoint her.

'I cannot stay at home all day, every day, *Maman*,' she said gently. 'It isn't good that you do so. You should go for a walk every afternoon. Pass a few words with Madame Castries. Visit Madame Garine. Make some friends.'

Her mother gave a shrug of her shoulders that was almost Gallic, saying a trifle sulkily, 'In Saigon it was easy, *ma chère*. We had so many friends – educated, wealthy people. People who respected us. Now, when Papa has no position...'

'You must forget the way that we lived in Saigon, *Maman*,' Gabrielle said firmly. 'Madame Castries and Madame Garine are neither wealthy nor educated, but they would be good friends to you if you would allow them to be.' Michel's car horn tooted loudly. 'Do you promise me that you will try?' she said, walking across to the door and opening it, pausing for a moment. 'That you will go for a walk and buy a paper from Madame Castries and pass the time of day with her? And that you will knock on Madame Garine's door and ask her if she would like to come upstairs and share a pot of coffee with you.'

Michel's car horn tooted again, this time more insistently, and Vanh said reluctantly, 'All right, *ma chère*. For your sake, I will try.'

Gabrielle gave her a dazzling smile, blew

her a kiss, and with the Moses basket and its precious cargo in one hand, hurried down the stone stairs.

The room Radford James and his band were using for rehearsals was above a bistro in one of the streets in the maze around the place de la Bastille. Michel's ancient Citroën coughed and spluttered down the rue de Rivoli, nearly coming to grief with a sleek Mercedes at the corner of the rue de Sévigné.

'What makes you so sure that Radford James will even listen to me?' she asked, turning toward the backseat to make sure that the Moses basket was safe.

The driver of the Mercedes was still hurling verbal abuse in their wake. Michel ignored him, saying complacently, 'Because he has already heard you sing.'

'When? Where?' she exclaimed indignantly. 'You never told me!'

A grin split his angular, almost adolescent features. 'He heard you the night of your last performance at the Black Cat.' He swerved into the rue de Birague, a cloud of exhaust fumes in his wake. 'There's something else I haven't told you.'

'And what is that?' There was a dangerous gleam in her eye. His voice was so sheepish, she knew that whatever it was, she wasn't going to like it.

He drew to a halt outside a bistro, the sound of rock music blasting the street from the upper windows. 'He has copies of all the songs you've written,' he said, making a speedy exit from the car.

*'Merde!'* she flared furiously, opening her own door, and then the rear door, hoisting the basket from the backseat. 'How dare you, Michel! That really is awful of you! Really—'

She broke off, forgetting her incensed indignation as the music hit her ears in a wall of sound. *'Tiens!'* she said in stunned amazement. 'How many musicians are in this rock band? Fifty?'

Michel laughed, leading the way inside and up a flight of bare wooden stairs. 'Seven at the moment. Three guitars, two bass, two pianos.'

'A Fool in Love' merged into 'Nowhere to Run'. At the top of the stairs they crossed a small landing and walked into a large room, bare except for the musicians and their instruments and a black woman in a red leather minidress, singing the 'Nowhere to Run' number in a voice that was a passably good imitation of Martha Reeves's.

'Fine, baby. Great,' a voice said dismissively. 'That's all for now, I'll be in touch.'

The woman looked as though she were going to argue the point, and then, as he turned away from her and toward Gabrielle and Michel, decided against it, shrugging a jacket around her shoulders and walking quickly from the room, flashing Gabrielle a look of frustrated fury as she did so.

'Well,' Radford James said uncaringly, standing with his fingers splayed on his hips in a gesture that would have been effeminate in a man less sinfully masculine. 'You're actually *here*, baby!' White teeth flashed the broadest smile that she had ever seen.

He was tall and loose-limbed, broad shoulders tapering down to a lean waist, the narrowness of his hips erotically emphasized by the tightness of faded blue denim. He was younger than she had anticipated, twenty-two or twenty-three, and his skin was so dark and smooth that there was almost a sheen to it.

She was flooded with a sense of immediate rapport, as if meeting for the first time someone she had always known.

'Yes, I'm actually here,' she said, laughter bubbling up in her throat as she put the Moses basket down and walked toward him.

He was the most beautiful man she had ever seen, and she knew that the rapport blazing between them was inextricably mixed with instant, almost overwhelming sexual attraction. If they had met a year earlier, she knew she would have had no hesitation in tumbling into his bed. But they hadn't met a year earlier, and she was married to Gavin, and the only bed she was ever going to tumble into was his.

Radford took hold of her hands, laughing down at her, his eyes telling her everything she already knew. 'Honey, when I saw you onstage I knew you were only a little-bitty thing, but hell, offstage you ain't no bigger than a minute!'

Gabrielle gave a throaty chuckle. She was wearing stiletto-high heels that added at least four inches to her height. She resisted the temptation to step out of them, and also the temptation to tell him that though she was petite, she had a big voice. He would find that out soon enough. As would Michel.

A smile quirked her mouth as Radford began to lead her toward the nearest piano. The songs she sang in the clubs never required her to give her voice full rein. She didn't know if the next few minutes were going to be a surprise for Radford, but she knew that they were going to be a shock for Michel.

'What would you like me to sing?' she asked, knowing that whatever it was, she would be able to do it just the way he wanted to hear it.

He looked down at her, an eyebrow rising slightly at her buoyant confidence. 'You know that this is a real long shot, don't you? I mean, I want a *big* voice as well as one packed with emotion. I *know* you have the emotion. But we're not a small-club band, and I don't want a small-club singing voice.'

'You're not going to get one,' Gabrielle said with sudden gentleness, knowing that he was nervous because he so desperately wanted her voice to be right.

Something unspoken, almost atavistic, passed between them. 'Okay,' he said softly. 'Okay, girl. We'll give it a try with one of your own songs. I've kept the structure and the basic melody, but you're going to find the treatment a hell of a lot different. Sit tight while we play it through and then, when you're ready, come in with the vocal.'

She stood by the side of the piano, and from the moment they played the opening riff she knew that Michel had been right. The sound was sensational. Blues oriented and gritty. And it was a sound that was backing *her* song. She looked across at Michel and flashed him a wide smile, trying to dispel the tension she knew he was feeling. It was going to be okay. Her nerve endings tingled with anticipation. It was going to be more than okay. It was going to be the start of a whole new career.

She stood very still for the few seconds before they began to play the song through for the second time and then, as the opening riff, honed razor sharp, hit the air, she launched herself away from the piano, dancing to the center of the room, the sound tearing out of her.

She never had to ask if she was good. The roar of applause from the band and from Radford and Michel, when the last note had been played, told her everything.

'Girl, you can sing,' Radford whooped exultantly, whipping them straight into 'Peaches 'n' Cream' and then 'I'm Ready for Love', song following song, some of them songs she had written herself and that Radford had already worked on with his band, some of them classic oldies. Only when *le petit* Gavin, overwhelmed by hunger, began to cry lustily, did the session come to an end.

'I guess that's it for today, baby,' Radford said as she wiped the perspiration from her face and lifted her crying son into her arms. 'How does it feel to be a queen of rock?'

'It feels great.' Her face was radiant, her heart still slamming against her chest, her pulse racing, perspiration trickling down her neck and her back.

He flashed her a dazzling, down-slanting smile. 'Wait till you give the same kind of performance under lights, honeychild. Then you'll *know* where it's at!'

She had undone her sweat-soaked shirt and the baby was nuzzling at her breast. He had never before met anyone like her. She was so petite, so guileless, so effortlessly sexy. And she wasn't about to take their mutual, almost crucifying attraction for each other to its logical conclusion. Her apologetic refusal to the unspoken question he had asked within seconds of meeting her was clear and unmistakable in her eyes.

He wondered why. He didn't believe for a moment that she was the kind of lady who would allow a husband and a child to hamper her natural inclinations. Not unless she wanted them to. And if she wanted them to, then it meant she had to be simply crazy in love. He wondered who her husband was, that he commanded faithfulness from a lady whose sexual appetite was, he was sure, as uninhibited and as wide-ranging as his own.

The open-air concert was to be held on the last Saturday of the month. For the next two weeks they met daily in the room above the bistro, Michel taking on the role of baby-sitter and audience as Radford had Gabrielle and the band rehearse numbers over and over, constantly altering the material, and improvising and discarding.

'That's *very* close,' he would say sometimes when they were all near to dropping with exhaustion. 'That's very close, but it's not quite it. Let's try it again.'

'You know that if this comes off, the record contract is in the bag, don't you?' Michel asked her, dangling *le petit* Gavin on his knee as Gabrielle nervously gathered together the dress she was going to wear, and her white leather stage boots, and her makeup.

'Yes.' She couldn't allow herself to think about the record contract. All she could think of was the concert. In two hours she would make her debut as a rock singer. And at least two of the songs she had written would get a massive hearing.

'I haven't forgotten anything, have I, *chéri*?' she asked, looking around the apartment, the dress and boots in one hand, her makeup bag in the other.

'No.' He was almost as nervous as she was. The concert wasn't just any old pop concert. It was going to be televised. It was going to reach an audience of millions. The cream of British and American rock groups had traveled to France especially to participate. The very best groups that France possessed had hustled to be with them on the bill.

'*Ça va*. Then I'm ready,' she said, her sumptuous red hair framing her face in an untamed riot of waves and curls.

Her mother came into the room, startled as always by Michel's easy, confident handling of her grandson. 'There is a letter for you, *ma chère*. It is from Saigon. And it is not from Nhu.'

'*Mon Dieu!*' Gabrielle did the impossible. She forgot about the concert, opening the envelope with trembling fingers, reading Gavin's untidy scrawl with a fast-beating heart.

'—and so I'm back from Da Nang now, and I think the Buddhists are going to run out of steam,' he had written toward the end of his letter. 'Nhu thinks they never had a chance since they can't offer any alternative political leadership. Your aunt Nhu is quite a girl! Very vital and very positive. She's taken me under her wing, and from now on life looks as if it's going to be very interesting indeed—' He ended by saying that he missed her like the very devil, and he sent her all his love.

'Good news?' Michel asked, his nervousness increasing. If it was bad news, he would never forgive her mother for having handed her the letter two hours before the most important concert of her life.

'Yes.' She held the letter close to her breasts for a moment, fighting an upsurge of tears. God, but she loved him! And she missed him!

'Then we'd better be going,' he said, lifting *le petit* Gavin up against his shoulder with one hand and picking up the Moses basket with the other.

She nodded agreement, blinking hard. Gavin would be horrified if he knew that she was missing him enough to cry from sheer longing. After all, *she* had encouraged him to leave her and go to Vietnam. By being there he was fulfilling her ambitions as well as his.

She smiled at her idiocy, the unshed tears clinging shimmeringly on her lashes. 'Yes, let's go, *mon brave*,' she said, walking quickly across to the door and leading the way down the stairs and into the street.

They did not perform until the second half of the concert, and afterward Gabrielle never could remember any of the prestigious American and British rock groups who preceded them. All she remembered was Radford saying to her, his eyes glittering like agates, 'This is it, baby! We're on!'

The opening riff boomed out over giant speakers. *Da-da-da-da-dum! Da-da-da-da-dum!* She crossed her fingers on both hands, threw a prayer up to heaven, and whirled onstage after him, mercurial dynamite in a black leather minidress and knee-high, stiletto-heeled boots.

The audience was with her from the very first moment. *'Do you love me?'* she belted out as the music stormed over them in a great majestic rock 'n' roll roar. *'Do you want me?'* As she danced downstage toward them, her hair burning red in the sunlight, her hips grinding, her feet stamping the rhythm, twenty thousand voices roared out assent.

They played their four scheduled numbers and the crowd howled for more, whistling and screaming, refusing to be pacified until they launched into yet another number. 'Okay!' Radford yelled to the band from his piano stool. 'Let's give them *"Lover Man"*.'

It was one of the songs that she had written, and Radford's arrangement of it was more blues than rock. Triumph and elation surged through her as she stood for a moment, suddenly still, gaining control of her breathing, and by the sheer force of her personality bringing the audience into a new mood with her.

*'Lover man, where have you gone?'* she sang, suddenly vulnerable, heart-stoppingly female, deliberately unleashing the touching, broken-edged quality in her voice that she had always used in the clubs to such staggering effect.

For a rock group it had been a daring choice to close with, and it was a sensation. As the last chord died away, the audience erupted in a storm of applause, shouting and screaming and stamping their feet. She could see Michel, offstage, whooping in exultation, and Radford, only yards away from her, punching the air with his fists.

The band was center-stage with her, hugging her and waving and shouting compliments back to the audience.

It was an incredible moment, a moment she knew she would never forget. And then

Michel lifted *le petit* Gavin from his Moses basket, holding him so that he could see her, and she knew that if only Gavin could have been there, too, it would have been more than incredible. It would have been the most wonderful moment of her life.

# CHAPTER SEVENTEEN

Life for Lewis, through May and June of 1966, was much the same as it had been since his arrival. Despite the constant stress and danger, there was a routine to his days that gave them structure and that even, on occasion, became monotonous. Day after day was passed with the same activities – patrolling the surrounding canal-infested countryside; ambushing any Viet Cong forces that were detected and could flush out; training the local Vietnamese militia units; administering civil operations such as medical programs and agricultural projects as well as military operations. Lewis's only relaxations were sleeping and eating. And army rations, supplemented by local produce, left a lot to be desired.

Sleeping was even less of a pleasure. Mosquitos, and a dozen other bugs that Lewis was unable to name, made nights a torment. Despite heavy spraying of insecticide inside the net covering his bunk, and lavish applications of insect repellent on his skin, some mosquitos always survived, crawling into his hair and settling on his arms and chest to feed from convenient capillaries.

Tam's laconic indifference to the blood-sucking pests never ceased to amuse him. She would swat them away, barely pausing in whatever task she was doing.

His team's euphoria at having Tam in the house, washing dishes and laundering and cleaning and sweeping, was short-lived. They had looked forward to flirting with her and teasing her, and they were sorely disappointed. Unlike most of the village girls, whose eyes were always full of mischief, and who laughed and smiled at the slightest opportunity, Tam was inscrutable. She did her work with flawless efficiency, scraping dried mud from the floors and from their boots, scouring the cooking pots until they shined, sewing up tears in fatigues. But she did it all with an attitude of barely veiled contempt, never speaking to the men unless it was absolutely necessary, and then only in a voice so ice cool and impersonal that they soon gave up any idea of thawing her into amiability.

Far from sharing his men's disappointment, Lewis was relieved by Tam's aloofness. A stunningly pretty seventeen- or eighteen-year-old in the team house and its precincts for six or seven hours a day could have been a sure-fire recipe for trouble. As it was, after the first few days, when the novelty of her presence had worn off, Lewis knew that he could relax. Even his optimistically persistent assistant team leader, Lieutenant Grainger, had given up trying to elicit a friendly response from her. If there was going to be any repercussions from having her as their cleaning girl, they were not going to be the sexual ones he had feared.

The only person she ever spoke to at length was himself, and he knew that she did so only in order to practise her English. She was a model pupil, listening avidly, never having to be told twice, returning each day with the previous day's grammar and vocabulary committed to memory, only her pronunciation being a little uncertain.

'By the time I leave Vietnam, your English will be good enough for you to apply for a job as an interpreter with the Americans,' he said to her one morning in late July as they came to the end of her daily lesson.

She looked across at him, and her eyes, normally devoid of expression, were curious. 'You cannot believe that I would do such a thing,' she said in charmingly labored English.

He pushed his chair away from the rough wood table and walked across to the cool-box for a vacuum bottle of drinking water.

'Why not?' he asked mildly. In the three months that she had been working at the team house, it was the first time their conversation had approached being personal. A tingle of triumph ran down his spine. If he could get her to talk about herself, then he might also be able to get her to listen to advice she badly needed, advice which, if he had given it previously, he knew she would have contemptuously spurned.

He returned to the table with the vacuum jug and two plastic beakers and she said, her eyes holding his, her curiosity touched with defiance, 'I am not learning English in order that I can help the Americans.'

He poured water into the beakers and handed her one of them, swatting away an insect that had landed on his arm. 'I know.'

A hint of a flush touched her tawny skin. 'You do not know. You cannot know.'

He ran a hand through his thickly curling hair. 'I do know,' he said again quietly. 'I know that you asked for English lessons so that you would be able to help the Viet Cong. I have always known that.'

In her eyes, curiosity and defiance had been replaced by stunned amazement. 'And yet you still taught me?'

He nodded, her incredulity and bewilderment arousing a wave of tenderness in him.

She frowned, and for a moment he thought she was going to retreat into her customary pose of careless indifference, and then she said, her voice troubled, 'I am sorry, *Dai uy*, but I do not understand.'

It was the first time that, addressing him by his title, she had not given the words a sarcastic edge. A slight smile touched the hard line of his mouth. If she wasn't careful, she would soon find herself treating him as a friend.

'No, I know that you don't, Tam,' he said gently, relieved that she was at last lowering the barriers that she had erected between them. He rested his folded arms on the table, leaning toward her slightly. 'Let me try to explain.'

'I do not believe you,' she said flatly when he told her of the atrocities committed by the Viet Cong against village chiefs who refused to cooperate with them. 'None of those things have happened here, in Van Binh.'

'Only because there is an American presence in Van Binh,' he said dryly.

'I still do not believe you.' Her hands were clenched tightly in her lap. 'The Viet Cong are freedom fighters. They are fighting for a free Vietnam.'

'They're fighting for a *Communist* Vietnam,' Lewis said, feeling his patience beginning to slip away from him. 'And if that's what you want, let me tell you that when you get it, you won't like it at all!'

'Why should you care?' she asked with a flare of her old spirit. '*You* are not Vietnamese! What is it to you what we Vietnamese do? If you want so much to be in Vietnam, just wait a little while and perhaps in your next reincarnation you will be born Vietnamese!'

She looked so pretty, her almond eyes sparking angrily, her waist-length black hair shimmering down her back, that his impatience died and he burst into rare laughter.

'There could be worse fates,' he said as Lieutenant Grainger walked into the team house, looking quizzically at them both.

For the first time since he had known her, Lewis saw a small grin edge the corner of her mouth. 'Perhaps, but not, I think, for an American,' she said naughtily, and with a gleam of laughter in her eye, she rose from her rickety wooden chair, and ignoring Lieutenant Grainger completely, she swept out of the team house, walking with eye-riveting grace across the compound to her washtub and her laundry.

'What was all that about?' Lieutenant Grainger asked, dragging his gaze away from her. 'Is the ice maiden beginning to thaw at last?'

'Maybe,' Lewis said noncomittally, irrationally annoyed by his assistant team leader's remark and his tone of voice. If Tam was beginning to thaw, it sure as hell wouldn't be in Grainger's direction. 'It's about time we set off for Tay Phong. Are the district chief and his cronies here yet?'

Tay Phong was the village farthest from Van Binh in his area. It was in a particularly vulnerable position, dangerously close to the network of waterways that the Cong used to smuggle supplies from the Cambodian border to their units. Lewis had a good relationship with Tay Phong's village chief that he wanted to maintain. If Tay Phong underwent a change of loyalty, becoming sympathetic to the Viet Cong, then he had no chance of ever again intercepting the supply convoys.

'Hoan is on his way up here now,' Grainger

said, referring to the district chief who was to travel to Tay Phong with them. He picked up his M-16, turning back toward the door, wondering what the hell pretty Tam had done or said to have provoked such unaccustomed laughter from his sober-sided captain.

Lewis strapped on his .45 service automatic and followed him. The sun seemed unusually bright, and he blinked his eyes uncomfortably as he strode across the compound to meet Hoan and the two members of his staff who always traveled with him.

*'Chào, Dai uy,'* the elderly district chief said cheerily.

*'Chào, Em,'* Lewis responded. His relationship with Hoan was a good one. He was a rare creature, a district chief who was unbribable and incorruptible. Today, however, Lewis knew that Hoan regarded himself as being off duty because he was going with them to Tay Phong only because he had a brother living there. The visit, made in the comfort of a water taxi, would give him the chance for a family chat.

As they walked down toward the village and the battered construction that served as a pier, Lewis turned his head, looking back at the compound. Tam had paused in her laundering and was standing, watching him. He grinned, pleased at the rapport that had suddenly sprung up between them, wishing he could have stayed in the team house, talking to her, rather than travel with Grainger and Hoan to Tay Phong.

The water taxi was a small engine-powered boat with a sheltered passenger compartment and was the common means of transportation from one village to the next. As Lewis stepped aboard, he was aware that he had the beginnings of a headache.

He sat beneath the shade, wishing yet again that he hadn't arranged to have a discussion with Tay Phong's village chief and to inspect its local militia platoon. He had a letter from Abbra tucked into the breast pocket of his tiger-stripe fatigues and he withdrew it, reading it yet again, his strong, hard-boned face softening slightly as he did.

She didn't appear to be seeing so much of Scott now that the football season was over. He didn't mind about that too much. He didn't want her getting so hooked on the game that she would want him to accompany her once he returned home. They would have better things to do than sit in the stands and cheer Scott on.

His smile deepened. The birthday party at the Polo Lounge sounded like fun. It was nice to think of them all there together, Abbra and Scott and his father, being a real family. He wondered whose idea it had been to have candles and a miniature football player on the cake and guessed that it had been Abbra's.

There wasn't too much else in her letter. She had been to Boston for a few days and waxed lyrical about the squirrels on the Common and the sun shining on the golden dome of the State House, and the winding old streets on Beacon Hill. He couldn't imagine why she had chosen the East Coast and Boston for a vacation when she could quite easily have driven down to Monterey or Carmel or even Mexico.

His head was beginning to throb, and he refolded the letter and put it back in his pocket, shivering slightly. There wasn't long to go now before he would be back home with her, and when he was, they would vacation together. Mexico would be a good choice. They could go to Acapulco and Oaxaca.

'Looks like we're going to be in for an uncomfortable ride, *Dai uy*,' Grainger said to him glumly as the water taxi approached the next village along the canal bank.

Lewis squinted into the fierce sunlight. There was a small crowd waiting at the make-shift dock. Black-garbed elderly women with baskets of farm produce, and farmers, cages of live hens at their feet. He groaned. Traveling with the villagers on a local water taxi was always a hardship, but today it would be unbearable.

His head was throbbing viciously and his limbs had begun to ache. If he had been back home in California he would have thought he was coming down with the flu, and he would have taken a couple of asprin and shrugged it off. In Vietnam the solution wasn't as simple. He could be suffering from anything, goddammit, and he had no access to any medication until they returned to Van Binh.

The water taxi glided to a halt and the chattering villagers loaded themselves aboard. He squeezed himself into a position from which he could keep a careful eye on the canal bank, knowing that Grainger would be doing the same on the other side of the boat. They never had come under sniper fire while traveling by water taxi, but there was always a first time.

He was beginning to feel nauseated, and determined that once in Tay Phong, his visit would be brief. He would inspect the militia, have a word with the village chief, and then he would go back to the team house and dose himself with aspirin and try to sleep off whatever it was he was coming down with.

'Are you okay, *Dai uy*?' Grainger called across from the far side of the boat, looking at him anxiously.

Lewis gave a brief nod. He was far from okay, but there was no point in whining about it to Grainger.

After a journey that seemed interminable, the water taxi glided to a halt in Tay Phong. Every muscle Lewis possessed ached as he climbed from the boat and began to walk toward the main street, Grainger, Hoan, and his cronies in his wake.

Tay Phong was like every other village in the province. There was one main street, hemmed in by shops and small houses made of grass and thatch. On one side the houses faced out over the canal, and a few sampans were tied up to wooden stilt pilings. Halfway down the street was the market square and a few more buildings: a Catholic church, a schoolhouse, both made of masonry blocks.

A pig careered across their path, a stream of children running noisily in its wake as they made their way to the village office, where the village chief was waiting to meet them.

'*Chào! Chào! Co van!*' the chief said buoyantly, greeting Lewis by his title of adviser and pouring out glasses of the local homemade firewater.

Lewis took the proferred glass reluctantly. Good manners demanded he drink it, and he did so in one swallow, certain it would either kill him or cure him.

'I have information, *Co van*,' the village chief said when the formalities of drinking the *ba si de* were over. He leaned toward Lewis over a table even more battered than the one in the team house. 'A supply unit is due to come into the area, a big one.'

Lights were dancing on the periphery of Lewis's vision, and he had to clamp his hands on his knees to prevent them from quivering. 'Are you sure it's coming this far south?' he asked, struggling to concentrate.

Usually it was only the offshoots of the big supply units that penetrated this far south. A main supply unit would be too big for his team and the local militia units to manage. They would need a backup force. Perhaps even a Special Forces 'A' team.

The village chief nodded his head vigorously. 'Yes, *Co van*,' he said emphatically. 'My informant is a member of the Viet Cong infrastructure who has discovered that his superior officer has been sleeping with his wife. The officer will be accompanying the supply unit and it is for revenge that he has come to me with information.'

'When he says a big supply unit, how big does he mean?'

It was common knowledge that there were at least two North Vietnamese Army regiments operating from just across the Cambodian border. The nearest province to them was Kien Phong, and in only one night's traveling the Cong, supplied from Cambodia with medicines and money and ammunition, could be deep in the province. From there, smaller units spread the supplies via boat and the labyrinthine canal network into the provinces of An Giang and Sa Dec, and as far south as their own province.

'Very big,' the village chief confirmed. 'The supplies are going to be brought in, not by the local Cong, but by the NVA themselves.'

Lewis groaned. He was feeling like death; all he wanted to do was to crawl into his bunk and pull a blanket over his head, and the chief was telling him that they were on the verge of a massive confrontation with North Vietnamese troops. 'When?' he croaked, aware that both Lieutenant Grainger and Hoan were looking across at him anxiously, knowing that there was something wrong with him.

'Four nights. Maybe five nights. My informant will come back to me and will tell me their route and checkpoints.'

'Okay.' Lewis rose to his feet, staggering as he did so. 'Let's go and inspect the militia.'

'Do you think you should?' Grainger said to him urgently, *sotto voce*. 'You're burning up. We should get you the hell back to camp.'

'Fifteen more minutes isn't going to make any damn difference, and if we're about to face the NVA, it would be nice to know that Tay Phong's militia is prepared.'

With Hoan at his side, Lewis inspected the troops, warning the platoon commander to be in a state of readiness over the next few days, and then, barely able to see for the raging pain in his head, and barely able to walk because of cramps in his legs and his feet, he struggled back to Tay Phong's crumbling jetty.

'For Christ's sake, *Dai uy*, what the hell are you coming down with?' Grainger demanded, terrified that he was going to have to call in a chopper to whisk Lewis to the nearest field hospital, and that in Lewis's absence the responsibility for organizing the ambush of the NVA units was going to fall onto his shoulders.

Lewis didn't answer. He couldn't. He was dimly aware that they had boarded a water taxi, and that it was mercifully free of the live farm produce that had accompanied them on their earlier journey. He was pretty certain he hadn't been poisoned. He knew damn well that he hadn't been in contact with any punji sticks, or any other poisoned booby trap that the Viet Cong were so adept at laying.

He tried to think what he had eaten in the last twenty-four hours, but his brain wouldn't function. Rats? Had he eaten any rat lately? Rat meat was a local staple and one that Sergeant Drayton often used in order to supplement their C rations. Chopped and cooked Chinese style with beans and flavored with the *nuoc mam* sauce that accompanied every Vietnamese dish, it was surprisingly palatable. But Drayton hadn't served any for over a week, Lewis was sure of it.

By the time the water taxi bumped gently against the canal side in Van Binh, he was leaning over the side of the boat, retching his heart out.

Very slowly, taking all of Lewis's weight on himself, Lieutenant Grainger began to half carry and half drag him back toward the team house.

Lewis knew that he was throwing up, and he knew that someone was holding a bucket for him, was murmuring words of comfort, but he didn't know who it was. As the unknown person removed the bucket and handed him a cloth to wipe his mouth with, and then a cup of water, he thought perhaps that it was his mother. His mother had always been gentle and understanding when, as a child, he had been ill.

He rolled back into his bunk, aware that someone was tucking a blanket in around him. He felt a fall of silken hair touch his face, and despite his abject misery, he tried to smile. Abbra. It was Abbra, of course.

'Thanks, sweetheart,' he mumbled gratefully, squeezing her hand before sliding once more into unconsciousness.

She didn't leave him, and in his brief moments of lucidity he knew that she was there, sponging his face and his chest, holding a cup of water to his mouth, re-covering him with the blankets he feverishly tossed aside.

'Love you,' he said as lights and colors whirled about him. 'You're a wonderful girl, sweetheart. The very best.'

It was morning when the fever broke. He lay, looking up at the base of the bunk above him, trying to work out where the hell he was. Turning his head slightly, he could see the wooden-floored, sparsely furnished room and a girl who was not Abbra sitting cross-legged on a mat, sewing up a tear in a pair of tiger-stripe fatigues. Vietnam. He was in Vietnam and Abbra was over eight thousand miles away.

'Welcome back to the world of the living, *Dai uy*,' Lieutenant Grainger said with a grin, handing him a cup of coffee. 'You had me pretty worried for a while.'

'Not half as worried as I was,' Lewis said dryly, easing himself up and resting his weight on one elbow as he sipped gratefully at the coffee. 'How much time did I lose?'

'Eighteen hours. The fever broke at about three in the morning. Since then you've been sleeping like a baby.'

From the far side of the team house Tam was watching him as she sewed. There was a strange expression in her eyes, a look almost of apprehension. He dimly remembered the gentle touch of feminine hands sponging his face and chest, holding cups of water to his mouth, even, dear God, holding a bucket for him as he vomited. He looked across at her, feeling grateful and more than a little embarrassed. He couldn't say anything to her in front of Grainger, not the things that he wanted to say, but as their eyes held he gave her an affectionate and appreciative smile.

The effect was amazing. Her apprehension vanished, replaced by an expression of overwhelming relief – and shy familiarity.

Later, after she had left the team house and he had dressed, he had walked across the compound to where she was laying freshly laundered fatigues out in the sun to dry.

'I'm sorry you had to play nurse,' he said, acutely aware of the soft curve of her breasts and the slender line of her hips beneath her cheap cotton *ao dai*.

She paused in her task, looking laughingly across at him, the familiarity in her eyes no longer so shy. 'I did not mind, *Dai uy*,' she said, her voice full of naughty mischief. 'You were not half so fearsome when you were helpless!'

It was no way for a cleaning girl to talk to a *co van* and a *dai uy*, but he did not reprimand her. As far as he was concerned, she had earned the right to speak to him as a friend, and he was enjoying their easy-going camaraderie.

In the days that followed, the lighthearted teasing of their new friendship did not take place when Grainger or Drayton or Duxbery or Pennington were within earshot. On those occasions she spoke to him with cool respect, and then only when necessary. But at other times, when he was teaching her English, or when Lieutenant Grainger was out on patrol with Sergeant Drayton and Sergeant Pennington, and Lewis was engaged with administrative work, then she would ask him about America, laughing with delighted incredulity at whatever he told her, and in more serious moments he would talk to her about her own country, educating her about the true nature of the Viet Cong, and what would happen in the South if they and their North Vietnamese masters were successful in their ambitions.

Tam had at first doubted, but gradually her disbelief had begun to fade. After all, if the *dai uy* said these things were true, then they must be true. The *dai uy* was clever, far cleverer than her sister and her brother-in-law.

By the time Lewis and his team and the local militia, supplemented by the militia of other villages in the area and by a Special Forces squad, left camp to intercept the NVA supply team, Tam had given Lewis her complete trust and loyalty.

It was dusk when the men filed out of the compound, making their way down to the canal and the waiting patrol boats that had been requisitioned from the navy especially for the night's operation. She watched them board the boats, and then walked back into the team house, making sure the mosquito netting was down around Lewis's bunk, that his second pair of boots were clean and mud-free, that there was clean clothing for him to change into when he returned. As she lifted the jacket of his green jungle fatigues, a photograph fell out of an unbuttoned breast pocket.

She picked it up and looked at it. It wasn't the first time she had seen it. It was a photograph that the *dai uy* almost always carried with him, but though she had caught glimpses of it previously, she had never before been able to study it at length. She knew who it was of, of course. The *dai uy*'s wife.

She looked down at the photograph jealously. She had thought that all American women were fair-haired, but the girl in the photograph had hair as glossily black as her own. And the *dai uy* had married her. He must have thought her very beautiful, which meant that he liked long black hair, and her own hair was far longer than the American girl's, and even more night-black. She slipped the photograph back into the *dai uy*'s pocket feeling immensely cheered. At least she knew now that she was physically attractive to him. And over the last few days, that had become very, very important to her.

* * *

Lewis boarded the head patrol boat, grateful for the special equipment. A possible confrontation with North Vietnamese Army forces was a very different ball game from a skirmish with the local Viet Cong, and the local Viet Cong were bad enough. He ordered one of the Vietnamese to squat in the bow and to keep a sharp lookout over the tall reeds that choked the canal banks. He laid his M-16 across his knees and mentally reviewed his strategy, hoping to God that he wasn't going to find any flaws in it now.

The branch canal that the informant had told them the NVA were going to use was one he was unfamiliar with, and he had had to trust his local militia commander's knowledge of the area to determine the best point to stage an ambush.

'Here, *Dai uy*,' the young commander of Van Binh forces had said unequivocally. 'There is an intersection here with a main waterway. If we diverge here,—' his finger had stubbed at the map spread out on Lewis's desk '—then we can converge on them from both sides.'

Lewis had nodded in agreement. It seemed an ideal point for an ambush. The only problem was that the NVA were well aware of every vulnerable position on the routes that they used, and they might be prepared for them. There was another worry too, one which he had discussed far into the night with the other members of his team. Their informant might not be an informant at all.

He could very well be giving them false information in order to lure them into a trap.

'In other words, we might very well find ourselves ambushed by superior forces before we have the chance to lay our own trap,' Sergeant Drayton had said dryly, as he cleaned his Colt .45 automatic. 'Not a very nice thought, is it?'

It wasn't, but Lewis had decided that it was a risk they would have to take. If worse came to worst, they would be able to summon air power. The patrol boats were radio linked to a USS aircraft carrier a mile out in the South China Sea, and helicopter gunships could be dispatched from the carrier's deck the instant they were asked for. It was a comforting thought, but he was fiercely hoping that such action wouldn't be necessary. He wanted the ambush to be as trouble free and as textbook an operation as their last ambush had been.

It was dark now, and the moon was full and high as the boats chugged softly down the waterway, deeper and deeper into what Lieutenant Grainger termed 'Indian country', country where the Viet Cong had complete control, country where they could expect, at any moment, to come under heavy enemy fire.

As they turned off the main waterway onto narrower, less-used canals, the undergrowth from the banks reached out toward them, low-lying branches flicking them with damp, insect-infested leaves.

'Christ, I hate this damned country!'

Sergeant Drayton whispered viciously as he swatted at a party of ants that were scurrying down the neck of his fatigues.

Lewis could cope with the ants, it was the leeches he hated. No matter what kind of operation they had been engaged in, when they returned to the team house, they would be covered with leeches. Burning them off with the end of a lighted cigarette was the most effective way to remove them, but out in the country it wasn't always possible to light a cigarette and then their unwelcome and painful traveling companions just had to be endured.

As time passed they began to move slower and slower, hampered by the water vines and reeds that choked the little-used channels.

Lieutenant Grainger looked across at him anxiously. 'How are we for time, *Dai uy*?'

'We have a little.'

They hadn't much and they both knew it. If they weren't in position at the intersection before midnight, then they ran the very real risk of running straight into the oncoming convoy of boats. And the kind of firefight that would ensue would be anything but textbook.

The Vietnamese militia commander crept toward him.

'We're nearly there, *Dai uy*,' he whispered.

Lewis nodded, signaling for all engines to be cut. As they glided over the fetid black water, he strained his ears for the sound of any other movement. Nothing.

'Here we go, *Trung uy*,' he said quietly to

Lieutenant Grainger. 'Let's hope to God it isn't a setup.'

It wasn't. With swift expertise he was able to string his troops out along both sides of the canal bank. The navy patrol boats were heavily armed and he had the .30-caliber machine gun that each boat carried offloaded and mounted in ambush position, to increase their firepower.

He flicked on his PRC-25, his portable receiver-transmitter that he was never without, transmitting softly to the commander of the local militia platoon that was on his left flank, checking for problems. The answer was negative and he called in Lieutenant Grainger who was with a platoon from Van Binh on the other side of the canal. 'Lima, this is Foxtrot, over.'

'Foxtrot, this is Lima,' Grainger's voice said, so quietly he could barely hear it. 'Go ahead.'

'This is Foxtrot ... Have you any problems? Over?'

'This is Lima. Negative. Over.'

They were all in position. The patrol boats, with their deck-mounted mortars, were discreetly out of sight several yards down the main waterway from the intersection. There was nothing for them to do now but settle among the soggy wetness of chest high reeds and wait.

As Lewis crouched in acute discomfort in the darkness, he was sure that he wasn't alone in hoping that their information was wrong, that if and when a convoy appeared, it would be Viet Cong, not NVA. If it was the NVA, then they were going to be in for a vicious battle. The North Vietnamese were outstanding soldiers, never giving way and never retreating. If the same tenaciousness and discipline could be bred in the soldiers of the ARVN, then Lewis felt quite sure that South Vietnam would have been more than capable of fighting its own battle, without American aid. But for some reason, in many units of the ARVN, tenaciousness and motivation were conspicuous only by their absence.

The radio crackled. 'Foxtrot, Lima, over.'

'Lima, this is Foxtrot,' he whispered into his hand mike. 'Over.'

'This is Lima. We have lights approaching. Over.'

The canal network was so labyrinthine that sampans traveling in a convoy at night habitually traveled with a small single light in the bows so that they could easily follow one another and not become lost.

'This is Pelican. How many lights? Over.'

There was the faint possibility that the sampans were being manned by fishermen. And if they were, the last thing he wanted to do was to come up on them with .30-caliber machine guns and deck-mounted mortars.

'This is Lima. A whole string of them. Eight or nine. Maybe a dozen. Over.'

Lewis muttered an obscenity beneath his breath. A dozen sampans in convoy were not local fishermen. All his units were on the one radio frequency, and he knew that all had heard his conversation with Grainger.

'This is Foxtrot to all units,' he whispered tersely. 'Stand by to attack. Over.'

Ambushing a fleet of sampans wasn't the straightforward task that ambushing an unprepared foot patrol was. Lewis knew that the NVA's first reaction would be to leap into the canal and to make for the banks in order to have the advantage of fighting on solid ground. Once that happened, it would be close fighting of the very worst kind, and he wanted to avoid it by decimating them with machine-gun fire before they even had a chance to hurl themselves overboard.

But it was an impossible ambition. The sampans were too far apart for them to be able to open fire on all of them simultaneously. It seemed to Lewis that even before he gave the signal for all units to blast the boats with everything they had, they were under answering fire. Nothing went as planned. The patrol boats were slow in moving out of their hiding place in the main waterway to give them support; the NVA from the tail boats were in the water and on the banks, raking them with fire from AK-47s even before the answering fire from the lead boats had been silenced.

Almost from the word go he knew that the operation was a debacle. Despite the explosive, savage spray from the .30-caliber machine guns and the ceaseless roar of fire from M-16s, the North Vietnamese kept hurtling toward them, Kalashnikovs at their hips, firing as they came. He knew he could expect no help from Grainger. Over the PRC-25, Grainger had yelled that he and his platoon were under heavy attack and were already being forced to fall back.

Lewis cursed the moon, so full and bright that it gave them virtually no cover. As he let rip with his M-16 at the crack North Vietnamese troops bearing down on them, Drayton leapt to his side, attaching a fresh belt to the flapping tail of his ammunition and then reloading his own M-16 and firing off another clip as the NVA steadfastly advanced.

As a fresh surge of troops from the sampans made the bank, Lewis hurtled past Drayton, racing toward them, a hand grenade, pin out, in his fist, his arm cocked as he threw and then dived for cover.

*'That got the motherfuckers!'* he could hear Drayton yelling exuberantly.

Lewis's first instinct, when he knew there were only eight or a dozen boats in the convoy, was that there was no need to call in air support. Now it was a decision he bitterly regretted. By not calling in the helicopter gunships right from the beginning, precious time, and lives, had been lost. He had called for them the minute he had realized the size of the operation they were involved in, but there was still no sign of them.

'Come on, come on!' he muttered viciously between his teeth. For nearly two minutes he had been unable to make contact with

Grainger. It could be Grainger had simply become separated from his PRC-25. Or it could be that Grainger was dead.

By now they were receiving the support they needed from the patrol boats. Mortar fire was deluging the sampans and silencing all returning fire from that direction. The main remaining danger was from the North Vietnamese who were on the water-logged banks, spraying everything that moved with AK-47 fire. If they once got away from the bank and spread out, they'd never be able to get the bastards.

*'Don't let them get away from the bank!'* he yelled across to Drayton. As he raced forward, firing as he ran, he could see one of the Vietnamese from Van Binh local militia, standing, feet apart, machine-gunning from the waist. *'Move!'* he shouted across to him. *'Let's get the bastards!'*

One minute the darkness was so full of fireballs and smoke and screams and shouted obscenities that he was both blinded and deafened, and the next there was silence.

He had been flat on his stomach, half submerged in water, firing, firing, firing at the remaining North Vietnamese. He raised himself up on one knee, looking around cautiously. From a distance of a mere three yards a wounded North Vietnamese was struggling to lift an AK-47 into a firing position.

'Oh, no, you don't, sonny boy!' Lewis said between clenched teeth. He lifted his M-16 with speed and unloaded six rounds into the

North Vietnamese's chest. The moon was bright enough for him to see the expression of horror on the soldier's face, and then his body sagged, collapsing in a sea of blood.

The silence was broken by the pounding of approaching helicopter rotors. They were arriving and they were too late. They no longer needed two gunships, they needed a dust off.

Of the twenty-four men who had set off from Van Binh, six were dead and four were injured. Even before Lewis had splashed across to the canal's far bank, he had known that Lieutenant Grainger was dead. All the men he had designated to that position were dead, their M-16s still in their hands, their faces toward the enemy.

He was well trained enough, and well adjusted enough, not to consume himself with guilt. He had planned the operation to the best of his ability, and in his superiors' eyes it would be considered a success. An American and five South Vietnamese had died, but so had two dozen crack North Vietnamese troops. And a convoy of supplies for the Viet Cong had been thwarted. But Grainger's death weighed heavily on him.

'I am sorry about Lieutenant Grainger,' Tam said to him with touching sincerity, and then she added fiercely, 'But if it was fate that an American must die, then I am glad that it was Lieutenant Grainger, *Dai uy*, and that it was not you!'

Despite Tam doing her best to cheer him, Lewis brooded miserably over Grainger's death. Grainger had been short, like himself, with only a few weeks to go before his tour of duty was over. And now he was dead. As each day passed, Lewis could feel himself becoming more taciturn and more somber. And for the first time he found himself counting the days until he would shake the soil of Vietnam from his boots for good.

Ten days after Lieutenant Grainger's death a report came in that a handful of North Vietnamese troops were holed up in a remote village. Whether they were troops who had escaped from the fight that had taken place on the canal bank, or they were fresh troops who had perhaps brought in a replacement convoy of supplies, he had no way of knowing. Either way, he had no reason to think that hunting them down would be any different from a score of previous such operations.

It was Tam who was filled with sudden, dreadful premonition.

'Do not go, *Dai uy*,' she said urgently.

He had smiled at her affectionately and told her not to be a silly girl, but she had persisted in pleading with him, and in the end he had said a little curtly, 'That's enough, Tam, you're behaving as if I'm your husband or your father!'

She had stared at him as if he had slapped her, and then had said quietly, 'Not my father, *Dai uy*.'

He had been putting maps into his map

case. Very slowly he finished what he was doing, the blood drumming in his ears. Surely she had not said what he thought she had said. And if she had, surely she had not meant it to sound the way that it had sounded. His own remark had been stupid enough. He couldn't for the life of him imagine why he had said the word *husband*. What he had meant to say was that she was fussing around him as though he were a member of her family, a brother or a father. And instead he had said husband. One look at her face, and the expression in her eyes was enough to tell him that she had meant exactly what she had inferred.

He was appalled, appalled not by the emotion he could read so clearly in her eyes, but by his own, immediate, answering response to it.

'I'm going, Tam,' he said as indifferently as he could manage. Dear God in heaven! Why hadn't he had the sense to see where their easygoing familiarity would lead? She would have to stop working for them. She couldn't continue to clean the team house, not now that he had admitted to himself how very much she attracted him.

There was a half-written letter to Abbra on his desk, and he slid it into a drawer. Abbra. He had never imagined that he could be unfaithful to her, but he knew that for one swift instant he had been unfaithful to her in spirit. He would not be so again. Much as he would miss Tam, and he would miss her dreadfully, their close relationship would have to come to an end.

It was as if she had read every word that he was thinking. 'I am sorry, *Dai uy*,' she had said, her eyes holding his steadily. And then, with devastating candor she had added simply, 'But I love you.'

'You can't love me!' His voice had been choked. Sweet Christ, but how had he gotten himself into such a mess? The last thing on earth he wanted was to hurt her, and if he had set out deliberately to hurt her, he couldn't have been more successful. 'We'll talk later, Tam,' he said, knowing that Duxbery and Drayton were waiting for him in the compound.

She had said nothing, but her eyes had said everything – that she knew what it was he was going to say to her, that she wouldn't be able to be his cleaning girl anymore, that he was never going to love her and take her back to America with him. In silent agony she watched him as he strode out of the team house and across the compound toward Sergeant Duxbery and Sergeant Drayton.

He didn't look back. Together the three of them began to walk down toward the village, where the local troops were waiting, and as they did so, Tam began to search feverishly through the breast pockets of Lewis's spare fatigues. The photograph wasn't there. She couldn't tear it up or burn it. Hot tears stung the backs of her eyes. She hadn't wanted to fall in love with him. She had hated him and had been determined to continue hating him. But he wasn't a man it was possible to hate. And now she loved him.

The faint put-put of engines could be heard, and she ran across to the door, hoping for one last glimpse of him. Because he had been wearing the same blue beret as his South Vietnamese troops, she couldn't distinguish him. She leaned against the jamb of the door, pressing her hands hard against her stomach in an effort to quell the dreadful presentiment of disaster that was churning there.

The village where the NVA were rumored to be hiding out showed no signs of them. Lewis was relieved. In his present disturbed state of mind the last thing he wanted was another confrontation with North Vietnamese. He ordered his men to search the surrounding paddy fields and dykes to make sure that the area was clean, and then ordered a return to Van Binh.

It was as their boats emerged from the narrower branch canal that served the village that the North Vietnamese struck. It was as neat an act of revenge as he had ever seen. In exactly the same way as they had ambushed the North Vietnamese, the North Vietnamese now ambushed them, raking them with blistering machine-gun fire from both banks, and sealing off the canal with a flotilla of sampans that he was sure were mined.

Duxbery was hit almost immediately,

screaming out in pain and clutching at his chest. Lewis leapt toward him, and as he did so a bullet hit him in the shoulder, lifting him from his feet. He was aware of pandemonium breaking out all around him and of Duxbery staring up at him with dead eyes, and then, shouting for the South Vietnamese to do likewise, he threw himself over the side of the boat, striking out for the thick, concealing vegetation that lined the bank. Bullets plummeted into the water and he took a deep breath, struggling to dive deep. Chokingly thick vines and reeds foiled him. His lungs were bursting, and when he at last broke surface, it was to find a North Vietnamese standing waist-deep in the water, pointing an AK-47 at him. The North Vietnamese grinned. *'Lai! Lai!'* he barked, gesturing with the machine gun for Lewis to wade out of the canal ahead of him. *'Move! Move!'*

# CHAPTER EIGHTEEN

For the next two months Kyle tried every trick in the book to pull a trip to Saigon.

'You've already pulled one three-day R and R trip to the big city,' his operations officer said sourly when Kyle demanded to know when the hell he was going to be listed to fly a ship down to the Tan Son Nhut air base. 'If you don't quit carping, the next time you see it will be when you're on your way out of this goddamned country – for good!'

'For Christ's sake, forget her,' Chuck said in exasperation. 'There's free tail all over this country and you want to make life hard for yourself by paying court to a chaperoned virgin! It makes no sense.'

Kyle knew it wasn't sensible, but despite his drunken visits with Chuck to the ladies of the nearest town, returning to Saigon and seeing Trinh again had become an obsession.

'What about the little lady back home?' Chuck asked as they flew troopers up to a landing zone that was reported to be cold.

Kyle grinned. Chuck's phrase was completely inappropriate for Serena. 'The *little lady* back home is a five-foot-ten blonde who is so wild herself she would make your hair curl!'

This time it was Chuck's turn to grin. 'She sounds like fun,' he said, flaring steeply to slow the Huey ready for landing.

'She is.'

His voice was so unequivocal that Chuck raised his eyebrows. He had Kyle marked down as a lot of things, but a devoted husband was not one of them. If he had been wrong, then the five-foot-ten blonde must be quite a girl. Kyle was the least likely devoted husband he'd ever seen.

For several days they ferried troopers into cold landing zones, spent hours laagering in wait for them, and then flew in to pick them up.

'For chrissakes, this is boring,' a fellow pilot said to Kyle as they sweated under a hot sun, waiting for the signal to crank up.

Kyle was in complete agreement. The tedium of waiting around for hours on end was far worse than the adrenaline-filled fear and excitement of flying into a battle zone.

'Look at this shit,' his companion said disgustedly, his finger stabbing at the magazine he was reading. 'Antiwar protesters marching on the White House. What kind of Americans are those? Why the hell aren't they marching in protest against Ho Chi Minh? And look at this fuckin' photograph here! This one was taken in England! England for chrissakes! What do the fuckin' English know about anything!'

Kyle looked across at the photograph with

idle curiosity. A group of antiwar protesters had marched on the American Embassy in Grosvenor Square and had refused to disperse peacefully. Fighting had broken out and several protesters had been arrested. There was a vivid photograph of one protester, banner still in hand, as police manhandled him into a Black Maria.

'Here, let me have a look at that!' he said suddenly, his interest quickening. He took hold of the magazine and then let out a whoop of disgust. 'Would you *look* at that! That moron is my brother-in-law, for Christ's sake!'

Chuck, who had been lying in the shade beside his Huey with a paperback covering his face, now removed it and opened one eye.

'No joke? That guy in the photo is your brother-in-law?'

'No joke,' Kyle said grimly. 'Christ. Given the choice, I think I'd rather shoot him than a gook! Have you seen his banner? "Long live Ho Chi Minh." I'd like to drop the prick into the middle of a battle zone being overrun by Cong and see if he'd still sing the same fucking song!'

Chuck sat up and reached across for the magazine, looking at it with interest. Lance's hippie-length blond hair and slightly effeminate features could be seen clearly. Underneath the photograph, in small print, it read, 'Viscount Blyth-Templeton being removed by police after leading a party of antiwar protesters with a petition to the American

Embassy.' Chuck didn't know very much about English aristocracy, but he figured that if Lance Blyth-Templeton was a viscount, then his sister, Kyle's wife, must be a lady or a viscountess or something.

He grinned. A five-foot-ten blonde, wild English viscountess must be quite something. Maybe he'd keep in touch with Kyle when their time in 'Nam was over. She was one lady he sure as hell would like to meet.

'Just *one* maintenance R and R trip to Saigon,' Kyle said pleadingly to his operations officer.

'What's the matter with you, Anderson? Aren't the women up here good enough for you?' his operations officer said bad-temperedly. 'Why the fuck should I give a three-day trip to Saigon to a warrant officer when I have captains lining up for the pleasure?'

'Because I've been flying my ass off for two months, that's why!' Kyle retorted furiously.

'Everyone flies their ass off. You aren't the only one banging Lady Luck and walking away in the morning without so much as a thank you, ma'am.'

'Look, this is real important to me. Just one three-day maintenance trip to Saigon.'

'Only if you say please,' his operations officer said without the least change in the tone of his voice or his facial expression.

For a second Kyle didn't register what he had said. 'I'll do anything. I'll...' The words finally penetrated his brain. 'Please! Please!

Pretty please!' he yelled exultantly, throwing his helmet into the air.

'Don't go overboard,' his operations officer said with a glimmer of good humor. 'It isn't all good news.'

'What's the bad?' Kyle asked, not caring.

'I'm scheduling you to go with Wilson,' his operations officer said, shaking his head in despair at his soft heart.

'And who am I supposed to drink and whore with while you pay court to little Miss Goody Two-Shoes?' Chuck said, disgruntled.

'Drop in at the Sporting Bar and fall in with some Green Berets,' Kyle said, opening his mail.

He had been surprised at how often Serena was writing to him. She wisely didn't mention Lance, but she made him chuckle with her anecdotes of a visit to a country house and contents sale with Rupert.

'For a wild woman, your lady at home is pretty good at putting pen to paper,' Chuck said, sifting through his own mail and then throwing it to one side in disgust.

'She's probably high on the novelty of it,' Kyle said with a carelessness he didn't truly feel.

After their previous year of separation, when they hadn't been in communication at all, he hadn't expected her to write. Nor had he expected that if she did, he would feel so appreciative. His own letters back to her were far less frequent, consisting of hastily scrawled postcards written whenever he was drunk enough to be maudlinly reminiscent.

Kyle was well aware of the daredevil reputation he had carved out for himself. Both he and Chuck were regarded as halfway to being crazy because of the risks they took. Whenever anyone called him crazy to his face, he simply grinned and agreed with them. Of course he was crazy. Hell, he wouldn't be there if he weren't!

'Those poor fuckers we're leaving behind wouldn't think you were quite so hip if they knew how you intend spending your three days R and R,' Chuck said dryly over the intercom as they cruised south toward Tan Son Nhut at one thousand five hundred feet. 'For Christ's sake, what is it with you? Have you never met a woman who was off limits before?'

'Nope,' Kyle replied, unperturbed. 'To tell you the truth, I don't think I have!'

Saigon shimmered in the heat below them, and he felt his stomach muscles tightening in nervous anticipation. Would she still be at the International? Would she remember him? If she remembered him, would she still agree to go out on a date with him?

'I swear to God I can smell that town from here,' Chuck said as they began to decelerate ready for landing. 'Swamp and mildew, stale perfume, exhaust fumes, and *nuoc mam*.'

'And sex,' Kyle said with a grin. 'Don't forget the sex.'

Chuck gave a snort of agreement. 'That town is so steeped in sex it reeks of it! And you, numbnut, are going to spend your time there holding hands, as if you were a bashful teenager!'

He didn't even bother to check in with Chuck at the Continental. Instead, he made his way straight to the International, bounding up the steps and into the lobby, his heart in his mouth.

She was there. For one instant, as she looked toward him, not recognizing him, her smile was polite and impersonal, and then it widened, recognition flooding her eyes.

'I'm back,' he said unnecessarily. 'We have a date, remember?'

His fatigues were still soaked with the sweat from his flight, a lock of dark hair fell untidily across his brow, and his electric-blue eyes were hot and determined.

A dimple touched the corner of her mouth beguilingly. 'It is not quite so simple,' she said, an undertone of laughter in her voice. 'You must meet my sister first and meet with her approval.'

'Lead me to her!' His grin was splitting his face. He felt as Alexander must have felt after conquering Persia.

Her amusement deepened. All Americans were crazy, but this one was certainly crazier than most. 'This evening, when I have finished work, then I will talk to her and ask her if she will meet you.'

Her last sentence had brought an uncomfortable element of doubt into the situation. 'Where would she enjoy dining most?' he asked, feeling that if a time and place were decided upon, a successful outcome was just a little bit likelier. 'The restaurant at the Continental? The Caravelle?'

'I think perhaps the Continental,' she said, wondering why, after eighteen months of being solicited by nearly every American who had crossed the International's lobby, she was now capitulating to this tall, lean, criminally young helicopter pilot with the reckless eyes.

'I'll book a table for seven-thirty.' It was a ridiculously early hour to be eating in Saigon, but he didn't care. He just wanted to be in her company, and if that meant being in her sister's company as well, then it was a small price to pay.

'I can't talk any longer,' she said softly as a boisterous party of European construction engineers entered the lobby.

He nodded, understanding at once. If she was overheard, or seen, talking to him with such familiarity, then the International's patrons would assume she was available and she would be overwhelmed by amorous advances.

'Right,' he said briefly. 'Bye.'

*'Chào,'* she said, the dimple in her cheek still in evidence.

As he strode past the engineers and out into the street he decided that it was time he came to grips with the Vietnamese language. Why on earth did the Viets use the word *chào* to both say hello and good-bye? It didn't make sense. For all he knew, they probably used the same word for other opposites, like stop and go, and friend and enemy. If they did, it was no wonder the American High Command had difficulties in understanding them!

'How was Miss Goody Two-Shoes?' Chuck asked him when he walked into their room at the Continental.

'Okay,' Kyle said, good-naturedly noncommittal.

Chuck had already showered and changed into jeans and a T-shirt, ready to hit the streets. He finished combing his close-cropped light brown hair, tucking the comb into his hip pocket, saying in amusement, 'So that's the way the cookie crumbles, is it? Miss Goody Two-Shoes really is a serious item and not a fit subject for bawdy speculation?'

'You got it.' Kyle stripped off his sweat-soaked shirt.

Chuck shook his head in mystification. 'Okay,' he said at last. 'If that's the way it is, buddy, then even though I'll never understand it, I promise I won't give you a hassle. As far as I'm concerned, Miss Goody Two-Shoes is your wife, your sister, your mother, and the Virgin Mary all rolled into one, and will receive all due respect.'

'Then start off by referring to her by her name,' Kyle said, pulling off his trousers and throwing them in Chuck's direction.

Chuck dodged the trousers. 'And that is?'

'Trinh, and for your information, it means

pure and virtuous.'

'How do you know?' Chuck was intrigued. 'Did she tell you that?'

Kyle walked into the bathroom and turned on the shower. 'No,' he yelled over the sound of the gushing water. 'There was a Vietnamese interpreter in camp the other day and I asked him!'

Chuck stared toward the open bathroom door. Kyle was really taking this thing seriously, far too seriously for his liking. After all, what the hell could come of it? Kyle was married. The girl was probably a Buddhist or a Confucian and even if Kyle got a divorce, there would be no way that her family would allow her to marry him. In his book, for Kyle to embark on such a relationship was absolutely pointless.

He shrugged his shoulders. It wasn't his business. He was Kyle's buddy, not his keeper. And he was wasting precious time. The bars and brothels were waiting.

'If you want to catch up with me, I'll be in La Boheme or The Sporting Bar,' he yelled, striding out of the room, knowing that he wouldn't be without a companion for very long.

There was a whole long afternoon to while away before he was due to meet Trinh and her sister, and for once Kyle was perplexed as to how he should spend his time. He couldn't do any heavy drinking. If he reeked of alcohol when he met her sister, then he would very probably never manage to date Trinh ever again. And he couldn't whore. Or could he?

He mentally debated the point while he toweled himself dry and changed into crisp, clean fatigues. After all, Trinh would never know, and if he didn't get himself some sex in before their date, then he certainly wouldn't get any during. He chuckled as he zipped up his pants. He was in grave danger of achieving the impossible. A three-day celibate R and R in Sin City. If word of it ever got around, his reputation would be shot to pieces.

As he walked through the lobby he ran into a Vietnamese wedding party making their way toward the Continental's tiny interior garden. The garden, with its mass of frangipani blossom and potted palms and gaily colored turquoise china elephants was a great favorite with local photographers.

He stood watching them. The groom was almost as slightly built as his bride, and they were holding hands, laughing across at each other, their hair and shoulders thick with flower petals. The bride was dressed in red, not white, and her friends twittered around her, as pretty as butterflies in their floating, pastel *ao dais*. For a few brief minutes they surrounded him and then they were gone, crowding ebulliently into the little garden.

He strolled out into the street. He was beginning to find the South Vietnamese a very attractive people. He wished to hell he had been taught more about their way of life and their customs when he had been at helicopter school. All he could remember was learning to call them dinks and slopes and gooks. His knuckles tightened fractionally. Anyone he heard referring to Trinh as a dink would very speedily regret it.

He paused for a moment before turning into La Boheme. Tu Do was massed with bicycles and cycles as it always was, but the cars honking for a passageway were American and driven by Americans. The dudes mobbing the sidewalk and dodging the street traffic were American. Neon signs advertised American brand names; Coke, Winstons, Levi's. The music blaring from American transistors was American music: James Brown, Wilson Pickett, The Temptations.

It was as if a monstrous wedge of downtown Los Angeles had been grafted onto the coast of Southeast Asia. And the Vietnamese smilingly serviced the invasion. They shined shoes and waited tables and cooked food and washed laundry and provided sex. For the first time Kyle wondered about the thoughts behind those smiles. He wondered what Trinh thought of the Americans in her city. He wondered what she thought of him.

'Saigon tea? You buy me Saigon tea?' a lady of the house said, curling herself around him.

Kyle slapped two dollars into her palm to keep her quiet, and looked around for Chuck.

'You number one,' his newfound friend said, winding her arms around his neck and rubbing herself seductively up against him.

Chuck was at the bar with a couple of marines, all of them with girls on their knees. All he had to do was walk across and join in the fun. He looked down at the girl, whose hand was now roving speculatively over the bulge in his crotch. She was very pretty, with fine, doll-like features and hair shimmering loosely down her back to her waist.

'You buy me another Saigon tea?' she asked winningly.

Kyle grinned down at her and then, surprising himself almost as much as he surprised the girl, he said, 'No. Today I seem to be right out of money for Saigon teas.'

The expression on the girl's face changed from one of winsomeness to one of incredulity and then disgust.

'You number-one cheap Charlie!' she flared indignantly, removing herself from him with all speed. 'You suck-suck!'

From the bar Chuck caught sight of him, shouting across for him to join them. Kyle raised a hand in acknowledgment and then shook his head. 'Not this time, buddy,' he yelled back over the deafening sound of Wilson Pickett's 'Mustang Sally'. 'See you later, back at the Continental.'

For the rest of the long, hot afternoon he kept out of trouble, restricting himself to a couple of beers. After that he turned to coffee, sitting beneath the awning of a sidewalk café, watching the world go by and spurning all offers of female companionship.

When he finally made his way back to the Continental, he saw Chuck and his companions stagger from a bar and half fall, laughing and uproariously drunk, into another.

He grinned to himself. It was a strange sensation being sober and celibate in a city so swingingly sinful. It was certainly an afternoon he would remember. Hell, it was an afternoon in Saigon so stainlessly pure, he would be able to tell his grandchildren about it!

He was glad that he had suggested they meet early. By 7:40 p.m. as a waiter led Trinh and her sister across to his table on the Continental's terrace, the surrounding tables were already beginning to fill.

He had been waiting for them for twenty minutes in an agony of impatience. For the past ten minutes he had been certain that they were not going to come, and then he had seen them, sumptuously dressed in silken *ao dais*, walking with head-turning grace in the waiter's wake.

As he rose to his feet his mouth was dry. He felt like a kid on his first date.

'My sister, Mai,' Trinh was saying to him. 'Mai, Kyle...'

'Anderson,' he finished for her quickly, knowing that she still didn't know his surname, as he, incredibly, did not know hers.

'I am very pleased to meet you, Mr Anderson,' she said with cool formality.

'Just call me Kyle.' As they sat down, Kyle

wondered if he had made a crass mistake. Perhaps such an invitation to a lady he had only just been introduced to was considered ill bred in polite Vietnamese circles. And he was certain that Trinh and her sister belonged to very polite circles indeed. As they had entered the hotel, and before the waiter had led them across the terrace, he had seen the proprietor bowing to them from the waist, greeting them warmly, an honor conferred on very few of the Continental's guests.

He ordered a bottle of chilled vin blanc cassis, and tried to redeem his thoughtless crassness.

'I'm very pleased to meet you, Miss...' He could have bitten off his tongue. He still didn't know her surname. 'Mai,' he said quickly, aware that Trinh was all too aware of his discomfiture and that she was having great difficulty in suppressing her giggles.

'I am very pleased to meet you too,' Mai said, her English charmingly touched with an unmistakable French accent. 'Our family has many Western friends, but they are not—' She paused, her sloe-dark eyes holding his. 'They are not army personnel. You understand what I am saying, Mr. Anderson?'

He understood perfectly. He looked across at Trinh, as beautiful as an exotic flower in her silk *ao dai*, her eyes laughing into his, and then he turned once more toward her sister.

'I know very little of Vietnamese customs and manners,' he said truthfully. 'But I do know that I want to see Trinh again. I understand the kind of girl she is, and the kind of family that she comes from, and that you are concerned for her reputation.' He cleared his throat, wondering what Serena's reaction would be if she could see and hear him. Would she throw the nearest available object at his head, or would she burst into shouts of disbelieving laughter? 'If you allow me to see her, I promise you that she will come to no harm ... that I won't take unfair advantage...' He was floundering and he knew it. He had never had these intentions before in his life, much less tried to articulate them.

'As our parents are dead, I am the head of our family,' Mai said, coming to his aid and looking too charmingly fragile to be the head of anything. 'If you wish to see Trinh, then you may do so, Mr. Anderson, providing she is adequately chaperoned.'

'By yourself?' Kyle asked, relieved that the inquisition, such as it was, appeared to be over.

Mai nodded, smiling a little shyly, and he was suddenly aware that she, too, was relieved that the business of the evening was over. 'Great,' he said, reflecting in amusement that if the sister's positions had been reversed, Trinh would have made a far sterner interrogator. 'Now that that's taken care of, let's eat.'

They started off with *canh chua* soup, a delicate mixture of shrimp and bean sprouts and pineapple and celery, and Trinh told him a little of her family history. 'We are a very old family in Saigon,' she said, sipping at her wine from a long-stemmed glass. 'My father was a mandarin and an adviser to Bao Dai, the last emperor.'

He listened, intrigued, discovering that she was neither Buddhist nor Confucian, but Roman Catholic, and that she had been educated in French schools in Saigon and had spent two years in Paris, at the Sorbonne.

As rice and finely chopped, tender beef wrapped in grape leaves followed the soup, he was aware that they were receiving several curious glances from the other diners. The majority of them were Americans from the embassy and the aid agencies, eked out by a handful of portly Vietnamese businessmen dressed Western-style. He knew very well what they were all thinking. Were Mai and Trinh high-class hookers? And if they weren't, what the hell was he doing squiring them around?

He was grateful when a fair-haired man about his own age walked across to a nearby table, escorting a Vietnamese companion who looked even more respectable than Mai and Trinh. She was, surprisingly, easily in her late thirties, and perhaps even in her early forties.

He looked across at them speculatively, wondering about their relationship. The guy didn't look to be army, his hair was far too long, and he didn't look to be American. He was deeply suntanned, and even though he was young, there was a web of fine lines around his eyes, as if he were accustomed to screwing his eyes up to look into the sun. As soon as he spoke, asking for the wine list, Kyle knew he had been right about him. He was an Australian.

'...where were you born in America?' Mai was asking him.

'Boston,' he said, dismissing the Australian from his mind, and wondering when he was going to be able to surreptitiously hold Trinh's hand.

'Well?' Chuck asked blearily the next morning as he dragged himself into the world of the living. 'Has the novelty of being a monk worn off yet?'

In the nearby twin bed Kyle rolled onto his back, resting his head on his hands. It was a very pertinent question. He had been able to hold Trinh's hand only briefly, when he had handed her into the taxicab that Mai had insisted they go home in, alone. That had been the full extent of the physical contact between them. Smiles across a table and a hot, urgent handhold. He thought of Trinh's delicate, flawless face and her laughing dark eyes, and his stomach turned a somersault as if he were going down a roller coaster.

'No,' he said, wondering for the first time where their relationship could possibly go. What it would lead to. 'No, I seem to be turning into a pretty damned good monk!'

Chuck groaned and pulled the sheet up over his head. 'Later,' was all Kyle could indistinctly hear. 'Tell me all about Miss Goody Trinh Two-Shoes, later.'

He did better than that. At lunchtime, in the lobby of the International he introduced Chuck to her.

Chuck was impressed. She was certainly something, every inch a lady but with that naughty light of laughter in her eyes that every Vietnamese woman he had ever met seemed to have been born with. All the same, if he were Kyle, he knew where his preference would lie. And that would be with the five-foot-ten, wild aristocratic blonde, in swinging London.

When they returned to camp, Kyle put his mind to the serious task of sorting out regular time in Saigon. Vietnam was a land that ran on bribes and corruption, and he saw no reason why he shouldn't sink to those depths himself, if they would get him what he wanted.

'You're an Anderson of the Anderson banking family?' his operations officer asked him, suddenly acutely attentive.

Kyle nodded.

'You're not shitting me, are you? Because if you are...'

'I'm not shitting you,' Kyle said, amused at how easy it was all going to be. 'All I want to do is to come to an arrangement.'

'Oh, I think we can do that all right,' his operations op said, grinning broadly, 'Yes, I certainly think we'll be able to do that all right. For a price.'

The price was astronomically high, but as far as Kyle was concerned, it was worth it. Before the month was out he was seeing Trinh at least two weekends out of every four. Mai still accompanied them on what Trinh termed their 'official' dates. But there were other times, snatched moments when she escaped from the hotel desk and they were able to be alone together. Sometimes they would walk through the back streets behind Tu Do, down to the river; sometimes they would walk in the park that backed onto the Presidential Palace gardens; sometimes they would sit drinking coffee in Broddards, a café that catered to Vietnamese rather than Americans. The idyll lasted until September, until Trinh said that she couldn't see him on his next free day because it was the anniversary of her mother's death and she was going to spend the day with Mai.

Kyle now knew enough of Vietnamese tradition and custom to realize that it would be useless to argue with her. Even though she was a Catholic and not a Buddhist, as a Vietnamese, ancestor worship was in her blood and her bones.

Now that he was beginning to understand a little of what made the Vietnamese tick, he was constantly exasperated by how ignorant his fellow Americans were about them. The Strategic Hamlet program was a case in point. Under Diem, and with American approval and American aid, peasants had been forcibly removed from their villages and farms and transferred to new 'fortified' villages, villages which, in theory, the Viet Cong would be unable to penetrate.

In regions such as the Mekong Delta, where the peasants did not live in concentrated settlements but in farmhouses strung out along the edges of the dikes, this involved taking them from the land that had been their father's and their father's father's, and no new allotment of land was given to them. The peasants, far from being grateful for their new 'safe' villages, resented the government and the Americans who funded the government. And this was all because they didn't understand that the plots of land, where their ancestors were buried, were sacred to the Vietnamese.

Some Vietnamese were removed from their land so that it could be defoliated with Agent Orange and made a wilderness in which nothing, not even Viet Cong, could survive. These vast areas were turned into 'free fire zones', where anything moving would be a legitimate target for American forces. Because of this, huge numbers of needless refugees were created. And the peasants' resentment was exploited ruthlessly by the Viet Cong.

If Chuck had been with him on the Saturday he was in Saigon and Trinh was unable to see him, then he might very well never have become drunk, might very well never have gone to her house to wait for her. As it was, he had a whole day to while away, with no prospect of even seeing her in the evening. He began drowning his sorrows at ten in the morning in the Sporting Bar, finding companionship among the Green Berets. By twelve he was in the most doubtful of all areas in Saigon, in Canh Hoi, behind the docks. Here, the only Americans to be found were black and the only ladies were dark-skinned Khmers.

It wasn't the first time he had been unfaithful to Trinh. He had been seeing her now for three months and he had had to find sexual release somewhere. But it was the first time he had so bitterly resented making love to a nameless whore, when the only woman he wanted to make love to was Trinh.

By five o'clock, back in the relatively respectable area of Tu Do Street, he sat broodingly over a beer in La Pagoda, the only bar that he knew where there were no girls to solicit the clients. If Trinh had not refused to see him, when it had cost him an arm and a leg to wangle the flight down, then the incident with the Khmer girl would never have taken place. By the time it was five-thirty he had convinced himself that Trinh was entirely to blame, that she wasn't appreciative of the lengths he had gone to in order to see her so regularly, that she was treating him shabbily, and he didn't deserve it.

He peered blearily at his Rolex. Five forty-five. Trinh and Mai were visiting her mother's grave, but wherever it was, surely they would be back by now. Surely there was no reason why she couldn't see him that evening.

He hauled himself to his feet. She would see him that evening. It was about time she and Mai understood the lengths he had to go to in order to fly south so regularly. Christ. He was paying enough out in bribes to fund the fucking war! And because it was the anniversary of her mother's death she wouldn't even see him.

'This shit,' he said to himself as he staggered out into the street in search of a taxicab, 'hash got to shtop.'

He knew where she lived, though Mai had seen to it with gentle firmness that he had never been invited inside. 'Avenue Charnier,' he said to the impassive-faced taxi driver, enunciating clearly with difficulty. 'The house with the orange walls.'

It had once been a very elegant house, but it was now beginning to show signs of decay. Not for the first time he wondered about Trinh and Mai's finances. They had obviously inherited money when their parents had died, but he had a sneaking suspicion that it wasn't very much and that only careful husbandry enabled them to continue living in their family home.

Swaying slightly, he paid the taxi driver. If they wanted money, then they could have it. He began to make his way unsteadily toward a white-painted front door flanked by verandahs. But they wouldn't ask for money. Not in a million years. Hell. They didn't even know that in Western terms he was rich, rich, rich. He hiccuped and jangled the bell. They would know when he told them about the bribes he was paying in order to fly down so regularly. He could hear the sounds of footsteps approaching the other side of the door. Light, feminine footsteps. Perhaps then Mai would cease her vigilance. Perhaps, at long last, he and Trinh could have a normal, loving relationship.

She swung the door open and stared at him, a mixture of pleasure and bewilderment and slight apprehension in her eyes.

'Kyle ... what are you doing here? Why...'

'Need to talk to you,' he said abruptly, reeling past her and into the house.

If she made any attempt to prevent him, he was unaware of it. The house had the same air of faded gentility on the inside as it did on the outside. The teak floors were highly polished, but the French period furnishings, heavy with ormolu and filigree decoration, were shabby and well worn. Through an open door he saw a family ancestral altar with candles flickering before it and he realized, a little sheepishly, that he had disturbed her at prayer.

'Where's Mai?' he asked, looking around. 'Want to talk to Mai as well.'

He had had enough dates *à trois*. It was time they all had a good talk, time he made it clear that three months of being chaperoned was all he was going to take. There were going to be some changes made.

'Mai is still at the family burial ground. I felt ill. I had a headache and a temperature and so I came home early, alone.'

He rocked back on his heels, looking at her in concern. She did look a little unwell. There was a suspicious flush of color in her golden cheeks, and he pressed the back of his hand against her forehead.

'Flu,' he said knowledgeably. 'You're probably coming down with flu.' It was only then, as he looked down at her in tender concern, that her words penetrated his drink-fumed brain. 'You mean Mai ishn't here? No one ish here? Jusht you and me?'

'You're drunk,' she said gently, taking hold of his arm and trying to steer him toward the now-closed door.

He resisted, standing his ground. He wanted to talk to her, didn't he? He wanted to tell her that he'd had enough of chaste kisses and infantile handholds. Christ. He was a chopper jock, a warrior, a war hawk who flew into battle with only Plexiglas, and tinfoil between him and the Apocalypse. His sex began to throb and harden. Three months he'd waited for her – three months on which on any given day he'd stood a crucifying chance of it being his last. He wasn't going to wait any longer. Only a dickhead would wait any longer.

'C'me here,' he said huskily, pulling her toward him. 'Love you, Trinh. Love you so much I'm dying by inches for you.'

At his touch she had started to tremble slightly, trying to pull away from him. He held her easily, lowering his head to hers, kissing her with pent-up hunger. Her hair slithered voluptuously over the backs of his hands. He could feel her small, high breasts beneath her silken *ao dai* soft against his chest.

'Oh, God,' he muttered hoarsely as unbridled passion roared through his loins. 'I've waited so long, Trinh. It's been cruel of you to make me wait so long!'

He knew she was struggling against him, and her struggles only inflamed him further. His hands were clumsy on the unfamiliar *ao dai*, but beneath the long, floating slit skirt he found the band of her silken pantaloons and began to pull them down roughly, his hands hot on the warm, smooth flesh of her buttocks.

*'No, Kyle! Stop! Please stop!'* she was crying frantically, squirming against him in a manner that nearly had him shooting sperm before he had even entered her.

There were no rugs on the floor, no cushions. As he pushed her down beneath him, subduing her with his weight, the shiny teak floor bruised his knees and grazed his elbows. Her fists were drumming vainly on his back, but he had his belt unbuckled, his fly unzipped. She loved him. He knew she loved him. She'd waited for this just as hungrily and as frustratedly as he had waited.

'Love you,' he said again as he pinned her

wrists to the floor above her head with one hand and guided his dick toward the warm, moist mouth of her vagina with the other. He forged deep inside her, feeling as if he were going to die with pleasure. *'Oh, Christ, Trinh!'* he gasped convulsively. *'Oh, Christ!'*

It was not going to be a long ride home. He was too drunk. But it was going to be the most meaningful ride of his life. He felt her nails scoring his back, heard her give a cry that sounded as if it had been torn from her heart, and then hot gold was shooting through him, his face contorting in a rictus of ecstatic agony as he cried out in primeval urgency, *'Oh, yes. Trinh! Yes! Yes! Yes!'*

It was a long time before he became aware of her tears sliding slowly against his shoulders. He had collapsed on top of her in drunken and exhausted fulfilment, losing consciousness. It was only as she tried to free herself of his crushing weight that his eyelids flickered open and he raised himself up on his elbows, looking down at her.

Her eyes were wide and dark, full of nameless horror. 'Trinh?' He eased his weight away from her, appalled by the sight of her tear-streaked face. 'Trinh! Don't cry! There's no need to cry!'

She sat up slowly, as if in great pain, and then pushed herself across the floor away from him, still in a sitting position, her silken trousers crumpled around her ankles. 'You have spoiled everything,' she whispered, her voice breaking in an agony of grief. 'I will never be able to see you again. Never.'

'No!' Dimly he was aware that he had ruined everything, that all the time he had been making love to her she had been fighting him every inch of the way. 'No, Trinh.' He was no longer drunk. He had never felt so sober in his life. He zipped up his trousers, buckling his belt, his hand shaking slightly as he did so. Christ, but he had been every kind of a fool. She was the most precious thing in the world to him, and he had treated her as if she were a two-bit whore from Tu Do Street.

He reached out a hand to touch her, but she shrank away from him, and he dropped it to his side knowing that the next few minutes were going to be the most important of his life.

'I love you, Trinh,' he said urgently, kneeling on one knee before her, feeling as if he were trying to regain the trust of a small, frightened wild animal. 'I love you and I want to marry you.'

It was true. He did want to marry her. She needed him as a husband in a way that Serena had never needed him and never would need him. And unless he was her husband, she would never be able to leave Vietnam and enter America with him when his year of duty was over.

Behind them, in the shaded house, the candle flames before her family altar flickered and flamed. He looked toward them, conscious of the solemnity of the vow he was making.

'I'm going to marry you, Trinh,' he said, taking hold of her hands and drawing her toward him. 'It may take a little time for the paperwork to be in order...'

How long would it take him to get a divorce now that he really wanted one? Would he have to start all over again? Would his previous divorce petition be held in his favor or be held against him? He didn't know, but he did know that he was not going to allow obstacles to stand in his way.

The first thing he would do when he arrived back in camp was write to Serena, explaining to her what Trinh's position would be if he had to leave 'Nam without being able to marry her. Perhaps, with Serena's cooperation, he could get a Mexican divorce. He would get his father's lawyers on it. They would be able to work something out. They would have to. 'We're going to be married and you're going to come to America with me, and it's going to be all right,' he said, loving her so much that he felt as if his heart were about to burst.

'And Mai?' she asked tremulously. 'What about Mai? I cannot leave her here on her own.'

He grinned. There was an old joke, marry an Oriental, and you become financially responsible for her entire family. It seemed to be true. 'And Mai as well,' he said, wondering what the hell his father was going to say when he arrived home in Boston with not only one Vietnamese girl as a souvenir of war, but two.

* * *

He wrote to Serena the morning after he returned to camp. Chuck watched him, sporting a headband of ragged cloth that gave him a piratical air as he studiously cleaned his Smith & Wesson .38. 'You're wasting your time,' he said as they sat together on his bunk. 'You won't get a divorce before you have to leave 'Nam. Even if you did, the army sure as hell isn't going to be ecstatic about you marrying a Viet. They'll make it damn near impossible.'

Kyle ignored him. *I'll always be glad that you flew out to Alabama before I left for 'Nam*, he was writing, resting the notepad on Chuck's locker. *What we've had between us is something I wouldn't have missed for the world, and something I will never forget. But I have to be able to marry Trinh. I have to be able to protect her. If you knew what life was like out here, Serry, you would understand.*

Strangely enough, he was sure that she would. Rich, spoiled and headstrong as she was, she was also uncompromisingly fair and if, when the recriminations were over, she could bring herself to be a friend to Trinh, then she would be the best friend that Trinh could ever hope to have.

'Put away the pen, Anderson, and forget about writing the great American novel,' his operations officer said sarcastically, striding toward him. 'We have a hot one. A reconnaissance squad needs picking up from the border.'

Chuck slipped his Smith & Wesson into its holster, grateful for some action. 'How near the border?' he asked.

'A half a mile,' the operations officer said, grinning. 'On Charlie's side.'

Kyle slipped the unfinished letter into the top drawer of Chuck's locker. 'You're not still pairing me with that dumb-shit cherry, are you?' he asked, referring to the company's latest new arrival who had been flying with him all week.

'You're flying with that dumb-shit cherry until he's right-seat qualified and as skilled as you in air-assault operations,' the operations officer said mercilessly, turning on his heel and striding away in the direction of the operations tent.

All through the briefing, as the operations officer gave them frequencies and ship numbers and suspected enemy locations, Kyle's attention kept drifting back to his letter to Serena. He would finish it the minute he got back to camp. With luck she would receive it before the end of the week.

'Okay,' the operations officer said at last, satisfied. 'That's it. Let's go.'

As he walked across to his ship, the cherry in his wake, he checked his gear. Pistol, flak jacket, maps. Helmet. He took hold of the base of his helmet, spreading it slightly and pulling it over his head. He would have to write a letter to his father, too, if he wanted his help in speeding up the lawyers.

He grimaced as he opened the Huey's door,

putting one foot on the skid and hoisting himself into his high-back seat. That letter would be even harder than his letter to Serena. He clicked the lever that anchored his shoulder straps to his wide lap belt, wondering how difficult it would be to take Trinh out of Vietnam and into the States if he wasn't married to her. Would she be able to enter on a visitor's visa? And if so, for how long?

He squeezed the radio trigger switch on his cyclic to the first click and said through his phones to his nervous copilot. 'Okay?'

The new arrival nodded. Kyle gave him a thumbs-up sign and rolled the throttle open to the indent starting position, squeezing the trigger switch on his collective. As the rotor blades began to turn, he wondered if perhaps it would be easiest to fly Trinh to England or to Sweden. She would surely be able to enter Sweden without any difficulty, and stay there, as a visitor, until they could marry.

He checked the gauge and nosed the Huey forward with a gentle push of the cyclic. But to make those kind of arrangements, he would have to level with Trinh and tell her that he was already married, and that he definitely didn't want to have to do that.

Chuck was first pilot in the ship in front of him, and as it climbed up over the trees at the edge of the camp, Kyle followed him, holding his speed down until they, and the accompanying ships, were all in formation.

Despite the trickiness of the area they were flying into, they met with no ground fire.

They flew north, over mountainous terrain, to a border area where Cambodia and Vietnam and Laos merged. Even when they located the reconnaissance party, they ran into no difficulties. It was a much smaller party than they had anticipated, and all the men boarded the first couple of ships, leaving Kyle and Chuck unloaded. It was only as they were preparing to take off, angry at being called out unnecessarily, that hell broke loose. The firing was so unexpected, so ferociously intense, that even Kyle lost his cool for a moment, muttering a frantic 'Holy Christ!' as his flight commander yelled over the radio, *'Go! Go! Go!'*

Kyle didn't need telling twice. He was being machine-gunned from what seemed to be every direction at once, and he knew as the Huey lifted off the ground that they were taking hits.

*'C'me on, baby! C'me on!'* he said savagely beneath his breath.

The Huey cleared the tree line. Over the radio he could hear shouted reports of other ships being hit. A steady stream of tracers flew toward him. He swore viciously. Some bastard had him in his sights and was concentrating entirely on him. He banked hard to the left, trying to lose the tracer fire, and almost immediately, as more bullets slammed into the tail rotors, he began to oscillate, losing control.

*'Skyhawk three! We're hit and going down!'* was the last terse, furious message Chuck

heard over the radio as the Huey tumbled brokenly from the sky, crashing down into the jungle canopy.

# CHAPTER NINETEEN

Gavin stared at Nhu across the candlelit table on the Continental's terrace. 'You mean your brother is in the South again?' he asked, careful to keep his voice low despite his incredulity. 'Here? In Saigon?'

Her eyes went quickly to the other tables around them. No one was paying them any attention. The young American who had been looking curiously in their direction when they had first arrived, was now deep in conversation with his two Vietnamese companions. She said very quietly, 'Not in Saigon. But nearby.'

Gavin's mind raced furiously. According to Gabrielle, her mother's brother was a full-fledged North Vietnamese Army colonel. If he could meet him, talk to him, then he would learn more about the war in five minutes than he would in a year of attending official American press conferences and ambiguously worded briefings.

'I want to meet him,' he said, laying down his fork and sipping a glass of water. 'Can you arrange it, Nhu?'

She didn't answer him for several seconds, and when she did, her voice was unsteady, betraying the agitation that lay beneath her veneer of unruffled composure. 'Yes,' she said, so quietly he could barely hear her. 'That is why I am here.'

Her reply was so unexpected that his hand shook and water spilled as he set his glass back down on the table. 'I'm sorry,' he said, wondering if he had misheard her. 'I don't understand...'

Her eyes were troubled. 'Neither do I, but I have shown Dinh the letters Vanh sent to me in which she says you can be trusted. And he wants to talk to you.'

Sheer elation sang down Gavin's spine. He had hoped that his family-by-marriage in Saigon would prove helpful to him as a reporter, but he had never envisaged a coup such as this. Gabrielle had said that when Dinh had come south in 1963, it had been on the express orders of General Giap. And Giap was Ho Chi Minh's right-hand man, the architect of the French defeat at Dien Bien Phu. He wondered what on earth Vanh had put in her letters that such a man would trust him, sight unseen.

He said hesitantly, knowing he would never forgive himself if his confession ruined his chances of a meeting, yet knowing he would never be able to live with himself if Gabrielle's uncle were to risk capture and death under the mistaken impression that he was meeting a fellow Communist, 'I sympathize with the North, Nhu. I think the American bombing campaign against northern towns and the killing of large numbers of innocent civilians is morally indefensible. But I am not a Communist.'

'Neither am I,' she said, a slight smile touching her mouth. 'I am a nationalist, and I support Ho. Although he is a Communist, I believe that he is also, first and foremost, a nationalist and a patriot.'

A waiter approached and she fell silent. When he had refilled her glass and moved away a safe distance, she continued quietly. 'And as a patriot I believe he will always place Vietnam's interest above that of personal ideology.'

It was a popular view. From everything he had read about Nguyen That Thanh, born seventy-six years ago in the village of Kim Lie, some 300 kilometers south of Hanoi, and known to the world by the alias Ho Chi Minh, Gavin thought that it was probably also correct.

'Are there any arrangements for me to meet your brother, Nhu?'

'I haven't yet been told. I had to meet you first and—' she blushed slightly, looking much younger than her thirty-two years '—and make my own judgment about you.'

He grinned, knowing that trust had sprung up between them immediately and that her judgment would be favorable.

The waiter approached again, removing plates and asking if they were ready for coffee. Gavin said that they were, and when the waiter was once again out of earshot he said curiously, 'I must confess I was surprised when you suggested we meet here, Nhu. Isn't it a very conspicuous rendezvous? Aren't we liable to attract attention?'

Her smile deepened. 'Have you never read that great story "The Purloined Letter" by Edgar Allan Poe?'

He shook his head, bemused at the unexpected range of her literary knowledge. Reading his thoughts, she said, unoffended, 'You forget that I was educated at a French school, Gavin. American literature was part of our syllabus in my last year.'

'It was part of mine as well,' he said, his eyes crinkling at the corners. 'But somehow or other we seem to have overlooked Mr. Poe. Tell me about his purloined letter. What does it have to do with us meeting here, at the Continental?'

The waiter came and served coffee. The terrace where they were sitting overlooked the plaza surrounding the old opera house, and as the hour grew later, the always-chaotic traffic intensified. Young Vietnamese pimps on souped-up scooters and Honda 50s zipped between Citroëns and Renaults as they transported their charges from rendezvous to rendezvous. The girls sat behind them, some in miniskirts so short it was doubtful if they were wearing anything below the waist at all, some in gossamer-light *ao dais*, their split skirts fluttering like streamers in their wake, and all with exotically painted faces.

She said, 'The letter was searched for in

vain. Under carpets, beneath mattresses. But because it was known to have been hidden, no one thought of looking in the most obvious place.'

'Which was?' he asked, wishing that Gabrielle were with him to enjoy the company of her delightful aunt.

Her eyes sparkled mischievously, reminding him so much of Gabrielle that a pang of longing stabbed through him, so sharp he had to physically prevent himself from crying out. 'In the card rack,' she said, gurgling with laughter. 'And the Continental is our card rack. Meeting openly like this, in front of all Saigon, will arouse far less suspicion than meeting furtively.'

They had drunk their coffee and then he had walked her down the steps leading to the plaza and had flagged down a battered blue and yellow taxicab for her.

'I will contact you,' she had promised, and then her eyes had become dark and urgent. 'But please remember, Gavin. Tell no one of who it is you are going to meet.'

He needed no reminding. Enormous trust was being placed in him and he had no intention of betraying it. 'I won't,' he said gravely. 'Good night, Nhu.'

She stepped into the taxi, and as it began to draw away she leaned toward the open window, once again smiling, calling out teasingly, 'I did not think an Australian nephew by marriage would be at all a nice thing to have, but I was wrong! Welcome to our family, Gavin!'

He waved, grinning with pleasure, and then turned and walked slowly back into the hotel. Despite the success of his trip to Hue, he was still very much a new boy at the press bureau and he had no idea if Paul Dulles would be cooperative about his disappearing on a story he was unable to even talk about.

He had a nightcap in the bar and decided that he would say nothing to Paul for the moment. There would be time enough to worry about Paul's cooperation when Nhu made contact, and that might not be for days, or even weeks. He slid from the bar stool and made his way to bed, wondering what Gabrielle was doing at that very moment, whether she was thinking of him – if she was missing him as painfully as he was missing her.

The next afternoon Paul sent him with Jimmy Giddings to JUSPAO, the Joint United States Public Affairs Office.

'It pains me to admit it,' Jimmy said, munching on a hamburger that was serving as a late lunch, 'but these biased announcements issued by the American command are almost the only source of our news. Investigative trips like yours to Hue are rarer than you might think.'

They turned into the JUSPAO building, passing an armed marine at the door. Above the entrance was a framed portrait of a smiling President Johnson. 'That guy sure has a lot to answer for,' Jimmy said as they began to walk through a maze of windowless corridors. 'He got America into this damned mess, but Christ knows how he's going to get her out of it.'

Corridor led into corridor, and just as Gavin was beginning to wonder if they were ever going to end, they came to a small theater crowded with newsmen.

'Here we go,' Jimmy said, finding a space against the rear wall and settling himself comfortably against it. 'The cheapest, most entertaining show in town.'

There was a chuckle of agreeing laughter from the reporters standing nearest to them, and then the noise level in the room died down a little as an American colonel strode across the stage to a lectern. Behind him was a large-scale map of Vietnam, liberally highlighted in blue and pink, and on a board by his side were pinned half a dozen statistical charts.

'The blue bits on the map are areas controlled by U.S. and allied forces, the pink bits are the areas controlled by the Cong,' Jimmy whispered as the colonel wished them all good afternoon and a soldier in front of the stage activated a large reel-to-reel tape recorder.

'What are the white bits?' Gavin whispered back.

Jimmy began to chew on a piece of gum. 'The white bits are so-called "movement areas", all moving toward being blue bits if you believe what the man up there is going to tell you. Personally, I don't.'

Gavin listened to a recap of the Buddhist disturbances in Hue, the descriptions of the horror that he had himself witnessed sanitized by specialist lingo. The reports of engagements between American troops and Viet Cong were treated in the same disorienting manner. Accidental civilian deaths were 'friendly casualties', Americans killed in action were referred to only by the letters KIA, and figures that looked horrendous to Gavin were described as being 'light'. There was a sheet on which was estimated the weekly kill ratio, the number of Viet Cong killed per American, the conclusion seeming to be that no matter the number of American dead, if numerically there were more Viet Cong dead, then the war was being won.

'How do they know that the figures for Viet Cong dead are correct?' he whispered to Jimmy. 'I thought the VC tried to recover their dead whenever possible?'

Jimmy looked across at him pityingly. 'They do,' he said, transferring his chewing gum from the left side of his mouth to the right. 'But whenever a platoon has engaged the enemy, the officer in command is asked how many Cong they hit. He doesn't have to have the bodies to back up his figures. He just has to think of a number and double it.'

'You mean the Viet Cong dead figures are estimates, and only the American figures are for real?'

'If you get any sharper, you'll cut yourself,'

Jimmy said with good-natured sarcasm.

'—American aircraft bombed targets close to Hanoi and Haiphong yesterday,' the colonel continued, 'destroying an estimated fifty percent of the North's fuel supply—'

'If we can't rely on what we're being told, why do we come?' Gavin demanded, sotto voce.

'Because it's easy,' Jimmy said, his tone indicating that it was a fact even a three-year-old would have grasped. 'And because only the military know what's been happening all around the country, each and every day. They may tell us only what they want us to know, but at least we get some sort of a coherent picture. You could spend weeks hitching helicopters with the troops, but you won't necessarily get any clearer a view of what the hell is happening.'

Gavin's mouth set in a tight, firm line. Jimmy, middle-aged and war weary, had settled for relying on the information being given out by the American military, but it didn't mean that *he* had to. The sooner he could hop aboard a helicopter with the troops, the better he would like it.

Two days later he got his chance. 'How would you like to cover the making of a free fire zone?' Paul asked as he strolled into the office. 'As the answer is obviously yes, get yourself down to the air base. There's a party of marines on their way to a place called Cam Lai. They're expecting you.'

It was his first time in an army helicopter. A

big, black marine grinned at him and handed him a helmet and a flak jacket. 'Don't worry, man, this ain't no heavy situation, just a safe little hop, a pleasant afternoon out in the boonies.'

Gavin looked around at the other marines seated on the floor of the wide-bellied Chinook. From the bored expressions on their faces, he figured he'd been told the truth.

The village they were flown into was made up of thatched-roof huts and paddyfields.

'Come on men!' the officer shouted as the marines began to bundle out of the helicopter into the stifling mid-morning heat. 'Let's git it on and over with!'

The first thing that Gavin heard above the roar of the rotor blades was the sound of desperate sobbing. Women were milling bewilderedly in the mud-baked streets, babies on their hips as they struggled with boxes and baskets of pitiful possessions.

The leading marine was already shouting to them to make their way toward the waiting Chinook, jerking his rifle to emphasize his words.

'How long have these people had to prepare to leave their homes?' Gavin shouted to the officer over the sound of the still-pulsating rotors.

'They were leafleted at nine this mornin',' the marine said, taking out a cigarette and lighting it as his men began to search the huts, ejecting wailing toddlers and terrified old people at rifle point.

'Christ!' Gavin felt as if he were in a lunatic asylum. 'It's only eleven now! How the hell do you expect them to be ready to abandon homes they've lived in for generations in just two hours?'

'Aw, they ain't got much stuff,' the officer said complacently.

Gavin wondered what would happen to his press accreditation if he socked an officer on the jaw on his first trip out in the field. One of the women, nearly dwarfed by a bundle of household belongings, tottered and fell as she was herded toward them. None of the marines made any move to help her to her feet.

'These are our *allies*, for Christ's sake!' Gavin yelled at the disinterested marines as he ran forward, taking hold of the woman's arm and helping her ease herself up from the dirt. 'We're supposed to be winning their hearts and minds, not terrifying the life out of them!'

The officer strolled threateningly toward him. 'You're goin' to make yourself very unpopular playin' the boy scout,' he said as the woman hurriedly picked up her bundle, clutching it close to her chest. 'Seems to me you should be askin' yourself why there's no able-bodied men in this here village. And the answer is, because they're probably all VC. If they are, then it'll be a pleasure to burn their village to the ground, and if they ain't, then I reckon they should be pretty glad to be goin' to a camp where they'll be protected 'gainst the VC.'

There was nothing Gavin could do. He stood impotently, white-lipped with rage, as the crying, protesting villagers were herded aboard the Chinook. God alone knew where they were being taken. The officer had said a camp. Wherever it was, it wasn't home and it never would be. Home was the village where their fathers had been born, and their father's father, and their father's father's father.

'We've got a problem, sir!' one of the marines yelled out, running up to them. 'There's an old man no one can move! Says his family shrine is here and he has to stay and tend it!'

'Assholes,' the officer said succinctly. 'Tell him this is goin' to be a free fire zone, and after today, anythin' movin' here will be regarded as VC and shot. Got that?'

'Yes sir,' the marine said unhappily. 'I've already told him that, sir, and he says he won't come. He says it's his duty to stay with the graves of his people. That if we want to move him, we'll have to kill him first.'

For one terrible moment Gavin thought the officer was going to give a laconic order for the old man to be shot. Instead, he said irritably. 'Okay. Leave him. We're behind schedule. Zippo the huts and let's be off.'

As the last of the villagers crowded aboard the Chinook, some with baskets of squawking hens, a couple of them with pigs in their arms, none of them knowing where they were going or what was to become of them, the marines set fire to the straw-thatched huts.

The smoke billowed thickly up into the hot, humid air. Aboard the Chinook the sobbing gave way to despairing whimpers and then to passive, helpless silence. Gavin climbed aboard and joined them, sick at heart. The old man had run off limping toward the paddy fields and, presumably, his family burial ground. Gavin knew that he wouldn't survive there for long. In a free fire zone nothing, man or beast, survived for very long.

'So you didn't like what you saw?' Paul said to him later at the bureau office.

'I didn't *understand* what I saw!' Gavin exploded savagely. 'Those people are our *allies*! America is supposedly in Vietnam to help and protect them! Can you imagine American or British generals in occupied France or Italy during the Second World War, ordering the herding of whole communities away from their homes to live in what can be described only as concentration camp conditions so that free fire zones could be created? The answer is that you can't, and if you want to know what the difference is, then I'll tell you! The difference, conscious or unconscious, is racial. If those Vietnamese I saw being ordered on to that Chinook at gunpoint and against their will had been white civilians, then the operation would have been carried out with a damned sight more civility!'

Paul leaned back in his chair, one leg

crossed over the other, his foot tapping the air and revealing a flash of a startling emerald sock. 'I thought you said the officer in charge was black?'

'I did. For all I know, the majority of black servicemen may have more empathy with the Vietnamese than their white counterparts, but the one I came across today didn't.'

His rage was so white-hot, so naive, that Paul suppressed a cynical smile. He could vaguely remember reacting the same way himself when he had first arrived, but that had been over a year ago. Since then, in order to survive, he had learned the art of remaining aloof from the insanity surrounding him. It was an art Gavin would no doubt learn too, in time.

'There are always two points of view to every argument,' he said, reaching for a glass and a bottle and pouring himself two fingers of whiskey. 'From the American military point of view, creating free fire zones makes sense.' He raised a hand to silence Gavin. 'Once the villages in a Viet Cong infested area have been destroyed, and their inhabitants removed to a safe place, then the Viet Cong have nothing and no one to shelter them. They become clearly identifiable targets. And they can be attacked without the lives of innocent civilians being put at risk.'

'If they are still there to attack!' Gavin snorted derisively. 'Which they won't be! And while they scarper off to new pastures, we destroy homes and communities and create hundreds of thousands of refugees. And that's another point!' He ran his hand through his hair. 'Why the hell are they referred to as refugees? They're *not* refugees, and calling them that distorts the truth of this situation. They're evacuees, and that's what they should be called!'

'That could be the beginning of the end,' Paul said dryly. 'Before you know where you are, even enemy WBLCs would be given their right name.'

'WBLCs?'

'Waterborne logistics craft.'

'What the hell are they?'

'Sampans,' Paul said with a grin. 'Come on, let's go to the Continental for a drink. I want to know why you described the camp the villagers were transferred to as a concentration camp.'

*It was a planned shantytown*, Gavin wrote later that day to Gabrielle, *miles from anywhere, with no paddy fields for the villagers to farm, and no trees for shade. All the surrounding ground had been bulldozed flat so that there was no vegetation to give cover to any Viet Cong. To keep the Viet Cong away, the tin-roofed houses were surrounded by barbed wire and watchtowers. The place was dirty, dusty, and utterly soulless. The refugees already living there were sullen and resentful, and who can blame them? If they weren't Viet Cong sympathizers before they were uprooted from their land, then they must surely be Viet Cong sympathizers now. But the Americans can't see it. This morning's operation was described officially as being a great success, the 'removal of several score villagers from a place of insecurity to a place of safety'.*

In his last letter, he had written about his meeting with Nhu, and had only hinted that he might meet Dinh, saying that he was 'looking forward to meeting the rest of her family quite soon'. Now he wrote: *I love you and I miss you, and I'm beginning to love this country too, or at least the un-Americanized bits! Tu Do Street has to be seen to be believed! It's like the worst parts of Las Vegas and Los Angeles all rolled into one and the clubs make the Black Cat seem a model of respectability!*

The rest of Gavin's week was spent covering the routine briefings at the Follies. U.S. air force and navy jets had begun a major campaign to wipe out fuel installations in the Hanoi–Haiphong area, and the briefings were even longer than normal, the hundred or so journalists in attendance asking a lot of questions about the escalation of the war.

He was alone in the bureau office, typing, when the door opened and to his utter astonishment Nhu stepped a trifle uncertainly into the room.

'Is it all right if I come in?' she asked hesitantly, looking around and seeing with relief that he was alone.

'But of course!' He was on his feet, pulling a chair away from one of the other desks so that she could sit down.

She shook her head when he motioned her

to sit. 'No. I am not staying, Gavin. I have come to tell you that the time is now. Dinh has sent someone to escort you to him.'

'When? Now? This very minute?'

She nodded.

'But I can't, Nhu!' he protested. 'I have to finish my article, tell my bureau chief—'

'That is precisely what Dinh does not want you to do,' she said gently. 'You are to leave now, without speaking to anyone either here or at the Continental.'

Through the screen door of thick, inch-square wire meshing, he could see a small Renault, a Vietnamese at the wheel.

'I can't possibly, Nhu! To disappear without a word would arouse far more problems than it would solve!'

'You are to leave a note, which I am to make sure your bureau chief receives,' Nhu said, unperturbed. 'And you are not to return to the Continental for a change of clothes. A change of clothes has already been arranged for you.'

He gazed around him helplessly. His half-finished article protruding from his type-writer read: *China has reacted by calling the bombing of the fuel installations in the Hanoi-Haiphong areas, 'barbarous and wanton acts that have further freed us from any bounds of restrictions in helping North Vietnam.'* For the life of him, he couldn't remember what he had planned to type next.

'You must write your note now,' Nhu said. 'The messenger Dinh has sent will not wait for you more than a few minutes.'

Gavin groaned. He had no choice but to write a note to Paul and disappear in the waiting Renault, but he was well aware that it was an action that could cost him his job.

'How long will I be away, Nhu?' he asked, reaching for a sheet of typing paper.

'I do not know. Three or four days. Perhaps a week.'

He scrawled: *Paul. Something huge has come up. Will explain all when I return, possibly end of week. Gavin.*

He propped it on Paul's desk, praying that when he returned it would be such a big story that forgiveness would be automatic, and followed Nhu out into the street.

'I am not going with you,' she said as the Renault's driver indicated to him that he should sit in the rear of the car. 'I am to stay here and make sure that your note is found and read.' She hesitated and then said, her voice trembling slightly, 'When you see my brother, tell him that I miss him.'

He nodded, stepping into the Renault's stiflingly hot interior.

The car sped out of the city through Cholon, the Chinese quarter, the driver remaining uncommunicably silent. Since he knew it would be a waste of time to ask where they were going or how long the trip would take, Gavin did neither. He sat back, looking out of the window at paddyfields and swamps and canals, wondering if they were on the road that ran northwest from Saigon to

Phnom Penh in Cambodia, and how far they could possibly go before being stopped and questioned by the police or the military.

Some ten or eleven kilometers from Saigon they careened into a small village looking much the same as the other villages they had driven through. This time, however, they turned off the road, bumping and swaying into a dusty alley between closely packed thatched-roof houses built of bamboo and corrugated iron.

'Are we here?' Gavin asked in Vietnamese. It was the first time he had spoken, and the driver's eyes flew wide at the shock of being spoken to by a round-eye in his own language.

'I return to Saigon,' he said uninformatively as two black-pajama-clad figures emerged from the nearest house, Soviet Kalashnikov AK-47 rifles in their hands.

The men began to walk toward the car and Gavin, suspecting that he was not going to be a passenger on his companion's return trip, opened the rear door and stepped out into the blistering midday heat. He didn't wait for the men to approach but took the initiative, walking confidently toward them.

'Chào,' he said, smiling tentatively and shaking their hands firmly.

'You are Mr. Gavin Ryan?' one of them asked in Vietnamese.

Gavin nodded.

'Your press accreditation card, please.'

Gavin removed his card from his shirt

pocket, and handed it to him. The man, in his black pajamas and sandals made out of discarded truck tires, scrutinized it as carefully as if he were a civil servant in a government office.

'Thank you,' he said, handing the card back to Gavin. 'Please follow me.'

Gavin hesitated for a fraction of a second. Behind him the Renault's engine revved into life, in front of him the door of the nearest thatched-roof house opened, revealing an intimidatingly dark interior. The man who hadn't yet spoken to him walked across to the Renault, exchanged a few words with the driver, and then the Renault began to back out of the alley, raising a cloud of dense dust.

Gavin turned and watched it for a moment. Then he followed the man who had been speaking to him into the house.

It took his eyes several seconds to adjust to the gloom. When they did so, he looked round him in astonishment. He had expected to find Dinh in the room. There was no one, just a few functional articles, a sleeping pallet, a table, two chairs, a grate for a fire, and a few cooking pots.

The Vietnamese handed him the suitcase that had been removed from the rear of the car. 'Are you armed? Have you a gun? A knife?' he asked.

Gavin shook his head and the man ran his hands swiftly and efficiently over him.

'Good,' he said, satisfied. 'You are to come with us, Comrade Ryan. This way, please.'

The Vietnamese who had so far remained silent kicked the cooking pots away from the grate with his foot and then squatted down, plunging his hand into the middle of a pile of cold ashes.

Gavin watched, mystified, and then his mystification changed to disbelief as the Vietnamese pulled hard, lifting open a small wooden trapdoor. As the man eased himself into the opening, dropping feet first out of sight, his companion turned to Gavin.

'This way,' he said again, and Gavin was almost sure there was a gleam of relish in his eyes as he motioned him forward.

If he had been as chunkily built as Jimmy Giddings, or as big-boned as Lestor McDermott, his adventure would have ended there, before it had begun, because there would have been no way Jimmy or Lestor could have eased themselves down through the narrow opening. As it was, he was almost as slight as the Vietnamese and with a last longing look toward the open door of the house and sunlight, he lowered himself into the claustrophobic darkness.

The shaft dropped into a tunnel, not high enough to walk in, but large and wide enough to wriggle along. It did not run straight. It zig-zagged, and every now and then there would be a cavity hollowed out in the tunnel's side, just deep enough for a human body to squeeze into. Sweat was pouring into his eyes and his breathing was harsh and rasping. He wondered how on earth the tunnel was ventilated, where it lead, and then, after about thirty-five to forty yards, they came to a second trapdoor which opened onto another shaft, which led deeper into the earth.

When he had entered the tunnel he had imagined that it led, after a few yards, to an underground hiding place. He never imagined that it would be so long and complex. There was bamboo lining the tunnel roof now, and they kept coming to intersections where other tunnels led off blackly.

Something scurried past his face, and he hit out blindly with his hands, barely controlling his panic. Had it been a spider? He hated spiders and he knew that in the tropics all spiders were likely to be poisonous. He was trembling violently, barely able to control his rising panic. It would be over soon. It couldn't go on for much longer. They would reach their destination. There would be light and air.

And the return? He wouldn't think about returning, only about arriving without disgracing himself by betraying his claustrophobia and his fear of whatever insect life was present but unseen.

Just when he thought he could continue no longer, faint light permeated the darkness and the Vietnamese in front of him scrambled from his belly onto his feet, standing upright.

Two seconds later Gavin was gratefully doing the same thing. He stared around him. The light was not daylight. It was the light of an improvised oil lamp, an old medicine bottle with a wick in it, and he was not in a shaft leading upward, as he had hoped, but in a chamber large enough to hold ten or twelve people. At a makeshift desk a Vietnamese wearing the green uniform of the North Vietnamese Army sat writing. The two black-clad Vietnamese waited respectfully for him to look up from his work. When he did so, he said only, 'Colonel Duong is waiting for you, Comrades.'

With every muscle in his body aching from the effort of his crawl, and his skin drenched with perspiration, Gavin followed his Vietnamese companions across the chamber and into another tunnel, this time one that was high enough to walk in upright. There was a dull rumble and the ground shook above them, a scattering of earth falling onto their heads. 'It is the big monkeys,' the Vietnamese who had done all the earlier talking, said to him. 'They are bombing the Boi Loi Woods.'

By big monkeys, Gavin assumed that his companion referred to the Americans. He wondered if Australians were also referred to in the same derogatory manner.

The chamber they walked into was as big as the previous one, but more comfortably furnished. There was a large table made out of packing cases and planks of wood, around which stood three men, all in North Vietnamese Army uniforms and all looking down at a large scale map. There were other boxes stacked against the wall which appeared to be serving as filing cabinets. And there was a hammock in one corner, and a smaller table on which was a lamp made out of an old menthol bottle, a dagger, a rifle, and a rice bag.

The men looked up, and the smallest of them, the one standing centrally and facing Gavin, said, 'I am Colonel Duong Quynh Dinh. Welcome to the tunnels of Cu Chi, Comrade Ryan.'

'I'm very pleased to be here,' Gavin said, trying to suppress his feeling of being entombed and to inject a note of sincerity into his voice.

Gabrielle's uncle looked far older than his forty-two years – the lean, wiry figure with not an ounce of excess flesh on his bones and a taut, heavily lined face seemed nearer to fifty-two.

He moved from behind the desk, walking up to Gavin, standing in front of him and holding his eyes for what seemed an eternity.

'I am told that you are a journalist and that your sympathies are with us, Comrade?' he said at last.

Gavin nodded. If Dinh was under the impression that he was a committed Communist, now did not seem the time or the place to enlighten him.

'And that you are my nephew-in-law?'

Gavin felt a tremor of relief. By publicly acknowledging the family connection, Dinh was giving him credentials in the eyes of the other North Vietnamese.

'Yes.' He unbuttoned his shirt pocket. 'I have brought two photographs for you, Colonel. One of them is Gabrielle and myself on our wedding day, the other is of your sister, Vanh.'

Dinh took them, looking down at them for a long time. Gavin knew that Dinh had not seen Vanh for several years, and that he had never seen Gabrielle.

'It is a long time since I have seen some members of my family,' Dinh said to him, taking a small notebook from his pocket and slipping the two photographs between the leaves. 'It is a hard price to pay for victory, but it is a price that I and my fellow comrades pay willingly.'

He motioned Gavin forward toward the table. 'Let me tell you something about the area you are in, Comrade.' He indicated a point on the map some twenty kilometers northwest of Saigon. 'This is Cu Chi district.' He circled an area of small villages clustered astride Route One. 'Here are the villages of An Nhon Tay and Phu My Hung, referred to by the Americans as the Ho Bo Woods. Phu My Hung is our area command post.' To the north of the area Gavin could see a faint blue line indicating the Saigon River. 'It is a district that was important to us in our war with the French, and that is important to us now, in our war with the Americans.'

'Because of its strategic significance?' Gavin interposed, trying hard to sound intelligent enough to warrant the confidence being placed in him.

Dinh nodded. 'Yes. As you see, the main road linking Phnom Pen and Saigon runs through Cu Chi, as does the Saigon River. We need to control these routes in order to bring supplies in from Cambodia.' He paused, and something that could have been a hint of a smile touched the hard line of his mouth. 'When I was a boy, this area was very green, very lush.'

Gavin knew that most of it was anything but green and lush now. A huge American army base had been built in the area, and in January a large-scale American military operation, code-named CRIMP had poured hundreds of troops into the countryside around Cu Chi in an effort to clear it of Viet Cong, and to secure it. In case they overlooked any Viet Cong, B-52s had then pounded the area with thirty-ton loads of high explosives.

'Were the tunnels here in January, when the area was bombed?' he asked, forgetting his claustrophobia as his reporter's intense interest in the story took over.

Again Gavin saw a faint glimmer of a smile. 'The tunnels have been here ever since the days when we fought the French. Every hamlet and village in the area built its own underground network where guerrilla fighters could hide, and from where they could launch surprise attacks upon the French Army. Now the tunnels have been repaired and extended. They cover an area from the Cambodian border to the outskirts of Saigon.'

If there had been a chair handy, Gavin would have gratefully sat down upon it. All the time he had been studying about Vietnam, preparing himself to come to Vietnam, he had never read a word referring to the enemy's use of tunnels. Paul hadn't mentioned the tunnels, nor had Jimmy or Lestor, which meant that they did not know about them. He felt like whooping with elation. When Paul read his story about Cu Chi, he wouldn't give a damn about the way he had disappeared without so much as a by-your-leave. He certainly wouldn't get the sack. He would get the press bureau's equivalent of a Pulitzer Prize!

'Let me give you some idea of the sophistication of our tunnel network, and then I will tell you why it is that I asked you to come to Cu Chi, and what it is that North Vietnam would like from you,' Dinh said, leading the way out of the chamber.

Gavin took a deep breath and followed him. He was beginning to feel slightly more acclimatized now and his interest superseded his fear.

For sixty yards or so at a time they would wriggle on their bellies like giant underground moles, and then they would scramble upright in a large chamber that served as a dormitory or a ammunition dump or a first aid station. There was even a kitchen.

'Where does the smoke go?' Gavin asked,

perplexed.

'It is ducted through several channels and finally escapes, greatly diffused, through ground-level chimneys a good distance from any tunnel entrance. Though most of our food is eaten cold,' Dinh said, a note of regret in his voice.

The strenuously physical tour continued. There were ventilation shafts and wells. There were false tunnels near some entrances, leading nowhere. There were dead ends. There were booby traps for any American soldier so enterprising as to discover an entrance and see through the false trails.

The booby traps were nearly Gavin's undoing. He was just congratulating himself on the way he had adjusted to the dark and the bodily stenches that poisoned the air, when there was a strange scuffling sound and Dinh wriggled into one of the hollows carved out of the tunnel's side that served as both a hiding place and a passing place.

'We will go no farther in this direction,' Dinh said, lighting a small candle to give light. 'It leads to a booby-trapped entrance. Can you see?'

In the flickering light of the candle, Gavin saw ahead of him, a mere three or four feet away, three huge rats reared on their haunches, teeth bared.

*'Jesus God!'*

He forgot all about making a favorable impression, about gaining Dinh's esteem. He jettisoned backward, his terror overwhelming. He was unable to turn around in the narrow tunnel, unable to move fast, fast, fast enough, and there was a gurgling animal sound coming from his throat as he tried to put distance between himself and the creatures of nightmare in front of him.

'They cannot harm you, Comrade,' Dinh said, chuckling. 'They are tethered by the neck.'

Gavin did not care. He continued to scramble backward, throwing the Vietnamese who had been accompanying them on their tour into noisy retreat. Not until he was again in one of the large chambers, the red clay walls civilizingly covered in looted U.S. parachute nylon, did he come to a sweat-soaked, shivering halt.

'You were right to give our unpleasant friends a wide berth,' Dinh said to him when he rejoined him. 'They have been infected with bubonic plague. If anyone should discover that particular entrance, a trapdoor can be lowered, sealing that part of the tunnel from the rest of the complex. The leash tethering the rats can be severed from this side of the trapdoor, and the rats let loose. Once greeted in such a manner, we do not expect to be troubled further.'

Gavin tried to say that he was certain they would never be troubled, ever again, but he was still incapable of speech.

'We will eat now,' Dinh said, saving him from disgracing himself further. 'And then I will tell you what it is that we want from you.'

All six of them ate together, the two Vietnamese who had initially escorted him through the tunnels, and the two middle-aged but exceedingly tough-looking North Vietnamese officers who had been closeted with Dinh when he had first arrived. From the lack of comment about the food, Gavin assumed that it must be their normal fare: cold rice supplemented by the merest sliver of chicken, and accompanied by water in tin mugs.

Gavin had never been so thirsty in his life, and his initial instinct was to gulp the water down. Then it occurred to him that there was no way that the water would have been boiled. He crossed his fingers. He had to drink, and he had to hope for the best.

When the food had been eaten, Dinh settled himself on a rough wooden chair behind the desk. 'Perhaps you have heard of a journalist by the name of Wilfred Burchett, Comrade?'

Gavin nodded. Wilfred Burchett was world-famous as being the journalist who, in the days of Dien Bien Phu, had interviewed and become a friend of Ho Chi Minh. He was Australian, no longer young, and because of his fiercely held political sympathies, was regarded by fellow journalists as something of a maverick.

'There are very few foreign journalists of the caliber of Mr. Burchett,' Dinh was saying. 'Journalists who report to the West the truth of what is happening in our country. Too many of them are misled by the false proclamations of victory coming from the American imperialists and their Saigon puppets.'

He paused, and Gavin felt a tingle run down his spine. Was Dinh going to ask him to assume the role of Burchett to his Ho Chi Minh? And if so, how could he possibly accept? He wasn't a freelance journalist able to write what he liked, when he liked. He was a news agency reporter. Whatever he wrote, even if it passed Paul Dulles's critical eye, it would be edited again in the Paris head office. When it reached the newspaper offices it was destined for, it would be edited again by a subeditor, who would put a headline on the story, place it in the paper, and cut it to fit. And the interference with the original story didn't end there. With agency stories it was customary for editors to merge the story with one on the same subject by their own correspondent.

To write stories covering Viet Cong activities, and to expect that they would be published in a form acceptable to the North Vietnamese, would be impossible for anyone but a freelance journalist with an established reputation.

'The Hanoi government has requested that you stay with us as our guest, Comrade,' Dinh said, confirming his suspicions. 'Like Mr Burchett, you will record our fight for freedom, and you will record the crimes of the American imperialists.'

Adrenaline began to pump along Gavin's veins. If he understood Dinh correctly, he was being offered the chance to go out on active operations with the Viet Cong. It was the kind of scoop that any journalist would sell his soul for. If the bureau refused to accept the story, on the grounds that there was no corroboration of it from any other source, then he would resign as a member of the staff and chance his luck as a freelancer.

'I am very honored to accept your invitation,' he said, wondering how long he was going to be their guest, and if, now that he had accepted their invitation, he would be allowed to communicate with Paul.

'That is very good, Comrade,' Dinh said unexpressively. 'The people of Vietnam are waiting for a historic moment, a moment when the whole nation will rise up in revolt. The revolutionary forces of Vietnam will very soon show the rest of the world what they can do, and you will have the great privilege of being with them when they are victorious.'

Gavin frowned slightly. They had been speaking sometimes in French, sometimes in Vietnamese, and though Dinh spoke in the same regional accent as Vanh, obviously he had misunderstood something. However optimistic the North Vietnamese were of eventually attaining their aims, no one could imagine that those aims were going to be attained in the next few days or weeks.

'When I return here, will I be met and brought by car in the same manner as I was this morning?' he asked, assuming that his assignment was to be an ongoing one.

'I am afraid you have not quite comprehended, Comrade,' Dinh said, a note of genuine regret in his voice. 'You will not be returning here because you will not be leaving here, at least you will not be leaving here for Saigon. My mission in the South is completed, and in five days time I shall begin the journey north, up the Ho Chi Minh Trail. When I do so, you will accompany me.'

Gavin stared at him. Of course. He should have known from the beginning. He hadn't been blindfolded on his journey to Cu Chi. Secrets that the Americans would have given a ransom for had been carelessly revealed to him. And they had been so because all along his hosts had known that he would never be able to communicate what he had seen, not unless they wanted him to communicate it. He wasn't their guest. For reasons that he still didn't comprehend, he was their prisoner.

'Can I choose to change my mind and refuse your invitation?' he asked quietly.

Dinh shook his head. 'No, Comrade. You have no choice. You have had no choice ever since the moment when you stepped into the car outside the bureau office.'

He wondered if Nhu had known Dinh's intentions, and was sure that she had not. His only consolation was that she did at least know who it was he had gone to meet, and she would be able to tell Gabrielle.

Gabrielle. He closed his eyes, knowing with dreadful certainty that he was not going to see her again for a very long time, that he was not going to see her again for years.